The Skriker

Pitch & Sickle

Book Three

THE DIABOLUS CHRONICLES

D K GIRL

The Skriker © 2021 by Danielle K Girl
Cover Art by Deranged Doctor Design

Edited by **Inspired Ink Editing**

ISBN: 978-0-6453274-3-4

CHAPTER 1

The figure striding from the woods had eyes of fire, and dangled the dead carcasses of a pair of hares in one hand. Wisps of smoke curled from the burnt hides, and the animals' heads were orbs of charcoal each. The scent of their scalded flesh reached Silas where he stood by the paltry fire. He was hungry enough that the waft was not altogether unpleasant.

'Supper is served,' Pitch declared, swinging his bounty carelessly.

He moved towards the fire like a terrible ghost, skin white as snow and eyes like tiny blazing suns. Christ almighty it was a sight, one that tightened Silas's chest and caused his heart to stutter beneath his ribs. He coughed, stoking absently at the fire they had lit to ward off the evening chill. Three days ago they had left the peacefulness of Ottelie's cottage, despite her protestations that it was not yet time for travel. After near on a week spent recuperating, Pitch was a mess of restlessness and would not be swayed from his determination to leave the Forest of Dean and return to Bishop's Castle where Lady Satine's farm awaited.

'I trust you did not set the woods ablaze as you hunted rabbits?' Silas scowled down at the fire. It was not a kind thing to say, he supposed, considering the daemon had seen to it that they would not go hungry that evening. But then again it was because of Pitch that they had no supplies to begin with. Ottelie had provided bread and eggs and an astounding array of sweet treats and cakes that should have sustained them for a week.

There was a half a loaf of bread and one egg remaining. Pitch's appetite was monstrous. Perhaps if he ceased his endless tapping of feet in the stirrups or the knocking of knuckles upon the pommel, he might conserve some of his energies. His agitation was exhausting to pay witness to.

'They are hares, Silas. And perhaps if I had burned this bloody wood down, it would see us reach our destination sooner rather than much later, as it seems your nag intends,' Pitch replied. 'Or are we to forever wander the forests of England alone, pissing against trees and sleeping on the dirt?'

Silas took a breath before he replied. One of them at least must stifle their temper, and the daemon had no talent for it. Especially not of late. 'Pitch, we have discussed this already. Many times.' He bit his lip, pausing before he spoke again. 'I do not decide Lalassu's course. I agree it is strange that we have not yet passed through a town, but there is reason for it, I'm sure. And we must act accordingly.'

Which was to say, Pitch should not have depleted their stores by sunrise of the second day, but Silas was hardly going to broach that subject once more. He did not favour another vicious tongue-lashing. It seemed the further on they journeyed, the more turbulent Pitch's mood became. It was likely he would have had them ride day and night if the choice were his. He muttered angrily beneath his breath when Lalassu stopped, late in the evenings, to afford them some rest. But when he was not cursing their need for sleep, he was mostly silent. Far too much so for someone who enjoyed the sound of his voice most other times. The modicum of calm the daemon had seemed to embrace while he recuperated in the cottage slipped away with each mile they travelled. And that intimate moment between them, lips within an inch of touching, grew more dreamlike with each passing day.

A pair of smouldering hares landed with a thump at Silas's feet. 'I caught them, you will skin them,' Pitch said, lofty as a king.

Silas looked up in alarm. 'I beg your pardon?'

'Why do you insist on saying that when it is clear you heard me very well?' Pitch replied, his irritation wrinkling his forehead.

He kicked at a jutting log, sending sparks flying from the fire, bringing it to life. There had been a lot of that of late, too. Lashing out at random objects: a low-hanging branch receiving a punch as Sanu took him beneath it, a rock in a brook where they had stopped to take water being sent flying with a well-placed kick. Silas had the sense of being near a pot ready to boil over. But if he dared ask if all was well, the glare he would receive could peel the skin from his bones.

'I'm not sure I know how…' Silas bent to take the hares in hand, but Pitch was there before him. Their hands met, a brief brush, before Pitch snatched the dead animals away.

'Damn it, Silas, must I do everything?'

Pitch had not called him Sickle in two days.

'I did not say I wouldn't do it,' he protested. 'Here, give them to me.' Silas reached for one of the carcasses that Pitch clutched about the neck. The daemon slapped at his hand, a sharp whip of skin against skin hard enough to wrench a gasp from Silas. 'What was that for?'

'Need there be a reason?'

'For god's sake, Pitch!' Silas shouted. 'What is wrong with you? Give me the damned rabbits.'

This time when he sought to claim the dinner bounty, Pitch pivoted on his heels, twisting to avoid him. A hiss came from him as he turned, and Silas would swear he saw the daemon wince.

'They are fucking hares, you imbecile.' Pitch spoke through gritted teeth. 'Leave it be, will you? I'll do it. Just keep the fire going.'

He shrugged into the faded brown leather coat that Ottelie had provided him. His own clothes were ruined beyond repair after Goodwich Castle. She'd sequestered an entire outfit, a white flannel shirt, a blue vest with tin buttons, and, most impressively, a pair of his favoured fall-front trousers, along with near-new lace-up boots. A farmer's garb. Though how the new Verderer had managed to source items that fit Pitch nearly perfectly was a wonder. The daemon had complained at the lack of a corset among the items but otherwise seemed quite pleased.

Silas had not been in such dire need of replacement clothing luckily. He doubted any nearby countryman could match him in size. Ottelie had laundered his dusty, ash-stained and bloodstained clothes and returned them to him as good as new.

'Pitch...please tell me...is there something wrong? Are you in pain? Perhaps we should rest here for a day –'

'No. We keep on,' he snapped. 'If you dare coddle me, Silas, I swear I shall separate you from your balls. Do you understand?'

Silas did his best to match Pitch's glare, but concern tugged at his brow. 'I'll keep my balls just where they are, thank you very much. And I am not coddling you, I am asking you a question. Just now when you moved, I saw that it caused you difficulty. Is it the wound in your stomach? Ottelie said it was too soon for you to be on horseback –'

'It is not the wound in my stomach. Don't bother yourself with my well-being.' He turned and began to walk away.

The words burst from Silas like a flight of swallows. 'It *does* bother me. You've eaten all we have, and a rabbit is hardly –'

'It's a bloody hare.'

'A hare then, damn it.' Silas balled his fists. 'But I know it is not enough for you. You've said as much before. Do you need...that is to say...would...it's just that I know –'

'Gods, what is trying to dribble from your mouth, man?'

'Company.' Silas spat it. He did not dribble. 'You need...company. You said once that what you drew from others was a natural painkiller for your kind.' What Pitch had said exactly, eyes heavy with need, was *pleasure does wonders for incubus blood*. 'So I just thought that perhaps...you needed...'

His words faded like the smoke curling from the dead hares. Good god, what had come over him? Despite being turned from the fire his face was warm. He could not chase from his mind the bittersweet scent of Pitch's breath as they had drawn so dangerously close upon Ottelie's bed. A kiss. That was all he was offering, of course. What harm in that, if it would restore the daemon from insufferable to barely tolerable?

The fire spat and crackled behind them, and Pitch stood in silence for far too long. Silas shook his head, ready with a curt withdrawal of the ludicrous offer.

'Do you *want* my company, Silas?' Pitch's voice slunk low, nearly lost beneath the soft night sounds of the woods. He stood perfectly still, like a hunter lying in wait.

Sweat beaded on Silas's brow. He felt light-headed; Pitch's question pounded in his ears. 'It's not like that...I was just...' Silas faltered. He was *just* taking leave of his senses, surely. If his heart thumped any harder, he'd have a broken rib to contend with.

'How very noble of you, Silas, to stoop so low. But have no fear, your virtue is safe.' Pitch held so tightly to the carcasses that Silas thought he heard a crack of bone. 'You cannot soothe what ails me. I dare say you'd be less use than a teacake.'

Silas's lips parted in a silent gasp. If he'd thought the daemon unwell before, he was certain of it now.

Pitch made his way to where the stump of a felled tree formed a perfect table on which to lay their supper. As Silas watched, lost for all words, the daemon dug his fingers into the ruff of a narrow neck and with the flick of a wrist tore away a strip of the hare's hide. The wet ripping sound sent a shudder through Silas's body.

'Go and tend to the fire,' Pitch said coolly. 'And stop gaping like a fool.'

With a scowl, and making a point of not jumping immediately to follow the curt command, Silas moved back to where the fire weaved and shone, thankful for its heat now as it chased away the chill that gripped him. Lalassu and Sanu watched on from just beyond the clearing, working their mouths against cropped grass.

Ankou and daemon ate in silence a little while later. The meat was pleasant enough once roasted, the company less so. Silas sat on one side of the fire, Pitch on the other, gnawing at his meat as though the creature still lived and he sought to ensure otherwise. His hands were unwashed, stained with the blood and muck that came from a disembowelled body. It did not make for pleasant dining surrounds, and Silas found he could eat no more than a few mouthfuls of the stringy meat.

'Would you like the rest of mine?' Silas raised what remained of his hare, impaled upon an oak's discarded branch. Pitch sucked noisily at a cracked bone, stealing the marrow.

'Hmmph.'

Silas supposed that to mean he would care for the leftovers, and he rose to his feet, grunting as his saddle-weary joints protested. He handed over the portion. Pitch snatched the stick without a look or a word and bit into the pink flesh. He had already stripped his own carcass bare of meat but was clearly not sated. Silas hovered, likely longer than he should have.

'You are blocking the light.' Pitch spoke through a mouthful. 'I'm sure you're enjoying the view, but I'd prefer you move.'

The view was distracting, certainly – flames always favoured Pitch's complexion – but worry curdled in Silas's stomach, along with the portions of hare. The daemon was withdrawing into himself, placing a distance between them that Silas did not understand. Nor relish.

It was lonely where he stood. And he realised it was likely the first time he'd felt that way since they had encountered one another.

Without a word he left Pitch to his gorging, and after tending to the horses – a gesture more beneficial for himself than the horses, who needed no real fussing over – Silas searched for a place to settle for the evening. Somewhere not too far from the fire. Lalassu nudged him towards a patch of moss-covered ground beneath a considerable oak. Without the mare's encouragement, the hidden natural bedding would have gone unnoticed. As he settled down for the evening, with a saddle for a makeshift pillow, gathering his coat about him, and shifting the pocket so he would not lie upon the bandalore, Silas kept his eye on Pitch.

The daemon lay on the far side of the fire. It was only the whiteness of his skin that marked his position, huddled in the bulge of the dead roots at the foot of the stump he'd used as a butcher's block earlier. The wood was still sticky with the hares' blood, their entrails glistening in the firelight. Silas did his best to sleep, but his mood did not lend itself to the calmness needed for such things, and he tossed and turned as the night deepened. Pitch's odd behaviour was but one thing to worry over. He rolled onto his back and touched at the pocket where the arrowhead nestled with all its vast implications. He had asked Pitch who should carry it as they prepared to depart, and the daemon had told him with much vexation that he should cast it into Ottelie's well.

'I don't wish to see the fucking thing again,' he'd declared, downing the very last of the Verderer's cider.

Perhaps Silas should have seen then that all was not as it should be with the daemon.

'No...no...' Across the way, Pitch struggled with his dreams again.

6

Silas sat up, debating the merits of trying to rouse him. The daemon had slept fitfully for several nights now. Mostly restless, as though no position he found made him content. He mumbled in his sleep, but the words were usually too distorted to make any sense of.

'I didn't know...' This time, though, he spoke clearly. If not for the fact that his eyes were shut, Silas might have thought him awake. 'He should not have been there. Raph...Raph!'

The name rose from him, weighed down with anguish. The daemon fell still. And though Silas waited for some time, he said no more and did not move again until the sky lightened and they rose to begin preparations to leave.

They rode on sometime later with the overcast day grey lit and damp. The twitter of birds as they rose to meet the morning mixed with the creak of leather from the saddles. Silas wove the loose reins about his fingers, seeking some distraction from Pitch's notable silence.

A half hour after they had set off from the campsite, the farmhouse came into view. It was some way up ahead still, just visible at the end of the forest-shadowed track they followed. A small affair, a main house with a red tiled roof surrounded by rather meagre fields that looked in need of a till.

'About fucking time,' Pitch sighed, the first words he'd spoken since they left the campsite. 'Move your arse now, Sickle.'

Silas started at the return of the moniker and was wholly unprepared for the dimple-inducing grin that was shot his way. For whatever reason, Pitch's mood had swung more favourably towards light. He clucked his tongue and urged Sanu into a canter, and Silas hurried to follow.

CHAPTER 2

They crouched like highwaymen on either side of a gap in a hedgerow, hidden from the sight of anyone who might have glanced from one of the small-paned windows of the main cottage. Silas took a quick look at the daemon, who knelt a step away. Pitch's eyes shone despite the dull, overcast afternoon, as though those flames he had brandished at Goodrich Castle were trying to force their way clear. Before now, Silas had longed to catch sight once more of that bright and brilliant creature who had forged a shield of fire to protect them from the downfall of the castle, a true guardian, rather than the sullen, listless companion he'd become over the past few days. But now that he glimpsed that entrancing power's return, Silas felt no better for it.

The daemon tapped his booted toe against the dirt in a manic rhythm as his fingers made an equally nonsensical pattern against his thigh. Pitch was feverish with calamity, prickling with anticipation, and it was deeply worrisome.

'Would you not tell me of your plan here?' Silas whispered, nodding towards the whitewashed home. If not for the laundry dangling upon a line beyond the main house, it would have appeared deserted. 'We really don't need to skulk about in the bushes –'

Pitch pursed his full lips, shushing him. 'Don't think, my dear Sickle. It is not becoming. Let me have my fun.'

'I'm not sure how asking for some bread and sugar constitutes fun.'

'That is because you are a terrible bore.'

Silas bit back a reply. He did not like this, not at all. Pitch kept his eyes locked on the simple wooden house, where dirty white chickens clucked and pecked their way about the yard. A lopsided shed, not quite grand enough to be called a barn, sat some short distance from the main house, and in between them lay a kitchen garden, where oncoming winter stripped bare anything edible.

'Might we be done with this quickly, then?' Silas said, tugging his coat free of a snagging twig, the bandalore a weight within one pocket, and the arrowhead, indiscernible in its lightness, in the other. 'We must get on.'

He sent a longing glance towards a nearby copse where Sanu and Lalassu waited, hidden. Never had Sybilla's company seemed more favourable.

'Then get on, for fuck's sake,' Pitch retorted. 'I am not keeping you here, and your fretting is becoming intolerable. I'll be dragged to your side once more, I'm certain. Satty wills it, so who are we to counter her precious demands? That red pile of shit I ride will see us rejoined, so go. I am fine, and having to assure you of this every moment of the day is fucking exhausting.'

Silas slid the daemon a sharp sideways glance. 'Really? *I* am exhausting?' he said, words crisp. 'You are desperately unaware of certain aspects of yourself.'

'I am infinitely aware of every aspect of myself, I assure you. And I'm also indelibly aware of how irritating your voice is. Now shut up.'

'I will not –'

'Shhhh!'

Good lord, he was a right bastard, there was no doubt of it. But Pitch certainly *looked* fine. Nibbling at his Cupid's bow lips, brow furrowed in nefarious concentration. Damn those bloody lips. Silas flushed even now to recall just how close he had come to brushing them with his own. He'd vacated Ottelie's bed after that near encounter and had not returned, choosing to sleep upon the strange carpet of flowers composing the floor – surprisingly comfortable – while Pitch sprawled in the new Verderer's bed.

Silas cleared his throat, focusing on the issue at hand. The daemon did appear healed. The gouged flesh at his belly had mended to a faint scar while they still rested at Ottelie's cottage, and the darkening in his veins, the evidence of the Blight's poison, had long since left him.

Outwardly he was a picture.

All the more striking for the informality of the clothing Ottelie had given him. Their haphazard nature, their poorly sewn hems and rough materials, suited him too well. Pitch had complained most bitterly about the lack of a corset vest for him to wear, as though that curious item of clothing were more important than all the rest. Ottelie had met his demands with a dismissive click of her tongue. But Silas had spent far too many moments imagining such an item upon the daemon, Pitch's slender waist accentuated further, an hourglass of curves.

Face warming, Silas looked to the farmhouse, chasing away thoughts of boned material and tight lacing. He rubbed absently at the rowan wood and holly bracelet that still hugged his wrist, a gift Ottelie had insisted he keep upon him.

Perhaps he *should* ride on and give himself time to clear his head and regain his senses.

Pitch snapped a spindly twig between slender fingers, and Silas jumped. 'Ah, now there we are. A man who knows his fists well, I'll wager.'

'What are you –'

Pitch hissed at him to shut up. The farmer, a thick-boned man with hunched shoulders clothed in a loose smock and sturdy boots, emerged from the shed. Of all things, it was a scythe he carried with well-practised ease over one shoulder.

'Wonderful, he'll do indeed,' Pitch muttered, eyes sparkling with pinpoints of gold.

'What are you on about?'

The daemon swung from vicious to innocuous in the batting of a lash. 'I simply admire a man who knows how to handle his scythe. But don't worry, my dear, yours is definitely bigger.'

'Now it is you who should shut up,' Silas growled, watching the farmer traipse off around the shed, disappearing from view. 'Enough of this, Pitch. Do what you intend here, and let us be gone.'

Pitch jumped to his feet. 'Very well, if you insist. But I should warn you, you may not enjoy it. Actually, I may be very wrong. You may well have a taste for bloodletting.'

This time his smile was not pleasant. It darkened his face in a way that caused Silas's breath to catch.

'Pitch...what the hell are you talking about?'

The daemon broke into a run, a gait he was remarkably proficient at when he set his mind to it. And his mind was clearly set. His lithe legs took him rapidly over the short expanse of open ground, an over-grazed paddock which was dotted with manure piles, and he was soon disappearing around the side of the main house, running opposite to where the farmer was headed.

'Shit,' Silas hissed.

Tobias Astaroth only worked in crooked lines, keeping clear of the straight and narrow.

A brief and sharp cry came from within the house. Silas swore anew.

No further sound reached him. Perhaps his ears had deceived him. Perhaps it was a pig in a sty that had squealed, and not the helpless woman of the house, surprised by the sudden appearance of an emerald-eyed stranger. Silas squatted there, clutching at the rough hedge like a child caught in a game of hide and seek, debating his course of action. Pitch would not be so foolish as to harm anyone here, surely?

Silas shook his head. 'He'll do no such thing. Lady Satine would have his head.'

If the daemon wanted to dart about like a thief, snatching food from unsuspecting countryfolk, then fine, let the fool have his fun.

For long, lonely minutes Silas sat with his racing thoughts. He was beginning to imagine the daemon had not stopped at the farmhouse at all but had set off running right past it, continuing on and leaving Silas far behind.

The idea made his pulse thump.

Throaty laughter floated upon the air. Silas peeked from around his rugged shield. He blew out a long-held breath. So, the daemon had not taken to murder. Pitch sauntered from the farmhouse, his arm entwined with that of a robust dark-haired woman whose skirts were hitched at the waist so that her ankles and boots were bared. Her pale pink apron was dusted with what he assumed to be flour, a sign that she had been at work in the kitchen. A basket dangled from her free hand. She was not a young woman. Her rounded face was weathered, and her waist did not curve with the hint of youth, but she beamed at Pitch as though she were gripped by the flush of her first endearment. He was speaking with her, but his mutterings were placed close against her ear and hidden from Silas. Whatever he said, he had her quite enchanted.

'Oh, blast you, Pitch.' Silas pressed the heels of his hands against his eyes, but he could not deny the relief that came with seeing the woman in fine form, rather than bloodied and bruised. Silas shook himself, irritated at his own thoughts. Pitch had damned well saved his life, more than once. He was capable of decent behaviour, and Silas should not assume the worst of him. His recent agitation would pass, surely. It was a moodiness that would shift, as it so often did with the daemon. Silas had to believe it. The alternative had him tense and unsettled. Another incident like that with the constable in the barn at Bishop's Castle was not worth thinking on. Pitch had loosed his temper upon the unfortunate man with terrifying ferocity.

Silas watched with nerves taut as the pair sauntered across the yard. Pitch ran a hand through his tousled hair, lifting it away from his neck and exposing the slender length of pale skin there. The woman pressed in close and lifted her chunky fingers to run them up Pitch's neck, tracing a line along the cut of his jaw and moving higher to the ridge of his cheek. She uttered gasps as she explored, and dissolved into childish giggles as Pitch tilted his head and kissed at her wrist. The woman's skirts swayed as she edged in closer. Silas pressed forward, into the unyielding sharp edges of the hedgerow, eyes narrowing at Pitch's lewd performance. All relief at having seen the woman unharmed was now crushed beneath a rising temper.

This was his *fun?* Seduction. Foul and deceptive seduction.

Silas should step out now and tell her exactly whom she dallied with. A daemon. An enchanter.

She should not look so delighted at his touch. Pitch was not hers to delight in. That was *his* guardian she fawned and cooed over. Stupid, bloody woman.

A thorn cut his palm where he grasped hold of the foliage too tightly.

Silas lowered his head. Christ almighty, what was wrong with him? Fatigue...hunger. There lay the blame, he was certain. Yes, he was ravenously hungry, and it was causing him to become ridiculous. Pitch could fuck the lady here and now if he so pleased, as long as he delivered that basket of food first. Silas raised his head. And his empty belly sank. The basket would not be arriving anytime soon.

The woman had let it drop to the ground in favour of freeing both hands so she could grasp at the daemon who played with her. The pair were locked at the lips, Pitch's hands upon the woman's cheeks, his mouth working upon hers. She tilted her head back to meet their slight difference in height, her body straining into him. Her hands searched at his back, finding their way low, cupping his arse. Pitch smiled into the kiss, and his own wandering hands fell upon the bulge of the woman's breasts. A moan escaped her, and she drove her mouth against him more feverishly.

'Fucking hell,' Silas growled. He'd not play Peeping Tom a second time. What he had witnessed of Pitch and the lieutenant in Mordiford had likely scarred him for life. 'Enough.'

He moved to stand but was caught short by a cry. 'What devilry is this?'

Silas dropped to his knees, concealed once more by wind-beaten foliage.

The farmer had returned. And he was not alone. All at once the seemingly empty farmhouse was awash with running men. One from the house, another from the shed, joining the farmer as he ran at the couple. They all bore weapons of some kind, crude as they were. The farmer with his scythe posed the greatest threat, while the younger man held a rake, and the third had armed himself with an obviously inadequate wooden bucket.

'Ma, what the blazes?'

'Take your 'ands off that woman.'

'Get 'im, Papa.'

The trio rushed at the couple. Pitch did not bother to disconnect his mouth from the woman's, but he did take time to lift his hand from her arse cheek and offer her enraged protectors a condescending wave.

CHAPTER 3

Silas knelt, frozen with uncertainty. To shout a warning was superfluous. It was clear that Pitch knew of the men's approach. He taunted them, even as they shouted at him, naming him all manner of obscene things in their efforts to have him loosen his hold on the woman. But he had no intention of releasing her. The daemon ran his hands down her back, settling splayed fingers upon the width of her generous posterior in clear view of the men who approached. She swooned against him, her own hands equally as adventurous in their mapping of his body, fingers disappearing beneath the layers of the daemon's clothes. If the woman was distressed, she showed no sign of it. Rather the opposite appeared true. She pulled her hand from where it searched beneath Pitch's flannel shirt, low at his waist, to wave back the approaching party.

'Leave me be,' she gasped, coming up for desperately-needed air before diving back in to suckle upon Pitch's lips as though she had not eaten in an age.

Her words were aimed not at the daemon who toyed with her so appallingly but towards the men of her household who sought to come to her aid.

'For god's sake, Pitch,' Silas cursed beneath his breath. 'Stop this madness.'

The youngest of the party, a buck-toothed man with thin shoulders, raised his rake. He was within striking distance, of that there was no doubt, and all that prevented Pitch from receiving a nasty blow was the woman he held. Her family would hardly strike out with her so near. But their rage was obvious, their eagerness to inflict harm could not have been clearer. And yet Pitch did not raise his head from his efforts.

'Get your fucking hands off her,' the lad shouted. 'Are you a madman?'

Silas flinched. Now there was a question. Could he be mad, perhaps driven so by his time on the Hellfield with a master wild enough to be called the Berserker Prince, or was Pitch just dangerously fond of a fight? A mixture of both perhaps?

The farmer afforded Pitch no opportunity to heed the orders given. He leapt forward, thrusting ahead the handle of the scythe rather than the vicious curved blade. He was clearly taking no chances with his wife so near to harm.

'Get back, Mary,' he cried. 'Unhand her, you bloody ratbag, or I'll knock your head off your shoulders.'

Using the tool like a lance, the man ran at Pitch and aimed not for his head but for his side, thrusting the rounded end of the tool into the daemon's hip. Pitch jerked but did not yield, and his arms did not fall from where they embraced the farmer's wife.

Another jab came, with enough brute force that a lesser man would have been knocked off his feet. But Pitch was neither lesser, nor man. He pulled his lips from the woman's face, and she uttered a cry, reaching for him, seeking to draw him back to her. Pitch grasped both her wrists in one hand and shoved them down, out of his way.

'I do not think your husband approves.' He was smiling. He had not stopped smiling from the moment the small mob had appeared baying for his blood.

'Stop it, Clyde,' the woman, Mary, cried. She shifted against Pitch's hold and made sure to place herself between the daemon and her bristling husband. 'You'll not harm him. Why the hell does it bother you anyways? You've not come near me in a bloody year.'

'Mary!' The farmer staggered, the scythe dangling in his slackened grasp.

'Ma!' The lad with the bucket was white with shock, though whether that came from his mother's intimate revelation or her wanton behaviour was anyone's guess.

Silas clenched the hedge's brittle branches, ignoring the pain of it. Indecision wracked him. He could step forward and put an end to this now, but would that raise the daemon's ire higher and cause more harm than good? What on Earth was Pitch's true intent here? He himself was hardly in any true danger. It was the humans that Silas feared for, the objects of Pitch's rough amusements. He blinked against the sharp memory of Pitch being beaten to a pulp in that barn at Bishop's Castle. Christ, he had goaded that raucous crowd there too, stirred their repulsion until it exploded from their fists.

And then he'd taken every blow with relish.

Silas ground his teeth. He must step in.

But Pitch chose then to make his own move.

He thrust the woman away. Mary stumbled, tripping over the discarded basket of stores. Clyde dropped the scythe and lunged for her. He caught her in an awkward stagger that saw them both topple to the ground, startling a trio of speckled hens that had wandered too close, oblivious to the tumultuous situation. Silas scowled at the fowls, as though they were to blame for this whole thing entirely. He prayed, to no god in particular, that Pitch's releasing of the woman signalled that his game was over.

The daemon held his slender arms aloft, as though in surrender.

'Gentlemen, please,' he said. 'Hold your tempers. Your mother, your wife, came to no harm, see? I'd say it is rather the opposite.' The two young men glanced at each other, confusion evident upon their faces. '*I'd* say she enjoyed every moment with me.' Christ, Pitch's smile was dreadful. 'Dare I say you might need to give your kitchen table a good rub down before you next use it...if you do not wish to add a salty tang to your supper.'

'Oh shit.' Silas groaned.

The buck-toothed man roared his indignation and raised his rake. He swung, albeit wildly, at the daemon. The lad was not diminutive, and there was decent force behind the blow. But Silas knew Pitch to be capable of rapid movement. He could have stepped from harm's way simply enough.

He did not move.

The prongs of the rake slammed against his back, and he bucked forward, sent teetering on his toes. The lad with the bucket made his move next, clasping the handle with both hands and throwing his body in a circle to gain momentum. The wood struck Pitch against the side of the head, and his chin jerked aside with the blow. Silas could see his wide smile still held in place, a trickle of blood already evident at his lip where the bucket had broken skin. He fell to his knees, jacket flapping about, and the farmer's boys set on him. Mary screamed her protest and fought to pull from her husband's hold as he cried hoarsely for her to get her wits about her and stop acting like a maniac.

But the true maniac was at their feet, hunched on all fours. Pitch grunted and shook with the blows levelled against him. The lad abandoned his bucket and used his feet instead to convey to Pitch just what he thought of him. Which was to say, very little. His dirty white smock danced about like a grim ghost as he threw his body into the assault. His brother shared his fervour and used the wooden handle of his rake to smack his message into Pitch's back. The daemon's face was hidden beneath the drape of tangled light brown strands.

He fell onto his side, curling in upon himself. His slender legs were tucked up against his belly, his delicate fingers clutched to his chest. As the kicks landed, he offered no resistance. He threw back his head, as though relishing the dreadful impact upon his body. His hair fell away from his face, revealing a steady stream of blood running from his nose and mouth. Pitch grinned through it all.

Just a week ago he'd been bleeding out on Ottelie's bed, his belly gouged, his skin etched with thin lines of the Blight-driven poison that had spilled from the spirit of the forest's glass prison.

He had barely begun to regain his strength. Now here he lay.

Silas tasted bitterness at the back of his throat, his breath coming in shallow gasps. 'You fool,' he whispered. There was no way his words could have reached the daemon, but Pitch looked his way. Just one eye was evident, gleaming through lengths of sweat-laden hair.

'Fear not,' he grunted in time with the blows. 'There'll be no constable here.'

Nonsensical words to those who stood about him, but for Silas they were crystal clear. He swore to all the saints and damned the daemon to hell once more. Pitch did not intend to punish these people the way he had that constable in the barn. Which meant this beating was for his own...pleasure. The daemon had, as Silas feared, placed himself back in the crude boxing ring all over again.

He ain't happy till he's hurtin'.

Gilmore's words, spoken what felt like an eternity ago now, but no less true.

The laughter was soft at first. A giggle really. But it soon grew, rising high to tickle at madness. Pitch laughed into the bloodied dirt, spewing forth shameless details of their mother's defilement. His obscene retelling brought on harder blows and incensed roars of derision.

'Lunatic!'

'Bloody cunt.'

'Mad bastard!'

Mary screeched at them to stop. But that was not what Pitch wanted. And the daemon was adept at getting what he wanted. Pitch sought the pain as feverishly as he sought sweetness. Silas pressed his hands to his ears, trying to stifle Pitch's unendurable laughter and his indecent lies until he could stand no more.

This was beyond a mere altercation between hot-tempered men. This was a battle of one man, against...well, against his daemons. Silas moved unsteadily, his shoulders heavy with the weight of it all, stepping into the gap between the hedges. If the family were not so engrossed in their punishment they would have noticed him easily.

They did not.

But Pitch did.

He stared from beneath bloodied strands, and something in his maddened expression shifted. His crimson-toothed grin wavered. The lad with the rake cracked it against Pitch's hip. The daemon jerked as though he'd been struck by lightning and slumped onto his back. He let loose with another foul-mouthed detail of an encounter that was pure fiction. For unless Pitch was capable of rutting in the blink of an eye, there was no way he had found his way beneath Mary's skirts in the time he'd been out of Silas's sight. Not unless she'd packed the picnic basket for him as he'd thrust into her. Silas turned away, pressing his lips tight. Pitch was toying with her, he had no doubt. Her protestations at his treatment bordered on hysterical, her flagrant behaviour likely to mortify her by the day's end. She was enchanted. But at least the daemon had not defiled her. Silas curled his fingers into fists. The entire family were enchanted in one way or another, to feed the daemon's twisted appetite.

Enough with this insanity.

Silas stepped forward, intending to interrupt the assault. He caught Pitch's eye once more. How the daemon's gaze burned.

All at once Silas was off his feet, hurtling backwards, an unseen weight slamming against his chest. He flailed his arms, seeking to stay upright only to find himself toppling. The ground bit at his arse, and his breath left him in a shocked gasp.

None of those near the farmhouse paid him any mind, too enraptured with the chaos there.

None, save for the daemon.

Pitch had managed to drag himself onto hands and knees again, and he directed his manic grin Silas's way. Silas read all he needed to know in the daemon's cruel expression. It was Pitch who had sent him flying. Sent him away.

'So be it, you bloody idiot.' Silas pushed to his feet, swatting at his dirtied coat with angry brushes. 'I am done with this.'

He stalked back to where Lalassu and Sanu waited. An inner voice screamed at him to turn back, to rescue the fool from himself. But Silas walked on. Pitch desired this madness, craved this harm. So be it. Let him have his torment, then. This addiction was beyond Silas's comprehension, and he could not bear witness to it. He'd not share in Pitch's pain.

The red horse could wait for her master. Silas would not.

And with the daemon's empty, broken laughter at his back, Silas swung into his saddle and held on as Lalassu spirited him away.

CHAPTER 4

S ilas leaned low against Lalassu's neck, his thighs glancing against the saddle, fingers loose around reins that were near buried in the endless, thick strands of her mane. She ran at a gallop, a breathtaking turn of hoof that not so long ago might have had set Silas screaming with terror. Not so now. He relished the stretch of her massive strides for it took him far away from that farmhouse. Away from the destruction there. Upon the pale horse's back he could gather himself, fix his resolve, and find a hiding place from the horrors about him. Silas went willingly where Lalassu would take him. So long as it was away. Far away from Pitch and his terrible beauty.

'What is wrong with the man?' Silas growled into a wind that flung his words back at him. Perhaps he was every bit as mad as the daemon, speaking to himself so, but his frustration boiled within, and releasing the words eased the tension. Pitch was supposed to keep Silas from harm, yet there he was, inflicting as much harm as he could find upon himself. Giving no consideration to who might see.

To who might be unprepared to endure such a sight.

'Faster,' Silas whispered. 'Faster.'

He asked too much, surely, for their pace already blurred the landscape and brought tears to his eyes. Lalassu responded, lengthening her body, straining forward until Silas was certain her hooves did not touch the ground at all. He settled deeper into the saddle, the cantle brushing against his arse, coat billowing about behind him. The horse's mane slashed about like a thousand tiny banners, its beautiful colours blinking snow white and sea green. Silas lost himself to the rhythm, crouching down against the mare until he saw only a shifting sea of her mane, silken waves dancing before him. With the thump of Lalassu's hooves came the thud of her breath, fired from flared nostrils.

Blast the daemon. Silas would be damned if he lamented over him a moment more. He drew in a deep breath, relishing his freedom in that moment. He was beholden to no one, and unchained from the calamity that was Tobias Astaroth. Perhaps Lalassu could run them until Mr Ahari, Lady Satine, and that godforsaken daemon were but a strange and troubling dream.

Far, far behind him.

He clenched the reins. No matter how much he enjoyed the thought of disappearing from all this, an interfering voice would not let him be. It insisted on whispering at him, calling on him to turn about and snatch Pitch away from those who brutalised him.

Silas concentrated on the rumble of Lalassu's hooves, letting the sound drown out the whispers. He could ride north. Perhaps all the way to Edinburgh Castle.

Now there was a thought. He could see for himself if the castle stirred any feelings, the way gazing upon the portrait of it had done at Mr Donisthrope's. Had that painting truly touched at a memory, or did Silas merely have a yet-undiscovered appreciation of fine artwork?

Dear god, how innocent he had been that day, following after the Donisthrope's housekeeper like an oblivious lamb to slaughter. Before the sun had fully set, Black Annis would inflict grievous injury upon him. And he would live despite it all.

Silas groaned, shaking his head at his stupidity. Upon his person he held an angel-made arrowhead and Death's bandalore. If Pitch was a maniacal fool, then Silas was the village idiot for imagining he could simply ride his way out of this predicament.

As if he could ride away from the likes of Lady Satine. A woman, or whatever she might be, who could possess a man miles from where she stood. Or Mr Ahari, whose home was a living entity. Or even Sybilla, a Valkyrie no less, loyal to her lady and no doubt more than capable of hunting Silas down and dragging him back to Bishop's Castle. Making his way to Edinburgh Castle was as likely as Silas sprouting wings.

He blinked, and his thoughts turned back to Pitch's display at Goodwich Castle, his back ablaze with twin torrents of light, protecting Silas from harm.

Despite himself, he shivered, gooseflesh rising. What a truly breathtaking sight it had been. Even as the world fell down around them, Silas had not, for the first time, been afraid.

And what had he done to repay Pitch's act? He had raced away in a headlong gallop, leaving the daemon lying in a puddle of his own blood.

The jump rose up suddenly, the remains of a collapsed wooden fence lying at an angle in the field ahead. Silas gasped and pressed up in the stirrups. He only just managed to avoid being sent flying over Lalassu's neck. The landing was brutal, the saddle coming up to meet his crotch in a cruel collision.

'Argh!' he cried, clutching at his groin, eyes watering.

Lalassu slowed into a trot, and Silas bounced about, balls screaming their protest. He cursed through gritted teeth, struggling to find the rise and fall of the movement. After an eternity the horse eased into a steady walk. He ran his hand along her neck, distracting himself from the ache between his legs.

'Would you take me north if I asked it of you?'

She whinnied softly, and he understood at once that he was a dreamer.

Neither the pale horse nor her rider was free. Far greater forces guided them, and Silas was their ankou.

He wiped at the pain-rent tears that had fallen and adjusted his seat. The sway of the animal and the melodic creaking of her tack lulled him, and they rode a long while with Silas lost in his own thoughts. When at last he blinked himself back into the saddle, Lalassu had taken them down a barely-marked trail – he'd not name the narrow slick of packed earth a road – one that meandered between fields that had not seen a grazing animal in some time. Ahead, a dark band marked the edge of a forest. The shy sun's last rays pierced the clouds and settled upon the towering oaks that dominated the landscape. The trees swayed beneath the weight of a strengthening breeze, giving a most disconcerting sense that they were more alive than they should be. He stiffened in the saddle.

He was not eager to spend time in another forest, most especially not at night. Or on his own, he thought, though he quickly wiped away that pathetic, childish lament. Good god, he could survive a night here alone if need be. He was a messenger of death, not one of the Order's clientele, ready to shriek at the slightest rustling in a hedge.

Besides, there was every chance Lalassu would continue straight through and take him to a village beyond.

He chose to ignore the fact that she had not done so in three days.

When Pitch had decided upon his ridiculous plan, it had been midafternoon, and now the weakness of the light spoke of the approach of evening. Night would fall with early November suddenness. The moon had waned to all but a sliver, and the darkness would be Stygian. His fingers twitched against the reins. So be it. If Lalassu wished to stop in the depths of the forest tonight, Silas hardly had a say in the matter.

The wind weaved its way through his hair, throwing the curls against his mouth. The strands still tasted of ash and the grody water of Goodrich Castle's moat. The length of his hair was becoming unruly, brushing below his collar. Ottelie had made no secret of her desire to take to him with a pair of shears, but he had refused. Not least of all because of a comment made in passing as they had sat about the fire in the cottage. Pitch had been taking his first tentative steps from the bed to the fireside, refusing Silas's offer of assistance, but giving him an appraising look as he hobbled by.

'The length rather suits you, I don't think you should cut it. Though you should trim your beard before it catches in your soup.'

So now Silas fought to free his hair from his lips, wishing very much that he had a strip of leather to bind it back. He touched his chin where the bristles had already begun to recover from Ottelie's attentions, rubbing his fingers across the coarse hair as Lalassu led them into the forest.

Disappointment swept him in a cold wave. He had actually hoped she might divert at the last moment and take them clear of the gloom.

'Who do you wish us to avoid, then, Lalassu?' Silas reached up the horse's neck to scratch at the place she favoured most. He played at laughter but his heart was not in it. 'What trouble are we in?'

He may have felt more at ease when in her saddle, but he was not so dull-headed that he did not recognise the furtive way the horse took them through the countryside, avoiding main roads and the sprawl of villages and towns. Silas had grown almost as frustrated with their meandering path as Pitch had. He'd have given his right arm for a comfortable bed rather than a mat of crunching leaves. The clandestine journey, and its implication, did nothing to soothe Silas's jaded nerves. Were they being pursued? Or was this just a precaution after the sinister encounter at the castle? He slid his hand into the pocket that cradled the arrowhead, careful to touch only the short, jagged splinter of wood left behind when the shaft was snapped. The blade tip was covered in a blot of wax to ensure he was not stabbed in the thigh as he rode.

If the arrowhead's owner were to appear, what would Silas face? A murderous avenging angel perhaps? The Watchers, Pitch had called them, those that had rebelled against the lord of Arcadia and made monsters out of men. Bloody hell, what tales he'd been told.

The hoot of an owl nearby nearly dislodged Silas from the saddle. He blew out a breath. 'Idiot. Get ahold of yourself.' He would be a snivelling bundle of terror by morning if he kept imagining Azazel hiding behind every tree and Nephilim waiting in the darkness.

He told himself that all that malarkey was Pitch's war, long since removed from this world.

Silas scratched hard at a knot of muscle in Lalassu's neck, and the horse tilted her head towards the pressure. 'I should be enjoying the respite, shouldn't I? Before long Sanu will gallop upon us, that dreadful fellow upon her back, and I'll be ruing the day I met him yet again.'

Lalassu tossed her head, peeling back her lips to expose the wedges of her yellowed teeth. As close to a sign of amusement, Silas decided, as a horse could make.

They slipped into the forest, following a narrow path that was likely used by woodland creatures alone. Lalassu's bulk pushed aside the narrow, reaching branches of hawthorn, while the undergrowth crunched beneath her broad hooves. The foliage was touched by the late autumn with many a tree flaming with the gold and yellow of the season. Silas raised himself in the stirrups to stretch his legs, his reticence fading.

There was none of the heaviness here that had come with entering the Forest of Dean. A dark weight had sat upon that place and needled its way beneath Silas's skin, but here, wherever they were, there was no such oppression. This was a forest untouched by the foul crush of the Blight. Silas's anxiety settled into a mere niggle, rather than the shiver down the spine it had been. He barely flinched when a scattering of redwings erupted from the undergrowth, and laughed at his own fright when a deer suddenly shot across their path. They travelled on, the light fading until all around him the trees were submerged by shadow. The clinking of Lalassu's tack set a hypnotic rhythm which lulled Silas into a doze. When the mare stopped, he sat bolt upright, blinking into the gloom.

'Right then, is that our lot for the day?'

There was rustling about him, the soft chirrup of night bugs in the leaves. The serenity was not interrupted by any awful singing, or belching, or other bodily expulsions Pitch was so fond of. It took some time to refocus his eyes to the night, but when they did, Silas was treated to a fantastic sight. Up ahead loomed several grey stone buildings pressed together at their side walls, each a differing height. The farthest from him was a single level, the middle made higher by a peaked roof containing an attic with tiny rounded windows, while the closest was by far the largest, a two-story section with white-trimmed windows and twin chimneys poking up from the roof tiles. No light shone through any windows.

'What do we have here, then?'

Someone's home he suspected, with the smaller buildings possibly storerooms.

Lalassu shook her head vigorously, shaking the reins in his grasp. Silas smiled, and dismounted. He wobbled about as his feet met the ground, and it took some shaking of limbs to have the blood circulating well enough that he was steady.

'Lalassu, I do believe you are my most favourite creature in the world right now.' His grin broadened at view of the night's accommodation. Tonight, there would be no sleeping on the ground. A welcome thing indeed. Mind, he'd not be sharing conversation or coffee with any other inhabitants. The place had an air of abandonment, with windows like empty, dark sockets. But at the very least he had a roof over his head, and if he were in luck, an armchair or even a bed to sleep upon.

He was imagining just such luxuries when the trickle of water caught his ear. It came from beyond the furthest wall of the house. He paced towards the sound, legs still a little shaky after the long ride. He'd been so busy exciting himself over the house, he'd not noticed the hulking outline of another structure nearby, made of the same tightly-packed stone as the living quarters. It had the look of a barn about it, with its high reach and broad girth. The building was perched just shy of a brook where flowing water glinted in the speckled light cast by the slender trace of the moon. The night had not fallen so dark as he had feared, and now with a fresh water supply discovered, along with sleeping quarters, his mood rose immeasurably.

He found himself upon a low-set bridge. With the smallest niggle of trepidation, he leaned over the capstones. The bridge had been built up hard to one of side of the building, and he saw down below him a great iron waterwheel, its lower section submerged in a small pond. This was not a barn at all, but rather a mill, and would have used the brook's flow to grind its wheel. It had not done so for some time, considering the heavy covering of duckweed settled on the pond's surface around the wheel's lower portion.

Up by the house where she had remained, Lalassu pawed at the ground and snorted.

'All right, steady on, I'll free you of your saddle soon enough.' Silas made his way back to her with a lightness in his step. She trotted to meet him halfway. 'Though I thank you for this place, I don't suppose there is a public house nearby where one might find a decent stew, perhaps a sharp ale?'

The horse nudged her velvet nose against his shoulder, urging him towards the front door.

Silas sighed. 'Very well then, so be it.' He ran up the stirrups and was reaching for the girth strap when she shied from him. 'You don't want your saddle off?'

Lalassu lifted off her front feet in a stunted rear, shaking her head in what appeared remarkably close to a no. The mare quick-walked in to meet him, and once again nuzzled him in the direction of the house.

'Fine, fine, I'll go inside.'

Lalassu nickered, her stormy coat flashing with moonlight. She rounded about and, with a flick of her heels, broke into a canter, racing off into the forest, back the way they had just travelled.

'Lalassu!' Silas called.

The thump of her hooves faded until he was left with the silence of a night-time forest. 'Well that is bloody wonderful,' he muttered, then louder said, 'You'd best come back with a pie at least.'

An owl hooted. The trees were still. Silas sighed.

The sudden disappearance of the pale horse was not preferable of course, but he was sure it was not permanent. A peculiar instinct, a curious new thing that had marked him since he'd first sat upon the mare, told him they'd not be separated long. She would return to him. He felt the inevitability like a reassuring spectre at his side.

That was not to say, as he gazed up at the building before him, that his foolish imagination did not thrust all kinds of unpleasant scenarios at him. What if another creature like Black Annis raged out of the shadows while he slept, or a maddened Verderer perhaps? This forest may well have a spirit too, one that could have deformed into something as monstrous as that in the Forest of Dean, by whichever nefarious adversary sought to do such things.

He rubbed his arms, bothered by the cold all at once. 'Gracious, man. Pull yourself together. Don't be such a meater, for god's sake. You're still standing, despite Annis and the Verderer. You're doing bloody well, I should say, what with being roused from eternal sleep and all.'

At some point he truly must stop talking to himself this way. But maybe later, when he was not alone, surrounded by scuttling forest creatures and without a daemon to fill the air with sound.

He winced, turning his thoughts from Pitch, and made his way up to the front door. It stood slightly ajar, the wood of the vertical edge having swelled too much to ensure it could close fully. Ruined by the damp no doubt. Even if he had wanted to, and he very much did, Silas could not shut the door tight. Mother Nature had seen to that. He shoved at it with his shoulder. The creak of the hinges was worthy of the best frightening stories, the ones where an unsuspecting innocent stepped into a menacing house and never stepped out again.

'Don't be a fool,' Silas muttered, fingering Ottelie's bracelet, finding odd reassurance in the hard, slender strips of rowan wood. 'Do not forget who you are.'

In truth, he *was* the monster people imagined when they gathered about a fireplace, drinking too much ale as a winter's night surrounded them.

He stooped to accommodate the low set of the door and stepped into the hallway. The floorboards groaned beneath his weight, and there was a disconcerting hole nearby, a shattered space in the wood that would have swallowed his leg had he stepped into it. Silas stepped gingerly down the hall, and the groaning and creaking went with him. But there was no further sign of damage upon the floor.

It became apparent that although the house was definitely abandoned, it had not been so for long. Cobwebs were aplenty, rife upon the multitude of landscape paintings adorning the walls, and draping every chair around a solid-built wooden table in the kitchen, but the scent of decay had not settled upon the place. The dust layers were not terrible. In fact the mantelpiece in the sitting room relinquished no muck when he ran his finger along its wooden surface. He checked every cupboard in the kitchen in vain, searched the shelves of the pantry with longing, but there was nothing edible about. A few pots sat upon the closed-range stove, an impressive appliance with an oven on either side of the firebox. Generous enough to keep the workers in the mill fed, he supposed, as well as the owners of the house. Silas sighed, running a finger upon the heavy iron kettle set upon the stove, imagining how wonderful a fresh cup of tea would taste right now. All at once it struck him that he need not *imagine* any such thing.

'There's plenty of wood about. I'll light a fire easily,' he mused out loud. 'Collect some water from the brook, perhaps a dandelion or two, and there you have it.' He nodded with self-satisfaction. Ottelie had taught him a thing or two about the offerings of the forest. If nothing else he'd enjoy a pleasant brew while he waited on Lalassu's return. He opened the back door, which was not nearly so abused by nature as the front. There, leaning against the stonework was a fishing rod and bucket. He snatched up the rod. A dull brass fly reel hung from the split cane rod. There was even a fly in the bottom of the bucket, with its menacing hook and tight weave of feathers, as though the owner had prepared to set off down to the brook but had become waylaid.

'Thank all the saints! There will be no god-damned rabbit tonight.'

Silas couldn't drive the smile from his lips. He gathered up the bucket, slung the rod over his shoulder, and set off to reel in his inevitable bounty.

CHAPTER 5

As it turned out, bounties were not so inevitable. Silas tied the fly, with its blue feather and dark brown hair, upon the line with deft fingers. If his stomach did not rumble so loudly, he might have stopped to marvel at how easily his thick fingers found their way about the sharp point of the hook and the delicate meagreness of the silk line. He might have been curious about how he knew to do such a thing so well, but hunger trumped such fancies easily.

Silas found a suitable spot, one where he could stand upon a delightfully flat rock just out from the edge. For an hour he stood there, casting again and again, and receiving not even a nibble. At least his casts were true. Fine turns of the wrist that again and again set the fly dancing upon the water's surface. There could be no doubt he'd known this sport in his past life, but that was hardly a revelation. Half the country likely enjoyed this pastime, and besides, he was not the best at it or he would have been roasting the rainbow skin of a trout upon that pan in the kitchen right now.

With far too much time on his hands, Silas's thoughts wandered. First of all to Pitch, pondering if the daemon had found his way back to Sanu, and if the pair might join them sometime soon, and then to Lalassu and where on Earth she might have gone. He stared into the water as it tinkled pleasantly over smoothed stones. Delightful as the sound was, the depths of the shallow brook were made ink black by the night, as though the riverbed had sunk into an abyss.

A terrible notion bullied its way into his distracted thoughts.

Christ, had he been doing just this at the time of his death? Had he taken a tumble from that jetty he'd seen in his vision, perhaps? A fishing trip gone terribly wrong? Perhaps the woman in lilac and her companion had heard his cry and come to his aid, arriving too late.

Silas pressed at his throat. The burn of the water as it shoved into him was far too easy to recall. He pinched the bridge of his nose, admonishing himself. Now was not the time to consider such things. Besides, he was not about to drown in the brook. He doubted it would pass his knees in most places.

The night sank deeper into coolness, the wind finding its way beneath his hair to drench his neck with gooseflesh. The cup of dandelion tea was seeming more and more worthy of greater attention with each passing second. Frogs had taken up their jolly call in the grasses around him, and owls made themselves known deeper in the forest.

'That is quite enough I think.' He flicked his wrist, intending to haul the hook from the water, but he did so with far too much fervour and the sharp point came whipping back towards him. Silas jerked out of the way. His boot slipped. And his feet whipped from beneath him.

'Shit!' Silas threw out his arms, as though the air might hold him, the rod flying from his grasp. Down he went, flailing and cursing. His arse hit the water first, water that was bitingly cold and quick to find its way into his trousers. The brook was shallow at least, that was a mercy. There was no repeat of the incident with the boggart, and he did not find himself tumbling into any angst-ridden memory of drowning. He sat with the flow tugging at his coat-tails. Certainly he did not relish the idea of reliving his death once more...and yet...he could not deny there was a part of him that wondered what might happen if he just laid himself down here. Sank himself into the water to find what secrets it hid. Would she be there again, the woman in lilac? Might he see her more clearly, and even know her name?

'I suspect there are more pleasant ways to take a bath.'

'Christ.' Silas scrambled to his feet, churning up the silt in his haste. 'Who's there? Show yourself!'

Laughter came from a corner of the mill. A figure stood there, too distant to make out entirely, but the silhouette was diminutive. Silas had felt no tingle upon his fingers to suggest he was bothered by a teratism.

'I'm afraid it's difficult to show myself any better. My candle is burnt out, and it's quite dark.' There was jolliness in the tone, as though they were ready to burst out laughing once more. 'I salvaged your rod.' The shadow raised one arm, brandishing the narrow rod that had flown from Silas's grasp as he tumbled. 'Did you have any better luck with the fish than I did? I only caught a tree root I'm afraid.'

Silas did not relax entirely, but the jovial tone of the stranger went some way to easing his tension. 'Well, then you caught more than I. I'm beginning to suspect that there are no fish at all in this brook.'

'I think you may be right.'

Laughter came from the darkness around the mill. The stranger stepped closer and caught enough of the moonlight to reveal features. A full-faced lad, clearly in the early dawn of adulthood. His sideways grin was set upon thick lips. Despite the fact that Silas was nearly double his size, the lad marched his way along without hesitation. He held a rod in each hand, and wore a peaked cap that sat at a precarious angle.

'My name's Charlie.' The young man swept the cap from his head. His light hair was cropped short, and apparently done so without the aid of a barber. Spiky strands stood upright in mismeasured lengths.

'Silas.' He nodded. An unpleasant thought struck him. 'Oh, my. Is this your home? I hope you don't mind that I –'

'No, no. You have me quite wrong.' He giggled, a high sound that suggested the lad may be younger than Silas first imagined. 'I'm merely passing through. I'd heard about the abandoned mill at the heart of Wyre Forest. I thought maybe it would make for a more pleasant shelter than the open air for an evening. Were you of the same mind?'

Silas nodded. The lad didn't need the full truth of it. 'I was, yes. But it seems you were here first and I've stolen your fishing spot. I will move on.'

His gaze flitted to the onyx-coloured forest about him, not relishing the thought of a walk through it at this hour.

'There's no need for that,' Charlie scoffed. 'Look at the size of the house. Have you been inside? There is even a sofa not entirely eaten by mice, and a mattress on the second floor which might not break your back. We could both stay and not bother each other at all.'

Silas eyed the young man. He seemed to be wearing all the clothes he owned, his body unnaturally puffed up by the layers. Baggy grey trousers swamped his legs, and a white smock hung down to his knees. Over it all he wore a patchworked jacket that was too wide for his shoulders and bulged about his arms as it struggled to hold in the layers beneath. He was more vagabond than ruffian. And if Silas was not mistaken, there was something of a plea in his offer to share the derelict house.

'If you are sure you don't mind?' If Lalassu considered this place safe enough to leave him, then Silas would consider it safe enough to remain.

More laughter came, a rasp to it, and it was not unpleasant. 'I suspected you were a decent fellow. I was watching you awhile before you took a dunking.'

'Oh.' He was not sure he enjoyed the idea of being spied upon.

'Nothing sinister, I assure you,' Charlie said quickly. 'You can never be too careful on the road, you understand? Do not take offence.' There was an air of desperation in the fellow's words. 'I'm not much in a fight, you see. Running tends to be my first port of call.' Charlie held out Silas's rod. 'It was amusing to hear you talk to the fish that dared defy your rod. Though I'm not sure that offering a snip of brandy was truly much of an enticement.'

Silas laughed, his surprise tilting the sound high. 'No? Should I have tried whisky, do you think?'

Charlie grinned, pushing full cheeks high. 'They make the finest of it where I come from. And apparently, if a fisherman is full of it, he is certain to catch the largest fish in the loch.' He burst out laughing, and the sound came from the very bottom of the belly.

Silas could not help but join him, even if the joke itself had been mild. All the tension from the past few days spilled free, sliding with the tears running down his cheeks. If anyone were to come upon them just now, they might think they had stumbled upon lunatics fresh from the asylum, but blast if it wasn't good to laugh till ribs ached.

'Now then, you are soaked.' Charlie gathered himself. 'We should go inside and set the fire.'

'Oh god, now that is a pleasant thought.' Silas shivered into his damp clothes. 'Shall we gather some wood?'

'No need. I have that sorted.' Charlie patted at a jacket pocket, and there came a metallic rattling sound. 'Some Lucifer matches, and the kindling I stashed earlier will have you dry in no time at all. Shall we go?' He shifted, turning about, and Silas spotted a clear and defined shadow moving with him. A darker patch in the dim light. Charlie was human.

Silas spared the brook one last longing glance. 'Yes, I'm fairly certain I've done all I can here.'

They set off towards the house.

'It will be good to have company tonight,' Charlie said. 'I was here alone last night, and I'll admit it, I did rather scare myself silly at times. Don't think badly of me, but I was a jellied mess for most of the night.'

The more the lad spoke the more certain Silas was that he heard a catch upon his words where the heavy lick of the Scottish brogue sat. A strange serendipity indeed that he had happened upon a dweller of the north, here in the depths of the woods. He should like to speak to the lad about Edinburgh Castle.

'The forest can be quite intimidating, especially at night.' Oh, how Silas knew it. 'But I don't believe we have any need for concern here.'

He wasn't about to tell the boy why he thought that, of course. Imagine the lad's face if Silas were to divulge that his enchanted horse had brought him here after he had fled from a self-flagellating daemon. Silas doubted Charlie would feel so at ease in his company then.

In that instant, the gulf between the ordinary world and his own yawned like a chasm. And the pang of loss was sharp.

'Well, I shall take your word for it,' Charlie declared. 'And if we are beset by monsters in our sleep, I shall blame you entirely.'

It was said in jest, of course it was, but Silas worried nonetheless. Both about the appearance of a teratism, and, though it left him with a vague sense of betrayal, the return of the daemon. If his foul mood had not faded, Silas did not enjoy the idea of Charlie being in Pitch's company.

'I'm sure it will be fine,' Silas said with more surety than he felt. 'Now where is it that you stacked that kindling? I'm also rather craving a cup of hot tea.'

'Wonderful idea! I'll see to setting the fire. Would you mind fetching some water for the kettle? The brook is clean, the water is quite delicious. I left a bucket at the back door you could use, rather than lug the kettle down there. It's a heavy bloody thing.'

'Oh, actually I took the bucket earlier and completely forgot it by the brook. I'll head back there now.'

'Excellent.' Charlie waved and scampered off around the side of the house. 'See you back here soon,' he called.

Silas made his way back along the path they had just travelled, teeth chattering as he went. He was drenched through from his waist down, his balls were shrivelled tight against the cold, his arse cheeks like two blocks of ice hanging from his rear. It was a short walk, and he was back at the brook quickly. The bucket was as he had left it, half concealed in a tuft of grass. He glanced at the water, and for the first time, he thought of the bandalore and the arrowhead.

'Oh, bloody hell.' He patted at his coat, searching for sign that the items had survived his embarrassing dunk in the brook. He found both in no time, his thumbs finding the satin smoothness of wood in one and the slick, thin blades of metal in the other.

Satisfied, Silas bent to retrieve the bucket.

A thud came from further up the bank. He straightened, his pulse quickening. He squinted, catching sight of a flash of silver, something writhing about on the muddy edge. His fingertips were cold but devoid of any tingling. The bandalore offered no warning, no hint of danger.

'Who's there?'

Another thump sounded, not a few feet from where he stood, another flash of silver, and the squelch of mud. Silas gripped the bucket tight, standing like a dumbstruck fool, staring at the small forms that danced about on the ground. A splash of water came. He barely had time to turn back to the brook, and a glistening shape was hurtling towards him. Silas cried out, hoisting the bucket to protect his face. A heavy weight landed against the wood and lurched about, dislodging the bucket from his grasp. It landed with a dull thud, its contents rolling free.

A trout.

It was bucking and flapping, mouth gaping at the waterless world. A childish giggle came from the brook, and a fine spray of chilled water caught Silas in the face.

For the ankou. In thanks. Eat well, said a familiar bubbling voice.

A greater splash followed. He turned away, hunching his shoulders as though that could help him avoid getting wet. At least it was only the back of his coat that took the drenching, and even then the spill did not soak through. Either way, he was not about to scold those who had splashed him.

'Thank you,' he called. 'Thank you so much.'

He could not be certain, but he would wager that odd bubbling voice belonged to the naiad who had spoken to him in a sun shower in Mordiford as Silas had dozed among the gravestones with a grim cat as company. The naiad had urged him on to the Forest of Dean and told him of the lost Verderer.

Silas gathered up the bounty, three fish in all, wide-eyed, gleaming creatures that would bake up nicely in that fine oven. He raised the bucket with its full load towards the brook, tipping it in thanks, as though it were a glass of the finest champagne.

'You are too kind,' he called to the naiad.

The brook bubbled and babbled and went about its merry way as though nothing of any consequence had occurred.

CHAPTER 6

S ilas may have been a poor fisherman, but he could cook trout to perfection. On his return from the brook, he had sequestered a handful of thyme from a neglected kitchen garden and, although woody, it had done wonders for the delicate white flesh.

He and Charlie sat side by side at the table in the kitchen, Silas having lowered himself with some trepidation into the woven cane chair on offer. The furniture creaked a protest but held his considerable mass, leaving him free to concentrate on the pan that was set between them, where the fresh-cooked trout lay like a treasure. There was no cutlery to speak of, nor plates, so they had waited until the meat cooled enough to dig their fingers into the pink flesh and gouge chunks free. Silas had groaned at the first bite into crisp, oily skin, and he had to restrain himself from lifting the whole fish to his mouth and devouring it like some kind of wild man.

'I'm not sure I understand how you managed such a feat,' Charlie said between morsels. 'But I don't think I've been as grateful for anything in my entire life.'

Silas smiled through damp lips. The lad was very agreeable company, and when he spoke, a most affecting dimple appeared in his left cheek.

'It really was most fortunate. I could hardly believe it when I cast my rod for one last try and the fish were biting at last.'

He was certain Charlie was aware that Silas had not taken a rod with him when he went to collect the bucket, but he had not raised the issue.

'Perhaps the river gods took pity on us and could not stand to hear us moaning any longer.' Charlie giggled. For it was a giggle rather than anything else, plied with a softness that often escaped men.

'Quite possible.' Silas took a sip of his dandelion tea. How pleasant it was to have such amicable conversation. Gone was the bluster and tension that came with having Tobias Astaroth at his side. It occurred to Silas that aside from the lieutenant this was the first human he had spent any amount of time with. And how comforting it was. 'A good thing you were here though. I doubt I could have set such wonderful fires.'

His coat and shirt hung on the two vacant chairs, set close to the firebox where they could dry. Silas had kept his trousers on, of course, and his undershirt, though its flimsy damp fabric clung to his hips in a most uncivilised way as it slowly dried in the warmth of the kitchen. He'd noticed Charlie's eyes flit to his chest more than once as they prepared the meal, triggering in Silas a mix of mortifying embarrassment and strange whirls of something else entirely.

'You flatter me, Silas, but it's an easy enough thing. I've been running away from home since I was old enough to walk. Learning to light a fire was rather essential.'

The lad was a master at the craft, if Silas were to judge. Charlie had discarded his patchworked jacket and smock, revealing a roughly-darned brown wool jumper beneath, but it was clearly not yet the last layer of clothing. It was difficult to tell just what body shape lurked beneath all the material. Silas assured himself that his eye kept straying towards the lad simply because he wished to show interest in the conversation, and not because an intense curiosity drew him there. Charlie glanced at him. His cornflower-blue eyes were kind, but Silas flinched nonetheless, and bit hard into the trout.

He swallowed and spoke into the comfortable silence. 'Was your home so very terrible?'

'Many would say not,' Charlie said after a pause. 'I had a grand roof over my head and food upon the table every morning and night. But I was...well, let us just say I've never felt a part of my own family, and I dare say they wonder what faerie circle I sprang from. I was most certainly not the child they thought they had given life to.' Charlie's cheeks were flushed from the heat. The fire highlighted the bright auburn flecks in his light brown hair. 'My father thought me a devilish changeling and sought to bring me back into line with a firm hand and a thrashing or seven.'

'I'm very sorry to hear that, Charlie.'

The lad cast aside Silas's heartfelt reply with a flippant wave of his hand. 'Thank you, but I am fine. Never been more free, actually. I intend to stay south of Hadrian's Wall the rest of my life, the further from Cook's dreadful haggis and Loch Ness the better, I say.'

Though Silas itched to enquire further into the lad's Scottish roots, now did not seem the time. 'Well, I for one am most thankful for your journey south.'

They sank into their own pensive silences. Silas watched the flames dance behind the grates of the firebox. His thoughts took flight, and damn if they did not land him back alongside Pitch at the castle. This would fast become an intolerable habit if he was to think of Pitch each time he saw a pretty flame. Silas sucked the oil from his fingers with far too much vigour. There was no need to ruin a perfectly good evening with thoughts of the daemon. Pitch would return soon enough, having sated his appetites, and if Silas were lucky, his mood would have lifted. There was no point in *worrying* about one such as Pitch.

They finished their meal and drank their tea, conversing with ease, discussing trivial things: the weather, the location of the long-gone inhabitants of the house, Charlie's love of chestnuts, and Silas's thirst for a decent ale. The lad did not pry into Silas's reasons for being so far off the beaten path, nor indeed anything too personal at all. Silas returned the favour. But keeping to plain discussion did not deplete his enjoyment of the company. In fact, it was likely *because* the conversation was so inane that it was so refreshing. Here there was no ankou, no scythe, no preternatural forces to fear.

The kitchen was a compact space, and the stove's flames were grand enough that most of the shadows were chased from the room. The same couldn't be said for one of the two doorless entrances into the kitchen. One was so coal black with darkness it was as though a wall stood there instead of a doorway. It caused him to shiver, despite the heat. Silas kept his gaze fixed instead upon the other entrance, which led to the sitting room where Charlie had already set a hearty fire in the hearth.

Charlie wiped oily fingers upon his trousers and stood up. 'Shall we adjourn to the parlour?' He mimicked the rounded mouth of the finest of lords, flourishing his hand towards the door with a half bow that set Silas smiling once more.

'However could I refuse such a fine invitation?' He played along, inclining his head and clasping his hands behind his back in a manner he hoped imitated those of fine blood.

'I should hope it would be impossible.' Charlie's cheek dimpled again, and he set off ahead of Silas, leading them into the cobweb-draped sitting room. There was but one option for sitting, a singular sofa, a highbacked, cushioned affair that might have been a soft pink in colour once but was now so marked with stains and faded in patches that it was difficult to say for certain. The frame was a beautiful dark wood, elaborate in its curls and carving, with flowing whorls at the tip of the upholstered arms and an extravagant design along the top of the back cushions: a crown flanked by fanciful botanicals. The seats themselves appeared comfortable enough and devoid of any evident decay. Silas placed himself on the far left and was pleased not to hear any squeak of springs or groans of framework. The spread of his thighs took up considerably more space upon the seat than Charlie's. His weight barely seemed to register upon the cushions. Whatever he hid beneath his layers was slight for sure.

'What a pity we do not have any whisky to finish the meal.' Charlie sighed, kicking off his well-worn boots, exposing thoroughly darned brown socks. He tucked one foot up beneath him.

Silas rested his head against the wood, his height overreaching the cushioned back, which would have been far more comfortable. 'Indeed, though I'm partial to brandy I must say.'

Charlie cleared his throat, a delicate sound. 'I do have something else we might enjoy.' He busied himself at the pocket of his trousers and withdrew a sorry-looking cigarette, almost bent in two after enduring the crushed confines.

Silas rolled his head to consider the thin curling of white paper. 'I'm not sure I am a smoker.'

'You're not sure?' Charlie said, much amused. 'Have you forgotten from one day to the next? Good gracious, Silas, whatever have you been through that you might forget such a thing?'

'You would be surprised.' Silas's laugh was unsteady.

'Then how about we discover something about you this evening?' Charlie made his way to the fireplace, crouching so he could lean in close to the weaving orange and reds to light the cigarette. The auburn in his hair was drawn out by the flames, making the spiky lengths appear far redder than it did other times. With his body silhouetted just so, Silas noted a slenderness to the lad's neck he'd not yet noticed before. He drew his eyes away, conscious of how intently he had stared. Christ, he could not even blame the evils of the drink for his wandering eye, nor a daemon's poisonous charms. Charlie took a long draw of the cigarette, setting the tip glowing. An earthy, woody scent, tinged with a hint of lemon, sprang upon the air.

Charlie made his way back to the sofa, extending the cigarette.

'Would you like some? It is cannabis. The doctors recommend it for a multitude of things. Wonderful for nervous coughs and insomnia, so they say.' Charlie took another puff as Silas hesitated. 'They even say it may go so far as to subdue a woman's hysteria.' He coughed and laughed in unison. 'Can you imagine such a thing?'

'Hardly.' Silas shifted in his seat. 'But I'm not sure I will join you. My dinner is still settling, and I'm quite relaxed as it is.'

Had he partaken of cannabis in life? He felt no repulsion towards the idea now but was not so sure he was ready to learn the effects of such a substance upon a once-dead body.

Charlie pressed the cigarette forward. 'At least hold it for me. I need to take this jumper off before I melt away entirely.'

Silas obliged, taking the white press of paper and plant between finger and thumb. Charlie grasped the hem of his jumper and hauled it over his head. The layers of clothing caught in his fingers, and his struggle to free himself exposed his midriff momentarily.

'Bloody hell, my clothing is attempting to suffocate me.' He bubbled with laughter.

Silas's grin froze. He'd not been wrong about Charlie being of slight build. The lad's waist curved above sharp hips with the slight swell of belly beneath his navel. There appeared to be bandaging of some kind further up his ribs, but much to his chagrin Silas's eyes pulled south, captured by the tilt and shift of the lad's hips as he wriggled free of his clothing, bringing to mind the gyrations of another.

Silas ground his teeth and cursed his flighty mind for letting loose thoughts of the daemon at such a time. It was not as though the pair were identical, anyway. And Silas, god forbid, had seen enough of the daemon to know. Charlie had none of the taut lines of muscle defining his belly and groin that Pitch did. The daemon was far narrower in the waist too, as though his skin were a corset itself. Charlie's middle was softer, fuller, and with no hint of the V-shape of muscle on Pitch that dragged the eye down lower, to that place between his legs the daemon adored so well.

Silas squeezed his eyes closed a moment. Bloody hell, what on Earth was he doing making such comparisons? He raised the cigarette to his lips and inhaled deeply. The warm heat flowed down his throat, mildly bitter and rough, his lungs dragging the smoke in. He held it there, refraining from taking a breath until he grew light-headed.

He exhaled with a small sound, pale smoke streaming from his lips.

'Changed your mind, then?' Charlie, finally freed of his jumper, smoothed out the shirts hidden beneath. Two at least, Silas would guess, yellowed at the cuffs and collar. Charlie repositioned himself on the couch, both feet beneath him now. His clothing billowed about him, trousers spread like tawny blankets about his legs. His bare skin was thankfully now covered.

'Well, I wouldn't mind a decent night's sleep.' He offered the cigarette back, but Charlie shook his head.

'Have another. You seem quite...distracted. Perhaps there is a lot upon your mind to bother you at night, Silas.'

Rather than answer, he inhaled again deeply. This time when he sought to hold the smoke in his lungs, it snagged there. He coughed, eyes watering. Puffs of pale white left his mouth in short bursts. Charlie laughed, taking the cigarette as Silas thrust it blindly at him, tears streaming. Once he had recovered, they sat in easy silence, passing the cannabis between them. One or the other would comment occasionally on how pleasantly warm the room was, or how fortunate it was they did not have to sleep outside. Wonderfully dull conversation. The smoke found its way into Silas's veins, laying as fine a haze upon his mind as it did the air of the sitting room. His muscles lost their knots, he slid down deeper into the sofa, and his eyelids grew a layer of lead. He could damned well not stop smiling.

The slightest feature of the room had his mirth bubbling.

'Do you see that?' He chuckled, pointing to a tear in the burgundy rug. 'Does it not look like a...a cockerel to you?' His laughter impaled his words, almost destroying them.

'Show me!' Charlie sucked at the last tiny morsel of the cigarette. 'Where do I see such an incredible sight?' He spoke rather loudly for such a quiet space.

'Just there? How can you not see it?' Silas's cheeks ached from grinning. And his arm seemed to float about before him like it had a life of its own. 'That is a cockerel, and it is marvellous.'

'Cockerel? You are quite mad, my dear chap. For that is a red squirrel if ever I saw one.' Charlie rocked forward, leaning to plant his hands against the rug but leaving his knees still upon the sofa, his arse high in the air. He squealed with delight. 'Yes, yes, squirrels I tell you. I would know them from any distance. There is a most formidable array of pines by the loch, where I live...lived...and there was a damned invasion of the blighters in their branches. My father despised them, as he did so many things.' Charlie's dimple was a living, dancing thing against his cheek. The roll of his tongue became more pronounced as his Scottish heritage refused to be subdued.

Pines by the loch.

A thought stirred, like a flag unfurling in the back of Silas's mind. But it was slippery as the proverbial eel. Pines. Loch. Blast it, he was so very terrible at catching eels.

'Oh wait!' Charlie declared. 'I see your cockerel, Silas. You are quite right. Not a squirrel at all. You are not only a great fisherman, you are handsome and good company and an excellent cockerel spotter.' His laughter shook him, and as he teetered there, half upside down, his shirts slid down his back and bunched about his neck. 'Oh, you should sit like this, Silas. The world looks so wonderful when it is topsy-turvy. It makes so much more sense than it did before. Hurry, the cockerel says you must.'

Silas's laughter jumped from him like a mad thing. 'How the blazes am I supposed to get this great lug of a body into a position like that?'

Despite his protest he drew his legs up and rocked about, seeking to set his knees upon the couch. Christ, he was not only broad, he was tall. So bloody tall. How had had gotten about without knocking his head a dozen times a day when he was alive?

'That's it,' Charlie encouraged. 'Now the other leg, then you should have it. No, no. Your left leg, Silas.'

'Which one is my left?' Silas guffawed. Goodness, his voice was deep. He'd not noticed that before.

'Oh shit, I don't think you have a left leg, how strange. Poor man.' Charlie sputtered, his chortles consuming him.

'Wait, maybe this is it.' Silas grabbed his knee, left or right he had no clue, and hauled it onto the sofa like a captain pulling up anchor. All at once he had done it. He was kneeling on the cushions. 'I did it!' he shouted, throwing his arms overhead in self-congratulations. The room spun, his body tilted, and Silas toppled over.

'Oh, I'm falling,' he said, simply.

'I'll catch you!'

Silas could not say what happened in the next moment, aside from it involving a clash of bodies, another roar of laughter, and a landing that saw him land flat out on his back on the rug with Charlie half-sprawled over him. Silas's ribs ached as he dissolved into a fit of laughter. Charlie bobbed against his chest as the hilarity shifted them both.

'Wonderful catch.' Silas sobbed, wiping at the tears.

He was faintly aware that it was all ridiculous, and all coming from the influence of what had lain in that roll of white paper, but how magnificent it was to ache from amusement and not more serious things.

'Thank you. I knew I would find my talent eventually.' Charlie sniffed, his head still set upon Silas's chest and showing no sign of moving.

Never mind, Silas decided, he was quite comfortable where he was. And far too exhausted to consider shifting. The fire snapped in its hearth, and Silas's eyelids fluttered. His body was loose and flooded with warmth. A wind had picked up outside, and it tapped at a loose shingle upon the roof. He tilted his head to gaze down at Charlie, who had grown silent. The lad's light auburn curls were even more mussed up than they'd been to begin with. He sighed, a contented and deep reaching sound.

'This has been a pleasant evening, Silas. Thank you for your good company.' Charlie adjusted his position, pulling his feet from where they still clung to the cushions. He slipped entirely into the narrow space between Silas and sofa, his head nestling against Silas's shoulder.

Silas's fuzzy mind registered how close they were, and that he should likely move to give the lad some space, but the rug was far too soft, the cannabis far too pleasant in his veins to bother. Charlie lifted his head. The lad chewed at his bottom lip, his eyes searching Silas's face. As though he sought an answer there.

'Is everything all right?' Silas murmured.

Charlie's full lips were damp. 'Very much so.'

Silas knew it was coming, but his addled brain chugged the message to him in slow, slow motion.

He. Is. Going. To. Kiss. You.

With a clear head he may have responded differently, he might have mumbled a refusal and found his way to his feet. As it was, he said nothing. And did not even blink as Charlie drew in, closing the space between them.

CHAPTER 7

C harlie's lips were akin to marshmallow. Silas had indulged in the airy, sickly-sweet concoction only once when Sybilla had offered him some of the candy treat before passing it on to Pitch, where it had been quickly devoured. When the daemon had kissed him at Lady Sybilla's farm it had still laced his lips, along with that strange bitterness. A combination not so unappealing as it might seem. Silas squeezed his eyes shut, banishing thoughts of the daemon into the darkness.

Focus, he admonished himself.

He should indulge in this moment. Was not everyone harking at him to wet his wick, or dip it...or whatever he was supposed to do to indulge his baser nature?

Silas fought through the fog that held his mind and body in a swaddle. But this was all wrong. His twitching cock and aching balls were betraying him. They should not rouse at this. Heat laced his spine as his body began to flood with arousal. Charlie lay half-draped upon him, his weight an insubstantial thing.

His tongue, a man's tongue, darted into Silas's mouth. It was a man's fingers that caressed his neck and explored the curve of his collarbone with breathtaking delicacy. Christ almighty, they could both be flung into gaol for this. This act they indulged in, it was foul, was it not? The swell of his member at the lad's touch was against the natural order of things.

Silas caught at his wild thoughts and took a stranglehold. What the hell did it matter? Silas *himself* was against the natural order of things. A man reanimated, brought forth from the grave. He smiled into the gentle explorations of Charlie's tongue. So bloody what if he imagined slipping his hand into Charlie's trousers and taking hold of the stiffness he knew he'd find there? The lad took advantage of the smile widening Silas's lips to probe deeper. Charlie's tongue darted between Silas's teeth, tentative, gentle, inquisitive. He responded and they toyed with each other, slipping in and out of the heat of one another's mouth.

'Silas,' Charlie whispered, sucking in a breath.

It seemed as though he intended to say more, but the words did not come. Silas rolled onto his side, lowering Charlie onto his back, his broad frame blocking the firelight from reaching the lad. For a while there was nothing but the slippery, damp sounds of their mouths united. Every so often Charlie would pull his lips free to indulge them upon Silas's cheeks where stubble must have been rough against delicate skin. He slid lower to take in the lobe of his ear before dancing kisses upon his brow. A sigh escaped Silas more than once. The man touched at him with the lightness of feathers. Silas ran his hand down over Charlie's body, tracing the curve of a shoulder and slipping to his back. Charlie groaned and returned his lips to Silas's own, his kisses more urgent.

He raised his knees, and they found a firm place against Silas's groin, pressing into the hardness there. All the while Silas floated upon his cloud, not entirely in the room, just distant enough that he could wonder if things were not going too far. It did not stop his hands from drifting though, running along Charlie's back, finding the roughness of bunched material there just below his shoulder blades. Charlie stiffened, and he pulled his lips from Silas's with a gasp.

'I'm sorry,' Silas said, though for what his hazed mind was not sure.

Charlie's breath came in quick intakes. A stick in the fire sizzled its protest at being consumed.

'No, no. You've done nothing wrong.' Charlie bit at his lower lip, swollen and red from the rub of flesh against flesh. He ran a finger down Silas's chest, the digit meandering this way and that over his ribs, travelling ever lower. Silas's heart stuttered. He ached, in the pit of his stomach and at the stiff column of flesh between his legs. His throat was narrowed with a simmering desire. But all the while it was as though he watched from a distance, viewing someone else's pleasure. As he had done at The Moon Inn.

Silas's breath hitched.

His eyelids fluttered, and he pulled himself from that place where he had knelt and watched the daemon with his lover.

Charlie's fingers landed upon Silas's waist, tracing the buttons that restrained his bulging cock. There was no denying Silas was stirred, no doubt at all that he enjoyed the taste of a man upon his tongue.

This was no enchantment, and he could not blame a daemon's trickery for the lustful heat that warmed him. Here was a piece of the man Silas Mercer had been. It should have been a welcome discovery, for all its troubles, but instead he felt only the crush of loneliness.

This was residuum of his past, but it lacked in substance. The revelation that he had a preference for cock was empty of any true worth. He longed to know more. Had he taken many lovers? Or had he been devoted to just one?

Charlie's fingers played over the two buttons on Silas's trousers, making light work of them, brushing soon at Silas's skin.

Had anyone shed a tear over his coffin?

He should have been thinking of other things, considering his current predicament, but even as Charlie caressed him, he could not help himself. He wondered if there was a mourner who still cried out his name in the night, as Pitch did for his mysterious Raph.

Silas flinched, staying Charlie's hand.

'Too much?' Charlie said.

'I'm...I don't...' Silas shook his head. God he could not keep a single thought on track. He was thinking too deeply on it all. If he preferred the white staff to the cloven inlet, then so be it. He should indulge to his heart's desire. The laws of men hardly applied to him, not anymore. Christ, Jane and Pitch did not hesitate to indulge themselves in whatever carnal pleasures took their fancy, why should Silas not do the same? 'It is not too much.'

He leaned in so quickly Charlie gasped. Silas loomed over the slighter man. He took Charlie's lips captive and sent rough fingers beneath the layers of the lad's shirts. Warm skin was silken to the touch, and Silas was breathless with sheer, raw want, nerves afire.

'Silas,' Charlie grunted against his lips. 'Silas...'

In answer Silas pressed in harder, slipping into that raucous place where desire ruled all. They both panted hard, bodies serpentining against one another as lust made servants of them. Silas took a handful of material and wrenched Charlie's shirts higher with no small frustration. He wanted the man laid out before him, naked and willing. But where he expected to find soft flesh there was roughness. The backs of his fingers rasped across the tightness of bandages.

The lad gasped and shoved his fists against Silas's chest, forcing him back.

'Silas, stop.'

He did so, but with a frown. 'Are you injured?' The inferno within ebbed. 'Did I hurt you?'

Charlie rolled his head back and forth against the rug. 'No, no you didn't. But perhaps I might hurt you.' He dropped his gaze so that he did not meet Silas's eyes. It might have been amusing, the idea that such a slight young man could do damage to one such as Silas, if Charlie did not tremble so.

'Tell me, what is wrong?' Silas said. 'We need go no further.'

The lad quietened him with a careful finger against his lips. The hint of fish and thyme lingered upon them. 'But I wish to. Silas, there is something...I've not been fair...' Charlie shifted against Silas, urging him clear. Once he had room, he took a deep breath and rose to his feet. Silas moved to follow, but Charlie stayed him gently with a toe against his shoulder. 'You are a good man, I feel it. And I have been long without company. If you will still have me, after I show you, I would take this as far as you will allow. Please know I did not intend anything nefarious here.' As Silas absorbed his words, Charlie pulled his shirts over his head, revealing in full the bandage wound tight around his chest.

'You say you are not injured...I don't understand.' Silas frowned.

A weak smile played at Charlie's lips, and he shook his head. He pulled at the string that fastened his trousers. His fingers, so recently upon Silas's body, worked deftly to release the tie. Silas's chest clenched, and the softening of his cock was halted in its tracks.

'I'm sorry,' Charlie whispered.

He closed his eyes and let his loosened trousers fall. He wore no drawers, all that he had was on display.

Silas stared, silent, lips parted with his surprise.

A man had *not* stirred him after all. A man had not kissed him deeply.

Between Charlie's legs it was dark and glistening. Silas stared at the mound of hair, curls and damp licks that were not so thick they could cover entirely the swell of plump lips beneath. A woman.

The notion of it was a struggle to comprehend in the fogginess.

Perhaps he should have said something, but Silas's mouth was dry, his erection once again slackening. Charlie unwound the bandaging about his...*her*...chest, her eyes never leaving his face. She wavered on her feet, still flush with the lingering effects of the cigarette. The bandage fell away, dropping to the floor like a collapsing serpent. Her breasts were pert handfuls of flesh with pronounced rose-pink nipples jutting into their newfound freedom. Red marks stung her skin where the bandage had dug tight.

'Would you lie with me now, Silas?' Her breath came in ragged gasps, and there was a fearfulness in her gaze that had been absent before. 'Or do you think terribly of me?'

He swallowed hard. 'I...no...I do not think terribly of you.' Through the cannabis cloud he knew that much at least. He rocked onto his knees, shifting in closer. His eyes drew near level with her breasts, and he wondered what it might be like to lay his head against them. Charlie was not the only one who could not catch her breath. 'What is your name?' he said, unsure what else to say.

'In my heart I have always been Charlie, though my parents named me Charlotte. A pity my body betrays me so.' Their grin was melancholy, a fragile thing. 'I'll not tell you my last name so that no one can demand it of you. My father is a bullish man of some stature, and he will not be satisfied until I am dragged back to him.'

'Dragged back?'

'Let us just say, I did not think much of his matchmaking, and will walk down no aisle I have been forced upon.'

She cupped her hands to his face. Silas hesitated a moment before he lifted his hands to rest lightly upon her narrow hips. The scent of her, heady and ripe, met his nostrils, and he struggled through the haze to discern if it pleased him or not. His cock did not strain and pulse as it had done before, but considering the shock of the turn of events, that was hardly surprising.

Charlie's blue eyes shone as she looked down at him. 'Will you lie with me, Silas?' There was an eagerness weighting her words. 'I've trusted no other so easily, but there is something...something about you that reminds me somewhat of myself. I think you too are no stranger to being alone, and that perhaps the world does not fit so well on you either. But if I have made a mistake, Silas, you must tell me.'

She dropped to her knees before him, and he had to lower his chin to keep her gaze. A gaze awash with trepidation. No, he misnamed it. That was desperation brightening her eyes.

'Oh, I am not certain that...' Her face paled, the spark he'd so enjoyed slipping from it. She moved to reach for her discarded clothing, and he despised how forlorn his words made her. Silas stayed her with a glancing touch. 'Charlie...you have not made a mistake.'

The cannabis worked its magic in his veins, urging him on. To lay with Charlotte would not be so terrible. Perhaps, he would find he had misjudged his tendencies entirely. That this nonsense with the daemon, the lingering glances, the rebellious way his thoughts returned to the kiss they had almost shared, and the one they had done so, was nothing more than that. Nonsense.

There was the woman in lilac, after all, the one who ran to him in his vision. The sight of her had brought on a sense of loss, of melancholy. Maybe he had loved her. Desired her.

Silas picked up the unravelled bandage. 'May I?'

Charlie nodded slowly. Silas gathered the end of the fabric and pressed it to her back, winding it beneath her arms and bringing it across her breasts. Charlie shivered and then moved to aid him. Together they wound the frayed material around and around, keeping the binding tight so she was as she had been before. As she wished herself to be. Once they were done, Charlie collapsed against him as though all the bones in her body had turned to jelly.

'You are a good man, I knew it,' she whispered, nestling into his chest. 'I chose this life for myself, but I did not account for how few good people I would find in it.'

Silas tugged his undershirt over his shoulders, slipping his past free with it. At least for now. 'I'm not sure if I am good, or bad, or whatever exists in between. I am just here.'

'And I am glad.'

There was that dimple, that unabashed smile.

Charlie placed her palms against his bare chest and pushed at him, urging him onto his back. She worked to free him of his trousers, and Silas lifted his hips to help her slide them clear.

Now he was as naked and vulnerable as she. Charlie took hold of his cock, working its relaxed length with smooth, hard rubs of her palm, bringing it back to rigid life. Silas let his head drop back and closed his eyes, relishing each stroke. He groaned into her rhythm, his body swaying to meet her grip. Too quickly he felt the curl at the base of his spine, the heat in his belly, that loudening song of lust. Silas sat up and cupped her face, bringing his lips to hers and sliding back into the comfortable familiarity of tongue against tongue. His arms dropped to gather Charlie to him, and he lifted her and swept them both around, laying her gently on her back. Her want made her moan, and her teeth nipped at him. She sought to bite at his tongue. His cock twitched with sudden life. Charlie spread her legs, and he found his place between them, cautious not to lean too greatly upon her, all too aware of how great their difference in size was, of how vast he felt above her. He ran his hand over her belly, down to where she was wet, waiting, ready. His finger traced the slippery mound, heated and swollen. Charlie writhed and whimpered beneath him, wrapping her legs about his hips, urging him down upon her. His cock slid against the velvet flesh between her thighs, her arousal hot as the inside of her mouth. His member, rock hard with need, bounced against the coarse hair that covered her intimate space, and he took shallow, hurried breaths that left him light-headed. He withdrew his hand, bracing himself over her. Taking a moment to watch her. Ensure that she was ready. He would not last long he feared, already beginning to shiver with the whisper of release.

Charlie's smile was thick with lust, her eyelids heavy. She reached between them and clasped her hand over his member, licking her lips as she guided him between warm folds. Silas leaned into her pressure, allowing her to take him in. He ground his teeth. She tightened around him, her heat searing his cock. A whimper left him. He pushed deeper, falling into her. Charlie cried out and Silas halted, fearful he had harmed her.

'Don't stop,' she cried, lifting her hips and throwing herself against him.

Silas groaned into his thrusts, seeking to keep each push of his hips steady and slow, but his lover had other plans for him. Charlie slammed up to meet him, her muscles tightening around his shaft. She scratched at his back, sweat beading upon her brow, a wildness storming her features. Silas met her frantic movements with those of his own, and they soared ever higher. He lost sight of the room around him, of the fire burning the room to cinders.

He lost sight of the person beneath him.

And found another in her place.

Silas squeezed his eyes shut, his thrusts gaining greater urgency. His veins were fit to burst beneath his skin. The room was filled with grunts and cries, sweat and musk. His body was aflame with the very basest of needs, and Silas rocked into it, soaring. He could not stop his mind from going where it wished. And with whom. Even in the darkness behind his lids Silas saw him. The flames dashed with emerald burning bright. Silas arched his back, his balls pulsed and clenched and flooded his cock with his climax. He spilled his seed, his body jerking in violent abandon. A cry tore from him, high and rich with sharp frustration. Somewhere in the distance he heard Charlie lose herself, he knew it was her body that bucked beneath him, understood it was her hands that clutched at him, but he kept his eyes closed tight so he might keep the picture there a little longer.

He shuddered through his fading throes. Gasping. And cursing the vile daemon who lay in his mind's eye.

CHAPTER 8

C harlie nestled in close against him, her knees tucked up to her chest.

'That was quite wonderful. Thank you, Silas.'

With his heart still thundering and his breath yet to settle, Silas was slow to reply. Certainly it was comforting to know that he was in full working order. And the pleasure had been immense, he'd not deny. But still...there was the small matter of where his thoughts had led him.

'You're welcome,' he said in the end, as though he'd opened a door for her and not taken her roughly, fiercely, with his thoughts straying and his mind vanishing her entirely and laying another in her place.

Her fingers found the rowan wood bracelet at his wrist, the only thing he wore. 'I like this, did you make it?'

'No. I didn't. It was a given to me...by a friend, when I needed a little succour.' He was gripped by a sudden urge, and slipped it free. Taking Charlie's hand he slid it over her fingers, onto her wrist. Though she was so much slighter than he, somehow the crooked wood fit her snugly. Not too large at all.

'But it's yours,' she exclaimed.

'And I'd like to give it to you.'

'It's beautiful.'

And seemed in its rightful place upon her. Silas had the Order behind him, and a daemon to protect him, but what did Charlie have? Christ, she'd not even had his *attention* while he was inside her. And the road she travelled was dangerous.

This felt right. Ottelie would not begrudge him the exchange, he was sure.

Charlie fell asleep quickly, making a sweet sound as she exhaled, a childish whimper that soothed Silas into sleep alongside her.

It was the cold that roused him. He woke to find himself draped in the folds of his coat and the fire burned down to a handful of glowing embers. Silas sat up.

'Charlie?' He scowled at the waver in his voice. He sounded like a child waking in the dark alone. 'Charlie, are you there?'

His answer was an unsettling creak of wood, coming from the hallway. Silas jumped to his feet, scouring the floor for his clothing. He threw on his undershirt and danced from foot to foot as he pulled on his trousers. One of his buttons had perished in the lustful melee. He stumbled, and his toe met the wooden foot of the sofa. Silas growled a curse, throwing on his socks, their odour quite overpowering, and pulling on his boots. He did not bother with a shirt, nor his coat. He raced into the hallway. The front door was ajar, spilling in the light of a dawning day. They must have slept for hours.

He felt keenly the absence of Lalassu, and wondered, not for the first time, where the blasted horse had run off to. He moved with deliberate strides, but at the last moment rethought his intention to simply step out. He had no idea what might wait for him there, what lurked beneath the eaves waiting for a fool such as he to rush out blindly. And he would be nearly blind, for the gloomy interior contrasted starkly with the fledgling light of the rising sun outside.

'Charlie?' he whispered.

The silence answered.

He did not tingle with the anticipation of a teratism here. In fact, he felt no ill ease at all, but it had unsettled him to wake alone. Perhaps he was abandoned. Silas leaned his back against the wall, brushing the faded strips of floral wallpaper long past their prime, and edged his way up the hall until he could see outside. He peered at the pathway beyond the door, searching for a hint of a shadow that might shift and alert him to a presence waiting on him beyond. There was none to be seen, save for the bobbing darkness of the wildflowers that had taken up residence alongside the rutted path. The wind was brisk with strength, and towards the brook the trees swayed back and forth in a pleasant rhythm.

Surely he'd not been such a dreadful lover that she had fled? Christ, how mortifying. But preferable of course to the alternative, that he had assumed too much of their safety here, misjudged the naiad's kind intentions, and now Charlie had met foul play.

Silas tensed at the thoughts.

Shit. Where were his wits? He should have taken more care. Instead he'd been fucking about. Quite literally.

A rattling of a door handle came from behind, a creak followed, and all at once the front door that had been so swollen with damp on his arrival, swung viciously on its hinges, slamming shut.

Silas hollered and jumped backwards, hands flailing at coat pockets that did not exist. He hissed at his stupidity. He'd left the bandalore in the sitting room.

'Silas? Is everything all right?'

He spun about, his hair catching at his face. Charlie stood at the far end of the hall, the back door open behind her, a basket in her hands. She had dressed in only her smock, her silhouette backlit, a bemused look upon her face. 'You look like you have seen a ghost.'

Silas shoved at his hair, looping it over his ears so he might not appear quite so dishevelled as he felt. 'Of course not. But the door...the door...' He pointed at the offending object behind him, aware that he was stammering like a fool. 'Are you all right?'

Charlie's smile twitched. 'I am very well. But you seem rather flustered.'

'I'm fine,' he said stiffly. 'I woke and there was no sign of you...I thought that perhaps...' He hesitated, caught in his own worries. He was not about to tell her what he truly thought might have happened. Besides, if he started speaking of terrible monsters and the Blight, or moody daemons, he suspected Charlie would laugh him off, more bemused than she was now. 'Well, I thought you had continued on your way.'

Her amusement softened into something gentler. 'As you can see, I have not. And I'll do no such thing, for I can see how greatly it would upset you. I'm sorry to have woken you so abruptly. I suppose I caused a draft when I opened the back door. That was quite the noise. But rest assured, it was not me storming off in a temper.' The dimple reappeared. 'In fact, I feel quite wonderful, very refreshed.' She tilted her head. 'How about you?'

'Oh, yes. Very refreshed.' But also curious as to how the door managed to slam itself shut when he could not force it closed last night.

Charlie headed into the kitchen with her basket of dandelions and other clippings, and he followed.

'Hmm. I'm surprised really.' Charlie set about stoking the firebox that was already stuffed with kindling. 'You were quite restless while you slept. I rather thought it might be I who woke alone, if I'm honest. I don't expect you to tell me anything about your life, fear not, but I've spent some time creating a wonderful story for you myself. About why you are here in Wyre Forest, I mean.' She struck a match and thrust it into the dry wood, where it caught and flickered. 'You are a fugitive, an outlaw, I imagine. Wanted across several counties for some dreadful act. But it was to avenge a loved one, so it's not without purpose I'm sure. Sorry, I have rather a macabre fascination with such things. I cannot get enough of the penny dreadfuls. Do you know they say there's a murderer in our family line? My great-grandfather took offence to a man who showed too much interest in his son. Beastly, don't you think? If it's true. No one will say more than two words about it. It is infuriating. I hope you don't mind that I've made you a criminal? I did so fancy the idea of bedding a lawless man.'

Silas's eyes widened. 'I truly don't think that I am lawless.'

Her laughter danced between them. 'But you're not sure? You are quite delightful, Silas. I don't think I've met a man more puzzling to me than you. A formidable giant to be sure. I suppose I should be quite terrified of you. I've met brutes on the road not unlike you whom I certainly *was* afraid of, especially when they learned what lies between my legs. But you...' Her gaze slid down his body, causing him to blush when her eyes stayed too long at his hips. 'You have the air of a startled deer about you, a wide-eyed helplessness that is quite endearing, and interesting.' She frowned at her thoughts. 'I wonder if you are not more lost than I am, Silas?'

He squirmed beneath her appraisal. She was sharp as a whip. Damn, it would be relieving to tell her the truth of who he was. Of teratisms, and magickal horses, angels, daemons and all the rest. Bring her penny dreadfuls to life in a way she could never imagine. He traced a whorl in the surface of the kitchen table. He suspected she would relish every word that came from him, and would not run. Despite what was best for her.

'You'll have to keep me as your rogue, I'm afraid, for I cannot tell you more of myself.' Really, he *could* speak of his employment with the Order. She might raise an eyebrow in bemusement as some did, or brighten with enthusiasm and gush at the exotic nature of his employ as did others. But he held his tongue, for he would only be able to speak in half-truths, and Silas did not enjoy the idea of lying to her.

Charlie studied him a moment longer and nodded. 'Then a rogue you shall be.'

She turned back to the firebox, where the fire had caught and the heat was already seeping into the small room. Satisfied, she moved to the basket she had set on the edge of the table. The wind rattled at loose windowpanes, and from somewhere within the house doves cooed.

'Are you hungry?' she said. 'I thought the leftover fish would be nice, and I gathered rowan berries. It is hardly a feast, but it will have to do.'

'Sounds delightful.' He cleared his throat so he might speak of more delicate matters. Namely the weight against his bladder. 'I just need to...I'm going to attend to –'

'You're going to take a piss.' Charlie's grin was alive with mischief. 'Silas, you were inside me last night. Feel free to dispose with formalities now.'

Good lord, whose daughter was this? And what fool was the man to imagine he could bend her to his will? He smiled at the notion and excused himself from the room. He returned to the hallway, careful around the gaping hole in the floor, and opened the front door. He followed the path down through the overgrown fenced area that might have been a fine garden once but was now the playground of whatever weeds could survive there. It occurred to him that he had not checked to see if the house contained a water closet, but he would not turn back, much preferring to walk out amongst the freer air of the forest and the whisper of the trees. He continued down towards the mill. It did not seem right to relieve himself too close to the house, or the mill, so he travelled a little upstream until only a small portion of the mill's dark shingles were still evident through the trees.

He unbuttoned his pants and relieved himself against a trunk with a contented sigh. His cock was tender to the touch, with some reddening near to the base. How long had it been since he'd engaged in such an act? Silas leaned a hand against the tree, enjoying the rough scrape of the bark against his palm. It looked to be a pleasant day ahead, mild but not uncomfortably so.

He stared about the forest as he pissed a warm stream into chilly air. He had expected some sign of Pitch before now, but was secretly glad he'd not yet arrived. Silas would need time to banish the vision he'd conjured of the daemon, gleaming emerald eyes and parted Cupid's bow lips gasping his name. Should Pitch appear now, Silas feared he could not look him in the eye.

A shiver stole along the back of his neck.

The crack of a branch disturbed the subtle chirrup of birdlife.

Dear god, do not let it be the daemon. Startled, Silas scanned about for a hint of him. A flash of reddish orange betrayed the quick scurry of a fox through the trees. He sighed. Charlie's assessment of him as a startled deer was embarrassingly accurate. Bloody hell, he was a servant of death and yet here he stood, jumping at the merest shadow. He shoved his cock back into his pants. And as he fiddled with the surviving button, he breathed in the clear air, inhaling until his shoulders lifted to accommodate full lungs. He exhaled through his mouth noisily, flecks of moisture escaping with the sound.

'Right then. Fish and rowan berries.' Silas planted his hands upon his hips. He did not favour the bitterness of the berries – Ottelie had assured him wrongly that they were pleasant – but fish would do nicely. 'Perhaps Lalassu will grace me with her presence by the time we are done.'

Another snap of dry wood came. This time from the forest beyond the brook. Silas braced, determined not to startle but resenting his decision not to grab his coat before he made his way out. At least his fingers were steady, no tingling bothering his skin, but a low prickle of caution stirred against his back. The wind made its lazy way about him, a briskness to its touch.

A shadow darted behind a swathe of ferns.

Just another fox. Or a deer. That was all. Silas sank his teeth into his lip. It was dawn, the forest was coming alive. That was only natural, and it should be a lovely thing to behold. It *had* been, before the Forest of Dean had stolen something from him.

Silas stared at the ferns. There was stillness there now. The birds were silent. The wind had lessened as though sheltering in the canopy of the trees. A sinking feeling dragged at his belly. A weight settled on the air.

'No,' he whispered. 'It cannot be.'

But he could not deny it. This pressure about him, the unnatural quiet, was all too reminiscent of the forest before Black Annis had attacked.

Silas grew rigid. Charlie was in the house alone, and he'd already been gone far longer than he should. He whirled about, breaking into a run. He reached the mill, and his boots sank into muddy ground, the moist soil sucking at his soles, slowing his headlong pace. A sound caught his ear, and he peered over his shoulder. Over on the far side of the brook, where the forest filtered the sun's rays and allowed only a smear of light through, a shadow burst from its hiding place among the bracken.

He squinted. It might have been a deer, frightened by his sudden movement. Whatever it was ran on four legs. It dashed low to the ground and was heavy enough to make a ruckus as it raced.

Away from him.

He had just turned his attentions back to the path when a scream shattered the preternatural quiet.

CHAPTER 9

S ilas found a turn of foot he'd not known himself capable of, cutting to shreds the distance that lay between him and Charlie. His heartbeat blurred into a singular hum beneath his ribs. His breath scorched up his throat. Panic and something shriller, undefined, bubbled beneath his skin. The front door was closed, but Silas did not stop to bother with the knob. He threw himself at the flimsy wood, and it shattered with pleasing ease.

'Charlie! Where are you?' An enormous thud resounded against the wall beside him, followed by a pained cry.

'Shit.' Silas dashed to the sitting room but stopped short just outside the doorway. A heavy sense of foreboding, of wrongness, impeded him like a wall. It was thick as fire smoke upon the place, crawling over his skin. 'Charlie? Are you all right?'

He forced himself into the room. And soon found his companion. Horror gripped him. She lay crumpled against the wall, curled up in a ball on the ground. Above her, a splay of cracks and a hollow marked where her body had met with the plasterwork.

A cloaked figure stood over her, his face nearly hidden beneath his hood. What Silas could see was vile.

Skin so white it seemed he'd never seen the sun, lips the hue of fresh bruises, and skin that stretched tight over a pronounced chin. The figure stood so still as to be a statue. Had Silas not glimpsed the features of a man, he might have assumed he was staring at a cloak hung upon a hatstand. The fiend's breath grated through his mouth, his inhales strained and stuttered.

'Get away from her,' Silas growled.

Dear god, this room reeked of acrid unease. And he did not have the bandalore upon him. It lay in his coat, which Charlie had folded neatly and placed on the sofa while he was out. Too many steps away.

'There you are.' The grating breath was harsh as a blacksmith's rasp upon a horseshoe. 'Ankou.'

Silas's blood raced through his veins. This creature knew him, knew Silas's truth. So this was no robber or cut-throat taking advantage of a solitary traveller. His eyes darted to the ground. A shadow clung to the fringe of his mud-caked cloak hem. Human, then? The intruder shifted, reaching for Charlie where she lay so alarmingly still.

'Don't touch her!' Silas ran at the fiend.

The hooded figure thrust an arm from beneath folds of rough grey fabric. A knife, narrow and fine, glinted in his grasp. Silas launched himself to one side with a grunt. He crashed into the flimsy side table next to the sofa, his weight destroying it as thoroughly as it had done the front door. Unwelcome shards of wood prodded at his side, but he had no time to investigate any injury. The cloaked intruder moved quickly, startlingly so, darting at his fallen prey like a hawk descending upon a mouse. Silas was forced into a cumbersome roll across the rug, snatching up one of the table's broken legs as he went. He kicked out as his attacker advanced. His feet found only the fluttering folds of the grey cloak. The man lunged, flaring the hood about his face, affording Silas a glimpse of what lay beneath as he scrambled to his feet.

He flinched at the sight, for it was no less appalling than the fowl miasma that clung to the room. The features were true to a man, but one who sat upon death's doorstep. He was gaunt, as though starving, pale cheeks hollow, the ridges of his eye sockets so pronounced it was as though his eyeballs were sinking into the skull.

And those eyes... Silas cursed beneath his breath. The intruder's eyes were solid pools of black.

He swung, aiming for the gut. The cloaked man twisted like a true contortionist, arching his body about to avoid the blow. There was something in the way he moved that had Silas recoiling. Did the fiend even have a spine?

The heavyset air bore down, quickening Silas's breath. His nerves jangled beneath his skin.

Wrong. Something was so terribly wrong here. He fought the urge to wretch.

The intruder righted himself and came again, arms outstretched though hidden in swathes of fabric, white fingertips peeking from the folds.

Silas grasped his table-leg sword in both hands, raising his arms and striking down with all the force he could muster. He landed a massive blow upon one spindly, reaching arm. The crack of bone rang out.

The man did not cry out. His horrid mouth-breathing did not falter from its rhythm. He most certainly did not let go of the knife. It was as though he had not noticed the strike at all. His broken arm fell to his side. The knuckles about the knife's handle were engorged, enormous compared to the bony fingers.

Silas edged back, arms spread wide in anticipation of attack. The intruder's black gaze did not leave him, and yet Silas had no sense of being *looked* at. The man was staring right through him as though mesmerised.

He'd like to believe it was an opium haze upon the man, an addicted lunatic housebreaking to feed his habit. Silas was no longer so naive.

'Leave, now.' He drew himself up, making use of all that bulk that normally irked him so. 'Leave us be. I'll not warn you again.'

He *must* draw the bandalore to him. But the intruder gave him no time for such efforts.

The sickly man shot at him, his speed blurring him to a grey sweeping cloud. If not for a glint of light upon his blade, Silas would have missed the strike. He threw up the table leg, a paltry defence against the mind-numbing speed of the intruder, and luck was with him. The blade stuck into the timber, the force of the blow pressing its tip clear through. The intruder's breath gurgled in his chest as he wrestled to pull the weapon clear.

Despite the use of only one hand, he set upon the task with the ferocity of a wolf upon a fresh kill, jerking his body in sharp, disfiguring motions. Silas fastened his hands to either ends of the length of wood, staggering against the intruder's frantic, robust energy. The attacker stood head high to his chest and stared straight ahead, unblinking. The knife's serrated edge saw it hold fast in the wood, and the jerking movement, the wrenching of the handle up and down, only served to bury it nearer to the hilt. Not that it deterred the intruder. Silas could barely keep his grip on the length of wood. The intruder's maddened strength belied his malnourished form. Silas leaned into the onslaught, desperate to herd the man back, perhaps trip him over his own feet.

But it was *he* who was in most danger of a fall.

Silas spared a glance over his shoulder. He was being inched back towards the sofa. If the intruder gained enough momentum, he might ram Silas into it, taking his knees from beneath him.

'Get back, I say.' He ground his teeth, grunting at the steam engine of frustration that bore down on him.

The Inverness coat with its hidden treasure was so desperately close. He fought to clear his head, to find that peaceful place he'd been in when the bandalore had heeded his summons at Lady Satine's farm. But the intruder gave him no respite, and the damned air seemed to have seeped into Silas's skull and draped itself on his thoughts. He was flustered, filled with an anxiety he could not quell. Silas shifted his plan. If he were to suddenly release his hold on the timber, the intruder's own momentum would throw him forward, affording Silas a chance to attack from behind.

He readied himself.

'Silas?'

'Charlie? Run away from here,' Silas cried. He dared a glance. She stood using the wall as a crutch, her face pained, eyes wide with terror. 'Run.'

The intruder let go of the knife and dove at Silas, his cloak billowing like a storm cloud about them. Silas cried out, tumbling back, the wood with its impaled knife flying from his grasp. The carved high edge of the sofa bit into his back, as the harsh drag of the intruder's breath fired against his neck. The sofa, a resilient piece of furniture if ever there was one, did not collapse but instead tipped backwards. The blow catapulted Silas into an awkward half-flip. Lengths of material enveloped him, and he landed in a painful, messy tangle upon the hard wooden floor. The intruder landed astride him, his hands everywhere at once, as though he searched for the tenderest places, skin most vulnerable to the nasty pinch of bony fingers. A curious crunching noise came with the fiend's searching, the grinding of a pestle in its mortar. All the while those glassy black eyes stared through Silas.

'Damn you, let me go.' Silas punched at his assailant.

Reed thin as he was, Silas could not seem to shift him. Nor catch at him. The cloaked fiend moved with such randomness, such jerky abandon, that Silas was reminded of an eel. Despite the injury made to his arm, the intruder was relentless. Silas could not predict where the blows would come from, struggling to protect his face from the gnarled fingers that pinched at him with no apparent rhyme or reason.

Silas pressed his hands against the intruder's chest, seeking to hold him at arm's length as some protection. He could feel each rib through the thinness of the man's shirt. How did such a wasted specimen have such strength? Their haphazard contest continued. Each time Silas thought himself free, the grey cloak was somehow there, blinding him, making him falter. It was as though the material were a living part of the intruder himself. With a frustrated cry, Silas lunged for a flailing hand. And at long last found a hold.

The pestle ground louder in its mortar. And beneath his palm came an odd sensation, as though he held on to broken crockery.

It struck him.

Christ almighty, the intruder had been using his broken arm to attack, and Silas now held it right at the spot on the forearm where bone had snapped beneath the skin. Horrid as it was, it was an advantage. Pressing his lips tight, Silas gripped harder, arm muscles tight with force.

A cracking came from beneath the grey layers.

'Fuck.' He hissed. And doubled his efforts. The arm bone was shattering in his hold. It must be agonising, but the cloaked man did not so much as gasp.

'Get off him, you bastard!'

Charlie appeared, all wild-eyed and flush-cheeked, standing over Silas and his attacker.

'Charlie, leave here! Now!'

But she'd not listened to him before, and was not doing so now.

She raised her arms. Wrapped between her clenched hands was a small knife, much too diminutive to have belonged to the intruder. She sucked in her breath and drove the point into the man's back. The intruder jerked and stiffened, the rasping breath catching in his throat. Silas snatched handfuls of the man's cloak, gathered it up, and heaved the intruder clear. His enraged throw was a sight to behold. The gangly man was sent soaring over the upturned sofa and hurtling towards the cold fireplace. The black-eyed creature crashed into the mantel, the loud crack of skull on stone reverberating. He landed on his back, half upon the brickwork of the hearth. His fathomless eyes were at last closed, his broken arm twisted at a gut-churning angle at his side.

'Are you all right, Silas?' Charlie still held her knife, and he saw that she trembled.

'I am. And you?'

He sat up gingerly, half expecting to find himself bleeding after the violating assault. The intruder's strange searching, needling touch had been less than pleasant. But there was no crimson about. He'd bruise for sure, but that was all.

'Yes.' Charlie waggled the knife, still in hand. 'I knew this would be worth lugging about in my boot one day. I'll have a headache for a while I suspect, but otherwise I'm fine. Are you sure you are well? He was really laying into you.'

'Quite sure.'

A flash of blue beneath him caught his attention. His coat, half lodged beneath the overturned sofa. He pulled it free, slipping a hand into the pocket where the bandalore should be. The wood was smooth and comforting against his fingertips, but he stifled a huff of frustration. Damn it, he'd performed badly. He should have been able to summon the bandalore, despite his distress. What use in having such a thing if he could not use it to defend himself?

To defend others?

'Did you see the way he moved, Silas? It was extraordinary. I've never seen a thing like it.'

'Nor I.'

The air had cleared. The unsettling weight lifted. Silas could think straight. Pity it was too bloody late for such things.

'Are you sure on that?' Charlie was impressively calm, despite the horror of the attack. Small wonder she'd survived so well on her own. 'Is there anything you'd like to tell me about your friend here?'

She jerked her chin at the prostrate intruder. His cloak spread around him like a spill of grey blood. His shirt, stained with unpleasant yellow and brown splotches, was torn badly, revealing the body beneath. Even from where he stood, Silas could make out the indentation of his ribs.

'He is no friend, I assure you.' Silas heaved himself to his feet. He could still feel the sting of the intruder's pinches upon him.

'Gathered that much. But what the bloody hell is he, Silas? There is something...' Charlie wrinkled her face, searching for the words. 'Wrong, about him. He looks nearer to death than life, like he's just stepped out of his coffin.' She shuddered. 'He is disgusting.'

Silas flinched. His fingers tightened about the bandalore.

'I have no idea who he is, or where he came from. But it is clearly not safe to stay here. I'm sorry. You should be on your way, as fast as you can.'

The pale horse had misjudged this place. Rather badly.

'What are you sorry for? You make it sound as though this were your fault.'

The girl was too perceptive for her own good. 'No...it's not like that. It just seems we should part ways.'

'Doesn't seem like that at all to me. Safety in numbers, I'd suspect. And as I don't believe you'd place me in any danger knowingly, then I can only assume you wish me to leave you, because it is you this....horror...was after. Are you sure there isn't anything you can tell me...about all this?'

He shrugged on his coat, watching Charlie's face as she stared down at the intruder with evident repulsion, lips tugged down, nose wrinkled. He was glad he'd not said a word of his truth to her, for he did not think he could bear to see her look at him the way she did the corpse-like figure by the fire. 'I have no idea who this is, if that is what you are insinuating. I am shaken, that is all. This sort of thing does not happen to me every day.' He scrutinised the floor as he lied through his teeth.

'Nor I. Can't say I mind either.' Charlie pressed the hilt of her knife to her temple and grimaced. 'Blast, that bastard threw quite the punch.'

'Did he say anything when he first appeared? Did he demand anything of you?'

She shook her head gingerly. 'Not a thing. I heard a sound in here and thought you'd returned. I took one step through the door and saw this delightful fellow on his knees over by the couch, sniffing about.'

'Sniffing?'

'Mmhmm.' She tapped the knife's tip to her chin. 'Strange as it sounds, he was sniffing at your coat.'

Silas felt the warmth drain from him. 'My coat?'

'Yes. Perhaps he was looking for the same thing you seemed so desperate to find in your pocket, just now?'

He blinked. The girl should be a private detective. She missed nothing. But was she right? Had the creature sought the bandalore? Or was it Silas's scent he'd locked onto?

Charlie was still waiting on his reply.

'I was simply checking that I had not been robbed. I have a few trinkets that are dear to me.'

'Fine.' She raised her hands. 'I'll not push you further on that, but he's not dead, so what do we do about that?' She brandished her knife. 'Should I finish what was started? I don't suppose it would be much different to the slaughter of a sheep, and I've done that before. I have to say, this is far more exciting than any penny dreadful I've read.'

Silas stared at her. 'Bloody hell, aren't I supposed to be the murderer so far as your story goes? And if I'm not about to slit the throat of an unconscious man, you most certainly are not. We will find some bindings and tie him to ensure he does not follow.'

It would have been wonderful to hear the thud of hooves through the forest right about now. But it appeared Silas had not one but two failed guardians.

Charlie shrugged. 'All right, as you wish. I saw some twine in the kitchen we could use.'

'As soon as that is done we will leave. I'll see you out of the forest safely.'

Charlie chuckled. 'How kind of you, sir. Though who will be protecting whom? That was quite the squeal you let loose when he pushed you over the couch.'

Silas recalled making no such sound, and he reddened with indignation. 'That is not what happened at all.'

'Very well.' She waved a careless hand and turned to leave. But something stayed her. She moved closer to the where the stranger lay, squinting down at him. 'That is odd, is it not?'

'What?'

'Blood. Or rather, the lack of it. I stabbed him at least three times, yet he's not bled a drop.'

They looked in unison at the blade in Charlie's hand. It was clean. They could have used it to cut up their abandoned breakfast fish.

'Please go and get the twine,' Silas urged, the unease curling about his insides once more.

'Absolutely. I think your idea to leave is a good one, Silas.'

All at once the cloaked man was on his feet, his head lolling back until the last moment when his chin snapped forward with a jolt that rocked his entire frail body. He snatched the knife from Charlie's hand and released a crackling, wobbling sound that might have been a scream in another life, but here it was like a rush of water gurgling down a blocked drain.

Charlie cried out, raising her hands to shield herself from the blow the intruder was readying to strike.

'Charlie, move!'

Silas raced forward, pushing her out of the way. He drove his free hand into his pocket, and the bandalore was there, ready for him. It all happened in a rush, a flurry of action and unconscious movement that saw the bandalore slither its string around his finger and jump into his grasp so quickly he had barely placed his hand in his pocket and he was withdrawing it again, weapon in hand.

'Stay back!' Silas roared.

He had thought to use the bandalore as he had done with the grave keeper, and wrap its string about the black-eyed stranger's neck. But the scythe did not fall in line with his plans. Its notes erupted. The blade bloomed into existence, the bandalore shape-shifting in a blink, the wooden discs gone, replaced with a weapon that rested somewhere between a scythe and a sickle. The handle was just the right length for his need, the blade more pointed than curved so as to strike a near target more readily.

The death blade's song was a sublime melody upon the air, very different in its timbre to when it sang of a teratism. This tune was quieter, with fewer rising notes, but as tantalising as any other.

Black eyes settled on him. Silas raised his weapon. His grip settled upon the familiar wooden curves of the shaft, those indents in the wood that were carved just for him. He shifted, his body, sliding into the most favourable position to strike, as though he'd cut at a man a thousand times before. The melody played along, holding him in its embrace. Shaping him, guiding him. Threading into his sinew.

And with one exacting swing, death's servant took the intruder's head.

CHAPTER 10

The headless corpse tumbled back towards the fireplace, its shoulders half buried in last night's ashes, tattered grey cloak covering much of the stone hearth. There was the faint and unpleasant scent of charred flesh upon the air. No blood ran from the ugly, catastrophic wound, as though the scythe had cauterised as it went.

Silas stared down at the grievous injury. Filled with the oddest sense of satisfaction, his body hummed with the echoes of the bandalore's song, even though the blade itself had ceased its melody the moment he'd delivered the killing blow.

'Oh shit, shit, shit,' Charlie whispered. 'Silas...Silas....'

The frantic way she croaked the words had Silas spinning about to face her. It took little scrutiny to discover what caused her distress. Charlie sat where he had shoved her, a few feet away, arms braced behind her, legs bent at the knees and spread.

She stared in horror at what rested between her feet.

The intruder's severed head.

Lengths of oily brown hair touched at where her toes poked through a hole in her thickly darned brown sock. The head had landed with the face turned upwards. There was some mercy in that the eyes were closed, but the intruder's lips were pulled back, exposing violet toothless gums opened wide in a final scream.

'Silas.' Charlie seemed frozen in place. 'Get it away...get it away...'

He studied the trail of fine white powder that meandered over the rug from the torso to where the head had landed, a trail as white as flour that marked the roll of the intruder's head after it left his shoulders.

'Silas! Move the fucking head!'

Her fevered shout snapped him out of his grim considerations. Silas took hold of a fistful of thin, grimy hair and lifted. The head was barely off the floor before the strands tore from the scalp with a puff of fine grey dust, and it landed with a thud next to Charlie's foot.

'Shit.' She lashed out, landing a kick against a hollow left cheek, sending the head rolling at speed towards Silas.

'Argh.' He lifted his foot to allow it to pass, and it rolled off the edge of the rug, coming to rest a moment later where the unevenness of the floorboards held it steady. It lay on its side now, and the damage caused by Charlie's desperate kick was evident, and curious. He'd not thought the blow strong enough to have done such damage, but there it was, nonetheless. The intruder's cheek was shattered like a dropped eggshell. Just above, near to the temple, there was a fleshless patch where the scalp had torn free, exposing the bone beneath. Silas realised that was where he had grasped the hair.

The hair was still gripped in his fist. With a derisive grunt he flicked the vile strands away. His throat tightened with disgust.

Charlie scrambled to her feet, rubbing her hands at her thighs as though she were trying to rub the skin clean off. She dashed past Silas.

'Charlie, wait.'

'I'm going to throw up!' she shouted, racing into the hall. 'Give me a moment.'

He was not keen to do so. He preferred she not leave his sight at all. 'Wait for me!'

Silas turned to follow her, and the length of his coat caught between his legs. He grabbed the folds of thick material, and his fingers touched something narrow and hard in his pocket. In all that had gone on, he'd entirely forgotten about the arrowhead.

What if this attack came from the very same enemy who had struck in the Forest of Dean? It did not seem too great a leap to imagine.

What a fool he was, dallying with Charlie. Silas and his pathetic attempts to pretend he was an ordinary man might yet get her killed.

Christ, if any harm came to her, he'd have no one to blame but himself. And how bitterly that stung. The sooner he had her out of this forest and on her way, the better.

A task made much easier if his bloody damned horse were to show herself.

He cast the dismembered body one last glance. The intruder at least would bother them no more. Likely he should have been repulsed by what he'd done, and no doubt he'd have a nightmare or two, but for now Silas could find nothing but the greatest relief at the creature's demise.

He hurried into the hallway. Through the gaping hole where the front door had once stood he glimpsed Charlie hurrying through the front garden, tugging on her patchworked coat, the strengthening morning light dancing off the flecks of auburn in her short hair. Sunlight dappled the branches, but he *felt* the silence, as much as heard it. Not a single bird called to the morning.

'Charlie, don't go too far,' he called. 'I'm not sure it's safe.'

'Can't be worse than back there, Silas.' She did not slow. 'Or whoever the hell you are.' Charlie vanished around the curve in the path that would take her beyond the mill and close to where, not so long ago, she had laughed long and hard over his fall into the brook.

'Damn it, Charlie. Stop.'

He could not blame her for her haste. He would no sooner have stopped either. Silas envied her that she *could* run from this. Leave this unpleasant waking nightmare behind, and not ever relive it. And he would let her do so, just as soon as he was certain no other horrors were about to beset them. In time he would let her run as far from this unfortunate encounter in the woods as she could go. But not yet.

Silas set off after her.

He surveyed the forest with narrowed eyes. What he wouldn't have done for a glimpse of a storm-cloud mane amongst the crooked trunks and swaying boughs. Or even a note of a dreadful tune. If Pitch had sauntered up the path right now, Silas might have embraced him with relief and saved a tongue-lashing till later.

He shook himself, setting his shoulders right. The daemon wasn't damned well here, nor was Lalassu. If he were to ensure Charlie's safety, he would have to rely on himself and none other. He exhaled. Christ, this day was off to a terrible start.

His gaze fell upon the brook, sparkling and dancing against the light, oblivious to the tumult. He paused with a sudden idea. Would the naiads carry a message on his behalf? To Holly Village perhaps? There was a water elemental there, Matilda. She had led Pitch to Silas when the harpies attacked in the graveyard. Surely the creatures borne of water could commune with one another? He could send off a call for help. Silas broke into a jog, buoyed by his plan.

The shriek erupted from the depths of the forest. Tearing at the air like it sought to rip every leaf from its branch. Silas staggered at the ear-splitting cry.

'Charlie! Where are you?' He rounded the side of the mill. 'Charlie!'

It was not Charlie who had cried out. No. There was no humanity in the sound at all. Whatever creature had loosened that noise was far from human. Silas reeled with terror at the thought of Charlie encountering such a creature.

'Charlie, answer me!' he shouted.

'Silas!' Her panicked cry came from up ahead, somewhere in the foliage beyond the mill, further along the brook.

'Charlie, where are –'

The shriek ripped through the forest once more, shredding an unseen path through all that was natural. Christ, the din was unholy. But what blasted direction did it come from? It was all and everything, no other sound could exist beneath it. Black Annis's dreadful noises, wails, and screams that had shuddered through him were those of a soul in torment, but what assailed the forest now was not borne of such weakness. There was a resolute strength in the shriek, a power that could drive a person to their knees if they allowed it to overcome them.

Silas curled his fingers into fists. Now was no time to stumble. The breeze stripped away the remnants of the piercing cry. He must find Charlie. They must leave this damned place. Together. He moved to head in the direction of Charlie's voice.

The splintering of undergrowth came from nearby. And a weighty splash soon after.

Silas darted back towards the brook. He spied movement just in time to halt and hide behind a conveniently placed birch. About a dozen paces from where he stood a figure ploughed across the calf-deep water, headed towards the mill.

Silas blinked in confusion.

If he were not so sure of what had befallen the intruder, he might have thought he watched the very same hooded man stride through the shallow water. His long grey cloak was blackened where the water soaked into the fabric.

'What the hell...' Silas breathed.

The figure moved unsteadily over the rocky bed, almost coming down onto a knee as he ploughed through the brook, but if this creature were capable of moving half as fast as the intruder inside the house Silas he should not be comforted by their clumsiness now.

He stuffed his hand into his pocket. His fingertips were warm with a gentle heat, but there was no telltale tingling as the bandalore's string found its place upon his finger. Mind, he hardly needed a magickal bandalore to tell him that something was very amiss here, but what exactly did he face? These were not teratisms that stalked him. He would have known it. The scythe would have known it. The blade was alert, clearly, but Silas's skin did not prickle, and when he'd taken the intruder's head, the scythe had not sung to him in the same way as with the Verderer or Black Annis.

He smothered the bandalore in his grasp.

What a pity the goddess had not seen fit to bless him with a better guide to life as an ankou. She'd gifted him a mystical weapon and then abandoned him. They all had, Lalassu, Lady Satine, even Pitch.

The cloaked figure reached Silas's side of the brook and clambered up the gentle incline easily. Silas was rigid with tension. Dear god, what if Charlie did as he had asked and came to him now?

'Stay where you are, Charlie,' he called. With a sharp intake of breath, he stepped from the birch's concealing embrace.

Silas raised his hands, and waved them about. The cloaked figure jerked his head to find him. His body turned a heartbeat later, sharp and rigid, like an automaton soldier executing a drill.

'Well you have his attention now,' Silas said grimly.

The mill loomed close, but nowhere near close enough to dash to if this stalker was as fast as the other. The snap of a twig behind him sent a cold trickle of dread working down his spine.

'Charlie?' he whispered without turning.

There was no answer, at least not by way of a word. Instead came the rasp of breath dragged across teeth and tongue.

Silas's breath stalled in his chest.

Christ, how many of these blasted things were there? He was light-headed with panic. Silas turned his head slowly, enough to see what stood behind him. Several feet away, further along the brook's edge, another cloaked figure stood, illuminated by shafts of light piercing the tree canopy. This one was different in shape to the creature that had entered the house, being much stockier of build. Silas's mouth was so dry he could barely swallow. He darted his attention back to the first figure. Was he closer? Silas could make out more details, the narrowness of his shoulders more evident beneath his cloak. The squareness of his jaw was illuminated by a random ray of sunshine. These were not, then, identical creatures.

God damn it, think, you fool, Silas raged against himself. *Move, damn it. Move.*

A rippling shadow edged through the undergrowth on the far side of the brook. A menace on four legs. Silas's heart sank. He recognised the shape, the solid mass of a stalking animal, shoulders hunched, body pressed low to the ground. He'd spotted this same creature what felt like a lifetime ago, when he'd made his way down here to relieve himself, his head sleep-addled, his body still humming after a night of blissful intimacy.

He was surrounded.

'Run, you bloody idiot!'

Charlie's desperate cry shook him from his overwrought state. She was hidden near the mill.

He must run these foul creatures as far from her as he could.

Silas let out a fractured, somewhat-crazed holler, drawing all the focus to himself. 'Come on, you bastards!'

And he ran at the brook like a man possessed.

CHAPTER 11

Silas's boots could not find purchase on the mossy, submerged rocks. He flailed about, stumbling his way across the shallow water. He was in very real danger of twisting an ankle. His coat dragged at his shoulders, and his determined steps splashed the water about, soaking his clothes and drenching his face.

The intruders followed.

His attention-seeking flight was succeeding as planned, but that plan was making his pulse thump in his ears. He was headed directly towards where he'd seen the shadow skulking. Perhaps this plan could have been better thought through.

Silas cast the bandalore blindly, flicking his wrist so that the wooden discs whirled out behind him, fearing that if he took his eyes off the way ahead, he'd find himself face-first in the brook. The bandalore whipped back along the string, having made no contact. But he hoped it might at least give his pursuers pause.

The bank was steeper on the far side of the narrow channel of water. Silas clenched his jaw against the strong suck of mud at his boots. With each step he flinched in anticipation of a knife's cut against his back, or the weight of a blow. Neither came. Silas raced on, his breath a searing, haggard expulsion from his lungs. He ran blindly deeper into the woods, weaving in and out of the trees in the desperate hope that the sudden changes in direction might afford him some advantage.

Perhaps there was weight to the idea, for although he could hear clearly the thud of footsteps chasing after him, they did not draw closer. He dared a glance back. To his left, the stockier of the cloaked figures paced through the thin cover of the scrub. To his right the other, the one with a square jaw, moved at a quicker pace, body held rigid as though a metal rod ran the length of his spine. But neither of them moved with any astonishing speed. Certainly nothing like the sudden flash of movement exhibited by the now-beheaded creature in the sitting room. Silas turned his gaze forward, narrowly avoiding a youthful oak blocking his path. He staggered, losing some momentum, and cursed his unsteady gait.

The high-pitched shriek rang out once more. The terrible sound seemed to unsettle the ground beneath him. Silas lunged for the steadiness of a nearby tree. The beast was closer for sure.

But that was what he had intended, he hurriedly, anxiously assured himself. For if all these creatures pursued him, they did not chase after Charlie. Silas had the bandalore, he had means of protecting himself. Or so he hoped. This would be his first fight against a multitude of attackers. His first fight without a daemon at his side. His gut turned at the thought. A handful of combat lessons, even with an angel for an instructor, did hardly a warrior make.

Silas quickened his maddened pace through the forest. He sent furtive glances about, seeking some sign of the awful creature behind those godforsaken screams. He could hear footfalls, the crash of bodies through scrub, but could make no sense of the shadows about him. His muscles ached beneath his ribs. Blast, he was tired of being set upon in forests. Was it too much to ask that he might take a quiet stroll through nature? The woods should be a place of serenity, not calamity. He was bloody sick and tired of terror besetting him in such a place. Granted, it was far less terrifying when that stupid bloody daemon was there with his impossible wings of flame.

'Damn you, Pitch,' he snapped. 'Damn you and your fucking madness.'

The iron-hard branch of a rowan tree flicked at his face, stinging his cheek, fuelling his anger. Silas's chest burned. His ankle had rolled more than once, and he feared that if he slowed at all, he might find his knees buckle beneath him. What exactly did he intend to do here? Run until he dropped? A shudder ran through his body. What if one of these bloodless fiends held a bow like the Verderer had done? Silas clenched the bandalore.

A shriek loosened from a monstrous throat again, as though sensing his rattled nerves. Silas tripped upon a root hidden beneath the sodden leafy carpet. His ears rang, echoing the scream that burrowed deep in his eardrums and threatened never to leave. But over that ringing, came another sound.

'Ankou.' Less a word, more the grind of stone.

Silas spat a curse and jolted to a halt. A slender figure stood up ahead, a spectre of lithe dullness beneath the heavy drapes of his grey cloak. *Another* cloaked intruder.

These interminable things bred as relentlessly as rabbits.

The crashing of footfalls around him fell silent. He did not dare look back. He needed no reminder of how dire his situation was.

'Come no closer.' He raised the bandalore and grimaced at the tremble so evident in his hand.

'You do not command them.' The intruder's bruised lips rough-handled the words, forcing them clear with a sound that reminded him of the fallen intruder's broken bones rubbing together.

'Then who does? Are you their leader?' The longer he stalled, the greater the chance Charlie had made her escape. 'I would have you call off your dogs, then.'

If only he were half as brave as he sounded.

At his flanks the other figures erupted with horrendous laughter. A cackling, wretched noise.

'Stop.' He clutched his hands to the sides of his head, the bandalore against his right ear. 'Stop it!'

Shared cruel amusement ballooned around him. Christ, it was awful. Silas doubled over, head aching, ears ringing. It was as though the laughter turned to liquid inside his skull and bubbled. What part of these creatures was *actually* human?

'These dogs of mine shall not be withdrawn,' the lithe one said. 'They have only just begun. You are right to cower, ankou. You are not enough.'

Silas blinked through the sting of tears, trying to keep the creature who spoke in sight. They had not moved, standing stiller than the forest about them. But something shifted beyond them, skulking through the undergrowth. The unmistakable bulk of the animal he'd seen earlier. Silas pressed his lips against a whimper. Could he take all three of these creatures *and* their beast?

A wolf, he suspected. There were the haunches, a long length of bristling tail, but what in god's name was wrong with the head? It was as large as Lalassu's but with one notable, troubling feature. One eye glowed red as a post box and bright as an ember, with the other nothing more than a pinprick.

'Back to your grave, ankou.'

The Speaker moved like a flash of lightning, tearing up the space between them. The beast lifted its enormous head, and the horrendous rending shriek rang out.

There was the culprit behind the dreadful sound. No wolf at all, but something monstrous.

The bandalore warmed against his ear, and the scythe began to play its tune. He lowered his hand, welcoming the delicate notes as they lifted over and above the painful cries of the beast. Silas's feet grew light, and he danced his weight upon them, moving with the scythe's song. He whirled about, his coat a blue sweep of colour around him. At his back the other two grey-cloaks waited, their midnight eyes upon him, still as statues in a gallery. He turned, completing a full circle.

The Speaker was almost upon him, cloak spread wide as a mist, his hood shifted to reveal the face beneath. Gaunt, skin sucking at bone, flesh the pallor of a dying man. Where the attacker in the house had held a knife, this fellow clutched a short-handled axe. At his back the red-eyed beast moved in loping strides, black tongue lolling. The gait was lackadaisical, as though daring Silas to run, and become the prey.

But Silas was done with running for today.

He threw back his arm and drew the scythe forth. The transformation happened quickly, in the flap of a butterfly's wings, and was every bit as delicate. The melody rose. In a heartbeat Silas held the rough wood in hand, the dull blade curving at its end. The scythe's pacific tune lilted and swayed, contrasting with the aggressive thud of Silas's own heart.

He swept the blade high.

'Stay back.' A pointless command, he knew full well, but he could not ignore the shadows at the Speaker's feet. These creatures were human...in some form at least. All about this encounter felt inherently *wrong*.

His hesitation was costly.

The Speaker drove his axe through the air, setting his aim at Silas's heart. At the very last moment, he banked right, coming at Silas from an angle. The alteration threw off Silas's aim, and he barely countered the blow. The blade cracked against the axe head, bouncing both him and the Speaker away from one another. Silas staggered back in a crouch but kept his footing. The Speaker did not fare so well, landing on his backside in a flourish of grey.

The red-eyed beast leapt, pushing off powerful haunches, soaring over its fallen master. Silas dropped to his knees, twisting the shaft, readying to fend off snapping jaws. But the creature had misjudged its leap and sailed over Silas's head. He threw himself into a roll, and when he braced himself upon his knees again, he found the Speaker back on his feet, axe at the ready for another assault. The scythe's melody still played, each note a guide. Silas followed the tune, allowing it to take him where it willed. The song spread his hands wide upon the shaft, it tilted the scythe until it was horizontal with the ground. And it whispered at him to wait.

The Speaker launched himself, whipping across the forest floor with that remarkable speed, axe raised overhead, face blank of all expression, eyes twin pools of nothingness.

Death's song led Silas in a vicious dance, tensing his arms, tugging at the muscle.

The scythe sliced into the Speaker's waist.

The blade travelled through the hips, making short work of the spine and ribs. Cutting through butter would have been more difficult. Like his headless brother before him, the Speaker did not utter a sound. A light dusting of white-grey powder rose from the ghastly wound, marking the path of the blade.

Silas watched as though set just apart from the reality of what was occurring. And in a very short time it was done.

The Speaker was rent in two.

The weight of the cloak pulled the shoulders back, seeing the upper body topple one way as the hips went the other. That fine ashen substance billowed as the severed parts met the ground. A harrowing sight, Silas would not deny, but his repulsion mingled with that same odd sense of satisfaction that had come with the intruder's beheading.

He pivoted on his knees, the scythe's aria raising its pitch, his movement rippling from him, impossibly graceful and fluid as the brook's waters. He was ready to guide the blade to where it was needed next.

He uttered an astonished cry.

There was sign of only one of the cloaked figures. He lay spread-eagled on the ground, sightless black eyes turned skywards, a massive gash in the side of his neck, one that had taken a portion of his shoulder. There was no blood of course, and the torn flesh had the look of spoilt meat. The ground around him was the colour of dirtied snow.

The red-eyed beast pushed itself clear of the bracken that had hidden it. Slobber dripped from the matted hair about its jaw.

Christ almighty, it was a massive thing. He suspected if it were to stand at full height, its ears would brush his chest. But it crouched low, coarse black hair hanging from its belly and brushing at the leaf litter. That strange eye pierced into him, its sheen the colour of a sun caught behind the glow of a grass fire. Its much smaller twin was a minuscule speck of crimson, as though the creature held the eye nearly shut.

Unlike the cloaked men, this creature held no shadow. As though Silas needed any reassurance of this beast's otherworldliness.

He adjusted his hold on the shaft, all too aware of his precarious stance. He needed to get off his knees; this position was far too vulnerable. But as the scythe's tune crept low, he listened. And what he thought he heard was a call to stillness. A note warning him to stay where he was.

Night-black lips peeled back from yellowed fangs. Menace rolled off the creature.

Christ, now would be a terrible time to have read the scythe wrong. Sweat coated his palms as the stand-off dragged on. His fingers ached from his tight hold upon the wooden shaft. The beast lowered its broad snout, shoulders bunching as it crouched lower still. Silas's stomach dropped, even as the melody fluttered about him.

'Get out of here!' The cry startled both man and beast. 'Go on! Get out!' A figure burst out of a clump of late-flowering brambles, charging forward with a flaming wooden torch. 'Be gone. I'm not scared of you, mongrel! Get!'

Charlie. Good god, the woman had lost her mind.

She held the narrow piece of wood like a lance, poking the flames ahead as she edged towards the crimson-eyed beast.

'Charlie stop!'

The beast growled, exposing fangs the length of Silas's fingers. It sank low, pressing its belly to the leaf litter.

'Go on with you!' Charlie cried. 'Last chance.'

She thrust the flaming torch into the beast's face. Silas clambered to his feet, panic making the movement stilted and cumbersome. With the creature distracted, he might reach it in time to stop it before it pounced.

He took just one step, and something miraculous happened.

The animal backed away from Charlie's flames.

'That's it, turn tail and run, you fleabag!' Her eyes danced with flickers of radiant light. 'Go on with you!'

Bloody hell, fear must have driven her to lunacy. Or was she truly enjoying this as much as it appeared? Whichever it was, her bold actions had the desired effect. The beast took a tentative step back, swinging its head towards Silas as though sizing up whether a meal was more readily available there. It twitched its tail, snapped its jaws, and did just as Charlie had demanded.

Turned tail and ran.

CHAPTER 12

Charlie exhaled, and the tip of the flaming torch sagged, the flames licking at the damp ground.

'Holy shit,' she gasped. 'I didn't think that would work.'

Silas was on his feet and at her side in a rush, dragging the scythe's base along the ground, gathering up a pile of decaying leaves in his wake. 'Charlotte –'

'It's Charlie.' A grunt of indignation.

'Charlie, are you all right?'

'That was a big fucking wolf.'

Silas eyed the length of wood she held. He spied bristles wrapped in cloth. Christ, she had come to his aid with a burning broom.

'Good god, Charlie, what were you thinking? I told you to run.'

Charlie's short, jagged hair was peppered with bits of the forest, and there was a graze upon her left cheek. 'Did you assume because I'd lain with you, I'd then do as I was told? My dear, my father is a lord, and I ignore him. You had no chance.'

He did not doubt that. 'It was far too dangerous. You might have been killed, Charlie.'

'And so might've you.' She wiped at sweaty cheeks. 'It looked to me as though you were frozen with fear, you poor man.'

Silas shrank back, stung. 'I most certainly was not. I assure you, I can hold my own in a fight.'

'Maybe so.' Her hand shook as she ran it through her cropped hair. 'But just now you looked like you were going to shit your pants.'

Silas stared at her. It was a good thing she and Pitch would never meet, Silas might not survive the outpouring of candour. 'I was simply pausing to take stock of the situation.'

Her laughter was dry as the snap of a twig. 'Is that what it was?'

The harshness of her words was out of place, and he saw that her bravado was not entirely robust. Her cheeks had lost their flush, and though she sought to cover her shaking with restless movement, it could not be ignored.

Should he offer his coat? Place an arm about her? Neither seemed quite right.

He spoke instead. 'Let us go. We should move on from here as fast as we can. There is at least one who has escaped.'

'Silas...' She paused to swallow. 'What in god's holy fucking name were those creatures? Did you see the size of that...that...hellhound?'

'A hellhound?' He ran cold at the thought. 'Do you think that is what it was?'

'Jesus, Silas, is that a possibility? I thought it a rabid wolf. Now you are truly frightening me.'

'I'm sure you are right...a wolf, I mean, it was most likely so, I would think.' Her suggestion caused him much consternation, for it may well be correct. That was no bloody wolf like he'd ever seen before. Were these fiends residents of Arcadia? He laid another curse upon the daemon for his absence. Between mouthfuls of sponge cake, Pitch might have given them the answer.

'*Most likely* it was *not* a hellhound?' Charlie chewed out the words. 'Shit, Silas. Come clean with me, before I go quite mad. I just saw you behead a...man, if I could call him that... with what must be the sharpest hunting knife I've ever seen, now there is...this...' She spread her hand towards the carnage that lay about them. 'Along with the fact you are seriously considering if that wolf we saw might be a hellhound. Who the hell are you?'

He dropped his gaze. How differently she had looked at him last night. But her talk of the hunting knife, and the wolf, told him she was seeing many things differently. That red eyed beast was no more a wolf, or the scythe a simple knife, than he was human.

'Charlie...I am...I am just...a...' Silas's attempt at a lie withered and died. 'Please, let us go. We will speak more of this when this forest is far behind us.'

Charlie crossed her arms over her chest. 'No, I think I'd rather you tell me right now why there are hellhounds and ash-men trying to kill you. And me.' A shudder ran through her.

How was it that she had not run away screaming by now?

'No. Now is not the time for lengthy discussion. Come, let us go.'

'Where are we going?'

It was a very good question, and he had no idea of the answer. 'Out of these woods, to begin with...' After that, well, who knew? He would worry on that when the time came.

The clear and unmistakable pounding of hooves reverberated through the trees. Whoever approached made no secret of it.

'Oh shit, what now?' Charlie adjusted her grip on her charcoaled broom.

Silas felt Lalassu's presence long before he sighted the pale horse, and his heart lifted. 'Steady on.' He touched at Charlie's raised arm, urging her to lower her makeshift weapon. 'It is all right.'

Lalassu emerged from the shroud of a hawthorn tree as though she'd been a part of it all along. His breath hitched. The mare was resplendent, her shimmering, stormy coat seeming to reflect the forest around her, those watery yellow eyes so wide the whites were visible.

'Bloody hell,' Charlie breathed. 'Now that is a steed to behold.'

'Indeed.' Silas smiled.

Lalassu danced towards them at a trot, tilting her head so that one eye was set upon Silas. His smile faltered as he noted the rider in her saddle, huddled low, reins slack in her hands. Her brilliant red hair contrasted with the horse's paler hue. The massive mare came to an abrupt halt, her back hooves sliding against the slippery undergrowth, snorting her excitement. Her rider straightened, and Silas found himself being scrutinised by a very familiar pair of amber eyes.

'Mercer, what the feck is goin' on 'ere, then?' Tyvain demanded. 'Got yourself in a spot, you great chunk of a man.'

She sat like a jockey upon Lalassu's back, her stirrups so short her thighs pressed nearly to her belly. Gone were the manly clothes she'd worn when last he'd seen her. Now she was dressed in a gown of black muslin with ruffling at the neck and wrists. She'd made some attempt to tame her wild auburn curls with a messy bun perched atop her head. They'd last crossed paths at The Atlas, where she'd ordered him a fish and chips he'd never gotten around to eating. Silas had had no inkling of what lay ahead of him then.

'Tyvain, what on Earth are you doing here?'

'Come to collect your sorry arse, ain't I?' Lalassu was restless beneath her, snorting as she pranced about the torso of the ash-man Silas had split in two. 'Came across these nags.' She waved a hand over her shoulder.

Silas had been too awestruck by Lalassu's sudden appearance to pay much mind to anything else, but now he saw she was followed by two other horses, a slender bay and a more robust piebald. Their reins were knotted at their necks, their saddles empty. The piebald nuzzled its pinkish nose at the ground, seeking to graze. 'Found them wandering about not far from here. I'm guessin' they belong to these sorry bastards, but they followed after your girl like love-struck drunkards.'

Silas frowned. 'My girl?'

Tyvain patted Lalassu's broad neck. 'Your bloody 'orse. Didn't get no smarter since I last saw ya, did ya?' Her gaze shifted to Charlie. 'But seems you've 'ad more than one distraction. 'O are you then, lad? One of these 'orses yours by chance?'

'The name is Charlie.' She set down her charred broom, apparently satisfied the new arrival wasn't about to cause them any harm. 'And no, I have no horse, but I cannot help but admire yours. Where did you find such an animal? She is magnificent.'

Silly as it was, Silas felt a pang of pride.

'Find 'er? You don't *find* this type of 'orse, she finds you,' Tyvain answered. 'Just as well too. I was bored out of my bloody mind in Kiddermister. One tea-leaf reading away from poking me own eyes out, till I got the call. Still, I could have done without all the drama of that bloody Astaroth.' Tyvain scratched at the ruffles about her neck, mouth stretched in a garish fashion as she worked at her skin.

'You've seen him?' Silas's pulse thumped. 'You've seen Pitch, then?'

Charlie was giving him a curious look, but he was far too intent on the Hag's reply to offer any explanation.

'Aye. And it weren't so pretty a sight as it normally is. But we'll talk on that later, when we ain't surrounded by more dead things than I'd like. You can 'ave the piebald, lad. I never did like 'em. I'll take the bay.' She swung a leg over Lalassu's shoulders, lifting it so high Silas had to quickly turn his head to avoid seeing a flash of what lay beneath the folds of her gown. She landed on the ground with a grunt. 'Bloody 'ell, if this 'orse was any damn bigger, it could shit in the clouds.'

Charlie leaned in towards Silas. 'Oh, I do like her.'

She said it softly, intended for his ears alone, but Tyvain was swift to answer. 'Just so as we are clear, these legs ain't spreading for ya, lad, but you can ogle me long as you please.'

Silas groaned inwardly. Was there a supernatural in existence who did not enjoy vulgarity? Charlie did not seem to mind though, a crooked smile still in place.

'Wonderful. I do enjoy a good ogle.' She did not correct Tyvain as to her sex. Silas would not do so, either.

'Sassy one, ain't ya?' Tyvain said approvingly. Before she put paid to any notion she was remotely ladylike, she pressed a finger to one nostril and snorted through the other, clearing it and barely missing the severed legs of the ash-man. 'Move that fine arse of yours now, Mercer. And as we go, you can tell me what the bloody 'ell 'appened 'ere.'

'I can tell you right now.' Charlie gestured at the carnage, nose wrinkled. 'Creatures from the very pits of hell attacked us.'

'Is that right? 'Ell you say?' Tyvain folded her arms, faintly bemused.

'Or someplace damned like it, yes,' Charlie declared.

'So the East End, then?' The Hag's eyes were piercingly bright, despite the fact that the weak morning sun barely filtered through the canopy.

'You are mocking me, and I don't much like it. At least I was here, when Silas needed help. Not a moment after.'

Silas stared at Charlie. Truly the lass seemed fearless.

Tyvain's chortle was chesty, shaking her ribs. 'Bloody 'ell, where did you find this one, Mercer? 'Ere I was thinkin' you would have a sizable pair of balls on ya, but now I'm thinkin' this lad will give you a run for your money in that department.'

'I can assure you Silas has no competition from me.' Charlie's grin was wry. 'And has nothing at all to be ashamed of.'

'Well, well.' Tyvain clucked her tongue. 'Seems you found many a way to keep yourself occupied whilst Mr Astaroth isn't about, Mercer.' She dug her toe into the ash-man's thigh. 'Aside from cutting people up and all.'

Silas might have flinched at the grisly observation were he not wondering how soon it would be before he could speak with her in confidence about Pitch. It was evident she knew he was not here, and didn't seem surprised. But Silas was not keen to speak of the daemon with Charlie near.

'We have had very few dull moments since meeting,' Charlie agreed, with way more enthusiasm than was warranted. 'I am quite exhausted.'

'I'm sure you are.' Tyvain might as well have licked her lips. 'Good for you, Mercer, those whirligigs of yours must be gettin' quite the exercise of late, considerin' the company you been keepin'.'

'Tyvain, enough.' Silas hid behind Lalassu, who nuzzled at him, her sheer bulk as reassuring as any shield. It was good to run his hands across her coat once more. 'Charlie is, I'm sure, speaking of the foul men who attacked us. She has been remarkably brave through it all –'

'She?' Tyvain sniffed, as though looking for the scent of the mentioned female. ''O's she?'

'Shit,' Silas muttered, then louder he said. 'He...I said he.'

Tyvain crouched down beside the ash-man with the torn-out throat, her skirts a puff of black cloud about her. 'Nah, ya didn't. But ain't that interestin'.' She might have meant Charlie, or the ashen figure she prodded at. 'Hmm, curious, curious, indeed.' Tyvain slid her thumb and forefinger against a grey-blue eyelid, widening it to reveal the smooth black orb beneath. The sightless orb was duller than Silas recalled. 'So is it lad or lass, then? What is your fancy?'

It was safe to assume her question was meant for Charlie, and not the corpse.

'Lad, and it is no fancy. It's simply how it should always have been,' came the reply. 'Sometimes the wrong skin gets put on the wrong soul, you understand?'

All at once the binding upon the lad's chest made great sense. And Silas saw he was not alone at feeling ill at ease in his own skin. Though their reasons were so vastly different.

Tyvain still held the ash-man's eye open wide, but her gaze slid up to Charlie.

'Aye. I understand, lad. Consider yourself 'eard, my boy.' She returned her attention to the dead man. 'But cock or cunny, tell me somethin', were you 'ere when these ugly feckers were still on two legs? Did they 'ave eyes on ya?'

Charlie nodded, raising her...no, his...charred broom. 'They did. And the hellhound too, though I chased it off.'

Tyvain raised a brow. 'What's this then?'

Silas spoke up. 'There was a wolf...but none like I've ever known. I thought it beholden to these men at first...but then, I could not say for certain. It seemed happy to take a bite of any of us.'

'As you can see.' Charlie gestured at the ash-man.

Tyvain paused in her scrutiny of the eyeball. 'The wolf did this, then?'

'It did,' Silas said. 'And would have come at us were it not for Charlie's flames.'

'Hmm.' Tyvain clicked her jaw. 'Well, that can't be meanin' anythin' good at all. Right bloody mess this is. 'O's watchin' ya, I can't say, but I'm guessing they ain't your friend.'

Silas's hand froze against Lalassu's neck. 'Watching us?'

Tyvain poked at the ash-man's eye. Her nail should have dug into pulpy, soft flesh. Instead it rapped against a solid mass, the ping of glass ringing out. 'Obsidian crystal...they was scryin'. You were being observed, me friends.' She busied at the folds of her skirt and from some hidden pocket produced a small knife, the blade as long and thick as her plump middle finger. Tyvain first dug the tip of the knife in beneath the eyeball, then placed her free palm against the dead man's forehead, her knee to his chest, and worked her blade deep into the eye socket.

'Oh shit.' Charlie blew out the words.

Silas winced, turning away.

'Stuck right in there, ain't ya?' Tyvain grunted as she worked. 'I'll not be feckin' 'appy if I break a nail.'

'What is she doing?' Charlie breathed.

'Look away.' Silas was heeding his own advice. But just hearing the Hag's efforts was bad enough. Christ almighty, she sounded as though she were killing the wretched thing all over again.

'I can't...' Charlie whispered. 'It's quite astonishing.'

'Aha! There we are.' Tyvain was triumphant. 'Oh, you want it then, eh?'

Silas dared turn back. Lalassu stood right up against Tyvain, who held the glassy sphere in an upturned palm. The horse's silky mane had once more come to life. The long fine threads lifting and sliding to cover the onyx eyeball in a tight cocoon. The lively horsehair retracted, leaving Tyvain's palm empty.

'Saint's alive.' Charlie's mouth hung open. 'That is some marvellous slight of hand you have there.'

Silas glanced at him, more sure than ever that Charlie was only seeing a half of what was truly going on before him.

'Yep, that's what it was all right. Just a trick of the eye.' Tyvain's laughter gurgled in her chest. 'Think I might go on a tour with your 'orse when things settle, Silas. Show off our tricks, eh? Handy kind of animal to have about.' She lifted the edges of her skirt and raised a booted heel, bringing it down hard upon the remaining eye. Cracking bone mixed with splintering glass. 'That's better.'

'Were they still watching us?' Silas gasped.

'Nah. I've seen obsidian used a couple of times by the Order. It's all nice and shiny when it's in use, and makes the 'airs on the back of your neck stand up. But when no one is scryin', the surface goes dull as ditchwater, just like these. I'd say the connection was severed soon as your scythe did its work.' Tyvain wiped her hands upon her black skirts and gathered up the bay's reins. 'I broke 'is face just 'cause I felt like breakin' things. What I'm seein' 'ere, its' puttin' me off me dinner. And I like me dinner more than life itself. Sooner we get the obsidian into the hands of the Order, the sooner I can get this feckin' corset off and get me appetite back. On ya 'orses. And you'll be comin' with us for now, lad.'

Charlie's cheeks flushed with excitement. 'Yes, ma'am.' He found his seat upon the piebald with a grace that declared this far from a first time in the saddle. 'You spoke of the Order. Tell me you are talking of the Order of the Golden Dawn.'

'I'll tell ya, 'cause I am.' Tyvain rose onto the bay in a rustling of fabric. 'Mercer didn't see fit to tell ya when 'e was balls deep? Go figure.'

Silas scowled at the devilish grin she cast him. 'I had not mentioned it, no.' He was last to mount, having to adjust the stirrups from Tyvain's shortened length. He settled into that comfortable place upon Lalassu's back.

'Whyever not?' Was Charlie a little breathless? 'Bloody hell, Silas, the Order is terribly famous. My lady's maid was obsessed with their shenanigans. She was constantly harping on about having a seance at our home. God, if the stories were to be believed, we had a household full of the dearly departed. A scullery maid in the cellar with a broken neck, a terrible drowning near the boatshed, a bloodied woman in one of the east-wing bedrooms crying out for the child she'd died giving birth to. The Order would have had to stay with us a month to be done with them all. Goodness, if you'd told me of your supernatural gifts before, I'd have dropped my trousers for you sooner.'

Tyvain nearly cackled herself off her horse. 'Gods,' she gasped. 'You are the least dull purebred I've met in an age.'

Purebred. Silas recalled Tyvain describing humans in just such a way at their first encounter in The Atlas. And on that occasion she had not spoken it nearly so kindly.

'I'm glad I can amuse,' Charlie said easily. 'I know many consider the Order full of charlatans looking to make coin from the gullible of society. But I suppose I know better now.' He turned in the saddle, finding Silas, who rode at the rear of the group. 'Might I ask, Silas, what is your gift?'

The heat drained from his cheeks. He was not nearly so excited by his supernatural gift as Charlie. He was death. And death was inextricably linked with sorrow. The idea of speaking his truth, of seeing the way Charlie's face would certainly fall, left him frigid inside.

Tyvain leapt into the silence, calling from up ahead where she'd goaded the bay into a fast walk. ''E's talented at lookin' dumbfounded.'

'That is true.' Charlie smiled, eyes brightening with a sudden thought. 'Oh my god, the fish! You summoned them from the water, didn't you, Silas? You can move objects with your mind. I see it now. Why the hell were you pretending to fish with a rod, and so badly?'

Charlie had presented him with a most suitable escape from the truth, and he'd not lose it. 'You have found me out. I can indeed move things with my mind. I just did not wish to frighten you.'

'I am not easily frightened. My father could not do it. Nor did long Scottish winter nights. You do not scare me now.'

Tyvain twisted in her saddle. 'Well, you've got balls, no doubt about it. Now let's get out of this forest before your rangy mutt decides 'e ain't done with ya both.'

CHAPTER 13

They joined a cart-worn road that once must have brought workers and carts to the mill but was now enduring a slow death by forest, the foliage creeping in over the potholes and ruts, reclaiming the worn ground. Tyvain had them at a trot until they at last broke out into the strengthening day and a landscape of open fields and pastures. It had not taken them long. Silas had thought himself well hidden in the depths of the forest but saw now that the world beyond was closer than he had imagined.

It was a pleasant, mild day, but Silas was only vaguely aware of such things. 'Would you mind terribly if I spoke with Tyvain alone a moment? You'll be quite safe, I assure you.'

Charlie smiled and drew the piebald in. 'I know I am, Silas, for you are here. Go on.'

Silas gave him a grateful nod and trotted ahead to draw up alongside the auburn-haired Hag. 'Tyvain, do you have any notion of what those creatures were?' he asked. 'They held shadows...I thought that to mean they were human...but they were anything but.'

'I've a few ideas of what set on you, and I don't like a bloody one of 'em.'

Silas knew better than to expect a reassuring answer, but he'd hoped for one less vague. 'What ideas?'

'Not for you to bother your pretty 'ead about right now.'

'I beg your pardon? I'd say I have every reason to bother about it –'

'Sure you do, but I still ain't sayin'. We'll let those 'o know these things decide on it.'

Silas pressed at the pommel, shifting his seat. Up here, upon Lalassu, he was far less disconcerted than he would have been standing upon the ground. The horse settled him, her movement as calming as a cradle for a babe, but even so, it did not chase away his consternation entirely. 'Are we returning to Lady Satine's place at Bishop's Castle?' *Is Pitch there?* He bit back on the question.

'Nah. We ain't. Just let me do the leadin'. You'll see soon enough.'

He huffed, irritation sliding warmly through his chest. 'Tell me *something*, for god's sake. Who was watching us back there in the woods?'

'You. There ain't no *us*. They were watchin' *you*. Not the random vagabond you fucked.'

'Tyvain,' Silas growled, all at once stung by insult. 'If you speak of Charlie in such a way again, I'll –'

She sniffed, slouching in her saddle. 'You'll what? Calm down, boy. And if you truly want to keep 'im safe, you'll not be fuckin' 'im again, and leavin' ya stench on 'im.'

'Excuse me?' Silas recoiled.

'Your scent, that less offensive to ya? Whateva' you wanna call it, knockin' creates a powerful energy. That's why the incubus and succubus are always frothing at the bit for a fuck. 'Ain't ya seen 'ow worked up your daemon gets for it? Surprised 'e 'asn't 'ad you flat on your back by now.'

Silas glanced at her. 'You do not seem surprised that Pitch isn't here. You knew, then, that we were separated?'

She nodded.

Silas twisted his fingers through Lalassu's mane. Somewhere in their depths was the obsidian eyeball. Christ, what a strange journey. 'He had become...most unreasonable. I could not speak any sense with him. He's prone to moods, but this was...' *Frightening, awful.* 'Well, he seemed...troubled.'

'Oh, that one is troubled all right.' Tyvain snorted derisively. 'Feckin' big bag o' trouble. I've not met many daemons, least not ones who bother to show themselves. Don't want their dirty little visits to our world to be known, most of 'em, snobby pricks. But I'm thinkin' that's fine and dandy, if they are anythin' like 'im. Ever since he sauntered through the doors of The Atlas a year ago, 'e's been a boil on everyone's arse. I'll be buggered if I know why the Lady keeps 'im around.'

'But he is all right?' Silas pushed.

Tyvain glanced at him. 'Sybilla's dealin' with 'im, thank the tits of all the saints. I'm sure she and the Lady will set 'im right, they 'ave before. Was too much for me. Lord knows why Ahari thought to send me to clean up Pitch's bloody mess. Guess I was closest by. Your 'orse turned up not more than a 'alf hour after 'e called and told me to put me riding boots on. But once I sent word back about the state Astaroth was in, they seemed kinda panicked. Changed their minds about me goin' anywhere near 'im. Was told to just keep an eye on 'im till Syb arrived.'

'Mr Ahari sent you to Pitch? How did he know...' Silas shook his head. He was raised from the dead and rode a horse that could show him a destination by weaving it in her mane. It was hardly astonishing that Mr Ahari in London might know about a daemon being beaten to a pulp in a countryside farm. 'Will Sybilla be taking him to the same place we are destined for?' He couldn't account for it, how the distance between them gnawed at him.

Tyvain picked at her teeth with a jagged nail. 'She will. You pinin' for 'im, then?' Her eyes were ripe with mischief.

'I am concerned.' He frowned. 'That is all. Considering he is supposed to be my guardian, I have every right to be.'

'Feck knows why you got stuck with 'im for a guardian. But you did fair enough on your own, so far as I can see.'

He held himself a little straighter in the saddle. She was quite right, but that did not vanish his worries. He'd not say it out loud, not in a dozen lives lived, but a knot of tension had unwound to hear that the daemon was in Sybilla's capable hands.

'Tyvain, if you'll not give me details, then tell me this at least. This sort of goings-on, bloodless men with skin of ash and wild hounds with embers for eyes, is it to be expected? I mean to say, should I have been prepared for such encounters? If so, I'll tell you I'm not much pleased with how the Order runs things.'

Tyvain's laugh whipped out short and crackled. 'Ever the gentleman, even when you are pissed off. No, Mercer. This ain't normal. Nothin' much 'as been normal awhile now. The world's tiltin'. The fact you're 'ere at all accounts to that. The Lady 'asn't raised 'er 'Orsemen in a whiles, from what I 'ear. So somebody sure is bothered.'

And Tyvain did not know the half of it. The incidents of the Forest of Dean were not yet known to her. Silas stopped himself from reaching to touch the arrowhead. He was unsure whether to mention it to Tyvain. The secret of it felt dangerous and much larger than them both.

'Will the Lady Satine be there when we arrive?'

'Your guess is as good as mine.' Tyvain shrugged. ''Er Ladyship ain't one for being too obvious.'

Before Silas could speak again, Charlie called out. 'I'm wondering if there is any chance of some food before too long? I'm starving.'

Silas wondered how on Earth he could think of food after what they'd witnessed.

'It's as far as it needs to be,' Tyvain returned.

Charlie did not baulk at the cryptic reply. 'All right, so how far is that? And will there be bread and cheese?'

Tyvain's chesty laughter resounded. 'Christ, I got rid of one boil on me ass to find another,' she grumbled, with good nature. 'Obviously you 'ave a taste for strange company, Mercer.'

She continued to chat away. He was aware of the drone of her voice, but the words themselves were lost. Silas was wrapped in his own thoughts, of headless corpses, obsidian crystal, and absent daemons.

'Aye! Mercer!'

He jumped, nearly losing a foot from a stirrup. 'What? Are we being followed? Where is Charlie?' He twisted in the saddle. The way behind was empty, save for a meandering herd of black cows grazing happily.

'I'm right here, Silas.' Charlie rode at his left, entirely unnoticed.

'Gods, where the feck did you go, man?' Tyvain tugged the pins from her bun, letting her auburn curls loose.

'Nowhere. I am right here. I have much on my mind.'

Charlie eyed him with considerably more sympathy than Tyvain. 'Your friend was saying that she passed a farmhouse not far from here on her way into the forest. They are likely to have a loaf or some milk to spare. Do you have any coin?'

'Coin?' It felt an eternity since he'd used such things. 'I have no idea.' Quite pointlessly he dug about in his coat pockets, as though something may have manifested there while he wasn't paying attention. His fingers brushed the arrowhead, and his belly fluttered. 'No, no I don't.'

Tyvain sighed. 'Here, take these.' She lifted her black skirt far higher than was decent. He turned his head at the sight of pale petticoats and paler skin.

'You told me not a moment ago that you were skinned.' Charlie reined the piebald in, guiding the horse in behind Silas and Lalassu so he could reach Tyvain's outstretched hand.

'Always pays to cry poor first,' the Hag said. 'See 'o will cough up, but I'm in no mood for starvin'.'

Charlie leaned out of his saddle to grab the meagre bounty. 'There will be no starving today.' The piebald shot off at his urging, in a trot at first, but quickly moving to a canter.

'Slow down!' Silas called. 'Don't get too far ahead.'

'Settle yourself. Won't do to fret over 'im like 'e is made of glass.' Tyvain was settling her skirts back about her saddle leathers. 'Didn't I 'ear 'im say 'e chased off your wolf?'

Silas watched as the distance between Charlie and himself widened. 'He seems to think so...chased off a wolf, I mean. Some of what he has said makes me think he is not seeing things as I do. I'm sure he didn't see the scythe in its true form.'

'You'd be right. He'll only be seein' what 'is 'ead can make of things, and what the supernatural will allow. Some purebreds are better at catchin' glimpses than other. Most are clueless, they don't have the right eyes to see, nor the ears to listen with.'

'I'd rather he was oblivious. Charlie is courageous, I dare say dangerously so.'

'Got your portion of bravery, then.' Tyvain laughed heartily at her own joke.

Silas stared ahead, lips pressed.

The Hag sighed. ''E'll be fine. Quit your worryin', it will drive you to drink. You're a funny one, you are. A man gets a second life, 'anded a blade come from death itself, and yet 'ere you are, fussin' over that scrappy laddie-lass, and workin' yourself up over the likes of Mr

Astaroth. I thought you too pigeon-livered to begin with, but I reckon I could get to likin' ya, Mercer. I'm sorry we didn't get to ya sooner, me and the 'orse. She was unhappy about it, me needin' to stay with the daemon. Thought she was gonna pick me up in her teeth and 'aul me 'ere for a moment. I barely said a word to Sybilla before we were off. I see why now.'

'I had thought myself safe.' He shrugged against the memory of Charlie's scream. 'Seeing as Lalassu left me there.'

'Maybe ya should 'ave been, 'o can say? But it's likely best you don't need to be relyin' on others to keep you alive. You 'andled yourself, didn't you? No 'arm done, 'sides bein' a bit pale in the face. Cheer up, Mercer. You ain't dead again yet, so all is well.'

He wasn't sure of that at all. 'Do your cards tell you that for certain? You are a soothsayer, if I recall?'

Charlie and the piebald were a diminishing speck up ahead. Silas urged Lalassu into a trot.

'I am, but cards aren't my tool of trade.' She slid a glance his way. 'I don't get no visions or nothin'. I don't gut chickens and see what lies ahead in its entrails. Nothin' so posh as that. The powers that be gave me guts that churn about and get all topsy-turvy when things ain't right. Me innards feel the changes comin'. And they 'ave been feelin' things stronger and stronger of late.' Her eyes did not leave him. He felt her gaze like a touch of the sun. 'I damned near puked me guts out when I laid eyes on ya in the carriage outside The Atlas.'

'That doesn't sound pleasant.'

'It weren't.'

He ran his tongue over his lip. 'Was that because you saw something...untoward...when you looked at me?'

If she did not answer, he would not mind.

'Told ya,' Tyvain barked. 'I don't bloody see things. It's just a *feelin'*. I knew you was important somehow.' She shifted in the saddle, and an unpleasant burst of noise came from beneath her skirts.

'Oh my god.' Silas crinkled his nose. 'Is there really a need for that?'

'You not listenin' to a word I said? This is 'ow it works, for the most part. I feel it in me gut, and it comes out eventually.' She slapped at her belly, her corset's thickness deadening the sound. 'When I got to that bloody daemon of yours, I thought I was gonna fill me drawers.'

Silas's skin prickled. 'Why? What was your gut telling you?'

'Can't put a name to it.' She sucked at her teeth. 'But I could see with my own eyes, 'e's not right. That crazy bastard had five officers laying into 'im by the time I got to Langley, and the craziest thing was 'e only bothered 'alf the time to fight back. Kept goadin' 'em on. That boy sets my bones rattlin' like no one else I've met. Could 'ave kissed Sybilla when she showed up.' She scratched at an armpit. 'Did 'e 'ave a go at ya, too? That why you left 'im?'

Silas was slow to answer. If he did not already regret his decision to abandon Pitch, and that was how he viewed it, as an abandonment, then he certainly would now. What if an officer had died, or a farmer for that matter? The fault would lie with Silas.

He rose and fell with the smoothness of Lalassu's trot. She set a quick pace, one that forced Tyvain's mount to nearly a canter to keep up.

'We had a disagreement about our course of action, that is all.' His cheek fluttered. 'I wished to continue to where Lalassu led us, he chose to...' He closed his eyes against the image that came. 'He came across the farmer's wife...and chose to linger.'

'Aah, so she did get screwed by the daemon, then. Gods, I've known an incubus or two, but 'e's something else that one. 'Is appetite is a sight to behold. 'Ope 'e's being kind to that fine arse of yours, Mercer. I'd 'ate to see 'im ruin ya.' Her dry cackle played at the air between them. 'Sorry, sorry. I've offended ya. I'll wash my mouth out first chance I get. Alls I'll say is it was probably a wise move of yours to get the hell out of there when 'e took a turn. Sybilla said this is one of 'is worse ones.'

'He has done this before?'

''Appened once or twice in the early days, so Gilmore says.'

'Gilmore? The chap from Holly Village?' The surly gnome, to be exact.

'That's the one.' Tyvain was uncommonly elegant in the rising trot. 'Likes a good chinwag, and a pint, after we've been joinin' giblets.'

Silas left that last comment well enough alone. 'What did he say of these turns?'

'Thinkin' I shouldn't be tellin' ya all this. Might not be my place.'

'I'm not sure you are the type to be concerned about such things.'

Her eyes widened, and she slapped at her thigh. 'Ha! There are those balls your Charlie was talkin' about. Best I keep talkin', then. So, 'ere you go. When the Lady Satine first took Astaroth in, she kept 'im confined in 'Olly Lodge for a good month or two. Now, truth be told, Gil didn't see much with 'is own eyes, the Lady banished everyone from the Lodge, but 'e's an earth elemental. What 'e couldn't see, 'e could feel. And 'e said at times it was terrible fearful. Said the screams could 'ave boiled your blood. Lady Satine was either givin' 'im a seein' too he'll not forget, or was tryin' to fix somethin' that was well and truly broke.'

'And you think he was having another of these turns...at the farmhouse?'

'You've got a twisted one at your side, make no mistake, Mercer. Maybe Lucifer kicked 'im out. Left us ta deal with 'im. They say 'is majesty has the shortest temper of all the Daemon Kings. Which must make it pretty feckin' short.'

Silas stared ahead, toying with Lalassu's mane as he matched her rhythm. He was keen to catch sight of Charlie again, to have him close by, but the road ahead swelled over a low hill and the piebald was out of sight.

'So you know of the kings...of Lucifer,' Silas said quietly.

'Aye, some. And seein' as you ain't faintin' off your 'orse, I'm guessin' you do too. Did you come back to life knowin' these things?'

'No. It has all been an unexpected...surprise.'

'So you and the daemon 'ave 'ad some pillow talk, then?' She sniffed.

He glanced at her. She didn't know about the curse upon Pitch's tongue if she assumed such talk was possible. 'Actually a boggart mentioned a few things –'

She spat. 'Feckin' boggarts, give me the willies.'

Silas didn't think much of them either. 'It was taunting Pitch about events in Arcadia.' He paused, watching her, but she didn't blanche at mention of the land where angels and daemons resided alongside one another any more than she had with speaking of Lucifer. 'The creature accused him of being a deserter from the legion of someone called the Berserker Prince.'

'Berserker Prince? I know they 'ave a daemon prince or two, but ain't 'eard of 'im before.'

They trotted over the rise. He spotted Charlie up ahead, the piebald at a walk. Beyond him lay two farmhouses, one sprawled across the road from the other.

'He went mad on the Hellfield,' Silas continued. 'And killed someone he shouldn't have...I think. An angel. One of Arcadia's own.' The words ran a little easier off the tongue now, and they did not choke him so thoroughly with their magnitude. 'Many of his soldiers fled, fearing they would be persecuted just for serving this prince. I don't know much more. Pitch wouldn't speak on it when I pressed him, but I know he was there when it happened. He admitted that much. And he was furious when the boggart spoke of desertion...do you think the creature was right?'

'I'd say if the truth of it is so hard to come at, ya best leave it alone. There'll be a reason no one is sayin' nothin', and when it comes to the Order they are often reasons ya don't wanna know. You seem to be worried' for 'im, saints know why, but I'd say the best thing you can do for'im, is to stop askin' questions. They shoot people 'ere for desertion, don't they? No tellin' what they do to 'em over there in Arcadia. Leave their strife to them, their battles ain't ours. Just keep 'is bed warm, and go about ya business together as you're told.'

Silas bristled. 'We do not have that type of partnership, I assure you.' Not outside of his head, at least.

'Truly?'E really 'aint bedded you yet?'

'No,' he said tightly.

Her low, crawling cackle stung. 'You're ever a surprise, Mercer. Keepin' an incubus like that out of your drawers is quite the feat indeed. I'm beginnin' to see why the Lady Satine picked you for a 'Orseman. Maybe you'll get things balanced for us again before too long. Now 'ow's about a canter, so as we can catch up with the lad? My guts are rumbling.'

She flapped her arms, shouting her mount into a faster stride, leaving Silas behind with questions that would linger unanswered a while longer. Lalassu surged forward, without an ounce of urging. He snapped his mouth closed for fear of dining on a bug, and in a few strides they had left

Tyvain in their wake. Silas fell into the hypnotic roll of Lalassu's lengthy strides as they thundered down the incline towards the twin farmhouses.

The houses were simple dwellings, single level, with the roof of the one on the right in bad need of rethatching. Charlie stood near to the front door, chatting with a thick-set woman in a pale yellow smock and red checked apron. The farmer's wife was not subtle in her appraisal of Silas as he dismounted Lalassu, and he took his time with loosening the girth before he turned to acknowledge her greeting.

'My name's Lorabelle. It is a pleasure to meet you, Mr Mercer.' The brown-eyed woman offered a calloused hand, her grip pleasantly firm, her smile baring darkened teeth. 'Your lad here has been telling me what happened. So sorry to hear it.' Silas sent Charlie a furtive glance, but the boy merely grinned. 'How frightening that must have been, having a wolf so brazen. Haven't heard of any in these parts for years. Thank the lord you saved him from the beast.'

While Silas gaped, his mind slow to find words he could use, Charlie stepped in. 'Never seen a braver man. The dog was foaming, rabid for sure, but Mr Mercer planted himself between me and it without a thought to his own safety.'

The woman, Lorabelle, fluttered her hands to her brown hair, swept back tightly against her scalp and knotted in a bun at the nape of her neck. 'My goodness, how chivalrous.'

Tyvain arrived just then, thankfully distracting Lorabelle and her batting lashes. 'And he saved you too, madam?'

The soothsayer's confused frown brought the first smile of the day to Silas's lips. 'What the blazes are you on about?'

'The rabid dog,' Charlie said pointedly, 'that attacked us earlier. I was telling Lorabelle here that we had to abandon all our belongings to escape it, and that Mr Mercer came most graciously to our rescue.'

Tyvain's acting skills required some work. She mingled a scoff with laughter. 'Oh, yes. Right 'ero 'e was.'

Lorabelle's's stunted lashes threatened to flutter themselves off their lids. 'Oh my, Mr Mercer, you must be parched after your encounter. Please do come in, you are welcome here. My husband is still out in the fields, but he'd be furious at me if I didn't offer you...some...refreshment at least. This way, please. I've got soup on the fire and bread just fresh cooked.'

Tyvain and Charlie followed after her, muttering with happy abandon about how generous a host Lorabelle was.

Silas did not move to follow. He glanced back, up along the road they had travelled. The countryside lay wide and open beneath a clear sky. Livestock moved about in fields; swallows darted through hedges. A peaceful scene. And he did not trust it at all.

CHAPTER 14

S ilas regarded the thick slab of bread with its covering of pungent, oozing cheese. His appetite was crushed to nothing, and his head was awash with the dozen questions he wished to find answers for. He gripped the edges of his chipped plate, trying to stifle thoughts of the ash-men and the wolf, and Pitch's wild, destructive behaviour. The kitchen smelled of rich gravy and slightly overbaked bread. A comfortable setting he might have enjoyed once. Now it just reminded him of his difference. This would never be his life, the quiet, demanding toil of a farmer and his family.

Instead, he'd been gifted a fine horse and a guardian with crumbling health, and sent out into a frightening, horrid world where enraged souls and men with ash for skin and glass for eyes sought to harm him and those he foolishly acquainted himself with.

He glanced at Charlie. The lad had no difficulty with his appetite, scoffing down his second lashing of bread, lips damp with oil. Christ, if that wolf had got its fangs upon Charlie, Silas would not have forgiven himself.

He pushed his plate away.

'Do you not like it, Mr Mercer?' Lorabelle's voice made him jump, coming from as close as it was. 'Can I get you something else?' She beamed as he looked up at her.

'No, no. This is most kind of you.' He brushed his loosened hair back behind his ears, his fingers snagging in the knots. He could only imagine what a bedraggled sight he must be. 'I'm sorry, it was quite an encounter...I ahh, I am still settling from it.'

Charlie and Tyvain chatted with the woman easily about such trivialities as the weather, the approach of winter, and the farm cat that had just yesterday birthed seven kittens. Lorabelle seemed to relish the company, topping up their cups with cider and laughing hard at Tyvain's dreadful jokes. Her eyes flitted too often to where Silas sat chewing upon reluctant mouthfuls, and he could not decipher if it was attraction or curiosity that drew her.

All at once his fingertips rushed with warmth.

Lalassu's whinny interrupted the chatter.

Silas stilled. Tyvain's sharp amber eyes found him.

'What?' Charlie spoke through a mouthful. 'Why do you both look like that?'

Lorabelle clutched the water jug to her belly. 'Is there something wrong?'

Lalassu neighed, a rough and throaty cry that ensured she'd not be ignored. Silas pushed back his chair. The bandalore rested quietly and deeply in his pocket, but he was coming to understand that he did not need the scythe to warn him every time something was amiss. His instinct did that well enough.

'Stay here, all of you.'

Lorabelle gave a startled squeak. 'Oh my goodness. What's wrong?'

Charlie rose too, and Silas thought he intended to follow despite the directive. The lad headed for the startled lady of the house. 'Nothing to fear. Mr Mercer will take care of it, I'm sure,' Charlie said with confidence. 'But I wonder if you have a mallet or something similar I might borrow? Preferably not a broom.'

Silas hurried out the front door. Tyvain followed close behind him.

'What's wrong with your 'orse?' she whispered, so loudly she might as well have spoken normally.

'I don't know.' He rushed towards the small yard where Lalassu and the other horses were being kept. The rustle of Tyvain's skirts moved with him. Lalassu was at the gate, pawing at the loose dirt. She tossed her head, sending a spray of fine sea-green strands into the air.

'Easy girl, easy.'

But she was not to be placated. The mare rose up onto her hindquarters, front hooves lashing. She neighed again, baring teeth. The piebald and bay shied into the furthest corner of the yard, seeking distance from the unsettled horse.

'Bloody 'ell, what's crawled up 'er arse?' Tyvain said.

'I do not speak horse, but I would guess she is unhappy,' Silas replied.

The mare's wide eyes, the colour of the straw, were set on something beyond Silas's shoulder. Fields spread out beyond the farmhouse and the barn set behind it. A small orchard was visible, the source of the cider, though most trees were skeletal with their lack of leaves and fruit. The farmhouse on the other side of the road seemed long abandoned, its roof trusses collapsed on the westerly side, and once-tended rose bushes now grew wild and woody. There was nothing obviously untoward, not at first glance, anyway. Lalassu avoided the reach of Silas's hand and paced along the fence line.

'Wait...looks like we 'ave some company.' Tyvain pointed back up the road they had travelled.

A wagon appeared over the rise that had hidden the farmhouses from view so well. The trailer was fully loaded with what Silas supposed were sacks of grain, and pulled by a pair of heavy workhorses. Its red wheels left a cloud of dust in its wake. The driver had his pair moving at a canter.

'What the blazes is 'e runnin' from?' Tyvain's words were more growl than anything else. 'And do we wish to feckin' know?'

'What's your gut telling you now?'

'That I ate too much damn cheese.'

Silas cursed and ran the short length of the garden that sat between the farmhouse and the picket fence marking the edge of the roadway. The day was bright, the sunlight seeming to glance off the white clouds and cause a glare. He squinted, trying to make out the driver. He could see they wore a cloak that billowed out behind them, and a wide-brimmed hat that managed to keep its place despite the frantic pace.

'Feck! Watch her,' Tyvain shouted.

Lalassu had grown tired of her confines. The horse ran at the fence and soared over it, mane and tail streaming like medieval banners behind her. In another life, Silas might have dashed out of the way of the oncoming horseflesh, heart racing, but in this one he merely stood and waited. The giant mare set the earth trembling beneath his feet as she landed beside him.

'Whoa there, girl.' He raised his arms, unafraid. 'What do you know, Lalassu?'

But she was not interested in his words, or Silas for that matter. The horse shied around him, her muscles rippling with the sharpness of the move, her eyes showing white around the wheat-field yellow, as she raced for the leaning picket fence. The piebald and bay squealed, bucking as the excitement spread to them, racing at breakneck pace around an enclosure far too small for such a thing.

'Mercer, what the feck is 'appening?' Tyvain hitched her skirts, tucking up the folds to reveal the stark white of stockingless calves beneath.

'Get inside, Tyvain!' Silas shouted.

Lalassu crashed through the flimsy fence, not even bothering to jump it. The heavy mare pounded up the road, set on a course aimed straight for the wagon, which continued its reckless pace.

'Don't be bloody ridiculous,' Tyvain snapped. 'I'm no 'elpless maid, you arsehole.'

The distance between wagon and pale horse shrank rapidly. Good god, what was the mare intending? The skin at his fingertips burned hotter, uncomfortably so.

'Silas,' Charlie called from the doorway. 'What's going on?'

Nothing good, he would wager.

''Is 'orse 'as lost its mind.' Tyvain spoke for him. 'Or she doesn't much like them draught 'orses.'

Whichever it was, Lalassu did not slow. There was barely a quarter of a mile before she would run headlong into the team of two. They were considerable animals, bred to haul great weights, nearer to Lalassu's own build of any horse Silas had seen so far. Combined with the weight of the laden wagon they pulled, they were a battering ram of force. God, he couldn't stand by and watch this. Silas dashed out onto the road.

'Lalassu, stop!'

'What are you doing, you fool?' Tyvain shouted. 'Let 'er deal with it.'

He would do no such thing. Silas broke into a run, racing after his maddened mare. 'Stop, stop now.' He swung his arms about, trying to capture the attention of the coachman. But there was no way the driver had not already seen the thunderous silvery-green charge coming for him, and he did not pull on the reins. Instead he raised his whip. The leather slashed down into the midst of the galloping draught horses, startling them into a flat-out gallop. The rumble of the wagon was like distant thunder closing in.

'You imbecile!' Tyvain screeched. 'Get back 'ere!'

He shot a look over his shoulder. 'Get Charlie inside. Stay away, Tyvain.'

He might not understand exactly what was happening here, but his body rang with alarm enough to want the pair well away. Despite his warning, the stupid, bloody soothsayer was following him, skirts lifted, sleeves pushed up, red hair bobbing about her head like an angry nest of wasps. 'Get back, I say.'

He found the bandalore, and it was waiting for him, the string weaving itself at once onto his finger.

Tyvain cried out. 'Fecking 'ell! Look at 'er!'

Lalassu reared, her muscles bunched hard at her hindquarters, her tail touching at the ground and spreading beneath her, bracing her as she stood on her hind legs. The wispy spread of her mane flowed out from either side of her thick neck, reaching wider and wider, drifting like the strands of a giant spider's web.

The coachman did not rein his horses in.

Further and further the pale horse's mane spread, wider than the coach itself. Christ, it *was* a spiderweb. A net cast wide.

The distance between the mare and the wagon was swallowed by the passing seconds. The driver at last shortened his reins, but not to stop. He pulled hard right, the savagery of the command drawing terrible screams of protest from the draughts. But if he sought to outmanoeuvre Lalassu's web, he had left his move too late.

Sea green flashed, and snow white gleamed beneath it. Lalassu dropped onto all fours, and lowered her head, like a bull readying for a charge.

Silas sucked in his breath.

The wagon ploughed across the few feet that remained empty between vehicle and pale horse. The widened lengths of Lalassu's mane swept forward, enveloping the dashing horses into their folds like a hungry mist. The draughts screamed, but the sound was cut short, and the silence was terrible.

The wagon bucked, the sudden stop propelling its back end high. The driver was hurled skyward, his whip flying from his hands. His cargo of sacks followed after him, arching high into the air.

'My god,' Silas gasped.

The wagon smashed back against the earth, back wheels shattering. The driver soared high for but a moment, propelled entirely over Lalassu and her storm-flashed spread of mane, before he and his cargo dropped from the sky. He landed just behind the incensed mare. She aimed a broad hoof at him, and though her head was lost beneath the web of mane she had weaved, she found her target.

The coachman's skull exploded in a plume of dust.

Silas stared at the filtering particles as they sprinkled down to land upon his cloak. A deeper grey than the others, but the same rough fabric and tattered edges sure enough.

The ash-men had found them again.

Barely had he made the connection when Silas spotted the first of the sacks begin to move. Material of faded grey, as though too long in the sun.

'Oh shit.' He'd been very wrong about the wagon's cargo. These were no sacks of grain.

'Tyvain!' he roared. 'They have found us.'

CHAPTER 15

The first ash-man clawed his way from the layers of his own cloak. He'd been bundled up like a grotesque child in swaddling cloth, and emerged now, contorting and stretching his way free. The others were dotted about him, at least five that Silas could count before a sharp sound drew him about.

He spun on his heels.

An ash-man stood not two feet from him, a brute of a figure, his raised hand wrapped with a nasty set of knuckledusters. The fiend's mouth widened, stretching already thin lips tight against gums that had lost most of their teeth. Silas stared into polished onyx eyes. His fingers were pained with the feverish prickling of a call to action. But before he could so much as twitch, the ash-man dropped to his knees and toppled forward, landing face-first upon the ground. A knife's silver hilt jutted from his bony back, buried deep in the vulnerable place at the top of his spine. Silas stared at the intricately carved handle.

'Wake up, you fecking idiot.' Tyvain ran on short but agile legs towards him. She grabbed the knife and wrenched it free of its bony prison. 'Where's your blade?'

His hand was still in his blasted pocket. Silas pulled the bandalore free, the discs warm against his palm. His fingers were sensitive with heightened alarm. 'Thank you.'

'Time for that shit later.' Tyvain ran past him. 'Keep your wits.'

Silas shook off the unsteadiness that came with knowing he'd very nearly been taken out and turned back to where the rest of the chaos lay.

Lalassu's swathe of mane had reduced from its complicated web form. The stricken draught horses now lay on their sides, broad chests heaving, so tangled up in their strappings they did not move. Remarkably they appeared uninjured. The shattered wagon spread about them like flotsam and jetsam.

The ash-men rose like horrid butterflies emerging from their cocoons, staggering upright, heads flopping about their shoulders as though they had not yet realised they had necks at all.

Tyvain released her knife once more. To their right, a cloaked figure fell before he'd yet straightened, the Hag's knife jutting from the centre of his chest.

Before Silas had time to blink, she pulled a second blade from somewhere in the folds of her gown, and another ash-man fell, this one on their left. The tall, spindly figure dropped as silently as his brother. A knife hilt stuck out from the delicate intersection of collarbone and base of the throat.

Silas stared at the soothsayer. The Hag was formidable in her knifeplay. He'd be well served to remember that.

Tyvain scowled at him. 'What? You think I'd last in the Order if all I could do was belch every time somethin' bad was comin'?'

Even if there had been an answer to give, Silas had no time to speak it. The remaining ash-men, four in all, rushed them from all sides. Lalassu reared, the glint of her coat a hail-rich storm cloud. She dashed towards the nearest of the ash-men, announcing her attack with a shattering bray. He saw the hapless figure raise a weapon, the sunlight catching at the blade he bore, before he was lost to view behind the bulk of the pale horse. Silas flicked his wrist, releasing the bandalore down its string. A gentle melody sounded, nothing like the tremendous, mesmerising song of the true blade but comforting just the same. The transformation into scythe was quick. A short shaft this time, resembling an axe handle, and suited to rapid angling. He braced both hands to its length. An ash-man ran at him, this one brandishing a short sword. Silas threw his considerable bulk into his thrust, but his attacker was not to be downed so readily. He parried the blow, not a hint of effort showing upon his expressionless, pale, ravaged face.

How foul the tinge of blue to his lips was, enough to cause Silas's own to curl. An odour wafted from the figure, like milk on the turn. Silas swung again, lower this time. The ash-man matched his move, dropping his blade, saving himself from being cut off at the knees. He shoved hard at Silas, forcing the larger man onto his back foot. Gathering himself, Silas was afforded a quick glimpse of Tyvain. She wore a grin best suited to the asylum, throwing her silver blades with deadly, precise aim.

The ash-man jabbed, and his sword point nicked Silas's coat sleeve. The scythe's notes trembled, their tune wavering.

'Christ.' He danced backwards. 'Focus, you fool.'

Silas fell back with a gasp, narrowly avoiding another jab of the ash-man's short blade. The fiend might hold the appearance of a hollowed-out shell of a man, but his fighting skills were not so vapid. Sweat clung to Silas's brow as they worked at one another. His opponent was formidable. Silas grunted and twisted and slashed, moved along by the melody. He tried desperately to recall what Sybilla had taught him of the fight, so he might gain advantage here. He was defending himself well enough, but that was all. Despite the moves the scythe gifted him, the way the notes dragged his limbs about, he was not bringing his enemy to heel.

You are not enough.

That is what the ash-man had whispered to him at the mill.

And damn it, the insipid creature may well be right. What if more of these intolerable beings were headed for the farmhouse? Charlie and their genial host were vulnerable.

Shit, shit. Silas's curses came with each misaimed strike. His fear made him sloppy, distracted. The ash-man hunched low and sprang fast, his swing aimed for Silas's head. With a desperate cry, Silas threw the shaft high. He managed to knock the attack off course.

But the misdirection did not work entirely in his favour. It drew him in too close to the ash-man, who took quick advantage. The blunt end of his sword cracked against Silas's temple.

Stars exploded in his vision. Silas's head snapped back. His teeth cracked as jaws slammed. From a distance he heard his own pained cry.

Silas staggered, blinking madly against the speckling that stole his sight. His world blurred and whirled.

'Oh, my dear, are you all right?' The voice was right at his ear.

No, it was closer than that.

The sound was deep in his head. Not the rasp of an ash-man, nor the rough bark of the soothsayer. A woman had spoken, her voice trembling with concern.

How Silas's heart stuttered to hear it.

He shook his head, swinging the scythe wildly as he fought the blindness that consumed him. Was it even the scythe he held? He was uncertain, dazed and pulled from centre.

That voice, though. God, he knew it.

His chest ached at the sound of it.

Laughter floated about him, high with lazy charm. 'I fear I am not fit to tend a garden after all.'

The scent of wet grass and the most glorious tinge of roses swept over him.

'Come now, Beatrice,' A new voice. The deeper timbre of a male, husky and bouncing with amusement. 'There was never any doubt of that. Serves you right for intruding, I'd say.'

He laughed, a sound that caught at the sunshine, and turned Silas inside out.

If his heart had skipped before, it positively thundered now. He could hear the roar of blood in his ears. Too loud. It sank the voices beneath it. The scent of roses vanished.

Silas blinked. The spots faded, and the day dazzled him. He squinted through the shimmer of sunstruck tears. The reek of curdling milk came at him.

And so too did the ash-man.

Silas was very much returned to the real world. The creature came at him with a body blow that lifted him off his feet. Silas went down in a flurry of foul language and a panicked shriek. Barely had he hit the ground when another was upon him, wrapping their arms about his legs. Another weight pinned down the arm that held the scythe.

'No, no!' Silas writhed and thrashed beneath the onslaught, desperate to keep hold of his weapon.

They were concentrating their assault upon the arm that held the scythe. It felt as though the entire wagonload of ash-men was upon his limb. But at least one of them straddled his hips, while another dug a knee into his left arm. Silas glared up at the fiend atop him. Drool dripped from slack jaws. He swung his head in time to avoid that vile liquid splashing onto his face.

Christ, how many of these forsaken things were perched upon him?

The ash-man positioned atop him shifted higher so that his knees pressed into Silas's underarms and his weight was upon Silas's chest. The movement shifted the lengths of the foul grey cloak he wore, sweeping it over Silas's face. Once again he was blinded, though there was no pretty scent of roses this time. The stench of rotten and ruined things made him retch.

Hands found every inch of him, sharp jabs, fleeting tugs, nasty pinches of skin that made him wince and writhe. This was just as the intruder at the house had done, mindless, incalculable strikes, as though they sought to tug his skin from his body altogether.

A hard tug came at the scythe, still clutched tightly in his grasp. They were trying to take the blade from him. He roared into the heated folds of material, the putrid air near to choking him. They would not have the scythe. Never.

There was a quickening against his fingers, a shift of wood from rough to smooth. The bandalore burrowed against his palm, as though seeking to hide itself beneath his skin.

'Silas! Fight them, man, they ain't that smart.' Tyvain's cry buckled with strain. 'You're built the size of three of 'em side by side, throw 'em off.' She cried out, launching a slather of curses at whoever it was she struggled with. 'Feck, 'ow many of these cunts are there?'

Too many to grapple with. That would have been Silas's answer should he have been able to cast a word clear. As it was he could barely catch his breath. The weight of the bodies atop him was smothering. Sharp nails dug at his outstretched arms and at his neck, scratches hot against his skin. He lifted his hips, the only part of him he could manage to raise off the ground, and bucked as though he were a wild horse attempting to unsaddle unwelcome riders. Fire slid down the side of his neck, a greater anguish tracing its mark along his skin. With horror he realised it was not nails but the tip of a blade.

'Are you frightened, ankou?' The ash-man astride him peeled back a layer and breathed foulness into the heat between them. 'Well, you should be. For I see you. And what a pitiful sight you are. The Lady did not choose well.'

A viscous strike landed against his wrist. Silas screamed. His fingers cinched around the bandalore. Christ, they could not have it. Every inch of him knew it. His body bristled with the need to covet death's blade.

Another strike came. Dear god, the pain was staggering. Unspeakable.

A shriek tore open the sky and split the earth.

But it was not his cry.

And the sound turned his blood to ice.

Was the moment not abysmal enough? Now the ash-men were rejoined by their fire-eyed beast.

They worked upon his wrist in violent concentration, running the blade back and forth as though they meant to saw the hand clean off. Silas's throat burned with his screams, but curse these monsters, he would not relinquish the bandalore. The ash-man above him snarled his displeasure as Silas's limb refused to be separated. Whatever blade they used did not seem fit to the task. Clawing fingers with their sharpened nails dug at Silas's hand, seeking to unwrap his hold upon the bandalore.

Neither blade nor bony digit could remove the god-given scythe. But Christ almighty, could the attempt have been made less agonising?

The ash-man growled, a watery sound from the depths of his sunken chest. Bursts of pain pinpricked other parts of Silas's body, against his ribs, his thighs, the curve of his ankle where the ash-men danced their blades upon him.

The shriek struck the air once more, slicing into his ears as surely as the blades against his skin. Silas moaned against the back of his teeth. He jerked and twisted against his captors. If he could just gain some purchase against the ground, find some leverage to raise himself, room to swing his arm, he might free himself yet.

The red-eyed beast roared, the bestial cry reverberating through Silas's assaulted bones. Silas groaned. He should never have ridden away from Pitch.

'Fucking daemon.' Dampness sprayed from his lips, the tang of copper touching his tongue.

A vicious snarl erupted nearby. Terribly close by. The weight upon Silas's chest lifted, burying him deeper beneath lengths of grey. The blade at his wrist ceased its wretched task, and his arm was freed. He sucked in a desperate breath, curling the bandalore in against his belly. He was almost thankful for the cloak that lay across his face, for it shielded him from seeing the damage done. He needed to stay clear-headed. Good god, how was it that he could move his hand at all? The pressure at his legs vanished.

Silas struggled, wriggling back and forth to free himself from the last of the ash-men still anchored upon him. An unsettling crunch came from nearby.

The snap of branches, where he knew none to be.

There were no screams, no cries, just the crack and pop of brittle limbs, and a low and menacing growl.

Silas fought his way free of the tangle of the cloak. At sight of his wrist he almost lost the small amount of cheesy bread he'd eaten. By god, it was a bloodied mess. He could barely make out the damage for all the blood that ran. The bandalore's string, red as a toffer's lips, slipped from his finger. The wood too was stained, turned dark by his blood . Silas slipped the bandalore into his uninjured hand, blinking against the light. He could make out only dark shapes, moving shadows. One of those shadows sank low, its length caressing the earth. The beast, he assumed. But it was too far away to even consider trying to strike out.

An ash-man was much nearer. The billow of his cloak marking his outline. Silas braced himself.

The bandalore's song rang out, but, most startlingly, the blade did not appear.

The discs whipped along the bloodied string, arching around the fiend and winding back to pull a noose around the man's neck. Silas leaned back, putting his weight into drawing the noose tight. He gritted his teeth and pulled harder. He'd learned in Mordiford, at the hapless gravedigger's expense, that the bandalore was a weapon too. And he'd not protest the stranglehold here. These were monsters, not a desperate man seeking to feed his family. He'd sheer that hollow-cheeked head right off those damned bony shoulders, blade or not.

Silas was aflame with indignation and simmering with rage. It cleared his vision, like wiping frost off a windowpane.

He found himself at the centre of a maelstrom.

At least half a dozen mauled and ruined bodies were strewn about him, their ash fluttering like snowfall in the midday light. A growl rose from the depths of Silas's chest, and he wrenched his arm back with all the force afforded to him. The bandalore's string tore through papery flesh and chalky bone.

'The Lady chose well enough,' he snarled at the black eyes that had never left him.

Those eyes were wide open as the ash-man's head tumbled from his shoulders, hitting the ground and sending white ash billowing like vapour escaping heated earth.

'Behind you, Mercer!'

Silas spun. A pounding, dangerous melody soared. With a maddened shout, Silas loosened the bandalore once more. Still the scythe did not show itself, but no matter.

The discs slammed into the ash-man's bulbous nose.

Shards of scalp and bone and glints of blackened glass sprayed in all directions. Silas's head thundered with a rush of blood. His body was so tightly strung there barely seemed enough air to force its way into his lungs. He vibrated with a fervour that frightened him, thrilled him. Christ, he wanted more of this.

Let them come.

What would Pitch think of him now? That disdainful bastard would have to marvel, surely.

He whirled about. 'Come on then. Who is frightened now?'

The bandalore's tune sank low.

Glowing orbs of red filled his vision. Bared yellowed fangs hung from gums black as night, and an oily green-grey substance dribbled from powerful jaws. Silas stumbled back, cradling his shattered wrist. Shit. He'd been right about the size of the beast, the creature's ears were level with his chest. Its tail reached higher still, a massive plume of black that reminded Silas of the feathers worn by carriage horses in a funeral procession. The animal dipped its broad head, shoulders bunching, preparing to strike.

Silas flicked his good wrist, setting the bandalore free, willing the scythe to burst forth. Where was the melody? It was too damned quiet.

To his true horror, the bandalore flew along its string barely a foot, and dropped limp, dangling from his finger, useless as a pendulum.

'Bloody hell.' Silas dodged right, but he was not fast enough.

The beast ploughed into the flying lengths of Silas's coat and clipped his side. The impact loosened a choked cry from him, and his head slammed down against rocky ground. Dazed, for a second time, he rolled to one side, trying to get onto his knees. His coat snagged behind him, and he cursed with all the fervour of a drunken sailor.

Silas grabbed at rich blue folds, now crusted with ash and dirt, desperate to free himself. The waft of rot hit him. A tremulous growl came from behind. Silas stilled, edging his head slowly so that he caught sight of the beast in the corner of his eye. It held the edge of his coat fast in its powerful jaws, the peeling back of its thick black lips giving the impression of a maniacal smile.

Damn it, the revolting animal was toying with him, like a cat with a paw upon an injured mouse's tail. Silas hissed. He'd had quite enough of being battered about. He lashed out with the troublesome bandalore, casting it behind him. But the angle was all wrong, of course, and he could not put his weight behind the throw.

The bandalore fled along its string well enough, but the trajectory he'd sent it on saw it curve in towards his back. The red-eyed monster released his coat and lunged, stamping its massive paws upon his shoulder blades. Silas hit the ground hard, catching his injured hand beneath him. He roared his unhappiness.

The beast tore into his coat. The rip of fabric seeming never-ending, as fangs as sharp and serrated as blades made light work of the material. The scent of dank and rotting things was about him. He would be one of those rotting things if he did not do something. The fragile clothing was hardly armour. In a moment his flesh would make a meal for the creature.

Why had the scythe forsaken him? Not a single note upon the air.

''Ey! Get on with ya, bloody bastard.' Tyvain's battle cry erupted nearby.

The creature yelped a lone note of surprise mingled with pain. The weight on Silas's back shifted. He pressed both hands to the earth, ignoring the excruciating protest at his wrist, and threw back his head, hoping to catch the beast in the nose. But his motion upwards met no resistance, and he found himself able to right himself onto his knees. He swayed there, catching a glimpse of the beast's long tail as the creature vanished behind the abandoned farmhouse.

'Feckin' 'ell.' Tyvain panted. 'I tried to knife the bloody thing three times. I swear my blades just bounced off the feckin' coat like it was made of iron or somethin'. You all right, lad?'

Silas got to his feet, all his joints protesting, his wrist alight with pain, the silent bandalore dangling from his finger. Lalassu stood a few paces away, regarding the place where the beast had vanished. She flicked her silver-green tail and appeared nonplussed about the fact that he'd almost become a monster's dinner.

'Mercer, you all right?'

'I have no idea.' He glanced at his injured wrist and inhaled sharply. Best he not look too closely for now, not while he was standing anyway, if he wished to remain that way. He was sure he'd just glimpsed the whiteness of bone beneath the blood. The bandalore distracted him, running itself up the short length of string and finding its place in his palm. 'I'm really not sure.'

He was exhaustion on two legs. If he could have curled up in a ball right here on the dirt, he wouldn't have minded. A sudden thought jerked him wide awake.

'Charlie...and Lorabelle...are they –'

'Fine. They're fine. Now 'ow's about we get the feck out of 'ere? I don't fancy meeting another wagonload of powdery pricks, or a black dog with a taste for ankou arse. Saint's taint, I should have stayed playing nanny to the bloody daemon –'

'Surely that was more than a simple dog?' Silas tried to frown, but his eyebrows ached. 'The beast was monstrous.'

'It sure weren't pretty. And yes, sweet'eart, it was more than just a simple dog. I was being farseeshish.'

He eyed her. 'Do you mean facetious?'

'Exactly what I said.'

'Silas!' Charlie ran towards them, face white with shock. 'Are you all right?'

People kept asking him that, but surely the answer was obvious. He was not all right. He'd been set upon, beaten, his hand nearly amputated, and the one weapon he'd thought himself capable of wielding had betrayed him in the heat of a battle.

'Oh my god, Silas. Your...your hand...' Though Charlie grew deathly pale, he reached a tentative hand towards the disgusting wreck of flesh. There was no doubt of it, there was a hint of bone showing through the gaping rough-hewn split.

'It is nothing.' Silas's hand was a red glove, but the flow at least had ceased. There were already darkening edges to the wound where the blood was drying. He would heal from this. As he had when Black Annis had impaled him.

Or had that changed too?

'You're in shock, for it is definitely something.' Charlie's words were thick with horror. 'Is it broken?'

'Take more than that to break 'im, I suspect.' Tyvain snorted. 'Right now only thing that needs doing is getting our arses on our bloody 'orses and getting the 'ell out of 'ere. I'll tell ya, I've never been more keen to knock on Old Bess's godsawful ugly front door than I am now. Sooner we get to the Sanctuary, the better. They'll sort you right out, Silas. Get your 'orses ready in double time, both of ya.'

Silas stared after her as she stomped her way back to the house. The quiet after the chaos was disconcerting. He couldn't quite feel his feet, and his heart still tried to beat its way out of him.

'Silas?' Charlie touched his elbow. 'She's right, we should go.' He tilted his head towards the wagon.

The downed draught horses had found their feet, miraculous considering the calamity, and both nibbled at thin grass by the roadside as though nothing untoward had happened at all. They were surrounded by piles of grey cloaks and heaps of ashen-dust. The wind worked the remains into the air, leaving it hazy.

At Charlie's gentle urging, Silas made his way back to the house. Lorabelle was passed out on her kitchen floor, a bundle of rags beneath her head.

'She passed out when she thought you were going to be run down by the wagon.' Charlie shrugged. 'She saw nothing of what came after. For the best I'd say. Why don't you sit down, I'll help Tyvain with saddling up the horses.'

He nodded, dropping heavily into the same chair where a short time ago he'd nibbled at his cheesy bread. The portion, now stiff with cooling, was still there, his bitemark upon a corner. Silas stared at it while Charlie and Tyvain readied the horses. Perhaps Charlie was right, and he was suffering from the shock of the encounter, for he could not keep his thoughts in order. They raced about in his skull, manic and wild. The taunts of the ash-man, or rather whatever lurked within the depths of the obsidian, haunted him.

The Lady did not choose well. Silas slumped in his seat. *Are you frightened?* Of course he bloody was. He was terrified. But not for himself. For Charlie, and Tyvain, well, perhaps not the latter now, considering, but certainly for the innocent woman whose hospitality might have gotten her killed. He had been so very frightened he would fail to protect them. Silas stared at crumbs beside his abandoned plate. And then there were the voices he'd heard, that odd, jovial conversation so very out of place in the heat of a desperate fight.

A hallucination caused by the blow he'd received? Or something more vital? A memory.

He wasn't sure how long he sat there before he realised he was still holding on to the bandalore. He slid it into his pocket. The wood thumped onto the floorboards, rolling beneath the table. Silas looked down with a start. A hole gaped where the pocket should be, the material ripped to pieces by yellowed fangs.

'The arrowhead,' he whispered, patting at the other pocket, which had escaped ruin. It was empty. 'Shit.'

The Arcadian relic was either a chew toy for the horrendous black dog now or somewhere out on the road where he had fallen. Silas dragged himself to his feet and made his way back out onto the road.

122

'What are ya doin', fool?' Tyvain called from where she cinched the bay's girth.

He mumbled about having lost something on the road, and soon Charlie and Tyvain joined him in the search for what he told them was a good luck charm. But the Hag gave him only the shortest time to look about between piles of ash and blood-flecked dirt before she ushered them all back to the horses.

'Enough. Your lucky piece will just 'ave to stay lost. You're dead on your feet, man, if you don't mind the pun. You need to rest, and we've got a ride ahead of us.'

Silas didn't have the energy to protest. The pain had lost its pincer edge, but god what he wouldn't do for one of Charlie's cigarettes now, or something else to dull his senses. Cider, or better yet, a Valkyrie's healing hand. They set out, with the farmhouse door firmly closed and their host tucked up in her bed. Her husband must have been at work a good distance away, for there was no sign of him despite the racket they had caused.

Just as well.

Silas urged Lalassu into a gallop, leading the others out. The further away he took himself, the better it would be for these people.

And the quicker they arrived at this Sanctuary, the sooner Charlie would be safe and returned to a life he could envy.

CHAPTER 16

P itch lay face down upon a mattress lumpy with uneven fill and wet with unpleasant things. He had lost the strength and desire to tug against his restraints some time ago, there was little point in such protest anyway. He was bound here with purpose, each wrist and ankle made prisoner. He groaned, and shifted one hand, seeking to breathe life back into fingers that were cold, a thumb that had grown numb. The cold, slender ring of metal encircling his wrist shifted, putting cruel pressure against pale skin reddened from constant rubbing. Fine chains ran from each cuff to circle about the bedposts. Each appeared as fine as a lady's necklace but were, he had learned, capable of holding a pained and mindless daemon in place, no matter how he bucked and writhed and screamed.

His captors had not restrained him to begin with. But he'd put up such a fight they had turned to harsher methods. They were familiar with him and were taking no chances.

Sybilla and the Lady Satine knew what he was capable of.

Knew exactly what he'd done to deserve to be here, trapped in this world of men.

He was spread naked like a hide at the tanners, with a needle being worked along his spine. The sheets were damp with his sweat and warm with his blood. His skin seethed with firey torment as they sought to wrestle him under control once more. He'd lost himself in the Forest of Dean, come slowly and surely undone. But the Lady Satine was determined to drag him back to rights, no matter how he longed to be done with it all, how he shouted and cursed and besmirched the names of all who refused him escape from his lot.

Gods, Lord Enoch was the master of exquisite punishment, Pitch would grant him that. To force life upon a condemned daemon, when he hungered for emptiness, death and the quiet it would bring, was exquisitely vicious.

'By all that is heavenly, Tobias, do you wish me to call back Sybilla so she might bind you tighter? Stop moving about, you are making this far worse than it needs to be.' The Lady Satine's voice crackled with irritation. 'The more you struggle the longer it takes. Why are you so determined not to accept some relief?'

Relief? If he had strength left to scoff at her, he would have done so with gusto, and spit every conceivable curse he could summon at her. Whatever it was that Satty needled into his skin, tracing her infernal point along the lines of that eye-sore of a tattoo, it could never truly relieve him. It diluted the agony of his flesh, certainly, and there was plenty to subdue, but it did nothing for the anguish of his mind, and that burden had only grown greater since the encounter with the Verderer.

By Raphael's festering crack, what a waking nightmare the Forest of Dean had been for this daemon.

Not only had he been defiled by the fae queen and felt her claws upon the darkest parts of himself, he carried now the echo of the terrible cries released when the Blight-filled prism shattered. What anguished sounds they were. He knew not what the Blight truly was, but he knew its noise, and it was as wretched as he. As the wails tore at him the spirit of the forest had stared, single eye piercing into him as hard as the breaking glass, as though the creature knew what lay within. Pitch's guts had twisted, and he felt something unravel deep in the dark edges of his mind. His ears still rang from that explosion of glass and horror. The echoing tenor made sleep, already elusive, now damned near impossible.

'Fuck off.' His protest was weak enough to be laughable. But Satty did not laugh.

'Not until we are done.'

He'd glimpsed her borrowed face, as Sybilla man-handled him onto the bed and stripped him of clothes stiffened with dried blood and dirt.

Satty's current face did not seem inclined to laughter, the swath of etched lines about dry and snarled lips said as much. He'd never seen the true form of the djinn who was now his master but he knew with certainty it would not be a crone whose hair was thinned and silver, and whose skin was darkened by long days spent toiling harsh land. Lady Satine possessed every inch of vanity he did, they had that in common at least. Whoever she embodied now, whether a shape she had shifted herself, or a witless human she had commandeered, they suited her purpose at this moment. Likely, her forgettable appearance made her invisible, free to come and go without comment. Free to play torturer and have no one the wiser for it.

'This can take a short while, or a long. That is up to you.' She was crisp as an autumn-dried leaf. 'No matter how many times you advise me to fuck off, and I've counted at least thirty such suggestions so far, I've no intention of leaving you this way. But you must stay still. We cannot afford to waste the amuletum, especially now we know that it will erode away each time you use your flame. I'd not planned on that, I'll admit. A good thing we learned of it sooner rather than later, but it will take some fixing.' A good thing? Gods, this woman had a strange idea of goodness. 'I have Mr Ahari sourcing an artifact that might aid you in focusing your flame, and steer it away from the parts of you that are compromised. It should mean you can avoid being reduced to a quivering wreck every time your daemonic energy is required.' Pitch snarled into the bedclothes, though even that small movement caused him ill. She'd sent he and the ankou on a pointless quest. What he truly needed was his vestige, the blade of bone created for him alone, the conduit for his flame. But the vestige had been stripped from him when they took all else away. 'Now, hold steady. And let's be done with this.'

He had no intention of being done with this. Once they had patched him up and he was no longer crushed by the pain of the wound at his back, she would deem him fit to carry on as before. And he knew himself far from fit.

Pitch rocked to one side, moving his weight as well as fatigue and dolor would allow. The coarse fabric, and jagged things beneath, pinched his balls.

'By Lugh's holy fucking bile, let me be.'

She shushed him, and dug her needle in. His cry wedged itself tiredly into the confines of his throat and went no further. He slumped into the sodden mattress. Satty was near to halfway done with the retouching of ink. Of amuletum.

Whatever the fuck that might be.

It did ease his suffering, that much was true. It was the same ink that formed the tattoo etched upon his back, in all its garish glory. An ironic marking, one he'd chosen in the throes of his grief when he first landed upon Lady Satine's doorstep. She'd asked him, while he sat dull-eyed with loss and confusion, what design he would prefer for the marking she would etch upon him to conceal the dreadful, weeping wound that scored his back and reduce its ferocious pain to a dull roar. In his daemonic form, a massive and frightening shape that it was, the damage done by an angel's halo had been awful but not so encompassing. A singular, but deep, laceration. In petty human form though it consumed his back entirely, with ugly, glistening welts and skin melted by a weapon borne of the creation fire of the Ophanim throne itself.

A hideous wound Lord Enoch had cursed never to heal, vengeance on his mind.

It could not mend, but it could be concealed. So Lady Satine had said. He'd barely heard a word of the conversation, lifting from his stupor long enough to answer her when she insisted on him choosing a design for the mark she would administer.

He'd chosen a pitchfork . One the humans gave their Devil in all the little stories they were so fond of creating. It suited him perfectly. And as he was in hell, he might as well dress the part.

Lady Satine settled beside him, causing the mattress to shift, and Pitch to groan.

He'd been splayed out like a carcass for hours now, in a windowless room with walls as black as soot. A subtle green glow, the sort that hung over the bogs in the depth of night, clung to the room, illuminating it weakly. There was not a candle scone in sight, nor furniture of any kind, save for the bed. He was going to need to piss at some point, but the idea of such great movement filled him with despair. He was battered and bruised, and not just from the farmer's fists, or the strike of the policeman's batons as they beat him into a vile stinking cell in that pathetic village. His encounters in the Forest of Dean had taken a deep toll. Reached right into that place within him that he strove so hard to quieten.

'Right, let's give this another go, shall we?' Satty leaned her arm against the swell of his arse cheek, using his body like it were nothing more than a tabletop to give her purchase. Gods, he wished he was a fucking table top. He would feel nothing then. 'Is that all right? Not too much pressure?'

He did not answer, and she began the needle's work at the middle of his back, where the skin was thinnest. He bit into the inside of his cheek where the skin was already flayed to buggery. His stomach churned with the swill of his own blood. He was starved and sickened and tired beyond measure. His refusal to lie steady, as she wished, was making this an enduring process. So be it. The longer it took, the better chance they'd give up on him entirely.

'Good, good.' Satty muttered, dancing pricks of pain against his skin.

When Sybilla had arrived to extricate him from the farmer's angry possession, her chest puffed with righteous disdain as only the Valkyrie angel could manage, she had found him lying in a pool of his own piss and blood, babbling through his pain and exhaustion. Pitch had assumed, very wrongly it turned out, that his altercations with the farmers would offer some relief from the ever intensifying throbbing at his back. Over the days spent recuperating in the sickeningly sweet surrounds of Ottelie's cottage, with the ankou fussing over him like an over-sized nursemaid, the discomfort had worsened and worsened. He'd been near mad with it by the time they set out. No amount of cake or ale shifted the pain. And with each hour he grew more fearful, more certain his agony would tip him so off-kilter he'd find his control slipping out of reach. And the interminable stirring at his core would strengthen. Unfold into something great and terrible. The restless, ceaseless tapping at his heart would call out, urging him to stretch invisible wings that ached from lack of use.

That was how he'd come to view the strange presence within. A sweeping, winged monster curled inside, always pressing for release, unhappy with its confines.

In Arcadia, he'd thought it a beast of war. He'd convinced himself it was borne of bloodlust and had a right to exist within him.

He was a Prince of the Hellfield, after all. A Dominion, as Lord Enoch had named his daemonic commanders.

The Dominion were mighty, terrifying and spawned for battle. So, what better than a wildness at his heart to aid him in felling the Nephilim and wiping the Watchers from existence? So what if the other princes felt no such stirrings. He was unique among them, then. Greater. More formidable. The blood had flowed, and he had soared. The monster's release was not a quick thing. The escape was gradual, the cage he held it in gradually rattling itself loose with each swing of his blade. They had feared him, those in Elyssiam and Arcadia both, and were right to do so. He had seen the consternation upon the faces of his own legion, on days when the unbridled, insatiable lust for the fight took him over.

The Beserker Prince.

Gods, how he'd relished the name. Taken the title like it were the very crown of Arcadia itself and placed it upon his head. Throwing himself into the fight with ever more reckless abandon, giving the beast greater and greater rein, allowing it to hammer at what was left of his cage of restraint until the bars broke, and the monster ran riot. The burn of it was intoxicating, astonishing, and utterly blinding.

So much so he'd lost sight entirely.

A sob snagged at the back of Pitch's throat, damning the memories for giving him no rest.

That fateful day upon the Hellfield his beast had glowed too bright. The Watchers, the Nephilm, the daemons of his legion, and the magnificence that was a Seraphim angel were made one and the same by the glare. He could not tell friend from foe, and had grown too savage to care.

He shone upon the Hellfield, as no prince of Daemonkind had a right too. And as he blazed, a mighty, splendid angel fell.

'Raph.' The name, that precious name, strained from him. His ruined throat contorted its beauty into a rough cry, taking a stranglehold that left him breathless.

'Now, now.' Lady Satine paused, and removed the pressure she'd put upon him. The bed creaked as she shifted, closer to him he suspected, for her words came right at his ear, causing him to shiver. 'What's done is done. It is over, and cannot be changed.'

'It is not done for me, it is endless.' He fairly barked his reply, like the animal he was. The wound he bore was permanent evidence of his wrongdoing. A memento of a fight he should not have fought.

'There aren't any words I can offer, none that will make much difference. I know that.' Her sigh was barely audible. 'But for what it's worth you should know the blame is not all yours. He should have known better than to ever place you in that gods-forsaken place where the wilds of war grow. He should have stepped in when he saw what it was making of you.'

Her words befuddled him, but his mind was weary and his body more so. He was in no mood to ask of whom she spoke. His sire perhaps? Or the Lord? Either way she was wrong. The blame was very much Pitch's own. 'I am...I was a Dominion, the spawn of a Daemonkind King, there was no other place for me to be.'

The dank air settled on him, pressing him into the mattress. The unnatural light, the swath of green that seemed to emanate from the onyx walls, embellished the room with an unearthly feel. Perhaps it was just that. Unearthly. And he'd been taken far away from a clueless ankou who eyed him with stupid wonderment, and there was no longer any need to worry that the Forest of Dean had rattled at his flimsy cage and disturbed a sleeping beast.

There was a silent length before Lady Satine spoke again through her foreign lips. 'There is another place, and it is here, and it is now. But I promise you this, Vassago, that when all is said and done, if you still suffer, if you still seek an end to this, you shall be set free. You have my word on that.'

Gods, how wretched must he appear for her to dare to use his true name. The name he could not utter, the name that Lord Enoch no doubt wished never to have heard. Prince Vassago, Beserker Prince of the Hellfield, and slayer of Seraphiel, the greatest of Arcadia's Seraphim angels.

'Just let me be.' He bit at the cushion of his cheek and tasted copper. 'I want no soothing.'

If he lay here long enough, perhaps he would vanish entirely. He would refuse to feed and fade away. This room was near enough to the cavernous, souless pit of the abaddon he *should* have been cast into to serve his penance.

Lady Satine moved again, edging away. ' Leave you be so you can sink into your doldrums?' She clucked her tongue. 'No. That won't be happening. And Bess won't have it either, you know. He's the master of Harvington Hall, I don't believe you've met. An impressive place he's built here. Almost as fine a Sanctuary as he made for me with Holly Village.' She prattled on, as though simply filling the dreary room with chatter would make everything all right. 'When you are up and about, I think you'll find it much to your taste. I daren't say it to any other of the Children of Melusine but I do think Bess to be the finest builder among them.' Pitch felt her words upon him, sure as a blow. He knew well of the Children of Melusine; half-human, half-fae, and exquisite craftsmen and woman. Inheritors of their royal fae mother's aptitude for building. They were the makers of Sanctuaries, sealed and secure establishments that were whatever their purchaser required: a hidden oasis, a stronghold for treasures, a magnificent, audacious manor on full display. The Children of Melusine could build a castle overnight and keep it completely hidden from all but the patron it was made for. He knew this because Seraphiel had had just such a place built for them, indulging Pitch's penchant for this world. They had fucked themselves near senseless, screaming like lunatics as they ravaged one another, and done so without a soul knowing, both here, or in Arcadia. Satty was still speaking. Gods, would she never shut up? 'Bess is going to want you to rise from your sickbed before too long, so the sheets can be washed at least.'

He grunted his disdain. Bess would be waiting a long while.

The lady exchanged her needle for a soft cloth, dabbing it at stains he could not see. He did not like Satty much on most days, he liked her less when she was gentle like this.

'You will endure, Vassago,' she whispered. 'You must.' An odd thing for her to say. He doubted anyone wished for him to endure. The Lord Enoch certainly did not. He had cursed his fallen prince with a wound that would not heal, and sentenced him to the eternal misery of the abaddon beneath White Mountain. An abyss from which few had ever returned, or done so with their sanity intact. But at the last moment the punishment had changed, he'd found himself banished instead, forbidden from ever setting foot in Arcadia again, and with none of the usual overbearing, humiliating ceremony, he'd been cast out by his own sire. As though Lucifer wished to ensure there was no chance he'd ever have to lay eyes upon his reprehensible spawn again. 'See this service to the Order as your way to redemption, if that is what you seek, or see it is as a life renewed. As I've told you, all that has occurred in Arcadia should be left behind. Leave the Beserker Prince there too.'

Pitch's attempt at laughter threatened to shatter his ribs. 'He is right before you.' A sweating, bleeding hollow shell of a creature who could never again utter his true name.

'No.' Satine said surely. 'I do not see him. This pitiful lump before me has no legion kneeling before him, he wields no vestige of angel bone for a sword. What I see is someone under great duress, yet still managing to fulfil his duty to the Order when he was asked. Admirable. The prince is no more. He has been banished, to the abaddon or here, it hardly matters. Let him go, and find yourself anew.'

A pretty speech, he was sure, and also utterly ridiculous. The prince may be banished, forbidden from taking his daemonic form, but that did not make him *no more*. This pitiful lump *was* him, no matter how Satty wished to delude herself. The stirring at his core might not be so strong as it once was, but it was not extinguished. The Forest of Dean, the fae queen and the Blight, had shown him that.

For reasons he could not fathom, Lady Satine had burdened herself with him, and she was as likely to regret it as Lucifer was to have sired him. When he arrived at Holly Lodge a year ago, spitting rage and spewing self-hatred, she'd told him he must be silent about his past, and put a lock upon his tongue to ensure it. He'd taken the punishment gladly. He desired more than anything to bury the reminders of his vile self. But then she had expected more of him. Placing him in the company of others, setting them in harm's way. Lady Satine could look after herself, but the same could not be said for Silas Mercer. The ankou was hapless, vulnerable as a newborn in many ways. He was also mildly beguiling and intolerably fine to look upon in a saddle. He did not deserve to be caught up in the lady's mistake.

Pitch rocked his head side to side. Heat built behind his closed lids, the sting of salt and guilt with it.

'Fuck, you vazey whore, will you not just leave me be?' He thrust his hips, but barely raised them from the bedcovers. 'Enough. I have had enough.'

Lady Satine sighed through the flare of sun-touched nostrils. 'I do not suppose to imagine how terrible it must be to endure the halo's wound as you do. The blade of a Seraphim strikes a formidable blow, and with the amuletum so thinned, it must be excruciating. Yet here you are, calling me foul things and fighting when others would lie still. You are every bit as formidable as the halo that struck you.' Gods, would this church-bell never shut her mouth? He needed to hear false declarations of his worth like he needed to be back in Sanu's saddle. He heard the tinkle of a glass, and the tap of the needle as she discarded the overflow of ink. 'I cannot heal you but I can lessen the burden you bear upon your body. The mind though is up to you. I offer you purpose here, and a chance to find a different side to yourself. There is need of you, Vassago. Will you take solace in that?'

A traitorous tear shoved its way free, disappearing at once into the dampness of the sheet. Gods, he was delicate, like an early winter frost upon a spiderweb, liable to fall to pieces at the slightest urging. The Forest of Dean had wrecked him. Reminded him, when he'd sought to forget, that he was as monstrous as any teratism.

'Need of me?' he rasped. 'If you have need of me to destroy your precious ankou then I shall not disappoint.'

'Your pain is making you insensible. You'll bring no harm to Silas.'

Her reply came with the drive of a sharp point upon tender flesh, right where his back dipped into a curve. Lady Satine's swing towards gentleness was done. He sucked a hissed breath through thinned lips.

'You are a fool to place me at his side.'

'It does not seem so, from the outside looking in.' Something warm and slippery ran across his skin, blood or amuletum, it was all the same. 'You did admirably, both of you, in that forest. Silas has come along well, as I had hoped he might. I am very much pleased to see such able Horsemen in my service, and I mean you with that, Mr Astaroth. Hopefully Silas has fared just as well without you these past hours. I'd prefer when next you feel the need to demonstrate an unnecessary act of self-destruction that you do not chase him away.'

He'd return to the insult later. 'Hopefully?' Pitch tried and failed to lift his head. 'Do you not know for certain how he fares?' His words fluttered like ailing butterflies, barely able to hold themselves aloft.

'Not at this exact moment, no.' She did not seem concerned in the least. So why then was Pitch bothering himself so? 'Lalassu is not with him. I sent her to Tyvain, who was nearest to where you were allowing yourself to be soundly beaten to a pulp, she was the first who could reach you.'

'You left him alone?' Pitch chewed at the words, tasting their sourness.

'Well, actually you did that.'

'Bitch.' Gooseflesh rose alongside where the needle worked.

The cumbersome oaf was liable to trip on his own laces and break his neck. Pitch's *unnecessary act of self-destruction* was supposed to have kept the fool safe. Far away from where wild things had begun to stir.

'I'm glad to hear your insult, just this once. It lets me know you've not yet surrendered.'

Whatever lies she wished to tell herself, so be it. 'Does the nag return to Silas now?' Fuck, it hurt to speak, the muscles of his jaw cracking with the effort.

'She does. And she'll not have left him anywhere she did not deem reasonable.'

Gods, what would that bloody horse know about what Silas considered reasonable? He viewed half the world with wide-eyed alarm, and the other with a wonderment that astonished Pitch on a near daily basis. Especially when the wonderment found its way to him, and he caught Silas watching him in a way that did odd things to his chest. Knotting it up and making it tight.

But awe would not keep the silly dolt fed. The ankou might be reasonable with his scythe, but he couldn't hunt to save himself, quite literally. If the nag had kept to the forests as she'd done the days before they parted company, Silas was likely as starved as Pitch.

He ground his hipbone into that uncomfortable place upon the mattress, letting it pinch at his skin. Why was he wasting what strength he had on considering the oaf? Let the fucking horse take Silas where it willed. The further he was from Pitch, the better.

'Lalassu will bring him here to Bess's Sanctuary eventually.' Lady Satine declared, as though reading his thoughts and taunting him. 'And we will have you mended, and back on the road where you are very much needed. You may well have noted that things are far from as they should be in this world.'

Pitch breathed vile words into stale fabric. He'd be fucked if he would continue on *any* way.

'I will not.' Pitch swallowed, the dryness of his throat paining him. But he found the resolve to twist at her touch, hot angry heat flaring through his middle but well worth it when he was rewarded with the clatter of the needle landing on wooden floorboards.

The Lady Satine muttered some very unladylike words. And this time her sigh was loud and demonstrative. 'Fine. I'll leave you for now, as you wish. I know you must be parched dry for I certainly am. I'll have food sent to you, it would do you well to eat something.' Her shoes scraped the rug-less floor as she moved to the foot of the bed. There was a touch at his ankle and at once the tightness of his binds relaxed, the chains lengthened, allowing him to shift his shoulders. If he had the impetus he could have bent his knees a little too, but he was fading badly, he suspected he might fall asleep before she made it to the door.

Lady Satine flourished a chamberpot from beneath the bed and set it within his reach, giving him a not so subtle reminder that for all the enormous things he was, there was a less impressive part that was fully human.

'I'll be back, and we will begin again. Rest for now. The amuletum you've allowed me to use should work its way deeper soon, you'll feel much better I'm sure, even with half the job done. And this melancholy you insist on wearing will vanish soon enough.'

Through heavy lids he watched her go. The door closed behind her and vanished into the smoothness of dark walls as though it had never existed to begin with. He was alone, finally. Pitch sank with his melancholy into the embrace of sleep, serenaded by the unyielding whisper of the Blight's mournful cries.

CHAPTER 17

To Silas's everlasting relief their journey was blissfully uneventful, with no sign they were about to be set upon again by ashen men and a deranged wolf. When they first left the farmhouse and the woman who lay like Sleeping Beauty in her bed, Lalassu had thrown out her astonishing illusions. Her replicas, with Silas upon her back, raced off in all the directions of the compass. Any enemy who sought them would be thoroughly led astray. Though he'd seen it once already, in the Forest of Dean, Silas still marvelled at the deception. Tyvain had wrinkled her nose, nonchalant, but fixing a keen eye on two of the racing, identical horses nonetheless. Charlie had seemed not to notice anything untoward, watching after the original with a sigh and a wistful smile.

They arrived at their Sanctuary shortly before sunset, after several long hours in the saddle, riding at pace. Grey clouds had rolled in to blot the sky not long before they arrived, and spitting rain had glanced upon them. He should have been relieved to see the journey's end in sight. Silas's belly dropped at the sight of Harvington Hall. The grand house was surrounded by a moat, one full to the brim with water. In fact, the hall itself appeared as though floating atop the surface. There was no land at all between the water and the brick walls. Swans glided without a care in the world, acting as though there was nothing terrifying about swimming at all. Silas's chest knit at the memory of Goodrich Castle, where that moat had become a heaving, writhing maelstrom of liquid intent on drowning them. He recalled being draped upon Pitch's back, clinging to the daemon so hard he was surprised he could take a breath.

'Come on then, don't piss about,' Tyvain called. 'I need me arse out of this saddle.'

She trotted them around the property, evidently knowing the place very well, to where a plain wooden bridge led them to the stables. The whitewashed wooden building was nestled behind the main house, which was actually a cluster of separate structures that huddled against one another in varying degrees of height, all peaked with elaborate chimney pots. Silas dismounted, using only one hand to brace himself, as his injured wrist still twinged and ached. Charlie had found him some clean rags in the farmhouse, and his garish wound was now wrapped in a strip of faded blue cotton, which had become stained with dark patches as he rode. He shook his legs, sighing with the relief of being able to stretch them again.

Lalassu nickered. And she received a reply immediately. The pale horse surged forward, pulling Silas into the darker confines of the stable. He caught himself just in time to stop a cry of delight.

Sanu was in the nearest stall. Pitch was indeed here. The great red horse had her head lifted, nostrils flared at the arrivals. Her sky-blue eyes fixed on him, and he marvelled once more. She had emerged from the Forest of Dean transformed, shifting from bow-backed nag to thunderous, splendid warhorse in what seemed the blink of an eye. That forest had affected them all, but none in quite so magnificent a way as Sanu. The red horse stomped a wide hoof against the ground, pawing at the generous layer of straw there.

'There, there, girl.' Silas felt himself an intruder as Sanu and Lalassu greeted each other with snorts and brushing of muzzles, but he could not help but get in the way, running his hand over a broad red cheek, just to ensure his eyes did not deceive him.

Pitch was here. He could have sagged with the relief.

'Didn't ya believe me, eh?' Tyvain seemed to read his thoughts. 'Told ya 'e'd be 'ere. You ain't gonna cry, are ya?'

'Of course not, don't be daft.' Silas glared at the back of her head as she led her bay into a free stall. The woman was incorrigible. He was certainly not about to shed a tear at sight of the daemon's horse. Still, it was a welcome sight. A burden seemed to lift from his shoulders.

'Bloody hell.' Charlie had entered last of all, leading the piebald. 'I thought Lalassu magnificent, but here is her match. Oh, and another! Aren't you a beauty?'

Silas had been too fixated upon Sanu to notice Sybilla's dapple grey stabled alongside the red horse. She was indeed a beauty, and Silas surprised himself with what relief he felt to find Sybilla close by. She was someone he could speak with plainly about all that had occurred, and someone who might just answer a question or two, if the Lady did not deign to show herself.

A rustling came from above, movement amongst the hay in the loft. Silas tensed but saw quickly that there was no danger of any ash-men or wolf lying in wait here. A stable boy clambered down the ladder, jumping down the last few rungs to land on the floor. His skin was nearly as dark as Sybilla's, with golden straw tangling in night-black curls. He rubbed at his eyes.

'Miss Flynn, you caught me nappin'. Mighty pleased to see you again.'

'What 'ave I said about that "miss" shit, Tom?' Tyvain handed him the bay's saddle and bridle before picking a length of straw from his hair. 'Thought your master might drag his great arse out to meet us. He still lounging about in 'is bed?'

The boy grinned, flashing a mouthful of wide teeth. 'He's been right busy he has. Worn himself out I think. Haven't seen much of him the past day or so. But I'm sure he'll be happy to know you're here.'

'Meh, doubt that.' Tyvain snorted, muttering something else unkind about laziness and tarts, and belched loud enough to startle Charlie's piebald. 'Let's go then. Tom's got things in 'and 'ere. If I don't eat somethin' soon, I'll fade fair away.'

Silas led Lalassu into the stall beside Sanu. The horse walked in eagerly, digging her nose into the bucket of chaff that awaited. Their host might be yet to greet them, but she was clearly aware of their impending arrival. And with the Lady's horses so evidently at ease, Silas's knots were fast coming undone. Now all he needed was to catch sight of the daemon and all would be well.

'They'll be good with me, sir,' the stable boy assured him.

'I've no doubt. Thank you, dear fellow.'

Charlie fell into line beside Silas as Tyvain led them to the main house.

'So, is this where I'm thrown into a dungeon before the Order makes me a sacrificial offering to appease their dark gods?' Charlie grinned. The fine skin beneath his eyes was dark. He was tired. As they all were.

'Good grief.' Silas was aghast. 'Whatever gave you such a notion?'

'Well, because I've seen too much. Like what happened back there...' He jerked his head. 'You know...at the farmhouse. Tyvain throwing her knives about like they grew from her fingernails, you dancing about with your blade and string...and Lalassu...well I'm not sure really what happened there. Those draught horses just seem to collapse at the sight of her.'

Silas eyed him as they walked. The lad might have only glimpsed half of what was truly happening, but that surely was unsettling enough.

'You are quite safe here, Charlie,' Silas said. 'I will see to that, I promise you.'

He could not shake a sense of guilt at the lad's situation. If Silas had not been so intent on pretending at being...well, human...Charlie would not be set in the middle of things. Silas would have sent him on his way immediately. Not chitchatted about trivial things...and then bedded him. He blushed at the thought of it.

'Oh I trust you, Silas,' Charlie declared. Thoughtlessly brave as always. Silas did not trust himself. 'And I hope that you might trust me enough to tell me exactly what I've stumbled into. For clearly you are in some kind of a bind.'

He slid a sideways glance at the lad. How understated his remark was. 'Charlie, I hope you understand, but the sooner you are away from all this the better. And even if I were able to speak to you about it, even if I knew much of it myself, I'd not burden you so. I don't need to tell you how dangerous a situation this is. You saw it well enough. We shall set you on your way, and though I'll miss your company, I'll be glad, for you will be safe.'

Charlie mulled over his reply for some time before answering. 'Very kind of you, Silas, to worry about me. But I can't say I'm eager to leave. I don't think I've ever felt quite so alive as I do now, you see. And I should miss your company too.'

Silas laughed, high with the note of surprise. 'Goodness, Tyvain is quite right. You are so very interesting.'

And astoundingly courageous, both in the choices made in his life, and the way he had handled the unbelievable occurrences since their meeting. Charlie was frightened, only a fool would not be, but he wore his fear well. Silas doubted the same could be said about him.

'As are you, my friend. It's been the most curious thing, but as soon as I was in your company I was at ease, as though we were familiar.' Charlie paused. 'Of course, we are now, aren't we?' He winked, and set off to catch up with Tyvain.

The Hag had a skip in her step as she waltzed up to the main house, which may just have been to escape the pattering rain that grew heavier as they walked. There was no sign of the limp she had exhibited on their first meeting at The Atlas in London, she was unhindered and in a hurry to get inside. Harvington Hall was actually three buildings, all of varying heights, topped with a swathe of jutting chimneys standing to attention upon the trio of light brown slate roofs. White-trimmed windows were set unaligned, giving the hall a carefree appearance. There was no uniformity of design, with guttering painted in different colours according to their section, and the brickwork varying slightly on each building. The gardens were a different story. They were all manicured and well-attended, trimmed and snipped into rigid lines.

They entered the house at its back, using a wooden door set with four panes of glass, an entrance more suited for the household staff. Tyvain seemed to delight in besmirching the cleanliness, not bothering to wipe her dirty boots before entering, smiling gleefully at the marks left upon the polished wood as her soles and the dirty edges of her gown left their mark. Though she continued to grumble about their host's failure to greet them, Tyvain was the most light-hearted Silas had known her.

She led them through to a wide foyer and up a neat half-turn staircase. The home's designer had favoured mixing different varieties of wood, which meant the interior was a mismatch of hues. The staircase was one such example, the flooring cut from deep claret mahogany, while the balustrade and the newel posts, shaped like obelisks, were lighter oak. Silas had yet to glimpse a tiled or stone surface.

'And I thought my mother was keen on her timbers.' Charlie laughed, plodding up the stairs.

They moved up three flights with no sign of any house staff, or Old Bess.

''Ere we go. You 'ave the corner room, Mercer,' Tyvain pointed to a closed door, right along the corridor. 'Lad, you take that one there, and this 'ere's mine.' She indicated the door directly ahead. 'Keep that in mind if you two intend any priggin' again soon, these walls ain't that thick, so keep it down.'

Silas sighed. Charlie rolled his eyes. Neither of them dignified Tyvain with a reply.

'Let's wash up, and by then we might have some attention. I'll see you both in the Lace Room, left of the front door. Can't 'ardly miss it. Be warned, Old Bess is a bloody awful card player, so if 'e offers to play ya, say yes. It will line your pockets. But for the sake of all the gods, do not let that silly git near the piano. Go on then, you'll find a change 'a clothes waitin' on ya, I'm sure. That's 'ow it works around 'ere.' She kicked her door closed behind her.

Silas gave Charlie a nod and stepped into his room. Iron-latticed windows afforded a view over the moat and the fields and woodland beyond. The grey day was settling, the heavy cloud drawing it faster to its close, draining the colour from the landscape. In the far distance thunder rumbled. At the edges of the moat a light mist had rolled in, as though the clouds had come to earth to rest.

Silas could hear Tyvain whistling in her room next door. He shrugged off his tattered coat and began unbuttoning his vest. Tyvain seemed happy as a lark. As though she had not been forced to knife several men and dodge a wolf with dripping fangs mere hours ago.

The Hag was right about the change of clothes. Laid out upon the broad bed with its covering of white satin and mustard-yellow pillows was a pair of grey trousers, a black linen shirt, and an exuberant red satin smoking jacket with a quilted shawl collar and cuffs. Pitch would have found it fetching, he didn't doubt, but it was far too ostentatious for Silas's taste. Still, he'd not complain; rather, he welcomed the chance to remove his bloodied, ride-weary clothes. He was most gladdened to spot a roll of clean bandages upon the dresser, alongside a washbasin brimming with steaming water.

Silas rolled up his sleeves and gingerly peeled off the dressing about his wound. The pain was dulled, distant, more akin to an ache than anything more troublesome. His eyes widened. The blood was well and truly dry, and already the bone was not quite so evident beneath the flesh, a thin film of muscle having crept in to cover it. He dabbed at the flayed edges of skin and worked at removing the blood that had dried in thick clumps about the healing wound. This was a part of being an ankou he could get used to: the quick healing. The deep puncture the arrowhead had made had taken just on a day to disappear entirely.

Thinking of the arrowhead had him rushing to bind his wrist again. He wished to speak with Sybilla as soon as possible and tell her all that had occurred, of course: the ash-men, the arrowhead, the red-eyed beast, Silas's increasing expertise with the scythe. All of that. But he could not fool himself. What he wished for most was to ask after the cursed daemon.

Had Pitch let those farmers beat him senseless? Was he terribly hurt? Tyvain had not mentioned any deaths, so the farmer and his sons must have been unharmed. But what of Pitch? What drove him to such brutal lengths?

Silas shrugged off his shirt and undershirt with irritated jerks of his shoulders. He did not know what infuriated him more, the daemon's appetite for blood and damage, or his absence when Silas had most needed him.

The clothes fit wonderfully, though perhaps the trousers were a little snug around his thighs. With some consternation, he pulled on the red silk smoking jacket. There was no doubt it was comfortable, and it rested well upon his broad shoulders. He no longer wondered on how it was he kept finding himself with clothes that fit so well. It was the least strange thing now in his life. The jacket had no pockets, and as the trousers were rather tight, he decided to leave the bandalore beneath the pillows. After changing his socks and tugging on a freshly-polished pair of black congress boots, he made his way downstairs. Tyvain still whistled about in her room, and he could hear the splash of water behind Charlie's door. But he was far too restless to linger in his own quarters.

Silas found the Lace Room easily. The front sitting room lived up to its name. There was lace on every surface, Battenburg on the side tables, draped on the backs of the chairs, set on the mantel above a wide-mouthed fireplace. The curtains were a finer design. He fancied them to be Coggeshall lace, though why he knew of it, who could say. The long swathes of material were needleworked with incredibly intricate floral patterns. He could not help but run his fingers over the fragile fabric. Beyond their white veil lay the ever-present waters of the moat. The dying sun made a last desperate stab through a momentary space in the clouds, reflecting upon the water with a strawberry stain. The mist gathered in closer. It would be dark soon, and, he suspected, very dark indeed.

Silas did not sit down, even though the gold-trimmed settee appeared quite comfortable. He could not bear the thought of being still. He found his thoughts returning to the stables. Sanu had appeared well rested when they arrived, no trace of sweat at her girth, her mane brushed silky, her eyes half-closed with contentment. Pitch must have arrived some time ago. So where the hell was he now?

CHAPTER 18

S ilas paced over to the fire, lit and blazing, though its heat could not seem to fend off the chill that had settled on him since he'd ridden away from the daemon. The considerable blaze was barely contained by its stone hearth. Flames danced their tips outward, and wiggled dangerously close to the intricate parquetry flooring, oak golden as honey.

'Mr Mercer, welcome to my humble home,' declared a warm voice. 'What a day you have had.'

Thunder marked the speaker's entrance with a dramatic thud. Turning on his heels, Silas started at who greeted him.

'Oh, my.' He bit his lip, aghast at his rudeness. But he had been quite unprepared.

The person who approached him wore the most stunning of gowns, sapphire blue, embellished at the bodice with tiny pearls and glinting stones. Those same stones gleamed amongst the yellow strands of his wig, a powdered affair that sat high upon his head, the paleness of it contrasting most astonishingly with olive skin reminiscent of Jane's warm tones. Silas took in the sculpted beard highlighting the heavy set of the man's jaw. He was being awfully brazen, but he could not help himself as his eyes travelled down to stare at the flatness of the corset upon the chest, and the curls of dark hair at the décolletage. At the man's neck was a prominent bump, which shifted as he spoke.

'So terribly sorry to have kept you.' He extended his hand. Chunky fingers were adorned with flashing rings of reds and yellows. 'I'm Bess, Master of Harvington Hall, member of the Order of the Golden Dawn, and your humble host.'

Silas nodded and took the hand offered to him. The grip was firm, but not too much so. Light grey eyes glinted with amusement.

'Goodness me, aren't you lovely. Hmm?' Bess said. 'I thought Ty was spouting her usual shitty nonsense when she said you were a sight for the eyes. I expected you to be rather hideous, wrinkled and hunchbacked, if I'm honest, because she does love to weave a tale.'

When faced with such blunt conversation Silas either stuttered a vague reply or said nothing at all. Here he chose the latter.

Bess rubbed at the back of his hand where a speck of black refused to budge. 'I do look a bit of a fright, wouldn't you say? It's been quite the couple of days. I certainly wasn't expecting so many visitors so quickly. Especially not one who would require so much...attention. Forgive me if the bags beneath my eyes could be packed for a sailing to the New World. I am exhausted.' He patted at the gown's marvellous blue fabric, his hand coming to rest just below the cinched waistline. 'I had intended to take a simple nap and be ready to greet you, but I passed dead away. No doubt I'll never hear the end of it from Tyvain.' His laughter fluttered about them, as warm as the room itself.

Silas knew he was staring, and it was abysmally rude. He pressed a thin smile to his lips. 'It is a pleasure to make your acquaintance...Miss...Mister...ah.' Christ, he must stop staring, but the sight was astonishing. Beguiling.

'Bess is quite fine.'

'Bess,' Silas acquiesced.

'I see from your face you've not met the likes of me before. Hmm? How about I simplify things for you, Mr Mercer. I am a man who enjoys a fine silk and a cinched corset. I don't much enjoy being dictated to about what I can or cannot wear. Humankind is so dreadfully dull on that point. And as I am only partly human, I see no need to work within their confines. I mean, truly, why should men be deprived of all this splendidness? The half of my blood that is fae simply screams at me to wear it. I enjoy pretty things, and is not Bess the prettiest name you've ever heard?' Bess of the pretty name and fae blood did not wait on a reply. 'I'll live the way I like, and to hell with those who pay it too much mind. Do you pay it much mind, Mr Mercer?'

He stared a moment longer. His first encounter with faekind had not gone well. But Bess seemed nothing like the queen of the bluecaps. He was warmth and comfort, where the queen had been winter's chill and danger.

'No mind at all,' Silas replied. 'That shade is very fetching on you, I must say.'

Bess's smile was as bright as the chandeliers that had swung at the Marquess of Ailsa's ball. 'My, my you are quite priceless.' He tilted his head, the wig wobbling. 'I do hope he has been gentle with you, Mr Mercer?'

'I beg your pardon?'

Bess swept towards the gold-trimmed settee, his gown accented perfectly by the embroidered pink fabric. He patted the seat, encouraging Silas to sit.

'I trust Tobias has not...how should I put this delicately...he has not taken what was not freely given?'

Silas paused halfway to sitting. Was the man truly suggesting what he thought? 'Not freely given?'

'His appetites are voracious. His methods untoward. He has not had you...or taken you when you might not –'

'Stop. That is quite enough.' He lowered himself onto the seat, his weight sinking him low. 'Mr Astaroth has done no such terrible thing.'

Bess searched his face, which Silas was sure was flushed red with his irritation. Pitch was many things, but...that...no. And he would not have them thinking such a thing of him. 'He enjoys a tease, but that is all. I have been left well alone. He'd not act that way towards me,' Silas said firmly.

Christ, if anything it was Silas who'd acted in an uncouth manner, kissing the daemon as he lay bleeding.

'Apologies. It is just that...well, I'm told he is an astonishingly strong incubus, with an appetite to match.' He touched again at the tiny black spot on his hand. 'And as he has not been well of late, and with the two of you having become separated, I feared that...well, that you had been forced to run.'

Now Silas hesitated, for some of the summation was not entirely wrong. 'I was not forced in the way you so unkindly suggested.' He still bristled at the idea. 'Tell me, is he recovered?'

Bess took a moment to reply. 'Not yet...' He fluttered his fingers. 'But do not worry, he will, recover that is. I'm sure.'

Was there uncertainty in his smile? Silas planted his hands upon his thighs, bracing himself. 'I didn't know what to do, and he did not seem to wish me to stay. I left him, and I regret it. I was terribly...angry at him.' *Frightened for him.* 'I thought he was deliberately trying to rile me, but I...I knew it deep down, that it was not the case.' He swallowed. 'Much happened to him in the Forest of Dean, and I fear he pretended that all was well when it was not. I should not have run.'

Bess placed his hand upon his. It was only slightly less broad than Silas's own. A tiny crackle moved between them. 'Silas – may I call you that?'

Thunder rolled beyond the walls, as though the weather enjoyed punctuating the man's question.

Silas nodded.

'Silas, you cannot be so hard upon yourself. You are so new to this world, and from what I'm told, doing a marvellous job of it. Tobias, I understand, can be...frightening...at times. I've not met him before, but I've met a daemon or two, and they are by nature rather intimidating. Those who are warriors, even more so. Sybilla tells me he goes out of his way to trouble you, much as he does all those closest to him. You did what you thought best. Think no more of it. You are both safe now. He is being cared for.' His radiant smile reappeared. 'And all the farm folk he stirred up remain alive and well, with quite the story to tell now.'

'What caused his turn, do you know?' Silas did not pull his hand away. Bess reminded him of Lalassu in a strange way, in how calming his presence was.

'We are not entirely sure. But whatever happened to you in the forest seems to have aggravated an old injury he has.' Bess watched the fire. The golden radiance highlighted flecks of shimmering silver in his grey eyes. 'But I think all will be well for now.'

'You think? How long until he will be healed?'

Bess's gaze was a gentle caress. 'Some wounds never heal, Silas, not truly. But we have done what we can to bring him comfort. We can do no more. Now it is up to him to gather his strength and resolve. He can recover, he has done so before. But as of this moment, he is still feeling rather sorry for himself. Tobias is weak, and has no desire yet to be strong.'

Silas swallowed, struggling to equate the daemon with a lack of desire. 'Well, have you offered him strawberry tarts? They help. Not scones though, he really abhors them. But tarts, now they are sure to pull him from his mood.'

He was rambling, but the blame lay with Bess, throwing him all off-balance with his words. Some wounds never heal? What nonsense. This was Pitch they were speaking of. The one who had stopped the world from collapsing down upon Silas.

Bess squeezed his hand. 'I will keep that in mind, Silas. The village bakery is a wonder. But you understand that as an incubus he will need...more...substantial replenishment than that?'

He blinked twice before the words sank in. 'Oh...yes, of course.' Damn that lump in his throat.

'Perhaps you would like to...'

'Bloody hell, no.' Silas pulled his hand free and stood up. 'You have it quite wrong. I understand his needs, but it is not like that between us. He has neither forced himself on me, nor have I offered my... services.'

'I understand. My apologies for offending you.' Bess lowered his chin so his lips were stolen from view. Silas swore he glimpsed a smile. 'Very well, we shall provide company for him. In time I'm sure he will be more amenable to sharing his bed.'

Gads, the fire was roaring. And the roughness in his throat would not shift. 'So I am to wait here, at the hall? It would not seem prudent to leave without my guardian.'

'That is not for me to say. I'm sorry.' Bess did at least seem genuinely sorry, but he'd rather have had the man's assurances.

'I don't know if Tyvain has told you yet of what we faced this past day, but it was...' Silas shook his head, touching at the bandage beneath his cuff. 'If not for them both, I think I'd not be standing here before you.' He'd held the shock at bay, but now it was impatient for release. His eyes stung. 'I am new to this. And there is so much I do not understand. They came at us, and I was so frightened that Charlie would be harmed. I didn't know how best to protect him.' His nails bit into his palms. 'Pitch was not there, and I was so...afraid.' Shit. He needed to rest, before he blurted out everything that ailed him.

Bess stood, the swish of his dress like the whisper of wind through pines. He came to stand before Silas, the billow of silk a soft barrier between them.

'He was not there, but you survived, nonetheless. Let yourself take note of that, Silas, that you are stronger than you believe. Izanami does not choose her ankou lightly.' Bess was tall; the solid man in the blue dress stood only a smidge beneath eye to eye with him. 'Lady Satine selects her Horsemen with even greater care, I'm sure.'

He tightened his fists, and the bite of anger was upon him. 'It would be wonderful if the goddess and the Lady Satine would deign to give me some insight into what they truly want of me. I should have been warned of the danger. I would never have brought Charlie into it if I'd known there was a chance we would be set upon by bloody ash-men and a crazed wolf. And now I learn that Pitch has been forced to my side when he should have been recuperating from older injuries. Do they have any idea of what trials he endured in that blasted forest? What that foul fae...' He stumbled, realising his company. Bess inclined his head, urging him on silently, no apparent offence taken. 'He was tortured so that I might escape.'

Bess's face crumpled. 'Tortured? Gods...that should never...that should not have been so. The bluecaps –'

'Were not in their right mind.' He swallowed hard, his anger ebbing. Yelling at Bess hadn't given him much release, only a sense of guilt. 'And I fear before long, neither shall I be.'

Bess attempted to warm up a smile. 'Now see here, Silas. There shall be no madness beneath my roof. At least, no more than already exists. This is one of the finest Sanctuaries I've ever built.' He glanced towards the window. The moat beyond appeared to be the only thing between them and the wide expanse of field and trees beyond. 'My Sanctuaries are more than just brick and stone, although these walls will withstand quite the punishment. There are safeguards in place here that you cannot see, fae wards I don't suppose your tired mind will want to hear of right now. But know this, Silas, for it is all I can offer you freely. You are safe. Rest, rage, grieve, fuck, feast. Do all or nothing of which you please, and Harvington Hall will protect you. I don't know what is planned for you, but I can make your stay here as pleasurable and as relaxed as you can dream.'

Bess touched his fingertips to Silas's hand. The strange crackling where their skin met came again, followed by a warm bath of peacefulness. He was sleepy all at once, but not so cotton-headed he did not see this for what it was. Silas was being manipulated.

'Don't coddle me, Bess.' He was in no mood for it. 'When might I speak with Sybilla? Or better yet, the Lady Satine?'

The man's sigh was feather-light. 'Come now, Silas, I think you know full well one does not simply summon Her Ladyship because one is having a bad day.'

'A bad day?' The words burst from him with a light peppering of spittle. 'You summarise this as just a bad day?'

Bess lifted his brow and wiped at his cheek.

'I'm sorry...' Silas muttered, but his anger had not yet cooled. 'Will you take me to Pitch? I would like to see for myself how he fares.'

Perhaps he was losing himself to panic, because he had the unreasonable idea that if he could just see Pitch, see the vibrancy in those emerald eyes, he would know for sure the daemon could recover. That despite Bess's talk of Silas having survived well on his own, he would not need to do any such thing. Bloody hell, he would march a host of nubile companions into the sick room himself, if need be. His pulse went awry at the thought. He was keenly aware of how dreadful the idea made him feel, but he'd said it well enough to Bess, Silas could not offer himself. Imagining such an encounter whilst caught in the throes of intimacy was one thing, consummating the act another thing entirely.

But blast it, why did Pitch deny himself?

Bess sighed, and he knew what was coming. 'Oh dear, Silas. I'm not having much luck saying yes to you, am I? You cannot see him, not today, I'm afraid.'

Silas lumbered towards the fire, reaching to brace himself against the mantel. That foul-mouthed lunatic was the closest he had to an ally in all this. They were both unwilling participants. They were both at the mercy of others. Silas blinked against the memory of the terrible cries wrenched from Pitch as the bluecaps tore into him. He had offered himself so that Silas might escape. And what was Silas's thanks in return? He'd fled while Pitch bled.

'Then when?' Silas demanded. 'I don't see why –'

'Old Bess can't take ya, so stop 'avin' a fit and sit your arse down.' Tyvain strode into the room with a bowl of plums in the crook of her arm. She sucked at the crimson flesh, juice glistening on her chin. She'd changed into a man's tailored suit, an admittedly fetching grey with a red kerchief at the pocket. Her red hair had been tamed into a slicked-back style and pinned in a low bun at the back of her head. 'Now if you don't calm yourself down, I'll lock ya in a room with Old Bess and 'is piano, and then you'll know true torment.'

'So wonderful to have you staying with me again, Tyvain,' Bess said coolly, though not without a glint of amusement. 'It is always a pleasure to have the Order's second most popular soothsayer in my residence.'

'Eh, feck off, you silly cow. You and me both know you ain't no soothsayer. Just a 'alf-fae tart with a knack for understandin' 'uman nature,' Tyvain said through a pulpy mouthful. 'Ya don't even pretend well with your tea-leaf readin'. Dunno why Ahari keeps bookin' ya up.'

'Well, likely because my adoring public ask for me. Perhaps they prefer me to a belching, wheezing old bitch they can barely understand?' He fluttered long lashes. Butter would not have melted in his mouth. And there was that infernal grumble of thunder in the distance again to add weight to the moment.

Tyvain snorted, the wet plum in her mouth like bitten flesh. 'Talk a lot of shit, don't ya? Tell me somethin' useful. Sybilla know we are 'ere? She with the daemon?'

'She does know you are here, yes. And she is with Mr Astaroth, yes.'

With a gleam in her eye, Tyvain said, 'Must be exhausted by now then, jumpin' up and down on 'is cock all this time. That's what keeps an incubus settled, ain't it?'

Silas coughed, shuffling his feet.

'I have no idea.' Bess returned to the pink settee, collapsing into it with aplomb. 'But I can assure you that is not what she is doing. He needed more robust attentions I'm afraid. Her Ladyship attended him herself for a while.' He glanced over at Silas who had straightened at his words. 'Though she is gone now, my dear.'

Tyvain harrumphed and dug about in her bowl of fruit. 'Well, I can't say I'm minding the peace and quiet. It's been a bitch of a day, I can tell ya. And that's without that bastard around. Now where the feck did I put it?' she muttered. 'Aha!' She pulled out what appeared to be a plum, smaller than all the rest and much, much darker. So much so, it appeared black. Tyvain tossed it suddenly at Bess, who gave out a startled cry but succeeded in catching it in his cupped hands.

'What the blazes, woman?' His cool poise snapped. 'You know I despise plums.'

'Didn't give ya none.'

Bess's eyes widened, and a quiet gasp escaped him. 'This is obsidian.'

'Clever, ain't ya?' Tyvain said. 'Mercer's 'orse tucked it in her mane while we travelled. I figured that was just as good as puttin' it in rock salt and wrapping it in a graveyard shroud as we could 'ave done. And I'm guessing the Sanctuary's sealed up enough that 'oever was scrying with it can't do so now.'

'We are both just oozing with cleverness today then, aren't we?' Bess responded dryly. 'Though I don't know what you expect me to do with this.'

'Nuthin'. You're good for buildin' and not much else, are ya, Your 'Ighness?'

Bess's face darkened. 'Now you are just being a bitch. Call me Your Highness again and you'll be sleeping in the stables.'

Silas looked between them both, though only paid half his attention to their conversation. 'Your Highness?'

'Nothing to bother yourself with, my dear,' Bess said. 'My mother was fae royalty, but the moment she lay with a human, they couldn't tear her title off her fast enough. And I certainly have no want of it.' He turned his focus to one of the orbs of glass, pinching it between forefinger and thumb like a jeweller regarding a gem. 'It's very pure, where did you find it?'

'In a man's 'ead,' Tyvain said through a juicy mouthful.

Bess jerked his head to face the soothsayer. 'What sort of man? Alive or dead?'

'Kinda in between, but mostly dead.'

'What on Earth are you talking about?'

Tyvain shrugged. 'Like I said, it's been a bitch of a day. I'll tell ya all about it once Syb is 'ere.' She scrutinised another plum. 'Oh Silas, in case you're wondering, your little rutting friend won't be about for a while. I figured that the adults needed to do some chattin'.'

Silas was too bothered to admonish her crass labelling. 'What have you done with Charlie?'

'Why do you assume I've done somethin'?'

'Because you have,' Bess replied. 'Spit it out, don't play with the poor man.'

''E's sleepin.' Tyvain wiped at some juice that had dripped onto her lapel.

'Sleeping?' Silas shook his head. 'But he was saying he was famished, when we arrived.'

'I knocked 'im out.' Tyvain waved off his objection. 'In a nice way, mind. Just a sleeping draught. Might 'ave a bit of a dry mouth when 'e wakes up, maybe an itchy arse, but fine otherwise. 'E don't need to 'ear or see any more fantastical shit. Soon as Old Bess plays with a few of 'is memories, we will be sendin' the chap on 'is merry way. And if you don't like it, remember this is your doin'. Think on that next time you've got a rod between your legs and wanting to stick it somewhere.'

He grimaced and turned back to the fire. 'Leave me be, Tyvain.'

'Gods, you're a sorrowful sight, ain't ya?' She cackled, slurping into another plum. She'd not bothered to enquire if he would like one.

'Tyvain, do everyone a favour and shut up.' A familiar voice drew Silas from considerations of the fire. 'Gods, the last thing I need right now is your squawking in my ear.'

Sybilla entered the room, done with tending her daemonic patient, and looking none the better for it.

CHAPTER 19

S ybilla dropped into the high-backed chair nearest the fire, unbuttoning her peach frock coat and stretching legs clad in black trousers and knee-high boots.

'Silas, it's so very good to see you again,' she said, untying the boot laces. 'You have been in for quite the trying time, haven't you? We have much to speak about.'

He wasn't sure if she referred to the Forest of Dean or Wyre. Either way he was surprised she knew anything at all of their troubles. They'd arrived but a short while ago, and Bess had informed them that Sybilla was still tending Pitch. 'There is much to discuss indeed.'

'How did you leave him, Syb?' Bess kicked off his slippers and pointed his toes towards the fire, the obsidian balls still in hand.

'Sleeping, at last. I finally managed to get a sleeping draught into him.' Sybilla sighed. 'Though he'd take nothing else. He is still refusing to feed.' Her words were brittle with fatigue. Silas noticed a smudge of black in her tight white-blonde curls, just above her right eye, unsettlingly similar to the stain on Bess's hand.

'Pitch is not eating?' Silas folded his arms, ignoring the dull ache that came from the wound at his wrist.

'Not yet.' Sybilla stretched her neck, kneading tight muscles. 'But I'm sure he will in time. He was exhausted but could not seem to settle enough to sleep. The draught will help. We'll see how he is when he wakes.'

'I would like to see him.' Silas watched the sway of flames. They were like miniature versions of those that had risen from Pitch's back as the castle had fallen down.

'I don't think that would be sensible, not just yet.' The Valkyrie was no more obliging than Old Bess. 'His treatment was robust, so his mood is...well, let's just say he is not at his best. Give it a bit more time.' Sybilla smiled, but it seemed to take an effort to raise her lips. Her face held a weight about it, dragging the skin down at the edges of her eyes.

'Speaking of eatin', I wouldn't mind a morsel or two meself.' Tyvain was considering another plum. 'Gonna need more than plums after a day like today.'

'Dinner is a few hours off yet. You'll just have to wait,' Bess said. Tyvain muttered her discontent, but the master of the house ignored her. 'Sybilla, I believe you'll be wanting to take a closer look at this.' He tossed the obsidian ball, which the Valkyrie caught smoothly. Her deep skin tones were not so dark against the orb, which was blacker than any black should be.

Sybilla's lip twitched as she turned it about in her fingertips. 'I for one have no appetite.'

Silas may not have Tyvain's gut instinct, but he knew he did not like the frown fixed on Sybilla's face, and he was not yet ready to know its cause. He kept the reassuring warmth of the fire at his back and led the conversation where his concerns were easier to navigate.

'Can you tell me anything of Pitch's treatment? How long until he might be up and about again?' She was far too slow in answering. 'Sybilla?'

But instead of replying, she cast a glance at Bess, and a silent exchange passed between them.

'You said he will recover.' A flicker of concern weaved through him. 'Did you not?'

'You lot all gone deaf? The man's askin' ya a question.' Tyvain wrinkled her freckle-dusted nose. 'We've all 'ad an 'ell of a day. Quit side-eying one another and tell us what's botherin' ya. If the daemon's dropped dead on us, then –'

'Tyvain, will you shut up.' Silas's raised voice dominated the room. The soothsayer lifted her auburn eyebrows. 'Just...please...be quiet.'

Old Bess was giving him a gentle, pitying smile. 'There, there, Silas. He is not dead, I assure you.'

But it wasn't assuring at all. There was a hesitancy behind the answers coming from Bess and Sybilla that was unsettling him in all kinds of ways. Beyond the windows the rain fell steadily now.

Christ, why was he so bothered? He barely knew his guardian, and what he did know wasn't altogether pleasant. But he needed reassurance that he'd ride out of here with the snide, acerbic daemon, like he needed a damn large brandy.

'Please, take a seat, Silas.' Sybilla fluttered her hand towards the partner of the chair she sat in, the one not two paces from where he stood, but Silas shook his head.

'I do not wish to sit, thank you.' He braced against the back of the chair instead, digging his fingers into the pale pink fabric. 'I would ask that you are honest with me about Pitch's condition. Tyvain told me that he's had this malady once before –'

'What I said was 'e's prone to goin' a bit bonkers.' Sybilla sent quick eyes to Tyvain, and the soothsayer blinked at her. 'What? It's true, ain't it?'

Sybilla pressed at her temples. 'There has been one occasion, when he first arrived, Ty. That is hardly a predilection.'

Tyvain shrugged a shoulder. 'Whatever the case may be, let's not waste too much breath on 'im. Got more to worry about, I'd say, and I don't need me guts to tell me that. Christ almighty, we just had to fend off some bastards with obsidian for eyes and chalk for skin, who tried to 'ack off Mercer's feckin' 'and before they sent in their bastard black dog – biggest feckin' thing I've ever seen – to try and finish what they started. Things are right messed up, I'd say. And I've got a real bad feelin' they are only going to get messier. 'Specially if them skin-and-bone bastards are what I think they are.' The soothsayer was watching Sybilla very carefully as she spoke, but the Valkyrie gave nothing away, her face smoothed of all but fatigue. 'Need me to tell ya more of what we saw?'

'No. I've seen enough.'

'Figured.' Tyvain sniffed. 'So? What are you and 'Er Ladyship makin' of it?'

Silas had no idea how Sybilla had seen evidence of their altercation, but it seemed unimportant in that moment. The room was hushed, as though it too held its breath. Flickering silver light at the windows marked the flash of lightning. The Valkyrie took her time in answering. She leaned down to work at the lace of her other boot, hiding her expression from Silas's view. 'The verdict is not wonderful, I'm afraid. Those skin-and-bone bastards, as you call them, were revenants.'

Bess cocked his head. 'My dear, do tell me I did not hear you correctly. Revenants?'

'I wish I could say otherwise, I truly do.' Sybilla sat up, kicking off the loosened boot. 'But there is no doubt of it.'

'Gods.' Bess scratched his beard, lips pinched as though he'd tasted bitterness.

'Feck. Well, that's gone and killed me appetite.' Tyvain discarded her half-eaten plum. 'Was really 'opin' you weren't gonna say it. Don't 'spose 'Er Ladyship got it wrong, and they were just a bunch of underfed, blind ruffians with an ankou fetish?'

'Gods, this is really not the time for your ridiculousness,' Bess growled.

'They were not ruffians, Tyvain,' Sybilla said quietly. 'Lalassu relayed details of the attack to Her Ladyship, and she is certain.'

Silas thought perhaps he'd heard wrong, until Tyvain spoke up.

''Is 'orse told 'er? What? The nag is some kind of carrier pigeon too?' The Hag laughed. Though Silas didn't find the discovery the least bit amusing.

'The Lady has a very unique connection with her horses, yes.' Sybilla said. 'She can see and hear everything they do. Should she choose.'

Her glance at Silas held a modicum of apology, as though she was well aware that this was something he deserved to know about earlier. Christ, he was grateful that near-kiss with the daemon had not taken place on horseback. He shook off the thought. Now was hardly the time for blushes.

'Well, that is, strangely, the least disturbing thing I've come across of late.' Silas edged back towards the fire as a chill took him. 'Tell me of the revenants, for I am not familiar with what they are, aside from bloody persistent.'

'Walkin' corpses,' Tyvain returned.

'Corpses?' Silas needed to remove the godawful red jacket he wore; it was stifling. 'The ash-men were...'

'Dead.' Tyvain launched an exasperated sigh. 'Not sure what part of walking corpses isn't makin' sense to ya.'

'But how is such a thing poss –' He caught himself. He was, for all intents and purposes, a walking dead man himself. 'So, how did they come to be? Were they raised by Izanami as I was?' Even as he asked it, he thought it unlikely. The goddess would not set her creatures against one another, surely?

'No.' Sybilla rubbed the ball of her foot, staring into the fire. 'You are nothing like those ash-men, Silas. They are souless, empty.'

'An' a lot fuckin' uglier,' Tyvain grunted.

'Then who raised them?' Silas wished he had a brandy in hand. 'If not the goddess, then who else is capable of such things?' A strange silence descended. Even Tyvain did not seem eager to speak up. After a few moments he could not bear it. 'Oh for goodness sake. Speak up, one of you, before I truly lose my nerve. I was hauled from my grave, told I serve death, and must remove maddened souls from this world. I've met naiads and grim and fae who tried to feed on me, or dance me to death, I really have no idea. I've been partnered with a daemon who has told me that Lucifer is truly a king of daemonkind, and that angels and daemons exist together in a fantastical place called Arcadia.' Sybilla's chin lifted at that, her eyes narrowing, but she let him continue. 'I am trying my level best to endure my new circumstances, but quite frankly, I'm at my wit's end. Pitch and I had a bloody castle fall down on us, for god's sake.' He held up his bandaged wrist. 'And now I've had corpses attempt to steal death's blade by cutting off my fucking hand, as Tyvain so eloquently said. I lost my guardian, and my horse abandoned me. I am tired, and sore, and very, very unhappy that an innocent lad's life was put in peril, simply because he kept my company.' It choked him even to say it. The idea of harm coming to Charlie was abhorrent. Perhaps their intimacy was to blame, but after only a short time in shared company, Silas knew he would miss the lad greatly when they parted ways. 'The absolute least you can do is tell me who wishes to see me parted from my limbs.' Blast, he'd sounded so convincing till that very last sentence, when his voice had cracked like porcelain.

158

Tyvain's lips shifted with a stifled grin. 'There's them balls again.'

Sybilla sat back in her chair, ignoring the soothsayer entirely. 'Tobias told you of Arcadia?'

Christ almighty, that was where her mind had gone after all he'd said?

'And Elyssiam and Azazel, yes.' Silas threw up his hands, buoyed on by his frustration. 'Along with rebellious angels who plotted a war, right here in this world, and Samyaza who created monsters out of men. Yes, I know of it. But only thanks to Pitch...you and the Lady have left me in the dark.' He very nearly shouted the last part, only just managing to retain some decorum.

Sybilla was studying him as though he were an oddity. 'Tobias has told you much.'

She seemed impressed, and he knew right then that she was aware of the curse upon the daemon's tongue. But before he could reply, Tyvain added herself to the conversation.

'Don't forget the boggart ya mentioned. Those gits have the gift of the gab all right. Blabbin' like no one's business.'

Sybilla's glare silenced her, and the Hag tucked herself into the corner of the couch, returning to her plums.

'All right, Silas,' Sybilla said smoothly. 'It seems you are informed of far more than I realised. But I'm afraid there is not much I can offer when it comes to saying who attacked you. I do not know who the necromancer is that raised those revenants.'

'A necromancer?' Silas said, in a small voice. 'This was...sorcery?'

Tyvain barked a laugh. ''Twas. It's still existin', despite the Order's mightiest efforts.'

'Tyvain, be quiet.' The words slid from Sybilla sharp as a blade.

'What?' the Hag muttered. 'Not like 'e's not gonna learn. Just sayin' it 'ow it is.'

Silas blinked down at the chair, as though some clarity lurked there in the pattern.

'How dreadfully disappointing.' Bess toyed with the length of dangling stones at his ear. He looked to Sybilla. 'How long has it been? Must be a hundred years or more, since maleficium has shown itself among the humans. When did you last deal with an occurrence of witchcraft or sorcery?'

Sybilla tilted her head against the seat and closed her eyes. 'It was August, sixteen hundred and eighty-two.' She winced, as though the memory stung her. 'Near on exactly two hundred years ago. I was foolish enough to believe that those witches at Pendle Hill were the last, and it was all done with. It has been so quiet for so long.' She rubbed at that place on her hair where the black mark clung.

Bess gathered up his skirts and rose from his place on the settee. 'How many revenants would you say?' He glanced between Silas and Tyvain. The Hag made a motion across her mouth, as though sealing it up. Evidently she was taking Sybilla's instruction to stay quiet to heart.

'There must have been twelve at least,' Silas said.

Bess's brow jumped. 'That many?' He turned to Sybilla. 'Our sorcerer is no novice, then.'

'No.' Sybilla returned. 'They are certainly not. Which is disturbing enough in itself. It means they have managed to stay beneath notice of the Order.' She paused. 'I heard no whisper of their emergence, yet clearly they have spent time honing their skills.'

'And now,' Bess said, 'the first we know of them is an attack on an ankou of the Golden Dawn?' He moved over to the windows as he spoke. He was not a slight man beneath his satin and petticoats, but he moved silently as a ghost. The random stutter of lightning in the sky behind him only added to the ethereal effect. 'Do you think they focused upon Silas because of his association with the Order?'

'I'd say it's highly likely. He was easy enough to discover. Word of his dealings with Black Annis would have spread, and there was the Verderer too, which I'm still to hear all about.' She tilted her head to regard Silas. 'We must speak of it very soon, you and I, so you might give me all the details. But I think it safe to say that you and Tobias have caused quite a stir in a short time.'

Silas stubbed his shoe against the rounded foot of the chair. He'd not disagree. But he needed to turn his unsettled thoughts from the daemon. 'They spoke to me, those...revenants...or perhaps whoever controlled them.'

Now he had Sybilla's undivided attention. Lalassu had been nowhere to be found when he was taunted by the ash-man. 'And? What did they say?'

160

Nothing bloody pleasant, that was for certain. Silas toyed with the quilted cuff on the too-lavish smoking jacket. 'That they are only just beginning. And, that I...I was not enough. That I should go back to my grave.'

Tyvain snorted but held her tongue. Sybilla's face tightened, and she stared down at her hands. She too, said nothing. Bess spoke first.

'Good gracious, they are melodramatic. And they definitely knew Silas to be ankou.' Bess stood framed by the window and brushed by the hint of a green glow that came from the mist beyond the windowpane. 'Theatrical, knowledgeable and skilled. Not a combination I would have hoped for. '

'Gods, I was truly hoping I was done with Azazel's maleficium.' Sybilla rubbed her hands over her face. 'But I see that is as likely as the Blight fading entirely.'

'Would anyone be so kind as to explain either of those things?' Silas said, firm as he could manage. 'Preferably both. I understand so little of the Blight, and nothing of this maleficium. Considering I have dealt with both, I do think I ought to know.'

Sybilla still studied her hands, as though all the answers lay there. 'You know already of the Watchers' time here on Earth, so you know of Samyaza's fall?'

He nodded. 'Some of it, I believe, yes. He was killed by the angels.'

A log rolled in the fireplace, sending up sparks.

'He was. They call it the Day of Ruination.'

'More melodrama,'Bess mumbled.

And he was right. The Arcadians did not scrimp on dramatic nomenclature. *Day of Ruination.* Christ, Silas thought, there could not be a more foreboding name for it. Sybilla continued. 'It was on that day that the Blight came to be, a grim consequence of angels gone to war. It is no small thing to bring down an Angelic rebellion and the stain it left could not be scoured away.'

Silas stared at her, feeling chilled despite the blazing fire. He was not sure what he'd imagined the Blight to be, but it was not this. Mr Ahari had told him that the Blight was a turmoil, a darkness at the heart of this world, one that had existed for two thousand years. Silas touched at his shoulder. The arrowhead that had pierced him, an artifact from the day of Samyaza's demise, was unfathomably old. Ancient. The Severance War Pitch had spoken of had raged for generations. And on Earth, lost souls had been tormented for century after century. 'I...I don't...' Christ, his mouth was dry. 'Mr Ahari told me something of ...of a strife that lurked deep in the world...Lady Satine once said it was at the heart of things, but neither deigned to tell me anything of it being made by warring angels — '

'Well, they are bloody busy, Silas.' Sybilla winced, stabbing a finger at her temple. 'With many things to occupy them. You were just fresh from the grave, perhaps they worried it would twist your delicate new mind, to tell you too much at once.'

'Tell me too much?' He grit his teeth. 'Are you mad, I've been told barely anything at all.'

'You've been told what is most important, Silas.' Her face shadowed. 'What it is you need to do. And that is to deal with the teratisms. Do you think every ankou receives a book on the entire history of the world each time they are given a blade?'

'Perhaps they bloody well should be.' He'd had quite enough of all this. 'And according to the lady I am not every ankou, nor do I carry an average blade. Did nobody think it important for me to know that some heavenly fight has...has somehow...' What in Christ's name had it done? 'Poisoned this world. If that's what it is? I think it is pretty bloody damned important. I'd not even know Samyaza's name were it not for Pitch.'

'You should have counted yourself lucky not to have known it, Silas,' Sybilla shouted. 'I wish to the gods I'd never heard it. Never lived in a world where either he or Azazel existed, for then I might have some gods-damned peace once in a while.' She snapped her mouth closed.

If a pin had dropped in the silence it would have rung out loud as a church bell.

Bess was first to speak, from where he leaned against the window frame. 'It has been a long week, my dear. Calm yourself. He did not mean any harm.'

'I know, I know.' Sybilla held up her hands, and cast Silas a rueful glance. 'I apologise. I should not have yelled at you, that was dreadful of me. I'm so tired I can barely think straight. It is best you speak with Mr

Ahari, or the Lady Satine about the Blight. That is their forte, not mine. I don't know why it has endured, or even what it truly is, only that it interferes with the vulnerable souls, just as you've been told. I know little else.' It was a lie, and they both knew it, but Silas nodded, not willing to argue anymore.

'So you've just thrown an almighty fit about talkin' about the angels,' Tyvain said, abandoning her silence. 'But you're gonna 'ave to do exactly that for a while longer. This poor bastard almost got smothered by a necromancer's revenants, 'e's gonna need to know somethin' about maleficium. And *dealing* with divine magick in humankind is kinda your speciality, ain't it, Syb? It's pretty much your entire reason for bein' 'ere.'

'Tyvain, by the saints,' Bess groaned. 'You can be a bitch sometimes.'

'Just sometimes? Feck, I thought I was much nearer to always.'

Sybilla groaned. 'It *is* much nearer to always.' She stood and padded in her sock-covered feet to where a drinks trolley held an array of cut-crystal bottles. Gathering a thick glass, she unstopped a decanter with a clear liquid, gin likely, and poured herself a generous serving. She held up the bottle. 'Anyone care for a glass?'

'Whisky for me, if you don't mind,' Bess called.

'Gin for me, thankin' ya.' Tyvain tugged the pin from her hair, letting her wild mop of red hair loose.

'Yes, please.' Silas dove in next. 'But a brandy, if you will.' He eyed the bottle, hoping it was filled high. He suspected he'd need more than a glass before the day was done. 'So, after all that...I'm not sure I want to ask but...divine magick?'

'That's right, Mercer. Just when ya thought them angels couldn't have fecked up this place any better,' Tyvain said, and belched into her sleeve. Bess tutted. 'Turns out Azazel is a prick, but a prick who knew how to teach an incantation or two to clueless men and women. 'E taught the purebreds the secret language of magick, divine magick. Made the very first sorcerers and witches, 'e did. Pity the magick was way too feckin' strong for their pissy little minds, and ended up killin' most of 'em, or making 'em mad as cut snakes. And a bigger pity that the magick keeps showin' up even after all this time, just every now and then, givin' Sybilla a reason to have to get out of bed in the mornin'.'

163

'Christ,' Silas whispered.

'Nah,' Tyvain snorted. 'He wasn't part of it. But a decent bloke, by all accounts.'

The joke, for he would assume it was that, was terrible and no one so much as snickered.

Sybilla finished with the gin, and reached for a bottle which was filled with the golden hue of whisky. 'Am I telling him about maleficium, or are you?'

'Was thinkin' ya couldn't do two things at once, seein' as you are pourin' so slow. Thought it might help ya speed it up.'

Silas wondered if he might see a glass fly across the room, aimed at the mouthy soothsayer, but Sybilla just shook her head. He thought he spied a fleeting smile on her full lips.

'I correct my earlier assessment,' Bess said, gazing out at the moat. 'You are a bitch *all* of the time.'

Tyvain harrumphed, and appeared quite proud of the evaluation.

'The Watchers had grand designs for this world, Silas,' Sybilla said. 'Their machinations grew bolder with time, when they realised how vulnerable to Angelic word and deed the humans truly were. Tyvain is right, Azazel, with his grimoires and sigils and velvet tongue, made the first sorcerers and witches, but the knowledge was never meant for humankind.' Silas watched her pour the brandy, silently begging her to hurry it along. 'Magick is not innate to man, not like it is for the fae or the djinn, or even the piskies, though even those magickal creatures would struggle to cope with the burden of divine magick. The power possessed by the angels comes from a far mightier source than what already exists in this world. So when Azazel made his magicians, there was always going to be strife. Maleficium was the result. A dark magick that fed on the nefarious intent of the sorcerer or witch until they lost themselves entirely. A corruptible magick that altered the very blood of the one who wielded it. Azazel could teach humankind the secrets and language of divine magick but it had been forbidden for very good reason. In the end, he made monsters as surely as Samyaza did.'

'Necromancers,' Silas breathed.

'Necromancers.' Sybilla set his glass of brandy down hard, next to the others she had assembled on a silver tray. Silas winced to see some precious liquid spill over the side.

'And, as you know, the Order ain't partial to monsters,' Tyvain said. 'It should please you to know, Silas, that you ain't the only one gettin' rid of undesirables.' She jerked her chin at Sybilla who purposely passed her by, without stopping to deliver the requested gin. 'Our Miss Valkyrie is known to do a bit of smiting herself. Ain't ya, Syb?'

The Valkyrie's face grew shadowed as she headed towards Bess, still at the window. 'Careful, soothsayer, or perhaps I'll decide that the tiny drop of djinn in your otherwise human blood is witchery instead.'

Silas stared between them. Tyvain caught his eye. 'Guess she ain't told ya what it is she does for the Order exactly?'

'No, she hasn't.' But then, he'd never asked. And now, he wasn't so sure he wished to know. His gaze darted back to Sybilla, who made her way towards him with the tray.

'That's right, ankou. You're gettin' it, I see.' Tyvain's smile was dastardly. 'Our lovely angel there is the Order's executioner. Keepin' all the purebreds safe from the witches and sorcerers 'o still show up on occasion and get too big for their britches.'

Silas took his brandy without a word, while Sybilla glared down at the tray, equally as silent.

'I swear you'll still be talking even when your coffin is six feet under.' Bess sighed. 'You make it sound so horrid, but it is absolutely necessary. Can you imagine if we had a world full of those like the sorcerer who created the revenants? They lose themselves, eventually, we all know it. And they'll be doing vile things to anyone who so much as stares at them the wrong way. They must be dealt with, I'm afraid.'

Silas met Sybilla's gaze. 'And you...deal...with them.' He breathed in the brandy.

'There's been no need for a long while.' Sybilla was firm. 'But yes, I do, and I must. Samyaza and Azazel coveted this world in terrible ways, Silas. Their legacies endure to this day, despite all that has been done to wipe away any sign of their presence. And there has been much done, believe me.' She sank back into her chair by the fire, which had burned down low.

'The Great Flood is my personal favourite,' Tyvain said, casually, as though she spoke of what she'd had for breakfast. 'Now there is one way to show you ain't 'appy about somethin'. Lord Enoch don't do things by bloody 'alves, that's for sure. Sent rains so hard and heavy they damned near drowned the whole world. Now that's impressive.'

Silas frowned, for he was doing an awful lot of that today, but he recalled something else Pitch had told him. 'Pitch mentioned a flood once...though he said it was blood that ran...Samyaza's. He thought it...likely an exaggeration.' Actually Pitch had been more unkind in his summary, declaring Lord Enoch a teller of histrionic tales. 'But there truly was a flood?'

Sybilla tilted her glass back and forth. 'There truly was. And it may well have had some of Samyaza's blood in it. It had been created to wash all trace of the angel away, to wipe out the Nephilim that hadn't already fled with Azazel to Elyssiam. It was supposed to have...erased...those with knowledge of divine magick, too. And for a long while it seemed as though it was the case. There was no sign of maleficium among humankind for hundreds of years. But it was not so easily extinguished, the bloodlines prevailed, and some of the grimoire had survived the flood. Over time the two found their way together. '

Tyvain set down her glass with a clank against the lacquered surface of the side table. 'And the Order of the Golden Dawn got their first witch hunter.'

'I told you I'd knock your teeth out next time you called me that,' the Valkyrie said, taking another sip of gin. 'But I'm too bloody tired to move.'

'Lucky for me teeth then.'

'I'll get up eventually, don't worry.'

Staring into the caramel brown liquid in his glass, Silas asked, 'What exactly happens...when you find evidence of magick?'

Tyvain drew her finger across her throat, and then mimicked a stabbing at her chest, and then mimed a hangman's noose. 'The Order, mainly Syb here, gets rid of 'em. Can't be lettin' it fester, don't work out well for anyone. She'll be goin' after ya necromancer soon enough.'

Sybilla scowled at the soothsayer, but did not counter her claim.

166

Silas shifted on his feet, all twisted about and unsettled. A headache was starting to bother him. 'And the Nephilim? Have any risen since the...flood?'

'Seen any giant feckin' footprints anywhere's about?' Tyvain snorted. 'Only giant I seen of late is you.'

'What she means to say is, no,' Bess said airily. 'The Nephilim bloodlines ceased to exist after the Flood. Or if they do exist, they have never again produced another of the kind that were here in the beginning.'

Silas needed far more brandy to cope with the deluge of information he'd been served. He almost wished he'd never demanded any answers in the first place. Bloody hell, he could have done with Pitch's careless presence. There was something in his derisive manner that was oddly comforting. As though troubles small or large hardly mattered a whit.

'Another drink?' He nodded at Sybilla's empty glass.

She held it out. 'You understand things well, Silas.'

He took the glass from her and made his way to the drinks trolley.

'Not that well,' Tyvain grunted. 'Ya didn't ask me.'

Ignoring the Hag's mutterings, Silas poured them both a considerable draught. The stopper rattled against the bottleneck as he set it in place. He'd not realised his hands shook so much. Silas made his way back to Sybilla, where she sat in her sock-clad feet, her frock coat discarded, and sleeves rolled. Even so dressed she held an air of strength that was hard to ignore, as though the warrior were always just below the surface.

Silas cleared his throat, passing her the drink. 'I think it best we speak of Goodrich Castle at the earliest possibility. Unless Pitch has told you already of what we encountered?'

She shook her head. 'He's not been in any state for conversation, though we know something of your trials by way of the horses. We must speak, but shall we allow ourselves a moment, another glass perhaps? There's been so much said already, and I'm quite certain you'll not tell me anything I'll be glad to hear.' She appeared so weary he would not disagree. The time spent with the ailing daemon had clearly worn on her. Christ, he wished to see Pitch with his own eyes. Tyvain's words kept playing at him. *If the daemon 'as dropped dead.*

Preposterous of course. It must be. It *had* to be. He grew ever more afraid of being set on his way alone. The world beyond these walls grew ever more terrifying.

Tyvain grunted as she heaved herself off the couch. 'Guess I'm makin' me own drink, then.' She scratched at her underarm as she went. 'I don't reckon' we'll be 'earin' anythin' we want ta hear for a while yet. And I reckon me guts 'ave known this was all comin'. Been tellin' me somethin' ain't right for a good year or more. Thought it was just the arrival of that daemon settin' me off to begin with, I couldn't be around the fucker without 'eavin' me guts. I know there's somethin' about 'im that will come to me in time, I've told Ahari as much, but 'e might as well pat me on me 'ead and tell me to be on me way, for all the shits 'e gives. Even after I foretold of Mercer's arrival.' She gave herself a self-congratulatory harrumph. 'I was 'aving the craziest dreams about a giant on a crystal 'orse. Then our ankou turns up. Now tell me that wasn't foretellin'?'

'It's more likely you'd gone too heavy on the laudanum,' Bess returned, skirts swaying as he made his way towards the group. 'Didn't your dreams include a giant with two heads carrying a bouquet of thistles in one hand and a figurine of a tiny devil with one horn in the other? The devil is human nonsense. Perhaps you fell asleep reading the Bible?' He took a delicate sip, fluttering his becomingly-long lashes.

Tyvain filled her glass to the brim. 'I stay away from readin', silly bitch. And that's what I saw. A giant galloping along with the devil tucked down the front of 'is trousers. I told 'Er Ladyship about them dreams too, and I reckon that's why she ended up puttin' Mercer and that arsehole together. My premonition.'

Bess nearly spat his whisky. 'Good gracious, you think highly of yourself, don't you?'

'Anyways,' Tyvain growled. 'I'm just sayin' that maybe I've seen somethin' about all this...bullshit...that's goin' on. The Order didn't see the necromancer comin', but maybe I did.' She darted a glance at Bess.

'Dear me,' Bess declared. 'Are you about to admit that you may have missed something in your signs?'

'Feck off, tart.' Tyvain glowered. 'I'm just sayin', it's possible. I see enough shit, and I write it all down. Seems like this is a bloody good time to check me scribbles, and see if there's anythin' there for us to know.'

'Gods, your journals are a scrawled disgrace.' Bess wandered over to the fire. 'A chicken has greater skill with a pen and inkwell.' He set another log on the embers, causing a burst of shimmering sparks to rise.

'Hmph.'

'If you want Bess to help you go through your journals just bloody say so.' Sybilla stretched her feet towards the reinvigorated fire. 'Why don't you make a start of it now? Give my ears a break. Silas and I will speak, then we will eat and then I will collapse into bed far earlier than is reasonable. I'll need to set out at first light tomorrow.'

'Where you gonna start searchin'?' Tyvain still stood at the drinks trolley, mixing a concoction that appeared to involve every bottle.

'Shrewsbury.' Sybilla looked to Silas. 'That is what the gravedigger said, did he not?'

Her question caught him off guard, and it took a moment to realise she spoke of the man in Bishop's Castle. George, the gravedigger who had been exhuming a corpse. He clutched at his glass, recalling how the bandalore had nearly strangled the poor man.

'Yes, it was Shrewsbury,' Silas said. 'He mentioned a tosher to be found in a pub there... Ah, I can't recall the name just now.'

'The Old Bell.' Sybilla had no such loss of memory. 'I'll start there. It's as good a place as any to begin the hunt. The Lady Satine and Mr Ahari will be informed of course.'

Bess held out a hand to Tyvain, fluttering it. 'Come on then. Let's go take a look at your scratchings. Shall I have Cook rustle up some cockles to tide us over? You enjoy them, don't you?'

Tyvain brightened. 'I've been known to eat a few. All right then. Lead the way, Your 'Ighness.'

'Call me that again and those cockles will be forced where you shall not enjoy them.' Bess gathered up his discarded slippers, and Tyvain grabbed her bowl of plums.

'You'd be surprised what I enjoy.' Tyvain snorted. 'Weren't your fairy grandma a princess? Makes ya one, don't it?'

'It's fae, and yes, she was. No it doesn't. Sadly, I can only dress as one.'

'Time to get spectacles if ya think that's what ya doin'.'

'Bess,' Sybilla called over the back and forth. 'Will you see to it that this gets to Albion?' She threw out something, which the Master of

Harvington Hall caught with a mild flick of the wrist, jewels sparkling madly. 'Alb has an aptitude for retrocognition. There is a small chance our necromancer has left some trace upon the obsidian.'

'Of course. He was in Leicester last I heard. I may take it myself.' Bess tucked the black orb down the front of his corset.

'Ah, now the poor bastard will peer into the ball and be faced with your 'airy chest on top of everything else. Gods save 'im.'

Tyvain dodged a slap, and the pair left the room in a flurry of insults and swishing of skirts.

'Will you come for a walk with me, Silas?' Sybilla took up her boots and slid them over her feet. 'I've had enough of being indoors. It feels as though I haven't breathed fresh air in an age.'

Silas glanced towards the windows. The rain had stopped at least, but it had come down hard. It would be damp and cold, and he was drained from their discussion already, let alone speaking of the castle. But he wished to keep in Sybilla's good graces, if there were any chance of seeing Pitch sooner rather than later.

He inclined his chin. 'Of course. Lead the way.'

Sybilla moved through the foyer, waving off a mealy-faced footman who seemed to emerge from the shadows. 'We are fine, thank you. Just taking some air.'

The man sank away behind the staircase that dominated the foyer. Sybilla opened the front door and strode along the short covered walkway and out into the evening. The entire world seemed bathed in the eerie green glow of the fog, but he had to agree, the fresh air was pleasing. The remnants of the rain dripped from the eaves, and clung to the shrubbery, glistening emerald. Silas shook himself. It would not do to think on the daemon every damned time something emerald showed itself. He took shallow breaths as he hurried across the stunted expanse of bridge that connected the hall to the land beyond the moat. The bridge was really just an extension of the walkway, and the section of water they crossed was no more than a few feet across, but he'd not stay above it any longer than need be.

Sybilla noted his quickened pace but did not comment upon it. They strolled along a garden path, avoiding the puddles that had formed. There was only the faintest murmur of unrest coming from the sky now, the thunder distant. Silas had only just begun to relax his shoulders when the shouting began.

CHAPTER 20

'**M**iss Blessington!' The cry came from the darkness to their left, somewhere towards the stables. 'Miss Blessington!'

Silas squinted through the topiary shrubs. Someone short and lithe ran at a fast clip towards them.

'Tom, whatever is the matter?' Sybilla, or Miss Blessington as it turned out, trudged towards the figure emerging from the curious green glow. His white shirt flapped about him, but his dark skin blended into the night, causing it to look as though only a ghostly shirt flew along the pathway.

'It's tryin' to eat me! You gotta help me.' The lad was squeaky with fear. 'Don't let it eat me!'

'Whatever are you on about?'

The lad dashed at them, drawing close enough for Silas to recognise the stable boy. He was wide-eyed with terror, arms flailing as though he sought to fly himself through the air and avoid his attacker. He crashed through a considerable puddle on the path without seeming to notice. Silas cursed his decision to leave the bandalore tucked beneath his pillows. When would he learn not to separate himself from the blasted thing?

'What is happening?' he asked.

'I haven't the faintest...oomph!' Sybilla staggered back as Tom threw himself at her, wrapping his arms about her waist. She regained her balance and stood like a startled scarecrow, arms outstretched, peering at the top of the boy's head. 'Tom, good grief, what has gotten into you?'

'A wolf,' he stammered. 'Biggest bloody thing I've ever seen. Eyes like coals. Followed me outta the stables.'

Silas tensed, condemning himself anew for not being ready with the scythe. 'That is the creature who attacked us. We did not lose it after all.' His wrist throbbed with the pace of his heart.

'If it is indeed that creature, it could not breach the Sanctuary borders so easily.' Sybilla peeled Tom's arms from her waist. 'Go inside, Tom. We will deal with this.'

'I don't have the...' Silas glanced down at the stable boy shivering behind Sybilla. 'The bandalore, it is inside.'

'I daren't say you shall have need of it.' Sybilla shooed Tom away. 'Go, now. And don't pay Ronin any mind if he grumbles at you for using the front entrance. Tell him I said so, and he's to get you a set of dry clothes. You are terribly damp. Now hurry, and stay inside until we return.'

The lad did not cause her to ask twice. He dashed off, making short work of the distance to the bridge.

'Come along, Silas,' Sybilla declared. 'Let us see this ferocious beast.'

Was she truly making light of this? He supposed she had not seen the creature to know how awful it was.

'I should really like to retrieve the scythe.'

'You do understand I'm a Valkyrie, don't you? I have a few years of experience with fighting monsters. Besides, Bess is the finest Sanctuary builder of his entire family. Save perhaps for his sister Jacquetta, but I'd never say that to his face. And Jacquetta has hidden herself away for a few years now, likely with enough coin and gems made from her commissions to last her several lifetimes. I digress, the point is that Melusine's Children are masters of Sanctuary building, and Harvington Hall is one of the finest. No one can enter these grounds if they intend harm to its inhabitants. You are safe here, Mr Mercer.'

'I was supposed to have been safe in Wyre Forest, was I not? Or else Lalassu would not have left me alone.'

That seemed to stifle Sybilla's airy mood. 'Well...that was unfortunate, yes. She most definitely did not foresee you being set upon. The revenants caught us all off guard, I should say. But the Sanctuary is another matter. Stand behind me if you will.'

'No, I am fine here, thank you,' Silas said stiffly. If asked outright, he'd not deny he was frightened, but Sybilla did not appear greatly alarmed. So he'd do his level best to appear the same way. Perhaps the lad had imagined the red eyes, the size of the beast. The night did tend to trick the eye.

Silas kept pace with the Valkyrie as she strode along the edge of the moat to where the wooden bridge led the road across it and on to the stables. It was the same way they had ridden in this afternoon, so he was vaguely familiar with the surrounds, but it had been light then, and now it was different entirely. The clouds held at bay any moon or stars to brighten the way. Instead the mist hung at the fringe of the moat, shedding its strange glow upon the bridge's bulk. The shadows cast beneath the rails appeared to shift like slow-waving flags in the breeze.

Sybilla paced across the bridge, the clack of her boot heels upon the wood announcing their arrival in no uncertain terms. Silas slowed upon reaching the structure and found himself at its edge, hesitant to move on. A generous portion of the moat water ran beneath this bridge, and there was yet no sign of the massive beast. His imagination was running away with him as spattering rain descended.

What if the creature lay in wait, like that blasted boggart, and it lunged at him as he moved across the bridge?

He'd be cast into those deep waters without a daemon to drag him free. Christ, he was being ridiculous, he was quite aware, and yet the fear had its pincers in him. Silas wiped at his face as the delicate rain fell. That caustic, consuming terror that had come with being submerged ran deep. He could feel it now stirring in his bones, swimming in the marrow. Those desperate gasps for air, the tear of the water as it pummelled his chest and filled him to bursting.

'Silas? Is everything all right?'

He could not answer truthfully. For if he did, he would say no. No, it was very much not all right. He might be death's messenger, but the weight of recalling how he died was almost pressing him to his knees.

'Yes, fine.' He was hoarse. 'I was just listening out for –'

The growl came at him from beyond a low hedge that marked the far side of the road. He froze, having no doubt what creature made it. The red-eyed beast stood hidden in the foliage. He knew it. How odd that certainty was. And yet, familiar. This surety, this sense of understanding was the same that came over him when he was in Lalassu's saddle. The growl came again, though this time it was all but hidden beneath the guttural roll of thunder. The storm had turned about it seemed, and was headed for them once more.

'Silas?' Sybilla said, once the rumbling ceased. 'Do you see it?'

'Not entirely, but it is here.' He squinted, searching for some hint of ruby red among the shadow-blackened hedge.

'And are you afraid?'

What an odd question. He frowned, ready to assure her he was not jelly-legged, when he realised what his reply would be. 'No. No, I am not.'

How very odd.

Silas took a tentative step towards the hedge. A great bulk shifted in its depths, and there was the glint of an ember's glow he recognised all too well.

'Easy now.' He stepped forward, one hand raised, as though that would fend off the creature if he was wrong about this. 'Easy there.'

And there it was. The whiff of dank and rotting things he recalled. Christ, he'd been so struck with terror as the ash-men set on him he'd not recognised it. Plus, the scent was not quite identical to the waft of the graveyard. This was richer, steeped in a headiness he did not quite recognise.

The beast made a sound, not unlike a whine, and the hedge shook so hard leaves fluttered down onto the wet soil. The thump of paws resounded as the beast fled. A coal-black shadow, large as a bear, loped off into the woods beyond the roadway. Silas exhaled, dropping his hands at his sides. A flicker of disappointment took him. A very different reaction to the last time he and the beast had been so close.

'What is it, Silas?'

He'd forgotten Sybilla's presence at all. She made her way back across the bridge towards him.

'I'm not certain.' A white light lit up the sky, lightning shot free from the approaching storm. He caught sight of something dull among the scattered leaves. Silas crouched down to peer more closely. The mud squelched at his shoes.

The arrowhead lay partly sunk into the wet soil.

'What the devil?'

He tugged it free and placed it upon his palm. It was the length of his shortest finger, and he drew no pleasure from remembering how it had buried itself entirely in his shoulder. Looking at it now, he wondered how he had endured the pain of it. The stunted piece of wood, the only piece of the shaft that remained, was still intact here. Two of its blades were jagged, with hooked barbs at their end, while the other two were as smooth as Tyvain's knife blades. Just as he recalled. The metal's colour resembled a smudge of charcoal, not quite black but not grey either.

He would never have spied it had the beast not drawn his attention there. All at once it struck him.

'Oh you fool, man.'

Silas raced his mind through earlier events of the day. The moment the beast had appeared, the moment it had soared over him, overshooting its leap and instead landing upon an ash-man, ripping the vile creature's throat away. The failure of the bandalore to liven, even as the beast's broad paws landed on his back during the second attack and its fangs tore at him.

His coat pocket, to be precise.

He'd thought Tyvain the one to free him with her knives. But adept as the soothsayer was with a blade, she had not driven the creature away.

The beast had simply found what it had been searching for.

Once it left with the arrowhead in its jaws, they had not been attacked again on the journey to the Sanctuary.

No one can enter these grounds if they intend harm to its inhabitants.

The beast had never intended any harm.

'Bloody hell! It wasn't trying to kill me at all.'

'Well, that was fairly clear. It just ran away.'

'No, not now,' Silas retorted. 'But at the mill, or the farmhouse, it was never after me at all. I think it was trying to take this away.' He held up the arrowhead.

Sybilla's repose faltered. 'Gods,' she breathed. 'Is that what I think it is?'

'If you think it is from Arcadia, then yes. Did Lalassu not...well...tell you?'

Sybilla shook her head. 'We did not know of it.'

'I suppose it's been either in my shoulder or in my pocket. But you recognise it well enough? That it is...' The name escaped him. He tried to recall how it had fallen from Pitch's lips. 'Nekhri.'

'Of course.' She looked up at him. 'And you know it too?'

'The Verderer's bow loosed it at me. And after Pitch gouged the blasted thing from my shoulder, he spoke of its origins. It was the arrowhead that led us to discuss Samyaza...and the Severance War.' Damn it, why did even that troublesome memory fill him with a sense of longing? Of loss? 'He said it could have come from an Elyssiam armoury. If sorcery has returned, is it possible that the Watchers have too?'

If she were to nod, it would officially become the worst day of his new life so far. He was not ready to face avenging angels.

'No.' She did not hesitate. 'The Watchers would have to breach White Mountain, Arcadia's stronghold, to make their way here, for that is where the flux points are, the only points of access,' she said, by way of hurried explanation. 'We would know if they were here. But this is worrying nonetheless. Our necromancer may know something of Arcadia, or at the very least they know the Order has these arrowheads in their possession and figured them significant enough to taunt us with.'

'They do? The Order I mean, have these?'

'Yes, and they are not so rare as you would imagine. The Ruination saw thousands of them released from both sides of the conflict. They still turn up every now and then in archaeological digs, to bamboozle professors and treasure hunters, along with a horde of other artifacts best kept out of human hands. Mr Ahari thoroughly enjoys spending the Order's profits securing them...the ones he knows of, at least.'

Silas gave her an absent nod, glancing over his shoulder to where the shrubs were still and no monstrous beast hid among them. He was thankful to learn it unlikely rebellious angels were about to descend upon the world just yet, but was not sure a proficient sorcerer was much more comforting.

'So Tom's wolf is the same creature you encountered with Tyvain?' Sybilla asked, taking the arrowhead from his palm.

'I have no doubt. There can be no mistaking the eyes.' Silas sifted through his thoughts. 'When we left the Forest of Dean, I carried this arrowhead upon me. It was in my pocket, until the creature took it from me.' He toyed with a new idea. 'Lalassu thought me safe in that forest...but she did not know I carried the arrowhead. With magick about...is it possible that it was this arrowhead that led the sorcerer's revenants straight to me?' Christ, Silas was an idiot. Pitch had told him, well, growled at him, to cast it into the new Verderer's well, but he'd not done so, and now he'd likely made himself, and Charlie, sitting ducks for the ash-men. He had the double misfortune of them having caught him after he'd separated from Pitch. Or perhaps that was a blessing. The encounter might have proved too much for the ailing daemon.

Sybilla cocked her brow. 'Splendid deductions, Silas. And yes, a tracing sigil is simple enough.' She rubbed her thumb against the splintered remains of the shaft. 'There is no evidence of it now, but once detected they are as uncomplex to remove as they are to cast. It seems you had a rescuer.'

'But who is its master?' Silas replied.

'Why would it need one? A magickal creature could counter a basic sigil well enough on its own. And the Order is not alone in wanting to see any traces of maleficium extinguished.'

As the last of her words fell, the scream rang out. The beast's cry was mercifully faint, but its clawing, agonised notes were as unmistakable as the red eyes.

Sybilla jerked her head to follow the sound. 'That is the beast?'

Silas nodded. 'The very one. Dreadful, isn't it?' Though not so bad now that he knew it did not come from any foe.

'I'd not like to hear it any closer, that is sure.'

'So you do not recognise it?'

'The sound? No, I'm afraid not. But I think I'm safe in saying it is no wolf. Likely it is one of the untold number of black dogs that haunt the British Isles. I've lost track of tales of them over the years. There seems to be one for every county. Bess will know more, but I think for now we had best speak more on what led to this pointed thing becoming one with your shoulder. Now, I'm not sure about you, but I'd like to remain outdoors. The air is clearer here, and I've spent far too long indoors the past day. The fresh air is bringing me awake, and I relish it.'

As did Silas. The openness sank into him like a balm working upon his tensions, nearly as soothing as a graveyard. But fresh air could not extinguish all his worries. He *was* relieved to know the beast did not hanker for a morsel of him, and that he had a strange ally of sorts, but that was not to say he was at ease.

'Let us continue on, then.' Silas brushed at the fine film of moisture on his jacket. By rights he should exchange the coat for more suitable outdoor attire, but rights be damned. And if he returned with a sodden jacket, he'd be able to exchange it for something more to his tastes. The notion moved his thoughts once more to the daemon. A short journey indeed. 'It is your time tending to Pitch that has kept you indoors?'

'Yes.' Short and precise. 'It has taken some doing to set him right. But right he shall be.'

Silas swallowed hard. 'Will he though? Be all right, I mean.'

Clasping her hands behind her back, Sybilla took a few steps before she replied. 'As well as he is capable, yes.'

That was hardly the robust assurance he'd sought. 'What on Earth does that mean?'

'Can we speak of the Verderer, and not the daemon, please?'

'No. We cannot.' Silas stopped still, a curl of anger licking at his insides. 'I need to know...damn it, I *want* to know what has happened with him. And not just today...not just of late...but what happened to bring him here to begin with. It is clear he is in the Lady's service under duress.' Pitch was being forced to ride at Silas's side. He did not do so willingly, no matter how much Silas liked to imagine otherwise. He'd thought a closeness had formed between them after all they'd endured in the castle but he'd been fooling himself, until this very moment. He'd seen too well the look upon Pitch's face as the daemon flung him away from the farmhouse with a flick of the wrist and a glare that could sear flesh from a bone. The daemon despised him. And now he thought he knew why. 'He has been pushed beyond his limits, has he not? Bess said it herself that it is an old injury that plagues him. Why would the Lady torment him so?' And make Silas the reason for his pain. 'She takes his tongue when he tries to speak of his life, for god's sake. How big is this mistake he's being so punished for?'

Sybilla walked just far enough ahead of him that he could not see her face, but he saw her shoulders stiffen. 'Mistake?'

'On our way to the Forest of Dean, I asked him how he came to be in Her Ladyship's service, and his reply was "a terrible mistake." He could say no more without losing his tongue. But it was clear to me that his servitude is a punishment.'

'Silas, we need to speak of other things.' She spoke low and measured. 'His past does not –'

'Don't you dare say it does not concern me.' Silas's anger bloomed like a struck match. Christ, he was exhausted and tired of half-truths. 'The Lady has shackled us together, she has made me a part of whatever penance he is forced to pay, and I do not like it. He protected me, he was *forced* to protect me, and it has harmed him. I am not blind, nor stupid, I can see that what he endured in the forest led to this. No wonder he could not stand the sight of me in the end.' Damn the crack of his voice. 'I am the cause of whatever besets him now. Do you think that does not *concern* me?' He was breathless, the words taking the air from his lungs.

Sybilla turned to face him. It was too dark where she stood to make out anything that might give away her mood.

'I can see very well that it does.' She was gentle. 'You have grown fond of him.'

His rage flickered. Silas blushed, turning his head so she would not see. That was the moment he realised they had walked across the wooden bridge and he had not noticed a step of it.

'I have grown...reliant on his company.' He walked ahead so he did not need to bluster beneath her gaze. 'And he despises me.'

'It is not you he despises, I assure you. He does not suffer in your company. Surely you must see that in how he looks at you?' She seemed to expect some answer from him, but he gaped at her like a fool. The Valkyrie had not seen the way Pitch's emerald eyes had gleamed with loathing. She was wrong. As he had been wrong to imagine, as they lay together on Ottelie's bed, that he'd seen need and longing where there had been none.

'I don't know what you –'

180

She flicked her wrist at his denial, sending it away. 'Very well, be that as it may, you should know that the Lady is not his tormentor. Far from it. Tobias came to her to avoid punishment.'

Silas stared at her back as she walked away, headed for the sweep of meadow beyond the stables. He ran to catch her before too great a distance grew between.

'Who wishes to punish him then?' He braced for her evasion and nearly tripped over his own feet when it did not come.

'The Lord Enoch.' They made their way through tall, wet grass, but Silas barely noted the damp stains upon his trousers. Nor the heavier fall of rain.

'Enoch?' he repeated uselessly.

'That is what I said.' Sybilla stopped them in the middle of the meadow, the tall grass whispering about them. 'You are clever, Silas, and tenacious. It won't do to have you so distracted by the past, so I will tell you what I can, and that will have to be enough. Do you understand?'

He nodded, suddenly dry mouthed. 'Yes.'

She didn't beat around. 'You asked Tyvain about the Berserker Prince on your journey here. You said a boggart had accused Tobias of being a deserter from his legion.'

'I did...but how do you...' He grunted. 'Lalassu. You must have been privy to the encounter itself too, then?'

'No, I wasn't. It is the Lady Satine that Lalassu communicates with. In turn the Lady liaises with me where she sees fit.'

Somewhere, far from where they stood, the storm mumbled its discontent.

'Was it true then?' Silas breathed. 'Pitch was in this Berserker Prince's legion?'

'He was.'

Silas stared down at the sway of foxtail. It was not that he had disbelieved Pitch's talk of the Hellfield, and his place upon it, but now it was irrefutable, and all the more awful. 'And he is a deserter?'

He lifted his head to find Sybilla watching him. 'Yes. He is one of those who fled the prince's legion after the fall of Seraphiel, in fear of the lord's vengeance.'

'Seraphiel?' The name was fair and delicate, and he did not recognise it. 'He is the Seraphim the boggart spoke of? An angel?'

Sybilla waved her hands, wincing. 'Yes. But it is best you never mention that name in front of Tobias. He cannot know that I've said anything to you of this, do you understand Silas?'

'Of course.' He rubbed his hands together, chasing away the chill that came with hearing some of Pitch's truth. 'He told me he was there, when this angel fell, but I had no idea how close to it he was.' Sybilla's eyes narrowed. He paused thinking she was about to speak but when nothing came he continued. 'When the boggart goaded him I thought he was going to tear the creature's head from its body. Pitch did not wish to talk about it, he made that very clear. How awful such an even must have been to witness...is a Seraphim an angel of some standing?'

Sybilla dropped her gaze, her laughter brittle. 'Some...yes. They are the highest order of Angelics in Arcadia, below only Lord Enoch himself. Seraphiel was their leader and become one of Enoch's closest confidants after Samyaza's betrayal. His death, at the hands of one who fought alongside him, was a terrible, senseless blow. Enoch...well, Lord Enoch did not take it well. Not only did he lose a Seraphim, he lost a Prince of the Hellfield too.' Sybilla rubbed at her arms, as though talk of the fallen angel and daemon chilled her.

'The Beserker Prince is dead?'

Sybilla worked her teeth at her lips, staring beyond him. 'No. At least not entirely. He was banished to an abaddon beneath White Mountain, Arcadia's version of the Palace of Westminster, if you will, only with far more dungeons. He is as good as dead there.' She definitely shivered.

Silas grasped at the slender bunch of grass nearest him. The world spun. 'So why does the Lady Satine protect him?'

Sybilla blinked, snapping her head towards him. 'The prince?'

'No, no...Pitch.'

'Of course.'

Silas waited for her to continue but she seemed distracted by something back towards the hall. He glanced that way and saw only the inviting glow of candles against iron wrought panes.

'Sybilla?'

'What's that?'

'If Pitch is a deserter, why does the Lady Satine protect him? I assume that is why he cannot speak of himself too deeply. It is a protection...' Gruesome, certainly, but he could at least fathom why such a thing might be necessary. Deserters could be shot here, in the human world, who knew what fate awaited them in a world of angels and daemons.

'Yes, yes, you have it.' She bit at the words. 'But I know little more of the whys and wherefores. I don't tend to question her ladyship's decisions, as you can imagine. Pitch is here, in her employ, and that's really all you and I need to know of it. Far stranger things have happened.' She gestured at him. 'Case in point. A man raised from the dead is quite a bit stranger than a frightened soldier fleeing a battlefield.'

'Yes...I suppose so.' His head ached and the rainfall had his clothes clinging too tight. 'Did Pitch's injury come from his time on the Hellfield then? It is a battle scar?'

'Ah, yes. It is.'

'It must have been a substantial wound, to bother him so much still.' One Silas had seen no sign of, not a scar upon that lithe body. 'Tyvain spoke once of when he first arrived at Holly Lodge, she said he was in a state then too.'

'Yes, yes. And Tyvain likes to talk far too much. You needn't worry on these things, Silas, it is all in hand.'

It was bothering him now, how she did not quite look him in the eye when she spoke.

'But it is clearly not. If he is still healing, he should not have been placed as he was in the Forest of Dean, where he would have to...to defend us as he did.' What did one call what Pitch had done, producing great lengths of flame from within himself, sending startling streams of glorious fire to fend off a descending castle and shatter a glass prison with just a touch. Whatever he might call it, it swept Silas with guilt. If he were not so inept, then Pitch would not have had to defend them both so well.

'We had thought it would not prove so...problematic, for him to do so. Measures had been taken. But it was not as though he had a choice. Your lives were at risk, and it was his role to defend you.'

'And he did so, very well. The Lady Satine knows this, surely?'

'Of course. She is well pleased...with both of you.'

Silas shook his head. 'I can hardly be compared to him. He was...quite marvellous.'

Now Sybilla's attention was on him fully, and her lips quirked with a smile. 'It is plain to see you think so.' She touched the tip of the arrowhead to her hair, scratching at the spot where evidence of the black mark had been washed clear by the rain. 'I'm sure I need not stress to you the importance of keeping Pitch's identity to yourself. It is not a pleasant fate that awaits a deserter. Keep him safe as he does you, and say nothing of his past. Let us deal with the rest.'

'Of course. I'll say nothing at all.'

'Good. I'm not sure if you have noticed, but it is pouring, and I'm soaked through.' She was quite right. The rain came down in a sheet that blurred the landscape. 'Shall we retire indoors after all? Find a quiet corner, perhaps some of those cockles Bess spoke of? They've been on my mind since he mentioned them.'

Silas could not say the same. Just the notion of eating flipped his stomach 'Yes, that would be fine.' He ran his hand through his hair, fingers snagging in sodden knots. 'Do you think it will be long before I can see him?'

'I'm sure it won't.'

Placated, Silas nodded. 'Good.'

Sybilla held up the arrowhead, its dull hue taking all the sparkle out of the rain that fell upon it. 'Come now. I fancy a pleasant restful evening before I set off early to search for our necromancer. You'd do well to try and enjoy the same, for I doubt it will be long before you and your daemon are called on once again to ride.'

CHAPTER 21

That night Silas slept fitfully, dreaming of a blackened forest and a hooded sorcerer who cast a nefarious spell, covering him in flesh-devouring spiders. In the dream, Tyvain laughed and pointed, while Charlie screamed as the spiders turned their sights upon him. Deeper in the forest, where Silas could not reach, Pitch swung from a hangman's noose tied to the boughs of an enormous, twisted ash tree.

His nightmares broke his night into pieces. And in the end he preferred not to sleep at all.

Silas was lying on his bed wide awake when the clip of hooves roused him. He made it to his window in time to see Sybilla heading off down the road on her dapple grey, trotting through a gloomy dawn-touched morning. He had stared in some confusion at the pair, for the horse, Hastings he'd heard her call the mare, appeared much broader and taller than he recalled. The silver tail flew far out behind it. He blinked, considered, and decided it likely the horse was as it seemed. Changed.

Why would Sybilla not be a Horseman too? She was far more suited to it than he.

Later that morning, Silas spoke with the master of Harvington Hall about the red-eyed beast, and Bess, of course, knew full well the creature that had crossed the Sanctuary boundaries. And of its name.

'A skriker,' he declared, through lips thick with strawberry coloured rouge. 'Though far from home and much bolder than I'd expect. I must say, I'm surprised you didn't recognise it as kin, for it certainly recognised you.'

'Pardon me?'

'The skriker are dogs of death. Their noses never miss it. They screech blue murder at the hint of a person's final days. It's thought they originated with the very first ankou, who was lonely as he swept his scythe about, gathering up his souls. Story goes the fae gifted him one of their own black pups to keep him company and ease his loneliness, and it was he who taught the beast to recognise the bouquet of death and dying. A pity he didn't teach it not to shatter eardrums each time it found the scent, what a dreadful noise they make. Some ankou still keep them, I believe, but most of the skriker live without a master now. Perhaps, your beast sought to change that?'

'Hmmm, perhaps.' He was not averse to the idea of a companion hound, especially on days when Pitch's sharp conversation grew too taxing. But it was something else the man had said that grabbed his attention most. 'You speak of other ankou...I suppose I hadn't stopped to wonder...if I was – '

'The only one?' Bess's laughter was kind. 'Dear me, no. Can you imagine if you were tasked with seeing to the souls of the entire world?'

He shook his head, with great fervour. 'I assumed that was not the case, that I was not the only one I mean, for it would take far more than a year to reach the farthest points of the Earth.' He moved on quickly from thoughts of the brevity of his role. 'But I did wonder...how many of us there were...and if I might meet another.'

'I don't see why not, but I'm not expert on the matter I'm afraid. Astonishing really, and I suppose it goes to show that I do really need to get out and about more, but I've not met an ankou before you, though I've certainly heard of your kind. Perhaps you could speak with Mr Ahari about it, next you meet, or the Lady Satine?'

He nodded, smiling politely, but none too certain either of the people mentioned were ever going to deem him worthy of visiting. He'd been left very much to his own devices so far as he could see.

'I will. Most certainly.' Silas paused. 'Might I see Pitch this morning?'

'I'm afraid not. Perhaps later today, my dear. We shall see.'

Silas did not see Pitch that day. Nor the next. And every time he asked after the daemon the answer was always the same.

'He is not ready.'

Two full days passed with little more to do than pace restlessly through the grounds of Harvington Hall. Sadly there was no graveyard on the property, and the weather was temperamental, the sun deciding against showing itself most days, with the cloud cover hanging so low it seemed you might touch it if you reached out from one of the attic windows. Drizzle was upon the menu each day, though that did not bother Silas. The spatter of cool rain upon his face grounded him. Its simplicity was comforting.

Not so comforting was the trek across the bridge he had to take if he wished to escape the wooden confines of the hall. Silas would scamper, there was no other word for it, across the sturdy stone bridge that lay across the moat, as if Black Annis and the Verderer both were on his heels. He'd whisk his way across with one hand never leaving the rough capstones, as though the parapet were a life raft he'd best not let go of.

He'd cut men, albeit dead ones, in half, beheaded them too, and yet here he was frightened as a babe at the sight of all that damned water around him.

He spent some time wandering the corridors in the futile hope he might just happen upon the sick room. But the halls were a labyrinth, and apparently endless. He took to the gardens instead. The fields that flanked Harvington Hall were not utilised by grazing stock. Instead they had been left to return to a more wild state. Fox sedge and reed sweet-grass grew in great swathes along the edge of the moat, nearly tall enough in parts to conceal him from any eyes that watched from the hall.

Silas was mostly left alone, as though all those about him sensed his disquiet and let him be with it. Charlie gave up inviting him to join he and Bess for a ride, after Silas refused for the third time. At dinner, as they ate smoked haddock and firm potatoes swimming in a cream sauce, his companions would chatter about a venture into the village that day, or the rabbits that had gotten into the kitchen garden again and how hilarious it had been to watch the gardener lose his mettle over it. Charlie and Bess discussed chess, of all things. It turned out the former was quite good at it, while the latter was atrocious, which surprised no one.

All represented trivial, menial discussions that distracted Silas at times and drove him mad with their inanity at others.

On the second evening he'd found Charlie and Tyvain engrossed in a game of whist. There was that issue, too, which vexed him. He wanted Charlie gone from here, far away, where he would be safe from all the strangeness that enveloped Silas. With all this talk of murderous angels and magick and necromancy, this was no place for someone so very human. But neither Charlie nor any of the others now appeared to be rushing his departure.

Everything was taking altogether too long.

'Not today I don't think, Silas.' Bess, resplendent in white satin trimmed with the sky-blue lace he seemed to favour, had been kind when Silas asked for the fourth time on the third day. 'Your daemon will come good, but it is not yet.'

Silas had scowled at him. To begin with, Pitch was not *his* daemon. Christ almighty, what was wrong with these people? They sat about as though each day was going to be as unharried as the one before.

'I could just take him his lunch perhaps?' Silas would have rolled his eyes if he'd witnessed someone else being so bloody pitiful. He was under no illusion that he bordered on woeful.

But all he wished to do was set eyes upon the daemon, to see for himself that Pitch had not left him entirely. They didn't even need to speak. In fact, it was preferable they didn't. The infernal bastard always seemed to stain conversation. This was a creature who had lain upon Ottelie's bed with his stomach gouged and his blood spilling from him, fluttering his lashes and flirting like he were at a ball.

What must he have been like upon a battlefield, fighting for his mad prince? Silas could not stop thinking on it, for he imagined it must have been an astonishing sight.

'He's not fond of a meal at the moment.' Bess had been gentle to begin with, but Silas could see his patience wearing thin today.

'He's still not eating?'

'Nothing at all...' Bess touched at the splendid powder-blue wig he wore that day. 'And I mean that entirely. He's refusing whatever...and whoever, we send him. But it is just a mood now, that fine body of his is healing well.' Bess patted his arm, which was most infuriating. 'Rest, Silas, enjoy the reprieve, for it will not last.'

He couldn't guess whether he meant reprieve from Pitch's company or the task at hand. Likely both.

And he tried to follow the advice. Silas spent the rest of the third day peeling potatoes with the scullery maid, which appeared to make the young lass grossly uncomfortable. She must have said a hundred times that he really oughtn't bother himself, that she was fine to do it. The housekeeper's eyes had nearly popped from her head when she found them there, in silence, a growing stack of curling skins before them.

'Mr Mercer...sir...there is no need for that.'

'I disagree, look at this pile.' He gestured at the small mound of potatoes before them. 'It is no bother at all.'

The housekeeper and the scullery maid had exchanged a glance, the maid had shrugged, and the peeling had continued in silence. Though Silas's thoughts were less quiet, bustling with all manner of awful things.

He could not peel potatoes forever. The task was soon done, and in the late afternoon, rain fell too heavily to consider yet another walk outdoors.

The corridors it was, then.

They were infuriatingly many, and all so identical in appearance that his wanderings often got him lost. The cluster of buildings that leaned against one another to form the entirety of the hall differed in size, the highest at four storeys, others at two and three. Beyond the wooded walls thunder grumbled, and jabs of lightning illuminated the corridor with silver light. Silas stood frowning at a brass sconce fixed slightly crooked upon the wall. He was certain he'd passed the damned thing once already. He glanced at the floor. There again was the curled lip of the rug where he'd tripped earlier.

He'd somehow gone around in a circle, despite having travelled up two sets of stairs and along the length of several hallways.

'What the bloody...' It dawned on him. 'Oh, you are an idiot,' he declared to the long, empty corridor.

He'd walked a trek just like this at The Atlas.

The Sanctuary, he was certain, was every bit as astounding as that place. And neither place would give him easy passage if it did not so

189

choose. The corridors would not take him where *he* wished to be if their master did not will it. And Bess had made it clear he could not see Pitch.

Searching for his room was a fool's errand. These corridors would shift and lengthen and replicate themselves until Silas was exhausted. He turned on his heels, muttering all manner of crude things, and strode back the way he had come.

'Fine. You win this.' He thumped his fist against the nearest door.

He was along the hall and almost at the top of the stairs when he heard the door open behind him.

'Silas? Did you knock?' Charlie stepped out of the room, dressed for a ride in snug-fitting grey pants and a man's dress shirt. He pulled on a riding coat, the shoulders a smidge too wide.

'Oh, apologies...I didn't realise.' The house had delivered him back to where their rooms lay, and he'd not recognised it. 'I was just...walking, and lost track of where I was.'

'This place does that, doesn't it? I somehow keep ending up either storming into Bess's room, poor luv, or striding out into the courtyard at the back, where the stables are. I can't work out if the house wants me to stay or get the hell out.' Charlie laughed, with no idea how close to the truth of things he was. 'Bess is such a dear, isn't he? He is talking of holding a dance at the hall and insists I am to wear a tailcoat if that is what I prefer. He'll have his seamstress make one for me. And a top hat, can you imagine?' He glowed as he spoke, a grin so wide it barely kept to his cheeks. 'Think of all the wonderful people that would come to such a dance. Oh Silas, I do like it here.'

Silas bit his tongue, quite actually. He'd no sooner cause that smile to falter than he'd poke his own eye out. 'I can imagine Bess throws quite the party.' In truth, Silas could think of nothing worse than dancing and frivolity right now.

'It's good to see you, Silas.' Charlie stood in the doorway, one hand resting upon the handle. 'I feel like I've barely crossed your path the past couple of days.'

He made his way back to the lad. 'I'm sorry, I should –'

'Hush now. I'm capable of amusing myself. Bess has kept me busy with endless card games.' He leaned in conspiratorially. 'Just between you and me, he is really a quite dreadful player but ever so keen. I'm just sneaking in a ride before he has me beating him at whist again. Would you like to join me? Lalassu would be happy to see you I suspect. And it would convince me you aren't avoiding me.'

'Oh, I'm not avoiding you. It's not that at all.'

Charlie winked. 'It's all right, Silas. I was just playing with you. You needed some solitude, anyone can see that. I am worried about you though. You've spent the past few days looking like a child whose dog has run away. You are very worried about your friend, aren't you? Mr Astaroth?'

Among many other things.

Silas tucked his hair behind his ears, ducking his head to avoid scrutiny. 'Yes. I'm sorry, it has been a challenging few weeks.' To say the very least.

'Bloody hell, do stop apologising. But tell me, are you all right, Silas? Truly? I've been wanting to ask you...since it all happened. You were astonishingly brave. How is your hand?'

He reached to touch Silas, who pulled away, tugging down his cuff. His flesh had healed completely by the first morning in Harvington Hall, the bone that had been exposed hidden beneath pale pink skin and sinew. Really, the bandages had been for Charlie's benefit, so he did not see how quickly Silas healed.

'Thank you, but I'm fine. What about you, Charlie? Really, I mean. You've seen some terribly strange things.'

To punctuate the moment, thunder rumbled. The storm that had threatened since they'd arrived was at last moving closer.

Charlie shrugged. 'I've been on the road and on the run for over a year. I've been terrified before, and seen stranger things.' His smile waned with the lie. 'I'll admit I've not liked my dreams much of late, but Bess has fixed me some brilliant sleeping elixirs. I'm grateful, I really am, Silas, that you have not sent me on my way. I'm grateful to the Order too, for letting me stay here. Weird as it may seem, I don't think I've felt this safe since I bolted out of the gates of Ald...' He coughed. 'Since I left home. I truly like it here, and I know you are worried for me, but I am fine really.'

'I'm glad,' he said simply. And he was. Charlie was amusing company, rock steady and unafraid. His bravery was formidable. And he was plainly and simply human, not reliant on any preternatural talents to survive, and yet had done so. It made Silas ashamed at times of his own reticence. But equally glad to know he'd not faltered when the moment came to keep Charlie safe.

'Do try not to worry about your friend. If there is anywhere he can get the care he needs, I've no doubt it is here.'

'He is not my friend.' Silas dove into his denial. 'We...we work together.'

'And that means he is not your friend?'

He chewed at the inside of his lip. 'That's not it.' Did daemons have friends? He doubted it very much.

'Well, whatever it is, try not to worry so much. It gives you wrinkles, and you look so much finer without them.' Charlie glanced back into his room. 'Hell, does it ever stop raining here? Perhaps I will ride a bit later.' China-blue eyes fell on Silas, and Charlie's grin danced. 'We could amuse ourselves in other ways, if you like? It might distract you.' The words were playful, flippant. There was no weight to them; Charlie expected nothing from him save for some momentary enjoyment. Warmth crept up Silas's neck at the blatant proposal. It would be a distraction, no doubt. What harm in surrendering himself to baser pleasure for a while?

As he considered his answer, thunder rolled, crashing onto the slates above. The windows in Charlie's room rattled, and the blast of sound shook Silas back to his senses. He recalled all too well how things had ended the last time he had lain with Charlie. There had been no distraction from Pitch at all. Rather the opposite.

Silas stepped back, putting distance between them. 'I'm sorry but I –'

Charlie held up his hand. 'If you apologise again, I'll be forced to hit you in the balls.' He laughed. How was he not a shivering wreck after all he'd witnessed? 'I understand, I truly do. Maybe tomorrow we can go into the village. The public house is pleasant, the ale not terrible.'

'I would like that.' And it was not a lie.

Charlie stood on tiptoes to reach his cheek and pressed warm lips there. He eased back onto the soles of his riding boots, leather creaking. 'Tell me, this friend of yours, I've heard him called Tobias and Mr Astaroth, but I wonder, does he go by any other name?'

Silas frowned. 'He has a nickname, yes. Pitch.'

An unnameable look slid across Charlie's face. 'Ah, there it is.'

'Pardon me?'

Charlie took his hand and squeezed it. 'I thought it *must* be him, after seeing you so bothered these past days.' He sucked at his cheek. 'Let us just say, I've heard you speak that name before.'

'Well, I'm sure I mentioned it when –'

'No, no,' Charlie declared airily. 'I know exactly where I heard it. You were naked and atop me at the time, and rather magnificently overcome with your climax. I thought at first you were calling me a bitch, which seemed odd, but each to their own. It was much clearer the second time.' He drew the door closed. 'Don't look so aghast. Blame the cannabis, if you wish, but don't you dare apologise for it.' He landed a cheeky pat against Silas's backside. 'I very much look forward to meeting your friend as soon as he is well. See you at dinner.'

Charlie waved his farewell and danced down the stairs, humming a jaunty tune. Silas stared after the lad, his face cold for lack of blood. Good god almighty. He'd sunk lower than he could imagine possible.

Silas wandered off in a daze, trying not to think on what Charlie had said. He found himself passing the library and mumbled a refusal when Bess invited him to join him by the fire. Silas could not bring himself to tell him he could not read. There was something intensely dignified about Bess, and it embarrassed Silas to even consider revealing his inadequacies. The Master of the Hall looked especially wonderful today too, his wig removed to reveal natural jaw-length silver-grey hair, rigidly straight and cut in a precise even line. He'd shaved clean the trim beard that had defined his jawline, and now only a shadow remained.

Silas kept on, cursing the labryinth this place was, but he should not have spoken so harshly, for the house retaliated by crossing his path with the very last person he was in the mood for.

'You still draggin' yourself around like a feckin' corpse?' Tyvain stood in a cosy room dominated by a billiards table. She was dressed in a sunshine-yellow gown that was far too busy and lace-ridden to suit her. She paused in her shot to regard him.

'No, I am not.' Though he possibly was.

One of the footmen who had tended them at dinner leaned casually against the wall, cue in hand. A striking lad, whose mother or father was clearly from the Orient. Silas supposed he should not be surprised to find Bess's household unlike any other, with the servants mingling with the people of the house so freely. The lithe, raven-haired lad studied his fingernails, not raising an eye at Silas's arrival.

He'd noted at the meal service that Ronin had no shadow, but he had no clue what type of creature he was, save for surly and profoundly good looking.

'Ronin's a natural, case you're wonderin'.' The soothsayer's preferred term for those with otherwordly talents, herself included, even though, strictly, she was human with a dash of magick. Divine magick from the angels. Silas shook off the thought. Tyvain chalked up her cue. 'You've met Kaneko at The Atlas, 'aven't ya? Well Ronin 'ere is like 'im. A tsukumogami. Eh, lad, what were you, back before you learnt to whip my arse at this game?'

'Sake pot,' he said with a disinterested sigh. 'Muramochi period.'

'Me least favourite drink,' Tyvain returned. 'Taste's like a spriggin's piss.'

'You would know, then.' Ronin's dagger-like look would have stopped anyone else dead, but Tyvain laughed, told him what to do with his cue, and turned her attentions to Silas. 'Fancy an arse kickin', Mercer?'

'No, thank you, but I do have a question, seeing as you mentioned The Atlas. Am I right in assuming that this house has the same...ah...talents as the pub? I'm having trouble finding my way about.'

She leaned across the table, lining up her shot. Her auburn hair, loose and wild, touched at the green velvet. 'That it is. Ain't she showin' you what you want to see, Mercer? Keeping you going in roundabouts, I expect. Searchin' for daemons, are we?'

The shot was clean, the ball slicing into the pocket without touching the sides. She stood upright, lifting her cue in triumph, a satisfied smirk on her lips.

'Not too bad for an old hag.' Ronin nodded, dark eyes brightening a little.

'Aye, get those pounds ready, Spriggin's Piss, you'll be partin' with 'em soon enough.' Tyvain shifted around the table, eyeing up her next shot. Now she stood with her back to him. 'You didn't answer my question, Mercer. Which is answer enough. If ya do find 'im, maybe you'll 'ave better luck than Ronin 'ere. Daemon weren't interested in a fuck with ya was 'e, Ronin? That must be what put ya in this mood. Don't get turned down often I bet.'

Ronin eyed her with disdain. 'Take your shot, Hag.'

Tyvain roared with laughter. ''E insulted your poor ancient cock, didn't 'e?' She shook too hard to take her shot, and it bounced off the cushion.

'I cared neither way. I was merely heeding my master's wishes. Mr Astaroth will come round eventually.' Ronin traced his pinky finger across a smooth black brow.

Silas inhaled, seeking to banish the thud of his pulse. An incubus had needs, that had been made abundantly clear. And it was not a good thing, he was sure, that Pitch had turned this offer down. But that did not stop a foolish twinge of relief. He realised he was staring at the handsome, sulky young man and quickly gathered himself. He muttered a goodbye and stepped back into the corridor.

'I think they are wrong,' Tyvain called out.

He leaned to peer at her around the doorway. 'I beg your pardon?'

'Wrong to keep ya away. It don't sit well with me. Don't let it sit well with you, either.' She burped into the crux of her elbow. 'Now off ya go then, keep searchin'. 'Ere, Ronin, 'ow's about a feckin' drink. It's near enough to evenin'.'

The pair began to bicker about who should serve, with Silas forgotten, the curious moment swept away. Was Tyvain's encouragement genuine, or was she amusing herself at his expense, urging him on in a fruitless search?

He frowned into his thoughts as he headed off down the hallway, tugging at his silver-grey lounge coat. There was no shortage of nice clothing available here at least, tailored exactly to his substantial needs. No shortage of refreshing beverages either. Tyvain had been right about one thing: it was certainly time for a drink. He'd head to the Lace Room and pour himself a brandy. Enough with this aimless wandering. A fine idea. It was a pity the house didn't agree. Sending him up and down stairs, through archways, and along hallways that looked all the same as one another.

He was at his wits' end when the tingling at his fingertips halted him in his stride. Silas stared down at his hands. The sensation was subtle, a far cry from the prickling that had come with the arrival of Black Annis and the Verderer, but it was concerning nonetheless. He'd left the bandalore in his room, tucked under the pillow as had become his preference. He wriggled his fingers. Bloody hell, surely a teratism could not find its way into the place?

Movement along the corridor drew his head up. The figure emerged directly from the wall. A stocky man with long, wild hair that hung to touch at the small of his back. He was dressed in misshapen layers of clothing, a mixture of fur trim and leather panelling. His beard was astonishing, dangling near to his generous belly. He was only faintly transparent, much the same as Addison, the unfortunate bleeding ghost who had come to Silas at the Donisthrope's home in Leicester.

The soul turned then, and Silas saw that the ghosts shared another unfortunate commonality.

Both had met gruesome deaths.

This man, in his middle years, had sustained an injury to the side of his head that had cleaved into forehead and cheekbone. His skull was cracked wide open, the pulp of his brain exposed. His right eye was a scrambled mess of wetness, dripping from the socket. Silas pressed his lips against a wave of revulsion.

You wish to see him.

The voice was in Silas's head, its nearness causing him to shiver.

Silas thought he knew full well whom the soul spoke of, but still he asked, 'Who?'

The daemon.

His heart stuttered. 'You would take me to him?'

You wish to see him.

Was it even a question? 'Yes,' he said quickly, as though the opportunity might slip from him like a dream.

Then the ankou's will shall be done. This way.

CHAPTER 22

The lost soul moved quietly, as one did when one had no corporeal form at all to betray them upon creaking floorboards. Silas, very much corporeal, possessed no such stealth. It was as though every single board declared his progress with a squeal. Questions were burning upon Silas's tongue, but he dared not breathe a word. He felt like a lad slinking from the house for a clandestine meeting. His nerves were taut and twinged at the slightest sound.

His guide did not pause. Thankfully this fellow did not bleed as Addison had done, and Silas was spared from having to follow a bloody trail through the house.

On they went. Moving up a flight of stairs here, down a corridor there, a turn right, a left, another flight of stairs. They saw no sign of any of the house's occupants, no housemaids or footmen anywhere in sight. The decorations grew sparse, as though the wing of the hall they had entered was rarely used. There were no runners upon the floor, not a picture on the wall or plant in its pot.

After several minutes, Silas dared speak. 'Your assistance is very welcome, but might I ask why you are aiding me?'

The bearded soul tilted his gruesome head. Silas could see the hallway ahead through the cavernous crack in his skull.

You are ankou-upon-the-pale-horse. Word has passed from house to house, forest to forest. It is said your blade swings with good intent. You have rescued those whom the Blight deforms and torments. For that, we are thankful.

'Rescued?'

Black Annis, the Verderer. Do you think they sought to become so twisted? He hadn't thought on them at all. Not beyond the teratisms they were. *Now they are free.*

Silas forgot for a moment the terrible state of the drifting apparition ahead of him and stared in wonderment. He'd not once supposed death's blade would be welcomed.

Make no mistake though, ankou, you will not loose that blade upon me here. Something akin to a snicker came from the soul, and with the thunder rolling it morphed into a growl. *Melusine's Child made this Sanctuary well. All beneath her roof are protected.*

'I understand. I intend you no harm, I assure you.' He hesitated. 'Do you have a name?'

The soul grunted, the sound flopping its way from between his shattered jaws. *Once maybe. I don't recall. I've been a long time here. Death passed me over once or twice, the likes of you rode by, but I kept myself hidden and turns out ain't much they can do if you won't move along. I was here long before the hall's foundation stone was laid, I'll be here after the whole place falls down and is nought but a pile of rubble again. Perhaps once the Sanctuary is gone and I can't hide so well, I'll wave you and your scythe down.*

'You hid, you say?' It would not be Silas who moved this lost soul on, not unless the Sanctuary fell down within the year. He experienced another pang of regret at the brevity of an ankou's existence. In a year, he might just be able to make sense of things.

Death is powerful, but careless. Once the soul is set free from the flesh, death considers its job done. It doesn't care much for those that are restless still, and not wanting to move on. That's what the likes of you are for. But there are ways of keeping clear of your scythe too, if a soul wants it hard enough.

'What would make a soul wish for such a thing?' The isolation of such an existence made Silas shudder.

A knife to the back, a quest left undone, a stolen chance at love. Things that make a man angry, a woman furious, a child anguished. Regret, fury, grief. Those are the chains that hold us here. And are the reason why the Blight can twist a soul into a teratism, and death can put her scythe in our hands and make a messenger of us.

The soul's head moved at an unnatural angle, and his gaze landed on Silas. A cold hand seemed to brush at the back of Silas's neck.

'What are you saying? That I – '

The spirit suddenly twisted away and raised a broad hand. *Hush.*

The very last thing Silas wished to do was hush. Had not the spirit just suggested that an ankou was borne of a miserable death?

'What is it?' he whispered, flushed with exasperation.

She is rousing. She has heard you finding your way.

'Who is rousing?' Silas sent a furtive glance back up the corridor. It stretched on so long the far end appeared black as a coal pit.

The house. The house rouses. You will need to follow a different path. Come, ankou. And do not stop when it seems you must. If you wish to reach him, you must keep going.

The soul rushed down the corridor. If Silas were not to be left behind, he must move, and now. The morbid conversation would have to wait. He broke into a run, cursing the calamity beneath his feet. The blasted wood snapped and popped like crackers. The horses in their stable could likely hear him. He had raced a few strides before he realised his feet were not solely to blame. The noise came from all around, the walls, the ceiling, and beyond, as though the house were shifting on its foundations.

'What is ha –'

A wall appeared out of nowhere before him. He stopped himself just short of a bumped nose against the woodwork. Where once an open corridor had led, now there was a corner, and a brand new passageway leading off to his left.

'What the bloody –'

Keep going I said, the soul shouted in his head.

Silas winced, pressing at his temple, but he did as he was told. He turned left, and had just taken a step when he was reprimanded again.

No. Ahead. That is where your path lies. Ahead.

Clearly the head wound had made the soul insensible. 'There is a wall here,' Silas cried with frustration. He pressed his palms to the wood, to

199

reassure himself that he spoke the truth. The oak panels were cool, as though the chill of outdoors lurked close behind.

Then find your way through. Such things would not have hindered you once, do you recall?

'No, I do no recall any such thing as running through walls.' Silas was gruff, running his hands up and down the smooth surface in search of signs of a secret panel. With the right placement of pressure, he may find a hidden door swinging. But it all appeared very, very damned solid.

You were a wraith before you were an ankou. Or did you suppose you went from coffin to servant so readily?

Silas held very still, while the house groaned and warped around him. 'Wraith?'

A ghost, a spectre, a phantom. We all choose our names as we see fit, and that is what I've chosen.

Silas braced against the wall, less steady than before. 'I barely remember anything at all, living or dead.' His frustration made him sharp. 'I came to while being hauled from my coffin and told that I was an ankou now and I had one year of service ahead of me. No one will give me a blasted straight answer about much at all. Now I'm learning from a wraith with its head cleaved in two that I was likely a ghost before now, one who had died unhappily at best, enraged at worst.'

There is no likely about it. A living man cannot be an ankou, only a wraith can. Do you know nothing of your death? When it was, at least? What was upon your headstone?

Silas balled up his fists. Perhaps he could punch this infernal wall down. 'I had no stone, and even if I did I could not read it. But I must have died on New Year's Eve, Mr Ahari said so. It was one of the reasons I was chosen as ankou, for the time.'

So then, which New Year's Eve? The one just gone, or much further in the past?

The question was like the lick of a whip. 'I don't...I don't know.' He leaned harder against the wall. God damn it, how long had he been dead for? He struggled to think straight, to bring to mind the dress the woman in lavender had worn. Was it fashionable? Or reminiscent of another era? 'Damn it, I don't know. Let me through.'

He thumped the wall. Quick sharp licks of sound came from beyond. And if he were a betting man, Silas would say that the ghost, the wraith, had laughed.

Much to learn, then.

Thunder was a beastly growl, deep and directly overhead.

Now come. Or she will fight us too hard for you to win. The moment is now. Find your way.

The prickling in Silas's fingertips lessened. Faded. The wraith was leaving him behind.

'No! Wait for me. Come back.' He pounded the wall. The resounding thud held a hollow timbre. 'Shit.'

Silas peered up the corridor, the house was luring him with false promises there, he knew it. But how the hell was he supposed to pass through solid walls? The wraith's instructions were all very well for someone who had no flesh and bone.

Do not stop when it seems you must. It damned well seemed he must stop now.

Silas stepped back.

Bloody hell, he must be truly delirious to do this. He took a few more steps back, thankful the house had thrown him into a corner where he could gain a run-up.

If you wish to reach him, you must keep going, that was what the wraith had said.

So be it, because right now, finding his way to Pitch was among the rare things that made any sense.

Silas shifted his shoulders. Thank god no one was here to witness this. They'd know for sure he was fit for the asylum when he bounced off the wall with a bloodied nose.

'One, two, three.'

He launched himself, rushing at the wall like a bull at a cape. Silas squeezed his eyes shut and leaned in with one shoulder.

Any moment now and he'd find himself rebounding from the hard surface.

The air dragged at him, and there came the oddest sense of being touched, feather-light fingertips seeking to take their hold upon him. His eyes flew open.

There was no wall ahead of him. He found himself in a new corridor, racing towards the top of a flight of stairs.

'Shit!' he cried – and tumbled down the stairs.

He managed to grab ahold of the banister, a rickety affair of pine, and save himself from a fall that might have broken his neck. No sooner had he steadied himself and the staircase vanished. He stood on even ground now, and just a foot before him a wall of stone bricked up the way. It reminded him of the ruined castle of Goodrich, the stonework was completely out of place in the more modern confines of the hall. Was he in a cellar of some kind?

Ahead. Go.

The wraith had not abandoned him at least. But he demanded the impossible. By some miracle Silas had made his way through a wooden wall, but one of stone? Silas laid his hands flat against the rough sandstone. It was warm as a hearth. Christ, what if he pushed through this to find himself in the middle of a parlour fire? The penalty for defying the house. His frustrations roared at once. He was tired of this chase.

'You will let me through,' Silas said, each word a concise, even snip of sound. 'Do you hear? I'll not stop until I find my way. So let me through.'

He shifted onto his heels, sending all his strength into his hands. The wall did not budge. Of course it didn't. He backed up and took a quick step towards it, shouldering the barrier. Fine dust sprinkled onto his boots.

'Oh, for god's sake! Let me bloody through.' The tingling at his fingertips flared, racing along his arms and scattering in his chest. It seemed to glance against his ribs, playing out a song against his bones. It was not a comfortable sensation at all, and it only served to flare his temper higher. The tingling moved deeper, creeping like worms into the soil, down into his marrow. A rhythm came upon his insides, a building melody being played out upon his heart, his spleen, his belly.

A song was played, not by the scythe, but by the scythe's master.

With renewed fervour, he eyed the wall. 'I am the pale Horseman. You. Will. Let. Me. Through.' Silas raised his arms and threw his weight against the barrier. His body hummed. There was a moment of resistance, a brief give, and Silas stood in an empty corridor.

202

The stones disappeared with no fuss or bother. No calamitous crash and tumble. They simply just *weren't*.

And he had made it so.

He quieted, and the melody withdrew from his innards, filtering into his fingertips once more, returning to the subtle tingle he was more accustomed to.

With his breath quick, Silas stared at the corridor ahead.

The quiet was the first thing he noticed. The hall seemed to hold its breath, all sounds of life left far behind. There was not a window to be seen. Nor any doorways save for one at the furthest end of the corridor. Its surface held a subtle shimmer of silver. Along the way, single candles flickered in their sconces against panels of wood so dark their rich brown appeared black where the candlelight could not reach. The wraith stood halfway between Silas and the door.

You found your way. Well done, ankou-of-the-pale-horse.

'Is he there?' Silas gestured at the door.

It swung open in answer. A faint grey-green light, like freshly picked sage, emanated from within. There was something else too, a denseness upon the air that was none too pleasant.

Tread carefully, ankou. There are some wounds even the angels cannot work their magick upon.

While Silas was still choosing his reply, the wraith left him. The bearded man, with his ghoulish ruined skull, pulled his furs about him and passed through the wall, causing the closest flame to shiver.

'Thank you,' Silas called.

Now he found himself in the position he loved the least. He was entirely alone. Behind him the corridor stretched itself so thin the candles set along its length could not glow bright enough to light the furthest reaches. A scuttling came from the shadows, some poor mouse trying to navigate the endless contortions of the hall. One by one the singular candles along the corridor shuddered and died in their sconces, dipping the passageway into a blackness Silas had not seen since the mines. He might have imagined himself underground if not for the rumbling presence of the storm outside, snarling like the skriker itself paced among the clouds.

Returning his attention to the room ahead, he crossed the threshold into the eerie marsh-green light within. The air inside was dank. It reminded him of that blasted barn with its crude boxing ring, and it was far too warm for a room with no fireplace. The walls held traces of the sage glow, with splotches of it more evident in some places, as though will-o'-the-wisps coated it like unfinished wallpaper. There were no windows to be seen.

His gaze fell upon the only piece of furniture in the room. A grandly carved four-poster bed set at the dead centre and taking up most of the usable space. Under the grey-green haze it was difficult to make out any colours except dark and light, but there were plenty of both upon the sheets. A great black stain rested at its centre, with fainter smudges fouling other sections of the once-white covering. Several flat pillows lay askew at the head of the bed, while a blanket was heaped in a tangled pile at the foot.

'Pitch?' he whispered. Shadows hugged the corners so deeply it was as though pieces of the room were missing. 'Are you here?'

The wraith must have made a mistake. This room was unoccupied. Despite the warmth, Silas shivered. He had followed the grotesque ghost blindly, never stopping to consider that the soul's intentions might not have been entirely good.

But the hall was a Sanctuary. Surely no harm would come to him beneath the nose of its master? His doubts crowded him, and he admonished himself for so foolishly leaving the bandalore in his room, beneath his pillow, like an infant hiding a tooth. Silas edged back towards the door, the oppressive atmosphere leaning against him.

A soft sound came from the far side of the bed. A whimper.

'Pitch?'

The noise returned, desperately quiet, but he recognised it still.

The daemon had not slept well while he recovered at Ottelie's cottage, and Silas had often heard him make just such a sound as he moved fitfully during the night.

Silas strode across the room. He had the strangest feeling that the walls were not fixed vertically and swayed in towards him in a barely-perceptible lean. The room was neither square nor rectangular, its angles seeming to shift in the corner of his eye. But whatever games the house might like to play with him, Silas had no time for it.

Pitch was here.

He was certain. His chest tightened as he approached the bed. The black markings there were a mismatch of shades, some reminiscent of blood.

'Pitch, answer me, are you...' Silas stared at the simply carved posts at the head of the bed. There was a silver chain attached to one of them. He traced its path across the pillows, over the width of the mattress, and to where it disappeared over the side of the bed. He sucked in his breath.

Ghostly-pale fingertips held a slack grip upon the slender chain.

He did not bother with making his way around the bed. It was at least as long as he was, and wide as four people side by side. Going around would take time Silas did not want to waste. He clamoured over it, and his hands pressed into the stains. Dampness clung to his palms.

'Oh god, what have they done?' he hissed.

He found the daemon a moment later.

Pitch lay on his side on the bare wooden floor, one arm raised to touch the chain. The air held a tinge of piss about it. Silas saw with horror that the chain was attached to a cuff, which was fastened about Pitch's wrist, an ugly, thick section of metal that made his delicate wrists seem all the more fragile. He was naked, his pale body aglow beneath the strange sage glow, except for where it was marked most unkindly by the same smudges of black that stained the sheets. His hair was a mess of sandy-tipped brown knots. Silas stumbled in his haste to clear the mattress, nearly finding himself with his face planted against the floorboards. He shifted onto his knees at Pitch's side, hands hovering. He dared not touch him until he knew what damage had been inflicted.

'Pitch, can you hear me?' Silas's heart knocked itself senseless against his ribs. 'What has happened here?'

He did not expect an answer, and did not receive one. He was not sure Pitch was even conscious. Silas touched at his hand where it fingered the chain. Pitch moaned and released what feeble hold he'd had.

'It's Silas. I'll not hurt you.' Any more than he had already been hurt. Silas's blood warmed. Christ almighty, Sybilla had known of this when they'd spoken. She had known that the daemon was tethered like a rabid dog in an airless, sealed room ripe with the scents of a man put under duress. Silas grabbed ahold of the chain, all his anger focusing him on this one object of torment. He wrenched against it, and the crunch of metal on wood came as the links bit into their bedpost anchor.

Once, twice, and three times he hauled his weight against it before realising his foolishness. This was a supernatural house built by a half-blood fae. Bess, if not Sybilla, would know how best how to restrain a daemon. Silas fought to clear his thoughts, his growing panic making him muddle-headed. He shifted along on his knees, seeking to place himself closer to Pitch's head. There was a stark white chamber pot set on the ground towards the corner of the room. The length of the chain would never have allowed Pitch to reach it, though wet splotches on the ground around it suggested he had at least tried.

Was it not enough to chain him, they must humiliate him too?

Silas's anger ran cold, and he was tempted to hurl the pot against the wall. He turned his attentions back to the stricken daemon. Pitch lay with his back to Silas, giving an unhindered view of the great tattoo there. The pitchfork-style design was smeared near unidentifiable by the mess of dark stains coating his skin, as though the tattoo itself had begun to melt, spreading out from his spine like a creeping tide of night.

Silas was nearly ill at the sight. Christ, this made no sense. They said they had treated him. Pitch should have been safe here. Bess had said that they had done all they could. It had been made to sound as though that involved care, not torture.

Silas leaned over him, wishing to see his face, to see some sign that there was life there. He gently pushed back the hair that had matted against Pitch's cheek. Silas noted the mottling of bruises upon his face, and the swirls of anger rose again. Any damage done at the farmhouse or the police station would have healed by now. These were fresh.

'Pitch, can you hear me? Please...say something.' It was the thunderstorm hugging Harvington Hall that answered with a distant, muffled crack of thunder.

Silas touched his fingers to Pitch's shoulder. The daemon was soaked with sweat.

'I'm going to lift you onto the bed, Pitch. Is that all right?'

He took a weakened groan as an affirmation. Silas worked his hands beneath Pitch's knees and shoulders and lifted. Bloody hell, he seemed even lighter than he had after Silas had carried him from Goodrich Castle, little more than an illusion. But illusions did not cry out as Pitch did.

The daemon showed the first signs of life, twisting weakly in Silas's grasp. 'No,' he gasped. 'I said no.'

Silas's gut twisted. Fuck, what had been done to him here? 'Pitch, it's all right...it's me.'

He laid Pitch down on his side, shifting the chain so that there was no danger of him lying upon it. Silas pulled away. The daemon rolled towards him, as though seeking the support once more, and fell onto his back. The moment he met the sheet, Pitch cried out, bucking his hips as though he'd touched broken glass. His limp cock slapped wetly at his thigh, and his arms were rigid at his sides, fingers clutching at the stained sheets. The chain slipped and slithered like a metallic snake.

'Shit,' Silas cried. 'I'm sorry...I'm sorry.'

He carefully pushed the daemon back up onto his side. Pitch's moans were pitiful. Never had he seen the daemon so vulnerable, not even after all that the Forest of Dean had thrown at them. Silas despised the sounds.

He moved to reach for one of the pillows to wedge at Pitch's back so he would not roll, when he glimpsed something strange within the smudged markings of the tattoo, a shifting of colour that caught his eye. 'What the hell have they done?'

Within the outline of the pitchfork much painstaking work had been done. Intricate, fine detail that must have been agonising so close to the bone. Hundreds of tiny welts, of varying length and designs, etched in a black very slightly paler than the onyx ink. Some were simple straight nicks, others were swirled into shapes that might be elaborate lettering, were he educated enough in such things to know.

Silas had had more than one opportunity to study the marking on Pitch's back, and he was certain these markings had been absent. That tattoo had been smooth and stark against alabaster skin. Now every inch of space within the design was filled to bursting with the intricate symbols. Little wonder he had been trapped down here for days, the tattoo ran the length of his body, from the crease of his arse to the base of his neck, spreading out into the two prongs that touched at his shoulder blades. And no small wonder Pitch was miserable, for his bindings made it clear the new work was not accepted willingly.

Silas's anger shifted into downright rage. He should march his way to Bess and demand she release him from this hellish room at once.

But doing that would mean leaving Pitch here alone. In this horrid room with not a window in sight, nor candle or fire to give it some life. Silas shook his head. That would not happen. *Could* not happen. He'd abandoned Pitch once already, and here was the result of it. Silas pressed his lips tight, cursing Bess and his sanctuary against the back of his teeth. It was a house of horrors. He rose to his feet and eyed the chain where it encircled the chunky wooden post on the further side of the bed. The post ran all the way up near to the ceiling, which meant simply lifting it clear to free him was not possible. Silas would need to break something, either the post itself or the chain.

He was a goddamned supernatural, was he not? He'd just walked through walls. These unimpressive chains would break.

Silas gathered the pillows around Pitch, who'd not yet made another sound. Once he was secured, Silas slipped from the bed and took hold of the links close to where they wrapped about the wood. He saw now they were bound so tightly there was no chance of wrestling the links up and over the height of the bedpost even if he'd wanted to. He wound a length around his palm so that his blood and ink-slicked hands could find purchase. The chain was deceptively fine in appearance, as though Bess had tied the daemon with something from his jewellery box. Silas hauled back. The tiny bones of his hand protested the strain; his shoulders screamed their protest. Though it may look like a woman's necklace, it had the strength of a ship's anchor chain. And big and furious as Silas was, it was not enough. Abandoning the chain, he grasped the bedpost instead. Fine. He would snap this post like a sapling then. But barely had he leaned his weight against it and the tremor sent through the bedframe had Pitch whimpering again.

'Shit, shit.' Silas hissed. Why the blazes had he not brought the bandalore with him? The blade would have made light work of the restraints. God, he wanted that blasted thing here now. He resettled his jacket, fighting to stay calm. Wild panic was getting him nowhere very quickly.

The bandalore. He needed it. He closed his eyes, shutting out the sight of the dishevelled daemon, closing himself off to the scent of anguish in the room.

He'd brought the scythe to his hand before, several times in fact. At The Atlas he'd done so twice, in the carriage and in Mr Ahari's office, then there had been the occasion at Lady Satine's farm. All of that had been when he'd barely known up from down.

He breathed in, then out again, slow and measured. Knowing for certain what it was he wanted.

'Come to me.'

The low, sweet note whistled beneath the distant rumble of the ever-present storm, and Silas nearly sobbed at the sound, for there was no other melody that caressed him that way. His fingers tingled. His heart soared with the tune of his own deadened blood.

A great thump resounded. Then another. The crash of a weight through timber. He stifled the urge to laugh like a madman. Christ, Bess wouldn't think much of this. Well Bess be damned. Silas didn't think much of his daemon being left in such a state. The melody guided him. Silas held out his hand, right beneath where he knew it needed to be.

The bandalore smashed through the ceiling and dropped into Silas's open, eager palm. The string slithered over his fingers, frantic in its race to find its place, looping in tight.

Silas swung.

The transformation was quicksilver. From wood to blade in a breath, the scythe burst from the discs, taking shape as a stiletto dagger, its deadly, narrow blade fixed in a handle of smoothed wood. Sparks flew, and the blade sliced through the bastard chain like it was a string of delicate pearls.

CHAPTER 23

'Pitch, can you hear me?'

The daemon muttered something low in reply. Not a groan at least, so there was that. The chain was broken, the scythe's song done, the bandalore deep in Silas's trouser pocket. But Pitch was still yet to open his eyes. Silas could not imagine a greater sight right now than a glimpse of clinquant emerald. He brushed back Pitch's sweat-drenched hair, easing it behind one ear so he could see his face. 'Please, open your eyes. We will leave here at once...do you hear me? There will be no more of this.'

A dangerously false promise. Did he imagine he could just pick up the naked daemon and carry him from Harvington Hall without hindrance? He could call on Lalassu, perhaps. The idea was discarded as soon as it came. Lalassu was the Lady's mount, her eyes and ears.

'Sickle.' The word brushed Pitch's lips.

Silas's pulse took an odd leap.

'Yes, yes. I'm right here.' Silas knelt by the bedside so he was nearer to level with the daemon's face.

Pitch's eyes were still shut fast. 'You should not be.' His voice was raspy, as though he'd shouted himself hoarse. Or screamed.

'I'm sure that's what they would prefer.' Silas's nerves frayed at their edges. He needed Pitch to open his eyes. 'Pitch, what has happened here? They told me they were treating you...but this is...'

Pitch sighed, a wheeze of breath that Silas could not decipher. The daemon shifted back, pressing back into the pillows.

'Fuck!' His cry was just short of a scream.

'Stop, stay still,' Silas pleaded.

'Get away, Silas, I do not want you here.' Pitch grabbed one of the pillows and threw it, rather pathetically, at Silas's head. He caught at the weak projectile easily, casting it down to the foot of the bed. When he looked up again he found Pitch staring at him. The daemon's eyes were dull, closer in shade to the curious grey-green light that illuminated the room, than the brilliant emerald he was used to. The sight filled Silas with dismay.

'Dear god man,' he said with some passion. 'You do not fare well. Tell me how I can help you.'

'Leave,' the daemon hissed, trying to levy himself up. His arm shook with the effort. 'Piss off and leave me.'

His body did not seem to be heeding instruction, the daemon was unsteady, sure to roll once more onto his back if he kept up his jerky movement. And Silas could not stand to hear his pained cry again.

'Wait, just wait, Pitch, for god's sake.'

Silas's next move happened in a blur. One moment he was on his knees on the floor, the next he was clambering onto the bed, boots and all. The mattress shuddered with his movement, and Pitch whimpered. Christ, that sound was all wrong from him. Silas moved with as much speed as he dared, never more regretful of his size.

'Just stay still,' Silas whispered. 'Lie down.'

He touched his fingers to Pitch's shoulder, coaxing him to abandon his unreasonable attempts to get out of the bed. The colour was washed from the daemon's already-pale skin, and there was no pinkness in his cheeks despite the sweat of a fever. The arm he braced against shook hard enough that Silas felt the trembling through the mattress.

'What are you doing?' How harsh Pitch's voice was, rubbed raw with distress.

'Trying to help you.' Was this helpful? He couldn't say for sure, but it felt right. 'Please lie down.'

Pitch stared down at him, lids heavy, as though keeping his eyes open was challenge enough, let alone finding his feet. Silas felt no relief when Pitch nodded and collapsed alongside him. Where was the vitriol, the snide retort? Belligerence was Pitch's modus operandi. But he was lustreless. The daemon breathed through parted lips, those twin swells of rose pink flesh the only piece of him that seemed untainted by his ordeal. But he breathed too hard for what meagre effort he'd made.

'Leave me alone, Silas.'

'I will not.' The room was fattened with despair and smelled too much of sweat and piss and surrender. 'I ask again, how can I help you?'

'You can stay away.'

'But I won't,' Silas said with conviction. 'I'll not do that again. I should not have let you go so easily at the farmhouse.'

What more he wanted to say caught at the back of his throat.

This intolerable being had sauntered into Silas's strange life and whittled away some of the loneliness and bewilderment and fear. When Pitch was around, with his barbed tongue and ridiculous appetites, Silas had little time left for self-pity and lamentations. Pitch made such things impossible, and foolish. It wasn't worth Silas's while to fall apart, for the daemon would mock and laugh at each piece as it fell, pointing out in no uncertain terms how pathetic it was to be so afraid of things he could not change. And he was right. In the daemon's company Silas found fortitude. In the daemon's company he was so often breathless and prone to foolish things. And he'd grown to like it very much.

Pitch's shoulder jerked, and a rough sound came from him. It took a moment to realise he had tried to laugh. 'You should have ridden as far from me as that nag would allow.'

They lay so close he could feel the daemon's breath against his neck.

'I was not so safe when I did that.' His words moved the hairs atop Pitch's head. 'So I'll stay here awhile I think.'

Pitch shifted, widening the small gap between them. He tilted his head back. 'You were not safe?' His gaze took in Silas's features, touching at his cheeks, his nose, and lingering upon his lips. Silas's skin seemed to tighten.

'All was well in the end. I'll tell you everything once you are up and about. It's been quite the few days.'

'Hasn't it just?' Pitch winced, as though tasting the words and finding them strange. 'I had hoped at times it was the very last of them.'

Christ, Pitch seemed so small and breakable just then, with little more substance than the unseasonable butterflies in Bess's gardens. Silas lifted his hand to touch the daemon, but he hesitated.

'I thought your injuries might have healed by now. But now I look at you...at this awful room...' He lowered his hand. 'They told me they were helping you. Was I lied to, Pitch? For if it so, I'll find us a way out of here. I promise you.'

Pitch lowered his eyelids, long lashes sweeping down like frail curtains. 'How brave you are, rushing us off like a knight to the rescue. But I do not need rescuing, Silas. I don't want help or healing, the sooner they bloody listen to a word I say, the better for all.'

Silas frowned, taking in the sparse room. Upon the floor, near to the door, was a scattering of food, bread and apple, as though a tray had been dropped. Or hurled there. A knot of uncertainty took hold in Silas's chest. Had he not been told that Pitch was refusing food ...and all else offered to him? Here now was evidence. Bloody hell, perhaps this was not the prison Silas imagined it to be.

'Pitch, you must stop this.' He stammered over the words, shaken at what he realised. The daemon was letting go, cutting himself adrift. 'I know you are troubled by old wounds, I know...I know you have a past that plagues you.' Green eyes settled on him at that, and shone more readily than before. 'But you must let them help you recover. We have things to do, you and I. The Order has much for us to accomplish yet, we cannot fail them.' He could not shift his eyes from Pitch's mouth, from the ruin and perfection of it. 'And I am quite terrible at hunting...you've seen it yourself. I can't go out on the road alone, it would be disastrous for all. Especially the rabbits...the hares, I mean.' He searched for sign of a smile, a sneer would have sufficed. Pitch closed his eyes once more. 'Pitch...Tobias, come on now. This is quite enough.'

His heart was thumping so hard Silas wondered if the daemon could hear it.

'They will find another nursemaid for you. They are not so rare, I'm sure.'

'No,' Silas snapped. 'They will not, for I won't allow it.' Christ almighty, he would not say goodbye. 'Pitch —.'

'Gods, just fuck off, you fool, before I hurt you.' A whisper, nothing more, seeping into the gloom with quiet resignation.

'Hurt me? I'd like to see you try it, right now. Come on then, do your worst.'

'That is not what I mean.'

'Then say what you mean.' Keep talking, throw insult, sneer and goad, but don't keep so still. Silas laid his hand on Pitch's shoulder, careful and sure not to go anywhere near where the tattoos lay, and yet still the daemon flinched.

'Why are you still here?' Pitch growled. 'Get out of my bed.'

Now there was a sign he was not in his right mind, if ever there were one. Silas watched the daemon drift from him, felt the creeping in of the darkness that lay in all the corners of this awful, quiet room. It was too damned quiet in here. He could only hear the drag of Pitch's breath through barely parted lips.

The blood churned through Silas's veins. His ears filled with the sound of his own pulse. Damn it, the bastard was not allowed to let go – and leave him all alone. He'd not allow it. And better yet, he could stop it. The realisation was the cool wash of clarity through despair.

Pitch was many things, incubus among them. And Silas knew now what such a creature craved. Touch, closeness, and rather a bit more but he'd not think too deeply on that. The point was, Silas could breathe life back into the shell Pitch had become.

He shifted himself with care, edging down so that he drew more even with the daemon.

'You do not get to have your way today, Tobias.'

Silas pushed onto his elbow and slid the fingers of his free hand into Pitch's hair, tangling them in damp gold-flecked curls. He cradled the back of Pitch's neck, holding him steady. Feeling him tense.

'What are you doing?'

Silas leaned in and gave his answer, before he thought better of it. His lips found the pillowy swell of the daemon's mouth. Pitch inhaled sharply, flinching. For a terrible moment Silas thought he would pull away, but all at once he yielded, straining up to run his tongue at Silas's bottom lip. They crashed together, a little cumbersome, their angle against one another made awkward by the way they lay, with Silas looming and Pitch kept on his side so there was no fear of pressure at his back. But Silas could not have cared less if they were upside down. His nerves crackled and his lips parted wider. Taking more. Pitch, sent his tongue deeper, following the ankou where he led. The daemon tasted of the same bitter sweetness Silas remembered from their encounter at Lady Satine's farmhouse, like an apple pie whose chef had added a dash too much cinnamon. It was not unpleasant. He had recoiled from the intimacy that day, but not now. Now Silas drank it in, melting into the unthinkable delicacy of Pitch's mouth. A soft moan came from one of them, maybe both, and Silas's prick ached with life, hard and upright.

The daemon clutched at Silas's neck, urging him down, drinking him in. Pitch, a man of flesh and blood and want in that moment, was coming alive again.

Taking what he needed.

And Silas offered what he could, willingly.

If there was any enchantment here, he couldn't give a damn.

Without breaking from the kiss, Pitch shifted his gracile figure, finding his way closer, naked and glorious. A hardness dug at Silas's belly. The press of the daemon's cock left him light-headed, choked with need. Silas's own arousal strained against fabric. Pitch's fingers glanced at his hip, and Silas shuddered. Christ, he was slipping, all sensibility tumbling away as they worked their lips against one another, tongues exploring wet heat.

Silas was afire with a flame he had no desire to escape. His hand slipped down to caress the back of Pitch's neck. He hungered to run his fingers along every inch of the man but he kept his exploration careful, conscious of the daemon's pains.

Pitch had no such hesitancy and explored Silas well enough for the both of them, fingers clutching, caressing, seeking. Desperate. They gasped into one another. The furnace at Silas's core would take an ocean of ice to douse. He was mad for air, but the thought of pulling away was unbearable. He let his fingers move cautiously, staying clear of the painful workings along Pitch's spine, moving over skin that would rival the finest velvets. Good god, the feel of this man was making it hard to breath. A moan escaped him, a small cry of want. He traced his fingertips over the faint rise of ribs, and the daemon shivered, releasing a fluttery cry that had Silas's balls tightening and his pulse tripping. He travelled lower to the curving dip of a narrow waist and along the jut of hip. Pitch was lean, too much so. He'd deprived himself, and it showed. But Christ almighty he was enticing, maddening with beauty. The daemon strained against him, ravenous, urgent, needing more, no longer satisfied to fade away. He slipped his hand beneath Silas's clothes and layers, digging his nails into his bare chest, finding anchorage. Silas's breath stuttered, he clutched at Pitch's hair like it were the only thing keeping him from being submerged. Perhaps it was.

The moment was sublime, and it was terrifying.

God, he ached to go further. To run fingers over the most intimate of places upon Pitch's body. What ecstasy must await there. But Christ, what a precipice this was. Beyond these beautiful curves lay something perilous, a path with no way back. Silas had known pleasure when he'd lain with Charlie, of course he had, but it had not been like this. So mixed with wild urges that sought to claim him, stirring his body in ways that frightened him. He could imagine giving away *everything* to feel this creature at his fingertips, to listen to the hungry sounds he made.

The daemon nipped at his chin and sealed Silas's fate with three words. 'Please don't stop.'

Silas swallowed, throat tight with desire. He stepped up to the precipice. His fingers took him over the edge, slipping down to caress the shallow valley between Pitch's arse cheeks, finding flesh of a new order of softness. The daemon...the man... swayed into him, groaning at his touch, as though someone like Silas were capable of driving someone like Tobias Astaroth mad with pleasure. It was intoxicating.

Silas cupped the daemon's arse, pulling him in, shivering as their cocks brushed against one another, separated only by a fine layer of cloth. A sigh escaped him as his hips rocked against solid desire. Pitch was panting into him, alive and full of need. He was vibrant again, and it was going to bring Silas undone. He pressed his fingertips into soft mounds of flesh. He'd not expected the silkiness, the perfect smoothness of Pitch's skin. The daemon had a brittleness to him that defied such fineness. He should not be so utterly mesmerising to touch.

Silas sucked at Pitch's lip, desperate to remain gentle despite the burn of arousal that was chewing him up like a wild beast. Good god, he wanted to slam himself against the man, he wanted to disappear inside him, to please Pitch until he was pushed so far beyond the hurts of his past he could not feel them. Silas kissed him with trembling restraint, pressing his lips to sharp cheeks and chin, and the creases at the edge of those undeniable eyes. The daemon writhed against him, his chest rumbling with growled pleasure. The noises sent heat racing into the base of Silas's spine and had his cock throbbing, leaking with tight hunger.

The encounter had slipped from his control, sliding far beyond where he had sought to go. Reason whispered at him, trying to make itself heard over the din of carnal pleasure.

This is madness. A moment you will regret.

But he already knew. And had gone too far to care.

CHAPTER 24

P itch had been doing very well with his misery, nursing it like a newborn that mewled and whined and ate at him. He'd starved himself of all the right things, the pleasures, the honeyed tang of offerings that Sybilla waved at him, and the handsome and pretty faces that the master of the house lined up like tin soldiers, sending them to do battle in his bed, to fight their way between his legs and drag him from his stupor.

Give him life.

He'd sent them all running, clutching at clothes and dignity. He'd not take what they offered. The Lady Satine may have subdued the agony of the halo's unhealed wounds, but she could not force his daemonic parts to heal. He did not wish to regain his faculties again. Fuck Satty and whatever crusade she would have him on. He'd not do it. And they should be fucking grateful for his protest. For even as he went unfed, denying an incubus' most basic needs, the restless animal within him paced in its cage, most unhappy with his decline. With each denial he made, each refusal to suck and feast and fornicate, he felt it roll and twist and threaten and it took more strength than he had some days to coax it to lie quietly with him, and abandon its revolt.

But then, after many long, lonely hours in a room that boxed him in as well as any coffin, even the wild thing lost its bite. Skulking down into the pit it dwelt in and curling in on itself, leaving him be. It seemed to Pitch that blessed, eternal nothingness was in sight. Waving its hands at a vile prince, calling him on.

He was so weakened, using his eyelids was a chore. Now, surely, those who tried to command him could see what a terrible guardian he made, what a hindrance to their cause. Now, *surely*, Satty would realise how foolish her attempts to bridle him were and he'd be set loose. The ankou would no longer be burdened with him. And if a fallen prince could not go back to the abaddon then he might find a hiding place here where he could wallow for a century or two. Hide himself away with his cursed memories and angel-sized mistakes.

Make himself a legend perhaps. A new monstrous myth the humans could frighten themselves with, a shadow in the depths of a cave, a creature of the moors, ever feeding their stories, but keeping his claws to himself.

A perfectly lovely plan.

Until this.

This moment when a cumbersome, meat-headed dolt blustered in and decided to play hero. Cradling a daemon and his misery, and breaking chains that should have stayed where they were.

The kiss was slightly cumbersome, wholly unexpected, and downright inconvenient.

Because now Pitch was ravenous.

He was clinging to the ankou like moss to a tree, burrowing into the mass of a man that loomed over him. Silas's tongue was urgent but cautious. He tasted like the salt of the earth and smelled like wet sandstone and slate. Pitch did not mind it at all. Silas's trimmed beard was coarse, scraping Pitch's chin as their mouths worked against one another. His thick fingers were rough-skinned, and clumsy with the man's nervousness, but by all the gods and their arseholes, it felt good. Better than good. Pitch could see straight for the first time in days. Maybe longer than that. Silas ran his hands along Pitch's body, tracing the curves, making a daemon shiver and groan, treating him as though he were a fragile sculpture of glass. That part unsettled Pitch the most, the fucking gentleness. He reached for Silas's hand where he'd paused, his broad palm covering Pitch's hip. And then he did something rather terrible.

Pitch begged.

'Please don't stop,' he whispered.

219

Silas obliged with breathtaking speed. His fingers found purchase on Pitch's arse and rocked their bodies closer. Their cocks brushed, separated by the unfortunate barrier of Silas's trousers. It was exquisite agony, making Pitch whimper. They were both rigid, the ankou every bit as swept up as the daemon, and they crashed against one another. Pitch did, at least. Thrusting and colliding into the hardness of the man, ignoring the pangs at his back. Silas was more cautious with his bulk and vigour, holding Pitch's weight, gripping tighter when rising desires nearly set him on his back again. The man's strength was impressive, balancing Pitch in his hold as though the daemon were not flesh and bone, but made of feathers, or the bubbles in champagne. He trembled, certainly, but it was not Pitch's weight that caused *that* strain. Silas hissed, leaving the collision of lips and tongues a moment.

'Christ, this is...' He couldn't seem to find more to say, but he was not returning his mouth to where it ought to be.

Pitch clung more tightly to the ankou's undershirt, and something unkindly near to desperation loosed his tongue.

'Do you not want me?'

Gods, how plaintive he sounded.

'I...I want you to be well.' Silas's words were so dented by desire they barely formed.

'Why?' He'd not intended to ask that question. Pitch edged his face away, so that he was not breathing into Silas's mouth as before.

'That is a terrible thing to ask.'

'I am a terrible creature.'

The ankou made a plaintive sound, his face creasing as though in pain. But thank the gods, he returned to his work. His fingers splayed to take handfuls of pliable flesh. With hands so broad Silas could be greedy, coveting an entire arse cheek, digging fingers into firm, giving skin. An adorable whimper came from the man, his eyes squeezed shut as though he were imagining this all a dream. As well he might. Pitch was no fool. He knew Silas struggled with many aspects of his reborn life. His cock hardening for a foul daemon would lie among them. And hard it indeed was. How that impressive member had not torn a hole in the man's trousers yet he did not know.

Pitch sighed into Silas's parted lips, relishing the taste of earthy things, of iron and cut flowers and loam. Gods, death had a pleasing tang.

Silas played his fingers along Pitch's warm crease, tentative but eager. Drifting down agonisingly close to the daemon's clenched balls, only to deprive him as he ran his fingers away again.

'Oh, fuck,' Pitch gasped, throwing his head back, leaving the warmth of the ankou's mouth.

'I'm sorry, did I — '

'Stop talking, keep going.' Pitch planted his palms against the side of Silas's face, capturing him, and leading him back to the kiss.

As Silas caressed him with infuriating carefulness, Pitch worked his hips against the man's belly, grinding their cocks hard against one another. The material caused a friction that was making Pitch's eyes water and his prick leak. Fuck, the ankou was barely touching him, fingers feather-light, but it was glorious. He was being filled without even spreading his legs.

Silas groaned, and took his precious lips away, moving to explore every inch of Pitch's face. Fluttering like a butterfly against eyelids, and whispering over cheekbones. He was as hungry as Pitch, devouring him, running his tongue along the length of his neck, panting like a horse ridden too hard. Fuck, what Pitch wouldn't do to ride this particular horse. But not yet, not now. Any pause to unbutton and free Silas's cock would mean stopping this ceaseless, perfect rhythm. They rocked into one another, the slight against the solid. Delicacy against the substantial. Silas loomed, large and wanting, gentle and considerate.

Gods, Pitch was twisting into so many desirous knots he could barely stand it. The ungainly, onerous ankou was turning him inside out and Silas had not even removed his coat or boots.

He tilted his arse, grabbing at Silas's hand and urging the ankou's fingers deeper. Down into the heat of the crevice between Pitch's cheeks. Deep enough to touch at the tight swirl of muscle there. They groaned in unison. Silas was shaking. Pitch's vision was getting hazy, a low burn at the base of his spine. Soon, far too soon, he was going to tumble over the brink.

If this was what happened when an incubus starved themselves, perhaps he should have deprived himself a long time ago. Pitch knew carnal pleasure well, he'd been a good friend to desire but this...this appetite...startled him. It widened his ribs so he might breathe, and sang at the place where the wild thing lay, lulling the beast deeper down into its pit. The heat that ran through him crept the length of his tormented spine, numbing the ache there. The agonies were sent racing away. He could move without flinching, he was slack and heedless and free. The humans imagined there was a heaven. Well, here he had found it, at the tip of a deadman's fingertips.

His incubus blood ran thick with relief.

All manner of sounds left Pitch, each one of them ripe with desire. He lifted his leg and settled it over Silas's thigh, securing himself there. Pitch was stretched wide. Cool air brushed at his taint and he shivered. Silas wasted no time in making his way to where Pitch was open, vulnerable to pleasure. His fingers skimmed again across a tight entrance, lingering for a heartbeat at that knot of muscle before moving on, searching deeper between the daemon's legs. He caressed Pitch's balls as though the taut skin was a glove upon a lady's hand.

Pitch choked on his bliss. His stomach was damp, his straining cock dribbling and fit to burst. Damn it, he'd not hold out much longer, but he did not wish for this intolerable carefulness to end. Being treated as though he were something precious. Deserving of gentle treatment.

The ankou was an imbecile to think so. But thank the gods for stupidity.

Silas played with Pitch's tight balls, rolling the hardened centres about in his fingertips. Fuck. Pitch cried out, arching his back. There was no pain. Only arousal, burning away the wretchedness.

Heat flooded him. He was filling to the absolute brim, the ankou working him into a frenzy with his ludicrously soft touch. Pitch ground his teeth. What a contrast this was to the angel's rough service. A bump and grind that left him raw, bruised and marked. He'd not complained, he'd relished the time that Seraphiel gave him. And there was nothing wrong with being thrown against a wall and fucked till you thought you'd split in half. But gods, this...this was tearing him apart in an entirely different way.

Pitch stifled a fresh cry, squeezing his eyes shut. He had not thought on Raph with anything but misery for a long time. He clutched at Silas's burly, muscled arm and held on for dear life. They grunted and moaned, sinking deeper into the roar of abandon. Silas murmured into Pitch's neck, words of heated desire that were foolish and desperately intimate.

'You are beautiful.'

The idiot was so wrong. Pitch was murderous, tormented and despised. But he wanted more.

'Say it again.'

'Beautiful.' Silas had his jaw clenched, suffocating the word. His broad chest rose in an uneven rhythm with Pitch's own, his eyelids heavy and allowing just a hint of the light brown of his eyes to shine through. The bastard smiled, his deviant hand still at work down below. He tilted his head to press his lips to Pitch's collarbone. His tongue slid along the curve of the delicate bone there, and ignited a brand new wave of shudders. The ankou had found a sweet spot, a tender place that made Pitch writhe. The angel had been first to discover it. Seraphiel, hidden beneath the layers of the lieutenant's body, concealed in his borrowed mortal disguise, had driven Pitch near feral with his attentions to that sensitive piece of flesh.

Pitch's rhythm faltered. Silas lifted his head, eyes blown wide with raw desire.

'Is it too much?' he whispered.

The man was going to destroy him with his unsettling concerns.

'Of course not.'

But Silas was not so easily fooled, and he shifted his attentions away from the tender place, freeing Pitch once more. The daemon threw himself back into the dance, breathing in the humus of the man who glanced a kiss against his forehead, and ran a finger along the velvet corridor deep between Pitch's legs. White heat tore up the length of Pitch's shaft.

'Fuck,' he cried. 'Gods.'

Silas's own cry, coming from a place deep and guttural, plummeted Pitch off his precarious edge. He rocked wildly against the solidity of the ankou as the wave soared through him and threw him like a seal upon the rocks, smashing him down into his climax. A scream came from a distance. Pitch's body shuddered and jarred, riding the enormous waves that tore through him. Pitch threw back his head, his jaw clenched tight, eyes shut fast as he spent himself in exquisite agonising bursts of warmth and wetness. He held on and Silas did the same. Pitch clutched at thick muscle and fine hair and did not relax his hold upon Silas's chest even as he shuddered into the final slackening twitches of release.

He was vaguely aware of Silas's hand moving from his arse, and finding its way to the small of his back. Even though he must have brushed at the tattoo the touch was painless, save for the delicious way it made Pitch's skin prickle. The ankou was shaking, his breath coming in short, stuttered bursts against Pitch's hair.

Blinking his eyes open, still dizzy and dazed with release, Pitch was surprised to find the room bright. That deplorable glaucous haze was gone, replaced by what he might assume was daylight if he were so inclined to study it. He was not. His head was too heavy to lift. He was nestled in against the ankou like a babe at the breast, his leg still cinched over Silas's thigh. His world warm and damp and heady with cum. Perfect.

The ankou's ribs heaved, drawing Pitch's eye down. He'd made a mess of them both. His own stomach was glistening, and his spill stained Silas's vest, but the dark spread on the ankou's trousers declared that he had enjoyed this encounter every bit as much. Pitch traced a finger through the sticky heat on Silas's clothing, making his way down to the man's waist.

Silas's breath hitched, his stomach clenching.

'I believe you will need to change your trousers.' Pitch's laughter jumped from him. He braced, certain pain would follow. None came. His slid his leg free from Silas's thigh, and found he could make the move easily, without discomfort.

Silas slumped onto his back, throwing an arm overhead. He was quiet for too long, and Pitch propped himself up on an elbow to regard him. The ankou's cheeks were flushed bright pink, and sweat coated his brow and imprisoned his dark strands. His pupils were still blown wide, smothering the light brown shade of his irises. The poor man appeared in some state of shock, but he couldn't seem to drag his gaze from Pitch's lips.

'That was...I...that was...' Whatever it had been he seemed incapable of operating his tongue well enough to describe it. Silas grunted, abandoning his attempt to articulate.

'That was something indeed.'

Pitch inhaled. The heady waft of sweat and spend perfumed the air, and the expansion of his lungs caused no displeasure. He settled back down beside Silas, desiring to stay where it was warm. He shifted his shoulders, and stretched his legs, testing his limits. For the first time in what felt like an age he was as near to whole as he could be. His thoughts were clear, his doldrums escaped, and his restless centre uncharacteristically pacific.

Damn it. Such pleasure was not what he'd sought. Pitch settled onto his back, his full weight upon the scars and violent wound it bore. Silas twisted sharply to halt him, muttering about taking care and not doing any harm.

Pitch pressed him away. 'Stop your fussing. I am fine, I feel quite well.'

And it was true. Not a murmur came from injuries new or old. He cursed the gods. Recovery was not what he had intended, certainly not what he'd wanted, but here it was. By Lucifer's balls, he was his own worst enemy. He'd made himself too vulnerable by denying himself so long. The ankou had caught him off guard, taking Pitch's protest apart with heedful touches and whispered nonsense.

He sighed.

In a while he would search again for a way to separate the lady's riders, but he needed repose first. For now Pitch would relish the thrum of release, and enjoy the blissful tiredness of completion, with the ankou's solid presence at his side.

All the rest could wait.

CHAPTER 25

S ilas struggled to catch his breath. His body hummed and rattled with the lingering burn of his climax. The daemon lay beside him, eyes closed, flat on his back, his belly and chest glistening with the spoils of their rutting. Pitch's cock, as lovely as the man it was attached to, was still lazily stiff between legs spread wide. His knee rested against Silas's thigh, as though them lying here together were the most natural thing in the world. The ankou turned his gaze to the ceiling.

Christ all-fucking-mighty. What had he just done? And how in heaven's name could such a thing have felt so exquisite? Shit, he'd not even removed his clothes, though he'd do so very soon. Pitch was absolutely right about the need for fresh trousers. Silas had come so hard he'd seen stars. He touched at his lips, tender from all the attention they had received.

The subtle kiss he'd intended to offer had morphed into something else entirely. He'd sought to aid the incubus, that was all. Not this...what in god's name was this, anyway? He'd not stepped off that bloody precipice, he'd swan-dived off it. Silas closed his eyes. By all that was holy, please let it have been a sordid dream. He winced. His clothes were soaked with the daemon's seed, his own drawers were ruined, and his fingertips tingled with the memory of the velvet luxury that was Pitch's skin.

Dreamlike, perhaps. But no illusion.

Pitch shifted, rolling onto his side and positioning himself so that his arse pressed against Silas's hip. The ankou bit his lip till his eyes watered, but that did not deter the treacherous lump between his legs from stirring.

Sweet lord, he needed to get out of here.

'Everything all right, Sickle?' Pitch asked with undisguised bemusement. Beyond the ebon markings that seeped from the reworked tattoo, he was pale as marble, and as smooth skinned. He'd not be out of place among the works of the finest galleries.

'Everything is fine.' At least, it would be when he could wipe the sight of Pitch's climax from his mind. Of how the throes of release had tightened his sharp lines and made fine veins bulge along his neck, the way he had clung to Silas as though the ankou were what kept him from being lost entirely. 'And you...did that...do you feel any better?' His voice cracked as though he were a pubescent lad.

Christ, would death be such a bad thing right now?

He must gather his senses and his dignity and get out of here.

'I feel quite well. You were surprisingly adept. Dead men appear to suit me.' Pitch breathed deep, his whole body moving, his arse pressing hard against Silas.

Damn it, get up. With Pitch recovered, he was certain to make this indiscretion intolerable. Their intimacy would be no unearthly moment for the likes of him. Unravelling a man, as he had done with Silas, was likely as common to the voracious daemon as breathing.

Get out of here, fool.

But Silas could not bring himself to heed his own warning. He could not shift so much as his big toe. The toe still in its boot, for Silas had jumped into bed with the daemon so quickly he'd not bothered to discard his footwear. His eyes strayed, taking in the svelte figure at his side. Silas's mind was a vicious traitor, recalling how Pitch had responded to his touch, how he'd gasped for more. His cock twitched.

Brandy. Bloody hell, he needed all the brandy in Bess's cellar.

The soft snore startled him. Silas held still.

There it came again, low and subtle. Delicate even. But unmistakable.

'Pitch?'

The tempered breathing continued uninterrupted. The daemon was snoring. Christ. Their encounter had put Pitch to sleep? While Silas tried to decide if that was insult or compliment, a flash of lightning filled the room with white light. Lightning...in a room with no windows.

With a frown, Silas lifted his chin. 'Oh,' he breathed.

The room was utterly transformed. No longer was it the bleak, dark space the lost soul had led him to. Two rectangular windows had appeared where there had been none before. Their white panelling matched that of the French doors which stood between them, opening out onto a small kitchen garden. Silas stared, astonished by the appearance of the view. A light rain fell, sprinkling down upon herbs and vegetables that glistened in a dying light which spoke of evening's approach. For all the wandering about he had done, at times feeling as though he were headed for the centre of the world as he traversed the halls and stairs, he had ended up nowhere more surprising than the ground floor.

The room itself was smaller than he'd imagined. Perhaps the shadows had widened it, given it the sense of being an endless abyss of darkness. The walls were framed in dark lengths of timber with whitewashed stone between. He glanced at the place where the bandalore had made its entrance. The ceiling was complete, unhindered by any blasted hole. Wonderful. He could slip away, and there would be no trace at all he'd ever been here.

Silas pressed himself up to sitting. Pitch moved suddenly, his arm reaching back, searching, finding Silas's knee.

'Where you...going...' he mumbled, his grip firm.

The racing pulse Silas had only just managed to quieten thundered again now. Did Pitch not wish him to leave? The idea made his skin prickle. But he could not stay here, no matter how the idea called to him.

'You should rest,' Silas replied. 'I'll not be far away.'

'Bring some sweetmeats, will you? And a tub... water as hot as you can make it.'

So, a footman was what the daemon sought, then. Silas should have been irritated at being ordered about so, but a tiny smile worked at his lips. That Pitch was now capable of demanding anything at all made him ridiculously pleased.

'I'll have Bess tend to it for you.'

'Hmph.' Pitch resettled, curling up amongst the rumpled, stained sheets, in a way that was making Silas's pulse leap.

He moved his bulk with slow caution to the edge of the bed, careful not to bounce Pitch about too much. Christ, the mass of this body was irksome at times. He was the veritable bull in the china shop.

His boots touched the floor, and Silas was on his feet. The squelchy dampness at his crotch was horribly uncomfortable, and just thinking on the cause scrambled his thoughts so badly he shook himself. Silas's gaze flitted to the daemon, and at once his mood darkened as he took in Pitch's back, with the multitudes of new markings along the inkwork. It was intricate needlework, the symbols so tiny and crowded together. He could not imagine how excruciating the process must have been.

He did not want to imagine it.

He tugged at the waist of his trousers. The heat had left his spend now, and a chill clung to his nethers. A change of drawers, then brandy. Much brandy. Mortification could come later, when he was good and drunk.

He moved to grab one of the pillows, the ones Pitch had not thrown across the room, and caught sight of the chain that had bound Pitch. Whatever reason Sybilla had for restraining Pitch like this, Silas suspected she had no need of it now. The daemon lay soft and subtle, his breathing even, though raspy.

He was fast asleep, and terribly charming for it.

Silas reached for the thin blanket bundled at the foot of the bed. He drew it up and over the daemon, whose eyelids fluttered with whatever visions sleep brought him. Silas moved with utmost care so as not to wake him. He tucked it about his shoulders, keeping it light about the daemon's back. He paused, leaning over the sleeping man. Colour had returned to his cheeks with rosy pinkness. His lips, those beguiling, pillowy swells, were pursed as he snored softly. His pert nose, with its tiny upturn, flared at the nostrils as he breathed. Damn it, he was breathtaking.

'Silas?'

'Shit!' Silas flew back, nearly tripping over himself in his haste.

He spun around to face the speaker. Bess stood just inside the doorway, a lacy shawl wrapped about wide shoulders fitted in lavender faille, rouge heavy upon his cheeks and lips, and his natural silver-grey hair tied back in a stubby ponytail.

'Bess...I was just...we...he seems to have improved.'

'As does this room.' Bess's gaze darted swiftly as a wren, moving from the windows to the broken chain to Pitch, and then to Silas. The blood drained from Silas's face. He felt quite unwell. 'Goodness, whatever did you say to him to bring him to his senses so well?' Did the man just wink at Silas? Oh dear god, let it not be so. 'He's not slept so peacefully since he arrived here, even with the draughts.'

'I didn't say anything in particular.'

'No. I'm sure you didn't *say* anything at all.' The silver in his grey eyes shone as they traced a path down Silas's front.

Bloody hell. Silas closed his jacket, layering one side over the other so he was sure all the nasty stains upon his front were covered. But the flutter of Bess's lip told him he was too late for such modesty. The man's amusement irritated him no end. It was all very well to snicker, but Bess had much to account for.

Silas stepped over to him, so as not to disturb Pitch. 'Can you explain to me why he was chained here like an animal? Were you stopping me from seeing him because he was unwell, or to prevent me seeing how he was treated?'

Bess sighed. 'I told Syb we should have removed that chain before now. It looks terribly savage. But there was need of it to begin with, I assure you. To protect him as much as us. Pain causes one to lash out in unpredictable ways. When he did not seek to harm us, he sought to harm himself. You saw that when you found him huddled on the floor, all but given over to his misery.'

A curl of trepidation ran through him. Silas had seen that, yes. But how had Bess?

'You knew when I arrived?' His tongue limped over the words.

'It is my Sanctuary, my dear, of course I did,' Bess said, without apology. 'And I must say, the Hall is quite upset with you. Finding your way despite her best efforts to the contrary. Her pathways are so rarely overcome by those without a lick of fae blood in their veins.'

Silas said nothing of the wraith. He'd not betray the spirit and risk losing his aid in the future.

Bess narrowed his eyes. 'Not only did you find your way, you freed your daemon, too. Most impressive, I must say.'

'That really must stop he is not *my* daemon.' His thoughts were in turmoil, thinking over all Bess had seen. His cheeks blazed with the shame of it.

'Don't fret. I barely saw a thing.' Bess laughed quietly. 'I'm no voyeur. Not mostly. I turned a blind eye when I saw where things were headed, but I did see you storm in here, no doubt cursing the lady and Sybilla and I a thousand times for what must seem our dreadful treatment of Mr Astaroth. It is not as it appears, Silas, I must assure you. His mood made this room what it was, and the festering sore it became needed to be isolated from the rest, for fear of the infection spreading. He made a prison for himself...at least his unhappiness and his soreness did so. And it was not us who kept you from him – it was Tobias who did that. He would not see you, not even after...well, after we had done what we could to set him well. He would not agree to any visitors, but most especially not you. So we left him be to wallow. For it was all he was agreeable to.'

Silas stared at the rouge-cheeked man. 'There are some wounds even the angels cannot work their magick upon,' he said softly.

Bess cocked his head, a strand of silver brushing his cheek. 'Who told you that?'

'I don't recall...Sybilla perhaps, or I dreamed it.' He brushed the enquiry aside. 'I've not slept well in a while.'

Bess regarded him with some scrutiny but seemed to decide against pushing further.

'Our friend here has been troubled sleeping too, until now. Shall we leave him to rest?' Bess waved his free hand towards the bed. A fur, a thick luxurious blanket of snow white, appeared over Pitch's sleeping form, emerging from the air like a descending cloud. Bess fluttered his fingers, and the fur drifted down to a perfectly gentle rest, tucking itself in around Pitch's slender legs, settling about his shoulders. A far more decent covering than the threadbare blanket Silas had set on him. A harsh snap of sound drew his attention to the far side of the room. A fireplace had appeared in the wall, framed with a wood mantel embellished with carvings of oak leaves and rowan berries. Cheerful orange flames burst to life behind a copper fire screen. 'There. More pleasant, wouldn't you say? I'll have that tub arranged for him shortly. I dare say he needs a thorough scrubbing. And the sweetmeats of course. I'll have Cook get on that right away.'

Silas flinched. 'I thought you said you were no voyeur?'

'And I am not.' Bess appeared mildly insulted. 'The Hall let me know when you were done. I was only privy to your pillow talk after.'

That was not soothing in the least.

They stepped out into the corridor, and Bess pulled the door shut behind them with a satisfied sigh. 'Sybilla will be so pleased at the news. She was worried for our Mr Astaroth, despite what she might say.'

He knew full well of her concerns, and she'd warned Silas not to breathe a word of their conversation, to protect Pitch. He'd no sooner put the daemon at risk than he would admit he was loath to leave his bed, but he'd seen the black marking on Bess's hand, the first time they'd met. The same that had stained Sybilla's hair for a while. Bess had undoubtedly tended Pitch on his sickbed. All he wished to know was why they had marked him so. Silas could easily enquire a little without giving away all Sybilla had told him in confidence.

'Bess, I wonder...what can you tell me of what was done to him here? I saw that there were an awful number of new marks made upon him...does that tattoo have something to do with the injuries he received on the – ' Bloody hell, he was terrible at secret keeping. The poor lovely bastard was doomed.

'The Hellfield?' Bess linked his arm through Silas's own, able to do so with ease thanks to his fortunate height. 'Don't look so aghast, you've not betrayed any confidences. I know Sybilla has told you something about your daemon's past.' Silas nodded, saying nothing in the hope Bess would reveal more. 'You have done us a favour and brought Mr Astaroth back to life...goodness, that is quite the twist, isn't it? An ankou doing the life-bringing.' Bess laughed, throaty and pleasant, but Silas was not quite so amused.

He stared ahead, his jaw tight.

Pulling at his lace shawl, Bess grew serious. 'Apologies. You must be quite overwhelmed by all that is going on, with Tobias and everything else.' Silas stayed quiet. The answer seemed obvious. 'The markings he has are no ordinary ink, as I'm sure you have realised. The tattoo keeps his true wound subdued...and hidden...a thankful thing for it is not pleasant to look upon. The mark also keeps the pain at bay. But what happened to you poor fellows in the Forest of Dean, when Tobias was forced to use his flame, eroded the markings in a way that was unexpected. He was quite beside himself with pain when you parted company, so don't take anything he might have said or done to you to heart. He was suffering.'

Silas stared at her, sick to his empty stomach. 'Why does an old injury still cause him so much anguish? Will it heal fully now, with the new markings?'

Bess considered his words over several slow paces. 'No, my dear. I'm afraid that is quite impossible with what was done to him. But it can be managed, and is being managed well.' He squeezed Silas's arm, a motion meant to reassure, no doubt. It did no such thing. 'And now that you have helped him satisfy his needs, and dragged him from his melancholy, I dare say it won't be long before the two of you are back upon the road, and dealing admirably with whatever it is that awaits you out there.'

CHAPTER 26

The journey back to his room was astonishingly easy. The corridor beyond Pitch's room led right to the main foyer of the house, where Bess bid him a farewell. From there it was a simple matter of travelling the flights of stairs to reach his room. Thankfully he encountered no one else on his travels. He'd feared a run-in with Tyvain, which would have been intolerable given his state and mood. Perhaps the hall was not so upset with him now for running her gauntlet.

The moment his door closed behind him, Silas tugged off his soiled clothes, jacket, vest, shirt, down to his drawers which were most ruined of all. A dreadful damp reminder of events.

A desperate time had called for a desperate measure. That was all. That was absolutely all.

Silas threw off his sodden drawers. His cock hung heavy, flaccid, as though it had not so recently tried to poke a hole through his trousers.

The evidence of his debauchery discarded, he stepped up to the washbasin and scooped his hands into the water. Icy cold. Just as well, it was exactly what he needed. Did the bloody house and its mysterious house staff know it all too well?

Silas splashed the frigid liquid against his warm cheeks, gasping at the shock of it. He rubbed at his face, trying to rid his nostrils of the lingering scent of Pitch and his release. He took another handful of water and applied it again harshly. Gooseflesh stood at stark attention all along his arms. The water was bloody cold but it wasn't settling his restless mind as he'd hoped. He snatched up a sky-blue washcloth that had been laid out for him and rubbed at his belly, moving down to his traitorous cock. He would remove all evidence of the encounter if it meant scrubbing himself raw. Christ. That was a terrible idea. The coarse fabric was not conducive to settling things at all. Casting the cloth aside, he snatched up another cupped handful of the wintery water and doused his rousing length. He gasped. The chill caused his balls to tighten and gooseflesh to run rampant about the rest of his body.

Shivering, Silas braced his hands against the dresser and took a moment to catch his breath.

Had he done such loathsome things in his life? Had he chosen to lay with a man and revelled in it so? He would admit, the landscape of the male body did not seem so foreign to him. It was not the intimacy that had shocked him, but who he shared it with. All else seemed right...seemed familiar even.

And there was Charlie, too. Silas had not hesitated to begin things there when he still thought the lad to have a cock.

But what of the woman in lavender he'd seen – and heard, if the vision that had struck him while the revenants attacked was more evidence? She had stirred him in some way, there was no denying. He knew her. But how deeply? Silas blew out a breath. She had certainly not stirred him as Pitch had done. And he already knew, to his horror, who had been on his mind when he was lying atop Charlie.

He pushed away from the dresser. 'Bloody hell, snap out of it.'

Whom he bedded, whom he desired, was hardly his biggest conundrum.

And this was a terribly-misplaced desire. For one, Pitch was not even a man, in the true sense of the word. Silas was losing his mind over a creature who could enchant a person to do anything they pleased. Ridiculous.

The encounter had been with purpose. Pitch needed to be returned to himself so they could tackle far greater concerns than where Silas might prefer to stick his cock. There was the small matter of Azazel's dastardly magick, not to mention teratisms and the Blight, born on a day of death and destruction and staining the world still, to be dealt with.

Silas would tuck himself back into his trousers and be done with it. Pitch would return to his philandering ways and dance from bed to bed as an incubus was wont to do. *Needed* to do, Silas reminded himself irritably. And he'd not be in one of those beds, for that would simply complicate matters where they were already vastly so. Silas would meet his own needs elsewhere. At least he'd discovered all parts of himself were in full working order. In fact, it was highly likely he was confusing a desire for Pitch with a baser desire for plain and simple fucking.

He stomped over to the wardrobe with its array of perfectly tailored items. He donned a pair of light brown trousers and a black shirt. Silas ran his hands through his hair in a half-hearted attempt to settle the wild locks, and rubbed at the short length of his beard, wondering if he should shave it off entirely. He decided quickly that he was far too tired to do any more than lie down on the bed, settle himself upon the hoard of satin pillows there, and close his eyes. A quick rest and then he would go and find the brandy he so desperately thirsted for.

He had fallen fast asleep when the tread of footsteps in the hall roused him. Silas kept his eyes closed, listening from a drowsy place of half-awakedness. Someone made their way up the uncarpeted corridor, but there was an oddness to the sound, an unevenness to the tempo that he could not place. The footsteps halted outside his door. Were he anywhere else, were he not half as leaden with sleep as he was, Silas might have been more attentive. But he was here, in Bess's Sanctuary, where even a house wraith was in alliance with him. Silas nestled deeper into his stash of pillows. The turn of the knob was overly loud in the quiet, the steady rain having slowed to a light drizzle. Whoever it was, was opening his door. Perhaps he *should* be concerned? Silas was considering rolling over to face the door when the visitor spoke.

'Sickle? Are you awake?' Pitch whispered, loudly enough that if he had been asleep, he likely would have woken.

Silas held deathly still. He wasn't even breathing. The only part of him that did not freeze was his turncoat pulse. It was a drummer gone mad. There was no way in any hell that might exist that Silas was ready to face Pitch. His stomach did an odd flip. Christ almighty, he wondered if he could ever look that man in the eye again.

'Sickle?' Pitch was not to be deterred.

He stepped into the room, his footfall deadened by the rug. Was he limping? There was definitely something uneven in the tempo. Silas braced, rigid as a tent pole. If Pitch touched him, he wasn't sure he wouldn't yelp like a startled pup. But no touch came. There was a clinking sound and then the most sublime waft of brandy. Pitch set what Silas imagined was a glass upon the side table. It was so near his head that if he rolled over now, he might find himself a hair's breadth away from Pitch's hand. He squeezed his eyes tightly.

'For later then,' the daemon said. 'My thanks to you.'

The last was said so delicately, so gossamer thinly, Silas might well have imagined it. Then Pitch was gone, the door clicked closed, and his uneven footfalls grew faint as he returned down the corridor. Silas exhaled and sat up, blinking into the dim light. A solid crystal glass was set on the bedside table. Silas reached for it. Pitch had left him a generous serving, one that took three large gulps to devour. The burn was delicious and heady. With a lung-clearing sigh, Silas made himself more comfortable, diving in under the covers and nestling into the feather bed with its multiple sheets and top blanket. He covered his head with the mass of pillows and sank into the warmth of a liquor-filled belly. Sleep rushed in quickly, and he drifted into it with a ludicrous smile on his face.

Pitch was back on his feet. And better than that, he was grateful for it.

Silas slept long and hard, through the night and into what he assumed was the next day, for the light beyond the windowpanes was far brighter than it had been when he'd lain down. The cloud cover had not shifted, but the storm no longer rumbled discontentedly and had settled itself into a steady patter of rain upon the shingles. Silas stretched out of the fogginess of a dreamless sleep. His arm tingled with the pins and needles of having lain unmoving for too long. His body was warm and pliable, and his mind floated where life had not yet trampled. There were no nameless terrors, he was no dead man, he certainly had not lain with a daemon.

He rolled onto his side, and the nirvana fled in a rush at the sight of the empty brandy glass. He shuddered as it all returned to him.

Silas threw back the covers and sat up, rubbing his face until he was composed enough to smooth out his clothes and put on his boots. He could hardly hide away in this room forever. Besides, he was ravenous with hunger.

He used the chamber pot, for a lengthy period of time. It seemed the heated stream of piss would never end, and it was a wonder he'd not wet the bloody bed. He slipped on a simple grey jacket, deciding against adding the bandalore to his ensemble for it hardly seemed likely Bess would allow a teratism to breakfast, and made his way downstairs. Silas ran his tongue against his teeth, tasting stale brandy. The daemon's whispered thanks was still loud in his ears. Silas flushed. It was appalling really, that he was so affected. He was being *thanked* for his efforts in the bedchamber, like he were a well-performing toffer.

He reached the foyer and stepped onto the intricate herringbone parquetry.

Pitch's irreverent laughter erupted, spilling from a nearby room. Silas stopped dead, stomach tightening. The daemon's wicked amusement was robust, untroubled.

'I liked ya better when ya were near dead.' Tyvain's drawl was rough with her irritation. 'You're a cheatin' cunt.'

'Goodness, such language from such a sweet, fine face.' Pitch feigned his shock with that fine edge of derision he did so well. He was most certainly returned to himself. All trace of that fearful melancholy vanished.

'You know what will be the best day of me life?' Tyvain didn't pause for an answer. 'The day I see in me tea leaves that your last is comin', daemon. Oh, 'ow I will drink on that day.'

'Oh sweetheart,' Pitch purred. 'I insist you tell me of that blessed event as soon as you know it, for I will join you in your celebrations. I can assure you.'

Tyvain barked a laugh so hard she dissolved into a coughing fit. The pair were not alone in the room. Silas recognised Charlie's giggle. But he failed to find any part of the conversation amusing. There was too much hint of the same resignation Pitch had shown in that dreadful room, where Silas had feared he was bidding a farewell. *I do not want help or healing.*

'Now you are done with cards,' Charlie said. 'Mr Astaroth, will you join me in a game of billiards?'

Silas was pulled from his thoughts by the notion of Charlie and Pitch in such close quarters. Mostly because he did not think it a good idea for the lad to risk exposing his secret to the daemon, who might enjoy playing with it like a cat with a mouse, but also because he was quite sick at the idea of the two people he'd been so intimate with starting a conversation.

God, he could not go into that room. His face alone would betray him, with its pitiful flushing and blushing.

He eyed the main door on the far side of the expansive foyer. A stroll in the gardens would be pleasant, despite the drizzle. Perhaps he could wander further and seek out a graveyard. He released a long-held breath. Now that would be a true pleasure. He'd almost reached the door, and freedom, when someone called to him.

'Mr Mercer, it is good to see you about. Can I help you with anything?'

Startled, Silas whirled about. Ronin stood there, his dark-eyed regard cool, his raven hair slicked back against his head, forest-green house uniform impeccable with its starched lines and snug fit.

'Oh, Ronin...no...no. I am just...I was...tell me, what time is it?'

'It is just after eleven in the morning, sir. You slept through dinner and breakfast, I'm afraid.' Ronin bobbed his head. 'Mr Astaroth is well again, and has been asking after you...very often.' Silas was sure the man stopped himself from rolling his eyes. 'But Master Bess insisted you be allowed to rest. He said you were quite exhausted. Mr Astaroth will no doubt be wanting to speak with you, now you are rested up.'

Now there was no rolling of the eyes but a glint instead. Ronin's steady gaze gave Silas the sense of peering into a bottomless pool.

'Oh? That is good to hear, that he is well, I mean.' Silas's words were boulders his tongue struggled to clamber over. But he also knew now why he was so famished. He'd slept through dinner and breakfast. It was likely the longest sleep he'd had since clambering from his grave.

'Shall I take you to him, sir?'

Silas blinked out of his thoughts. Him? To Pitch? Dear god, no. 'Of course. Thank you.'

What else could he do? Scamper away like a frightened mouse? That would not do.

'There is brandy in the parlour, waiting for you, sir.'

Well, there was that at least. 'Wonderful. Thank you very much.'

'I'll have some poached eggs and fresh toast made for you too, if that is to your liking?'

'Indeed, thank you again.'

He followed along behind the footman, casting a forlorn glance towards the main door, relinquishing his bid for freedom. Ronin took him across the foyer and back down to the foot of the staircase, halting in front of the door to the right of the railing, where that unsettling laughter had first caught Silas's ear.

The footman paused with his hand upon the doorknob. 'Be sure to let me know if there is anything else you need, sir.'

A new life would be grand. 'Thank you.'

If only he'd woken in the dead of the night when everyone else had gone to bed.

Ronin opened the door, and Silas stepped into the parlour.

CHAPTER 27

As luck would have it, Tobias Astaroth was the very first person Silas set eyes on. He stood by one of the wide windows, silhouetted by the greyness of the day. His hair was loose but slicked back from his face with oil, leaving the curls at the end unburdened and brushing the back of his neck. He wore black stovepipe trousers with his preferred fall front, a white satin shirt, sleeves rolled high, and a vest patterned in black and an emerald that rivalled his eyes and seemed to accentuate his narrow waist even more becomingly. Despite knowing he should look away immediately, Silas could not tear his gaze free. The clothing was to blame, he saw, for the hour-glass appearance. For it was not a vest at all but a tightly-cinched corset, tailored to resemble that item of clothing. The hug of bone drew the eyes to Pitch's hips, and lower, as he leaned to retrieve a glass from a table beneath the window.

He looked so...well.

Silas's skin flamed, and he would have given his life, his second one at that, to be as diminutive as Gilmore, capable of disappearing behind the high-backed chairs that dotted the comfortably furnished room. Pitch turned his head and found Silas across the room. His eyes glittered like a dragon's hoarded treasure. The daemon's lips lifted, his smile bright with unspeakable things.

'Silas.'

The single word threatened to unravel the one it named.

Silas offered him a nod. 'Pitch.'

'By the gods, 'e lives,' Tyvain declared heartily from where she sat opposite Bess at a card table placed near a subdued fire. 'I thought Old Bess 'ad chopped you up and put you in last night's stew.'

Bess tossed his head. His new wig, a fine pile of pale pink curls, danced about his ears. 'Woman, if anyone is going in my stew, it will be you. How are you feeling, Silas? Rested? Hungry no doubt?'

'Quite,' Silas returned. 'I am famished, but Ronin is seeing to my needs.' He grimaced at his choice of words and kept his gaze far from Pitch, quite sure of the delighted, salacious mirth he'd find there.

'We have missed you, Silas.' Charlie stood by the billiards table, blue eyes beaming, cue in hand. He wore a morning coat of light cotton, its shade of lavender bringing to mind the woman of Silas's visions. The collar and cuffs were cut from a deeper hue of violet, and the design suited the lad well. 'I'm so glad you are here. I was just about to be soundly beaten by Mr Astaroth I suspect. I'm told he is quite the player. But, Mr Astaroth, do you mind if we wait awhile before we begin so I can speak with Silas?'

Pitch was the consummate vision of grace as he dipped his head. 'Of course not. It appears Mr Mercer could do with a drink.'

'Shall I pour you one, Silas?' Charlie was all enthusiasm.

'Please.' A triple at that, despite the hour.

Charlie downed his cue and hurried to where Silas still lingered just inside the door, toying with the idea of making a dash. The lad put paid to the notion though, linking their arms and ushering Silas towards the drinks cart, which lay thankfully on the opposite side of the room to where Pitch stood, watching. This was the same room where Silas had come upon Tyvain and Ronin before he'd gone on to overcome the hall's obstacles and sweep a naked daemon into his arms. It was a far more intimate space than the Lace Room where he'd spoken with Sybilla of angels and sorcery. At some point, he'd have no option but to move closer to Pitch.

'You must have been dreadfully tired, you poor thing,' Charlie said, selecting a glass. 'I thought you'd never wake.'

'And now you 'ave, you owe us, Silas,' Tyvain sniffed. 'It's been 'ell keepin' your partner amused while you snored away.'

She gathered her cards and shuffled them. Bess waited on her to deal, toying with a length of pearls about his sturdy neck. His wardrobe seemed bottomless. He wore now an exquisite gown of winter-sky blue, with thin lines of red satin criss-crossing the corset. Bess's eyes were upon him.

Damn it, every pair of eyes in the room was upon him. And he felt the emeralds most of all.

'Hag, you truly thought you were amusing me?' Pitch snipped. 'I thought you were attempting to bore me to death.'

'Gave it me best shot.' Tyvain shrugged. 'But the fates aren't done with ya yet, I 'spose.'

Silas flinched at the offhanded comment, recalling the terrible state he'd found Pitch in.

'What is your poison, Silas?' Charlie asked.

'Brandy,' Pitch declared. 'A pitiful drink, but there you go. There is no accounting for tastes, is there?'

Christ, Silas would not disagree with him there.

'Mr Astaroth, can I serve you something while I am here?' Charlie declared brightly. 'Do tell me what fabulous drink it is that delights your tongue, and is not so terribly pitiful as a mere brandy?'

His sarcasm was bold and at the forefront. Silas nearly choked on his stifled laughter. But it would not do to allow Charlie to see him amused. It would only encourage the lad to spar with the daemon.

'What delights my tongue?' Pitch curled the words like serpents. 'I'm not sure I can speak of my tastes in such delicate company.'

Silas winced. Tyvain was right. Pitch was far more tolerable when he was indisposed.

'Goodness, I would hate to forfeit our game by fainting fair away,' Charlie returned with absolute precision. 'Best I serve you a brandy. I fear it's all my delicate sensibilities can handle.'

Tyvain snorted. Bess raised a lace fan from his lap and fluttered it over his mouth. Pitch regarded Charlie with a look all the more disturbing for how unreadable it was. The lad seemed unperturbed though, turning his back to pour out two glasses of syrup-brown brandy.

'For you and I, Silas.' He upturned a smaller sherry glass and very deliberately filled it half-full. 'And for our brandy-despising friend.'

With a rather deviant grin, Charlie passed Silas his glass, tapped his own against the rim, and offered a cheers. Once they had each taken a sip, and Silas's eyes stung with the heavenliness of the drink, Charlie leaned in close.

'Dear Silas, Mr Astaroth has the tongue of a viper, but I see now why you were so readily distracted when we were together.'

He coughed into his mouthful. 'I beg your pardon?'

'You know exactly what I mean. He makes my hair stand on end, but he is absolutely, sublimely stunning. I doubt you realised you were between my legs at all.' Charlie laughed softly, without any trace of bitterness or indignation. But Silas stared at him aghast. 'Don't look so horrified, Silas. We lay together just once. It hardly means we are beholden to one another. It was lovely and all, you are every bit as easy on the eye as your...friend, but I see very clearly that even if I *had* harboured thoughts of keeping you to myself it would be quite impossible anyway.' He slid a sideways glance to where Pitch pretended to be intent on something outside. 'Tyvain did not lie when she said he has been difficult to occupy. I do think Bess was nearly ready to come and shake you awake hours ago.' He smiled through another sip of brandy, clearly enjoying Silas's failed attempts to find any words to say. But then Charlie grew serious. 'I'll not tease you anymore, Silas. I see it makes you very uncomfortable. But I have to say, I'm concerned for you. I heard Tyvain say last night that Mr Astaroth is your guardian.' He frowned. 'Clearly he was too unwell to protect you from that beast and those hideous men...is he well enough to do so now? I would hate to think of you being set upon like that again.'

The question chased clear any lingering embarrassment, for it was a serious one indeed. Silas delayed a reply with another mouthful. His empty stomach was making fast work of the brandy, its soothing edges quick to find him. 'Of course,' he said. 'We had some challenges well before I met you, and he was injured. But now he's had time to recover properly, I'm sure all will be well.'

'Good, very good.' Charlie nodded. 'I don't suppose there is any chance you will tell me what evils you two are partnered against? For I can get nothing from our host, sadly.'

Silas shook his head and Charlie sighed, with theatrical aplomb.

'Well, it is quite clear that by the happy chance of our meeting, I have landed in the middle of something quite astonishing. I've never felt quite so alive in my life.' He downed the rest of the brandy in one gulp and poured another.

Silas stared into his glass. The lad might be excited by their encounter, but it filled Silas with concern, and not a little guilt. If he'd sent Charlie away, scared him off the instant he'd stepped from the shadows of the mill, he would be well clear of danger. At least, the supernatural kind. As soon as he was able, he must take Bess aside and see what arrangements could be made to move Charlie on.

Tyvain let loose with a curse that would have made a clergyman shrivel. Bess's laughter lifted, throaty and delighted.

'Charlie, my dear, did you see?' Bess clapped his thick hands. 'I beat her. I actually did it. And all dues are yours, my sweet child. You are a marvellous teacher.'

''E's a pain in the arse,' Tyvain grumbled.

'And a terrible server of drinks. Are we to have this game or not?' Pitch left the window and moved towards the billiards table, limping discernibly, favouring his left leg. There was the explanation for the uneven footsteps last night.

'What is wrong with your leg?' The words bristled with more urgency than Silas intended.

'My leg? Hmm, perhaps it was all your weight upon it when we –'

'Pitch, answer the question,' Silas snapped. Why had he ever thought following that damned wraith was a good idea?

'I would, if I knew the answer.' Pitch laughed carelessly. 'Perhaps the Lady Satine is not so clever with her needle as she thinks.'

Silas cringed at thought of how long that needle must have worked to lay down so many marks as he'd seen.

'Now, Silas, do stop pestering Charlie and allow him to come and play with me.'

There was the serpent again, coiling itself around the daemon's words. Silas did not want Charlie anywhere near the blasted man.

'Dear Mr Astaroth,' Charlie said, with airy disregard. 'I do not allow Silas to do anything to me that I do not approve first. Now, if you are so impatient to be resoundingly beaten, then let us begin.'

Pitch arched fine eyebrows. His gaze flicked between Silas and Charlie and the dawning moment was all too clear. A shadow passed across his face, unreadable as the daemon so often was, chasing away whatever emotion had fluttered to the surface.

'I do enjoy a thrashing. Shall we begin?' Pitch's Cupid's bow lips stretched. 'Silas, come and watch me play with your little friend. You quite enjoy watching, if I recall.'

'Oh god,' Silas hissed. His glass was in real danger of shattering.

Tyvain's chesty laughter broke out. She slapped at her knee. 'Someone needs to tell me what the blazes that's all about, and soon.'

Silas glared at Pitch from across the room.

Charlie squeezed his arm. 'He does rile you ever so easily, doesn't he? I should think you might have to work on that, if you are to survive this pairing.' With a wink, the lad made his way across the room, stopping by Bess and placing a hand upon his shoulder. 'Will you save a game for me?'

'Of course, my lovely. You are the only thing making this dreary place tolerable right now. Have you spoken with Mr Mercer of my offer?'

'Not yet. No.' Charlie glanced back at Silas, who still clutched at his brandy glass. 'Bess wishes me to stay on at Harvington Hall, for as long as I like.'

'Oh,' he said. 'I see.' He saw, and did not like it.

'He is a delight,' Bess declared with lazy strokes of the fan. 'I've not enjoyed such company in a long time, and deplore the idea of such a lad being out on the roads alone. Charlie has said there is nowhere he needs to be, so why not be here?'

Silas frowned at Bess, his temper simmering. 'Do you really think that would be wise? I thought he need only stay until...' Christ, he should not have started that sentence. 'Surely Charlie is not at risk now and can leave without threat to his safety.'

Surely, after days spent here, the lad no longer smelled of *him* and could return to a simpler life where the walking dead did not set upon him, and daemons did not eye him like prey.

''E should stay.' Tyvain frowned down at her cards, picking at a spot on her chin. 'Serendipity is best not to be ignored, Mr Mercer. You two came across each other in a way that ain't necessarily random, is all I'm sayin'.

The laddie-lass 'as got a place 'ere now.' Her belch was astoundingly guttural. 'See? There you 'ave it.'

'Aha!' Charlie raised his glass. 'There you go, Silas. You are not rid of me yet.' He tottered with his enthusiasm, and Bess laughed as he reached up to steady his newest resident. 'See, I'm in very good hands, am I not?'

How many drinks had he had before Silas arrived?

'Charlie, I don't think that this is the right –'

Pitch sighed. 'Oh for fuck's sake, Sickle. Must you always look like a kicked cat and ruin everyone's fun? Now, Charlie, do come along and play with these balls. I'd like to see how you handle them.'

Christ, it was as though their sordid coupling had never occurred. And perhaps that stung more than the daemon's barbed tongue.

Charlie giggled, far too delighted.

'Pitch, that's enough.' Silas's simmering anger was nearing the boil. Brandy on an empty stomach did not seem such a grand plan now. Where were those damned eggs and toast? 'Leave him be. I'm warning you. I'll not have you manipulating him.'

'Silas, thank you for your concerns, but I can handle myself,' Charlie declared.

But the lad had no idea whom he dallied with. Silas remembered all too well the unfortunate attendant upon the train, and the young woman, Mabel, in The Moon Inn, tripping over themselves as the daemon toyed with them. Oh god. Thinking on The Moon Inn fouled Silas's temper even more. For that led him to think of the lieutenant. He pressed at his temple, the pang of a headache beginning. Bloody hell, he hoped he would never have to face that poor man again.

'Are you well, Silas?' Bess asked, right beside his ear. He'd not seen the man rise from his seat to join him.

'I'm fine, thank you.'

Pitch leaned low against the table, arse high, readying his shot. A vision of hard sculpted beauty, his chin tilted to tighten a slender neck. He said something to Charlie, who laughed before leaning down next to the daemon, demonstrating an angle he thought best suitable for the shot. Silas's throat tightened.

How could such a small fire make a room so intolerably stuffy?

'This act of his is just that, you know, don't you?' Bess said in a low voice. 'I think he does not take well to pity, not even the hint of it, so he's blustering about like a peacock prancing. Determined to show he is in control. For you to have seen him so low, let alone carry him from that pit he'd dug himself into, will not go down well with him.'

Silas tugged at his collar, the skin damp beneath. 'It was concern, not pity. And what is so wrong with either?'

'Much, when you do not believe you deserve them.'

'I see.' Silas set down his glass, clacking glass against wood. He didn't bloody *see*, at all. Why the hell was Pitch so offended by the idea of someone showing an ounce of sympathy for his plight? 'Bess, excuse me. I think I'll go and see how the food is coming along, if you don't mind?'

'Come and go as you like, Silas. You need no permission from me.'

He hurried from the room, ignoring Charlie's call to join them at the table.

CHAPTER 28

The rain had barely ceased since they had arrived at Harvington Hall and it did not stop now, the pattering upon the shingles and windowpanes a soothing distant murmur, overtaken at intervals by the grumble of thunder. The unsettled weather suited his mood very well as he stood in the foyer, torn with what direction he should take.

Though his belly would protest otherwise, food was not what he craved. Silas's need was baser. There beyond the wooded barrier of the main door, he might find what he sought, for what would soothe him was not the oily odour of eggs and bread but the loamy, mildewed scent of the graveyard.

The front door shifted against its hinges. The knob rattled, the latch clicked, and the door shifted open. Icy, damp air raced in through the slick gap.

Go where your hunger leads you, ankou-of-the-pale-horse.

The wraith kept to the shadows that hung like a sooty veil beside the door. Silas caught his breath. God almighty, he'd forgotten how ghoulish the dead man's death wounds were.

'My hunger?'

Do you not crave?

An odd question, but his answer was stranger. 'I do. I struggle to find such...peace...restfulness... anywhere else.' He knew the wraith understood. The soul spoke of Silas's hunger for the quiet sanctity of the restful dead, the rasp of gravestone against his fingertips. The cemetery was more appealing than all the brandy in the world. 'Is there a graveyard in this village?'

The wraith shook his dreadful head. Silas glanced away as loose skin flapped.

Sanctuaries are not built on such places. You will find one just beyond the village, outside the Sanctuary line but near enough that you should have no fear.

'The village is within the Sanctuary too?'

This Sanctuary could survive a siege. The wraith's reply bubbled with something akin to amusement.

'I see. Well, I thank you...for all that you have done.'

And you. For all that you shall do.

Well, that was not ominous at all. The wraith left him, blending back into the shadows and taking his grisly self away. Silas rubbed at his arms. The day was far too brisk to traipse about without a coat. He'd make a quick return to his room before stepping out. Silas turned to head back to the stairs.

Ronin strode forward, scowling, coming from the corridor beyond the staircase. His expression smoothed to blank when he spotted Silas.

'Oh, I thought I felt a draught,' he said. 'Is everything all right, sir?'

'Fine, fine. I am just going for a walk –'

'But your eggs –'

'Sorry, I expect I'll find some breakfast in the village.'

Before the too-attentive footman, with his fathomless brown eyes, could stop him, Silas strode out the door. He'd survive without the coat. He passed without hesitation from the cover of the eaves and across the squat, solid bridge that would take him to dry land. The downpour had withdrawn to a fine mist. Fortunate. He was not about to get soaked. Not yet, at least. He broke into a jog as he cleared the bridge and found himself in an exposed section of garden. He only slowed once he reached twin lengths of topiary shrubs, each cut into triangular shapes, which afforded protection as he dashed from one to the other like a common thief.

He considered heading to the stables and riding Lalassu into the village, but he abandoned that idea with haste. As wonderful as the mare may be, she was also the Lady Satine's servant. He wished for solitude, and he knew now that he had no such thing upon her back. That was the sort of world he resided in now, one where his horse was capable of tattling. This foray would be done on foot, but blast it, he really should not be wandering about without the bandalore at least. Especially if he were to step beyond Sanctuary boundaries.

He glanced back at the hall.

He could call the bandalore to him. He was quite astute at it now. And practise was surely a good thing, was it not? Silas shook his head. The calamity that may ensue as the bandalore broke its way out of the hall, likely shattering a window, would draw far too much attention. And who knew what retribution the hall might inflict if it grew tired of his continual efforts to demolish her fine perfection. He'd punctured more than one hole in her interior as he'd summoned the bandalore to Pitch's abysmal chamber.

Damn. That memory threatened to douse the thrill of his adventure if he thought on it too long. Silas spun about, and stepped straight into a great muddy puddle, foetid water slashing at his leggings and inching its way in at the top of his boot. The squelch of mud was all too like that horrid quagmire at Black Annis's bower. The sky released a pattering of rain down on him, bleakening the mood.

Silas grunted, flicking at dampness upon his sleeve. 'She is done with,' he muttered.

God help him if a small puddle of mud stopped him in his tracks. Blast it all, he was going to have this stroll if it killed him. Again. Christ almighty, whichever way his thoughts went, they found something unpleasant to contemplate. Now the wraith's comments about his death plagued him. The hacked up creature had challenged Silas to recall a pivotal detail of his demise. How long had Silas been dead?

And as it was with so many, many other questions, he didn't know the cursed answer.

Silas growled at the clouds, at the mud, the crickets with their ceaseless chirping, anything unfortunate enough to be nearby. One moment of peace. Was that too much to damned well ask for?

He'd find this pissy graveyard, and he'd plant himself among the headstones and find some quiet, come hell or high water.

He moved on, pitying anyone who might attempt to halt him now. He was ankou-on-the-bloody-pale-horse, was he not? And he wanted a moment alone.

Silas fixed his mind on more pleasant considerations. Like the wiry, prickly lengths of a gooseberry bush there, the dart of swallows in the hawthorn, the unseen creatures that caused the branches to shiver as they scattered at his passing. He actually had no clue where he was headed. For all he knew it may be entirely the wrong direction. But he didn't care, so long as it was outdoors where he could breathe. Besides, there appeared to be only one main road as an option, and his feet drew him along it, as though they too knew something he did not. That notion threatened to sour his recently-recovered mood all over again, so he settled into walking, and admiring the view. The hell with the rest of it.

Nature proved a masterful panacea for a foul mood. If there was somewhere other than a graveyard that could soothe him, it was the woodlands. Preferably those without a maddened Verderer, of course. The stroll was untangling his knots well, the rain held back as though not daring to fall, and he filled his lungs with deep, slow breaths.

He'd walked a full, pleasant ten minutes when the hairs on the back of his neck stood to attention. He was struck with the feeling of being watched. There was a faint tingle beneath his fingertips, but it was so distant he thought perhaps he could blame the energies of the storm for it. The ever-present bank of ominous cloud seemed to threaten but did little else, muttering and flashing at a distance, the tempestuous clime prickling the air.

A squirrel darted up a nearby oak, the scrape of its claws evident in the quiet. He scowled at the flash of orange and brown and carried on. If he were to start at every scampering woodland creature, he'd be mad by nightfall. His temper was still alight. And right then, if an ash-man had dared show himself, he would have happily throttled him with his bare hands. He was quite done with being pinched and cut at.

Gracious, he was inordinately cranky. But it was quite a refreshing change from being frightened and unsteady. He was rather enjoying it. Maybe some of the daemon's temper had rubbed off on him.

Silas threw back his head, a snap of laughter escaping him. Good god, what a terribly poor choice of words in that thought. Far more tangible things than a mood had rubbed off on him. Soaked him actually.

'Silas.' He shouted at himself, startling some birds in the hedgerow. 'You are appalling.'

Which was very true, but it did not stop him chuckling away to himself for a while. He must be harebrained from lack of food. That was it surely, for it was not amusing at all, the whole sordid encounter with the daemon. Horrifying, really. Without a doubt. But by god, just thinking on the ethereal softness of Pitch's skin was waking up the slumbering traitor between his legs, and here, as he strolled in his own company, causing no harm to anyone, he decided he'd not feel bad for it. He'd worry later about the implications, about the emotions that had arisen as he lay with Pitch. For now he'd enjoy playing with the memory. With being filthy. With being very human.

Harvington Hall fell from view behind him, and he found himself surrounded by fields. A typical English countryside with lush pasture and grazing livestock mixing among meadows left to nature's wilder hand, full to the brim with swaying wildflowers and long grasses. He was enjoying memory of the delightful whine that had come from Pitch as he came, arching and straining in Silas's arms, when the long grasses far to his right shook and crackled with the pressure of something large moving among them.

Silas suppressed a shiver.

He handled his momentary fright roughly, shoving it back down where it could not interrupt his thoughts. There were no revenants or teratisms lurking about here. Bess had told him, he was safe, and he knew it. The movement could be explained. A wandering sheep, perhaps. Even a fox, though the disturbance seemed caused by something larger than those sly hunters. But whichever animal it was had as little interest in him as he did in it. The creature was moving away, weaving its way through the grasses until there was nothing to show for it at all.

CHAPTER 29

The village of Mustow Green was insubstantial, a short stretch of high street with a lopsided collection of residences and stores along its length. Wonderfully unremarkable.

Silas wiped at his face and shook the droplets from his hair. The rain was still no more than a fine mist, but his walk had been long enough to ensure the moisture made wilder the black waves that hung damply from his head. He should have thought to tie up the ever-growing strands. They brushed his shoulders, some teasing even lower. He could do with a shave too. Perhaps he'd seek out a barber after he'd visited the graveyard. Already the walk had done him a world of good, even without the graves, though he'd had to pause a moment once he heard people nearby. He'd gotten himself worked up along the way. It wouldn't do to stride into town with pants bulging. Recalling the bloodied ruin of his wrist and the fear he'd felt at harm coming to Charlie when the ash-men had attacked soon put paid to any arousal.

A ruddy-cheeked gent passed by, pushing a barrow full of empty potato sacks. He was a solid man, with flat cheeks and an impressively high forehead.

'Excuse me, sir,' Silas said. 'Could you direct me to the churchyard, I hear there is one just beyond the village?'

The gent appraised him from toe to top of his head. 'You must be from Harvington, then.'

Silas nodded, surprised at the rapid assessment. 'Well, yes. I am. How did you know?'

'Doesn't take a genius.' His smile was genuine. 'You're on foot, and you aren't from the village. Harvington's the only place of note around here. And you look like someone of note.'

'Well, I don't know about that, but thank you. Ah, the churchyard?'

'Church is out down Persher Lane, near the smithy's.' He pointed the way, a narrow laneway some way further down the high street. 'Ten minutes on foot, not much more.' The man adjusted his hold on his barrow, clearly readying to leave. It was then that Silas's stomach decided to make itself known. The growl was formidable, and acutely horrifying. Silas pressed at his belly.

'Do excuse me.'

The man with the barrow chortled. 'Old Bess not feeding you up there?'

'Oh, it's not that. We have been very well cared for. I skipped breakfast, I'm afraid. My mistake.' Silas glanced up at the sky. The drizzle grew heavier. 'You have had quite the rainfall here of late.'

This was pleasant. Menial conversation.

'We get all kinds of odd weather about here, but all of it involves the rain in some shape or form. Never lets up. The storms that blow in are quite the thing too. Did you hear it yesterday up at the hall? Not a lick of rain but the biggest clap of thunder you've ever heard. Near frightened me into my ale. You must have heard it?'

Yesterday afternoon he'd been occupied with other things. 'I don't recall.' He cleared his throat. 'It must grow tiresome, all this dampness?'

He may not know much of Sanctuaries, or the power that built them, but he suspected the weather and Harvington Hall were linked. If a living house, then why not pliant weather?

'We put up with it, 'cause of all else,' the barrow-man replied. 'No better place in the world to be than Mustow Green if you ask me. Small slice of heaven. I couldn't tell you the last time we needed a doctor called here. The last bloke moved away after a year or two out of boredom. Never known the crops to fail here, and that cattle plague in sixty-five? Didn't come anywhere near us, though it wiped out the herds across most of the country.'

Silas raised his brow, feigning surprise. The man spoke of the plague, thirty years old, as though it were as commonly known as London itself. For Silas it was like listening to another language.

'Neighbouring villages won't even let us enter our produce in the county fairs no more, on account of the size of our pumpkins and the like. They say we've got the pixies and the sprites working for us.' He loosed laughter that rumbled in time with the thunder, much amused by such an absurd idea.

Silas blinked. 'How extraordinarily silly of them.'

There were more passers-by now, and Silas was drawing attention. All of it pleasantly congenial. A tip of a hat there, a nod there. Curious but kind smiles all round.

The barrow-man lifted his load. 'Now if you are wanting to get some food in that belly, you've got the pub of course further along, but I'd say go for a pie at Nora's bakery.' He jerked his chin in a vague direction. 'She'll see you right. Best pigeon pie you'll ever eat.'

Silas muttered a thanks, staring in the direction he was being ushered. Bess had spoken of the bakery, spoken highly of it, if he recalled. As much as he still longed for the graveyard, the idea of steaming golden crust and oozing gravy had him salivating. And perhaps they would have a supply of strawberry tarts.

Bidding the barrow man a farewell, he waltzed down a cobbled street remarkably devoid of mud and potholes considering the inclement weather. He tipped his nonexistent hat and muttered good mornings to all he passed. He was all too aware of the eyes upon him, and that number seemed to grow as he walked, as though word had spread and all and sundry were popping out to take a peak at the new arrival. He'd not been in company of such numbers since the Marquess of Ailsa's ball.

By the time he reached the bakery, marked by the tantalising smells emanating from the shopfront and a hanging sign with a loaf of bread, Silas fairly dashed inside, setting the jingling bell upon the door into a frightful cacophony.

'Oh my goodness, you startled me, a big lad like yourself running in here.' The freckle-faced woman behind the counter laughed, Nora he presumed. 'Hungry then?' She wiped her floured hands upon her gingham apron. Her svelte figure suggested she did not sample her wares very often.

'My apologies, I was just...I was...' Good god, he had been running like a scared hare from a wolf pack. 'I've been told you bake a wondrous pigeon pie.'

'Mr Richardson sent you here, then?' She rolled her eyes. 'Gracious, if the man could win a woman's heart by drumming up business, he'd have had what he's after long before now.'

Silas smiled at her, settling down from his bullish entry. His lips parted at sight of the morsels on offer. Breads were piled high in baskets on low shelves behind the counter, dark ryes and lighter loaves speckled with sunflower seeds and dusted with flour. There was a glass cabinet beneath the wooden counter, filled to brimming with delicate pastries and vibrantly-coloured cakes and slices. Cherries glistened atop wobbling jellies, and astoundingly large blueberries crowned a tart whose pastry was utter perfection in gold. *Christ*, Silas thought, *Pitch would lose his mind in this place.*

'Pies are fresh out of the oven out the back. Anything else I can get you, then?'

With his mouth watering and his eye on a particularly exquisite chocolate eclair oozing yellow cream, Silas readied to order. Bloody hell, he had not a penny on him. His empty stomach fell.

'I'm afraid I've left my coin behind. I'll return at once.'

Nora made a dismissive sound, her amber eyes bright. 'You're from Harvington. Master Bess will put it right. Don't trouble yourself.'

'Are you sure?'

'Of course.'

'Thank you, thank you so much.' Good god, he was starving. 'I'll take an éclair, please.'

Nora slid out the tray of eclairs to fill his order, revealing what had been lying behind in the crammed cabinet. Strawberry tartlets, nearly hidden behind an enormous sponge cake.

'You have strawberry tarts,' he exclaimed. Idiot. He was sure the woman knew her own stores.

'Fresh done this morning. Shall I pack one for you?'

'Oh, three at least...his appetite knows no bounds.' His words skipped from him. 'These will be gone before I can set them on a plate.' Silas snapped his mouth shut. Bloody hell.

'Tell you what, I'll give you six, with the last thrown in for free.' Nora's eyes sparkled, her grin wide. 'I've not seen a man grow so excited over discovering strawberry tartlets in my store before. I hope your gentleman enjoys eating them as much as you enjoyed finding them.'

His face warmed. 'Oh, no...it's not...' *Your* gentleman, *your* daemon. Christ. 'Well, it's just that I've heard very good things about your bakery from the Master of Harvington Hall. And I know quite a few of his guests...enjoy...strawberry tarts, not just my gentleman...the gentleman that...you see?' If she did, she was a wonder. *Stop talking, Silas.*

'Ahuh. Well, whatever it is, it makes your face light up. You're a handsome man to begin with, but you are very lovely when you smile like that. Anything else, my dear?'

Silas tugged at his collar, where it seemed too tight for his throat. 'A couple of teacakes, if you would. And just that pie. Thank you.'

Nora settled his selection into a dented silver tin and tied it up in a gingham cloth. She stepped out the back to retrieve the pie, wrapping it in paper before handing it over. The warm parcel fit snugly into his palm, and the scent nearly made him groan.

'Thank you, once again.' Silas rushed from the store nearly as quickly as he'd arrived in it. Now more than ever he was ready for the solemnity of the graveyard. To sit himself among the graves and breathe in the dankness. Death had become a strangely desirable armchair, and now he had a piping-hot pie to go along with it.

A cart laden high with straw and pulled by a skinny mule blocked his path. Silas dodged around it with a grace that surprised even him. But he was quite turned about. Which way had he come into town? He'd been too busy muttering good mornings as he headed to the bakery. He enquired of a young lass as to the direction to the churchyard. Her ringlets bounced about beneath a pretty peacock-green bonnet. She giggled as she pointed out the way and bobbed an unnecessary curtsy as he left her. Her demeanour brought to mind poor Mable from The Moon Inn. He wondered if the lass had recovered from the things she'd witnessed through the peephole. Silas tightened his hold on the gingham cloth, swinging the tin and its ridiculous tartlets with more vigour than was warranted.

The sooner he ate his pie the better.

Silas found the laneway, leaving the stares and liveliness of the high street behind. The passageway was short, merging with a new path obviously intended for foot passengers only. No carriage could have travelled along the narrow way between skeletal birch trees, stripped naked of their leaves.

A fresh scent hit his nostrils, and he could have cried out with the pleasure of it. Grave dirt, its richness was like no other.

Silas broke into a jog, which took him over a low rise in the ground. Beyond it was a simple church and its even simpler yard. He nodded with satisfaction at the sight of the tilted headstones within hallowed grounds surrounded by a low stone wall. Another few paces and he would be at the dilapidated gate. Silas frowned. Another few paces and he'd step past the misty drizzle of rain too. He could see quite clearly that no rain fell upon the churchyard. He glanced up at the sky. The clouds covered all, offering no explanation for the pronounced curtain of moisture between him and the yard. The Sanctuary border perhaps? A reasonable assumption.

And if it were the case, then the Sanctuary was but a handful of steps away if anything untoward approached him.

He pushed forward, and the air swelled with the earthy tang of mould and loam. Silas opened with care the rotted gate that hung by one working latch and stepped across the threshold.

There was not much to the place, barely a dozen graves, and the church had clearly seen its best days long ago. The roof had caved in in parts, exposing the beams that gave the structure form. The arched door must have been an impressive chunk of wood to fill such a wide gap, but it was as decimated as the church roof, with only a portion hanging from each hinge.

There was a scattering of coloured glass upon the two steps that lay beneath the empty doorway. Despite the lack of roof over most of its interior, the church was oddly shadow filled. But he was not disconcerted. Or afraid. This was *his* sanctuary.

Silas set down the wrapped tin on a moss-cradled stone seat, just inside the gate. He spread his arms, threw back his head, and exhaled, as though he had summited a formidable mountain.

'Wonderful,' he declared to the empty yard.

The air hugged him, a comforting blanket of dank, pastoral weight. It was with some surprise that he noted the yard was well-maintained. The grass was clipped about the headstones and was the refreshing green of a golf course. There was even a fresh bouquet of early-blooming winter clematis resting on a particularly grand headstone in the middle row. The stone was carved with roses and ivy, the name of the deceased a flourish of elegant lines. Silas regarded the inscription with irritation, lamenting his lack of reading skills.

But overall, he stood deeply content. like a farmer surveying an abundant crop. If only he could bottle this contentment and carry it with him, for the respite of Harvington Hall was temporary.

The ride would continue.

And god knew what else awaited them out there. He closed his eyes.

Play their game and win, Pitch had told him once.

A pity then that Silas had no idea what the game was, let alone how to win it. And now there was the trouble of Pitch's incapacitating ailment. What if it struck him down again? Fooling about with caresses and kisses was one thing, but it was clear far more had to be done to bring Pitch back from a terrible brink. Those marks upon his back were not easily forgotten. But it was more than that. It was the melancholy that had taken him.

Damn, it had been painful to witness. The emptiness that Silas had heard in his voice, the listless way he lay upon that bed to begin with. The look on Pitch's face when he'd thought Silas regarded him with pity had been caustic. And that room...a reflection of his mood, according to Bess. Cold and devoid of light, oppressive with surrender.

Silas knew himself lonely, but Pitch...Pitch had been carved hollow.

Keep him safe. Sybilla's words.

And Silas dared imagine he could. He'd beheaded a revenant, cut another in two, defied a defiant hall, and summoned the bandalore at will. Was it foolish to imagine he could do as the Valkyrie asked? And protect the daemon, as Pitch would protect him?

His eyes flickered open, adjusting to the return of the light. A soft mist had moved in, clinging to the boundaries of the graveyard, like a fine veil offering him privacy. Silas's fingertips came alive with gentle sensation. It was not the sharp alarm that came with a teratism, more a low, dull alert that spoke of having his wits about him. He straightened. Cautious, but not concerned.

Wood shifted somewhere within the derelict church, a pale of timber creaking within the darkened space. He would have blamed the wind, if there were any to blame. The breeze, like the rain, stayed away from this churchyard.

Silas made his cautious way closer, drawn to the building. Whatever stirred his senses lurked there. He was nearly able to peer in through the doorway when a white cat emerged from a hole in the stone foundations, slinking low to the ground as though witnessed midhunt.

Silas relaxed. 'Hello there.' The cat raised its head, pinning him with eyes as white as its body. Lips drew back to reveal a jaw filled with jagged teeth. 'Not the prettiest of them, are you, poor chap?'

A grim. He knew it as readily as he would know a sheep or a cow.

The grim cat's answer was to settle on its haunches and lick its arsehole.

'Very well then.' Silas chuckled. 'I'll give you some privacy.'

He heard stirrings within the church once more. Silas stepped closer and peered into the darkness. The shadows, those that huddled beneath the last of the roof, were moving.

Growing larger.

Shifting towards him.

A guttural growl came from the wreckage. And a glowing orb of red watched him from the gloom.

CHAPTER 30

'Where do you think you're goin'?' the Hag barked at him from where she peeked around the parlour doorway. 'Bess know you're 'eadin' out?'

Pitch raised a sculpted brow, tucking away the coat he held so it was hidden behind the open front door. 'He's not my mistress. I'll go where I like.' Limping like a pathetic cripple, he pressed fingertips into the offending hip. The patch-up job that had been done on him left much to be desired. There was no pain, but the stiffness that stemmed from his lower back was abominable. He could not stretch his right leg into a full stride.

'Seems to me they put a lot of effort into settin' you right.' The crone was still carrying on. By Malik's taint she was irritating. 'Don't you go botching it all up with a back-alley brawl or nothin'. There's more important things to be doin'.'

Pitch regarded her the way he regarded tripe, which he despised. 'Like what, pray tell?' Like he had prayed a day in his life. 'I'm not sure I count following around after an ankou who needs instruction on how to blink all that important. I'll admit, this is all rather tedious.'

'That right?' Tyvain gave him a wolfish grin. 'So you're just manhandlin' Mercer's coat out of boredom, then?'

He did not like this bitch at all. Would anyone really mind if he scorched the soothsayer completely out of existence?

Pitch layered on his smoothest grin. 'Something like that. He is inordinately attached to it. I thought I might bury it in the manure pile behind the stables, and see how long it was before he shed a tear over its disappearance.'

'Mother Mary's tits, you're so fulla shit I can see it piled up behind your eyes.'

'I can arrange to bury you in the manure as well. It would be no bother.'

'Ah, feck off, ya silly bastard.' Tyvain chuckled.

It irritated him to see her bemusement. She was not unsettled in the least by the glare he sent her.

'But good luck findin' 'im. Mercer couldn't get out of 'ere fast enough soon as 'e laid eyes on ya.' She nodded at Pitch. 'Left 'is coat behind he was so quick about it. Ya should probably take that as a sign the man don't want you buzzin' about, but far be it for me to tell ya what to do.'

Pitch stepped outside, making sure to slam the door so hard the soothsayer's teeth should have rattled. He bundled Silas's coat under his arm. He'd be damned if he'd bother to keep it hung so it wouldn't wrinkle. The bandalore pressed at his ribs, hidden in the folds of a freshly mended pocket. He'd found the scythe after a very short search of the ankou's room, buried beneath his pillow, as though that hiding place would never be found. Pitch moved as fast as his stiff joints would allow, all the better to be away from this hall and its inhabitants. He was absolutely not taking Silas his coat because it was damp out, and bloody cold, but because the idiot had left behind the one thing that did not render him utterly useless. Without the bandalore the giant oaf was vulnerable.

Pitch reached a shrub tall enough to conceal him from anyone watching from the hall and buckled forward, hands pressed to his knees. He was a little breathless, and something twinged at his hip. The human body was pathetic, wonderful to play with, with all its nuances, but pathetic just the same. Gods, he despised this wretchedness. Once he'd recovered his wits after the wholly unexpected dalliance with Silas and his vexing tender attentions, Pitch had found himself returned to vigour with a new disability. The amuletum had done its work to banish the agony of the halo's mark, and Silas's hands had done wonders to sate a daemon's hunger, but the bodily flesh had not recovered so well as he expected. It were as though some of his joints had melted into one another when he used the flame, the injury worst of all where hip met thigh upon his right leg. As he'd lost himself under Silas's fingertips, he'd felt the damage come undone, the ease of movement return to most places. But not there. Hard as he had come, astounding as the feel of the ankou upon him had been, it had ended too soon.

But Pitch had done more than enough pitiable begging in that bed. He'd allow a basilick to eat out his eyes before he'd ask for more, just a bit more, to set him to rights.

If the next time he used his flame he turned into an immovable lump then be it on Lady Satine's head. The djinn with her mysterious motives, had chosen poorly when she'd accepted his deliverance. He couldn't imagine what had driven her to such a length, a great debt to Lucifer perhaps, or a misguided belief that a subjugated prince might strengthen her precious Order. Either way, she'd learn soon enough how foolish she'd been.

Pitch resettled Silas's coat over his arm. Until the lady came to her senses, he supposed he was stuck with the stupid, bloody ankou, and his firm fingers and concerns. Lifting Pitch out of the ruins of that horrid castle with the tree trunks he called arms, and fussing over him like an intolerable nursemaid in that woman's dreary cottage. Caressing him back to life amid vile stained sheets and desolation, handling him so gently even Pitch himself had been convinced he did not deserve to break.

He hissed his irritation to the dampness.

Now the imbecile was wandering about without his coat and likely to catch a bloody chill, all because he'd been so desperate to extricate himself from Pitch's company. He'd practically flown out of the parlour.

Had their encounter been that intolerable?

Pitch ran his hands down the sides of his corseted vest. Beautiful, Silas had called him, and the words had done all manner of strange things to Pitch's pulse. But what else would he be *but* beautiful, really? If he was to be trapped in human form forever he was certainly going to do so in the finest version of himself he could imagine. Pitch had made sure that this body bore no resemblance to any other he'd ever worn, just as he'd been ordered. And he'd created something quite magnificent.

'Only a man bereft of his senses would not have enjoyed it.' He declared to a sparrow who did not seem to care much at all. 'Besides, he was rigid as that branch you are perched upon. He enjoyed it. Obviously it was all too much for our bashful ankou. But he need not worry, for it won't happen again. I'm not some poor damned beggar who needs his charity.'

The tiny bird spirited away in a bluster of frantic wings.

Pitch continued on through the gardens and down the road until he reached the village of Mustow Green. The stiffness in his leg made the journey more tedious than he would have liked. And now there was an ache at the crease of his thigh. He scowled at it and the mud that insisted on clinging to his delightful double monk strap shoes. His lack of coat was going to disturb some sensibilities no doubt, but he was hardly averse to such things. Silas's coat was no use at all. The monstrous man's clothing would swamp him. These curves were best left unhidden.

Sauntering down the main street, Pitch drank in the vast number of stares that came his way. He spotted more than a few residents who took his fancy. He nodded at the coy smile sent by a flaxen-haired woman whose face carried a pleasing swathe of wrinkles, and a chap with thin lips and a pert arse, who winked at him as they passed. It was unfair, really, to waltz among the purebreds with his incubus blood fairly boiling beneath his skin this way. He could have seduced any one of them to suck his cock right here upon the high street, if he had so wished. And well he may do if they remained at Harvington Hall too long. Silas would not return to his bed for the pleasure of it, he was sure. The ankou had come to rescue him, and even that rested uneasily with the oaf. Pitch had seen the look upon his face in the parlour, and it was not one that suggested Silas desired anything but distance between them.

Pitch's smile slipped ever so.

He spotted a gent stepping out of a barbershop, hat in hand, hair glistening with newly-applied oil, and by the gods he looked familiar at first glance. Pitch stopped so quickly his hip pinched. But it was not as he'd thought. The lieutenant was not here. Thank all the fucking gods. He wanted no opportunity to bollocks up that man's life another time.

The fuck in Mordiford had been a mistake. Pitch had always enjoyed Edward Charters's calm company, well before Raph chose him as his vessel. In fact it was likely *why* the angel had chosen him to begin with, but now Edward was a painful momento that Pitch should abandon. The angel was gone. How many times must he stick his cock in the man to have that sink in?

An uneven cobblestone caused him to stumble.

'Are you all right, sir?' A grubby-nosed lad watched him from the steps of the grocers.

'Of course I'm all right,' Pitch snapped, bunching the coat deeper under his arm and continuing on his way.

'Good day.' He winked at a woman who was being bothered by two infants at her skirts. One of the brats chose that moment to fall on its arse and bawl its displeasure, but the mother did not take her eyes from Pitch.

'Oh...good...good...'

He didn't bother waiting for the rest of her stuttered greeting. The mealy-mouthed child was intolerably loud. He eyed a pile of horse manure on the road up ahead, considering which way around he would take to avoid it.

A looming, unmistakable figure stepped out of the bakery across the road. Pitch stepped straight into the pile, still steaming and warm. He barely noticed it.

The ankou clutched a bundle wrapped in gingham in one hand, something wrapped in paper in the other. He looked as flustered as only that man could. Silas nearly tripped over his own enormous feet in his rush to be free of the store. Pitch snickered.

Had a lass batted her lashes at him?

The attention of all the passers-by shifted from Pitch at the ankou's entrance. There was no competition so far as beauty was concerned. Pitch would not easily lose that crown, but gods the oaf was large. Likely people feared being trampled by the giant of a man, with his powerful shoulders and purposeful stride. He was built like the runt of a Nephilim litter.

Silas's shadow fell across the bawling child, who craned its neck to peer up at the broad man. He seemed to consider stopping to enquire about the mewling babe, which made Pitch's stomach turn. There was only so much of the man's considerations he could bear. Pitch almost cheered when the ankou glanced at the paper-wrapped package in his hand and continued on.

He followed, making a pleasant study of Silas as he kept a furtive distance. His hair was more wild and unkempt than Pitch knew the ankou preferred, but it suited him all too well. Without his long coat to hide it, Silas's posterior was a sight to behold. Pitch had not taken a hold of it when he'd had the chance, too busy melting beneath a thick-fingered touch, and he regretted it.

Silas stopped to speak with a lass in a pretty green bonnet. She pointed out directions, fluttering lashes and swooning like there was no tomorrow. The oaf was oblivious. He thanked her, his eyes already on the way ahead, and set off. Right, Pitch decided, enough with the clandestine tailing of the man. It was time to declare his presence.

'Sila –'

A bay pulling a tray laden with tin milk pails chose that moment to shy, rattling her load free right in front of Pitch. Calamity rang out. And the only person in the village who did not seem to exclaim at it was Silas. The ankou disappeared down a laneway as Pitch cursed and glared his way through the ensuing hubbub. By the time he'd found his way around the chaos, Silas was nowhere to be seen.

'Fuck.'

Tracking down the woman in the bonnet, he put on his sweetest smile.

'That large gentleman who spoke with you...tell me where he was headed.'

She regarded him, her fingers tight upon her floral skirts, her pink lips moist. She was wary. He'd been far too forthright, fallen back to his commanding ways. At times the propriety of humankind drove him to distraction, and this was one of those times.

'I'm not sure I should say. Might I ask what you want of him?'

He stared at her. What a brilliant bloody question. What the fuck *was* he doing here, scurrying after Sickle like a lost pup. 'I...I just... Good day to you.' He turned on his shit-stained heels and carried on with all the refinement his limp would allow. High time he returned to the hall. Or better yet, he'd find the alehouse in this miserable place and drain it of its supplies.

'He asked for the churchyard,' the woman called out, and Pitch stopped. 'It is down Persher Lane. You'll see the blacksmith's on the corner. I could show you, if you like?' How congenial she'd become all of a sudden. 'I see it's likely you are trying to return his coat to him...are you not?'

He turned to look at her, stepping out of the way of a burly gent who moved too close. He sought to catch Pitch's eye, but the flirtation was ignored. Of course Silas would be headed for such a place. To sit among the rot and loss. He sighed.

'I am indeed.' Pitch patted at the coat beneath his arm. 'He does tend towards forgetfulness. Not altogether right in the head sometimes my friend.'

He thought she might comment on his own lack of outerwear, but she gave him a shallow smile and gestured up the road. 'This way. I'll show you.'

The woman led him to a narrow laneway, one a person might streak by if they were in a hurry or too distracted by the sight of the blacksmith, a well-muscled specimen, streaked with black soot and all the other grime of fireside work. On another day Pitch would have happily drunk in the man's fine form, but this day the sight of the black smears on the smithy's body brought to mind an unpleasant comparison to the amuletum needled into his own.

'There you are, then.' The woman in the bonnet of green did not even wait for his thanks.

Pitch watched her walk on, wondering if she would at least sneak a glance back at him. She did not turn.

'No accounting for taste.' He tugged at his corset vest, setting the boning more comfortably, and headed down the laneway.

His uneven, cumbersome strides seemed to stretch the journey endlessly, but at last the churchyard came into view, woeful as it was. There was barely a handful of gravestones to be seen. What a lonesome place to desire. The ankou was both stuffy *and* strange. Granted, far less stuffy than Pitch had imagined. His fingers curled, just thinking on how the man had stroked away all trace of a prince's wreck and ruin.

He searched for Silas and spotted him at once, standing before a ruined church like a witless dolt. He appeared frozen in terror as he stared at the red-eyed beast that slunk from the depths of the dilapidated building.

'Silas,' Pitch shouted, running into the yard. He flung away the ankou's coat, and summoned his flame to hand. It was not quick to ignite, sputtering and crackling through him. It was too soon. 'Move!'

The beast padded down the short flight of stairs that led out of the church and onto the grass. The massive creature would look Silas in the eye if it raised its head enough, and it was now hardly a few feet from him. Yet, the ankou made no move to flee.

Pitch's heat rose, and there at his core the familiar stirring began. A shadow of its former self, but woken just the same. What in Dagan's name was wrong with the fool? This must be the creature Silas's little bedmate Charlie had spoken of, the monster that had sought to take pieces of the ankou for its supper. Pitch might have forgiven the beast had it devoured Silas's lover, but he could not allow it to feed here.

Silas turned his head. His mouth was open, brow furrowed. Perhaps he shouted something, but the roar inside Pitch's head drowned it.

He raced through the headstones, all stiffened joints forgotten.

Pitch drew back his arm. Fuck, the limb was as heavy as the blacksmith's anvil. But at least the beast's attentions had shifted from Silas to Pitch. The creature's red eyes blazed, one large as a crown, the other smaller than a sixpence. It moved past Silas and sank back on its haunches, gathering itself to leap.

'Pitch, no!' Silas's voice cut through the roar.

No? Had the ankou gone insane?

'Run, Silas.' Pitch readied to cast the flame, wincing. His ribs burned, and not as they should. The flame was piss-weak, fluttering like a candle in a draft-filled hall. His arm ached so hard he could barely keep it raised. Gods, he was a piece of shit. The ankou needed him, and Pitch was a failure once more.

Anger tapped at the hole inside him. His innards twisted in a way he did not recognise, or enjoy. Silas was definitely shouting at him, but the ankou could cry himself hoarse. If Pitch was in such disrepair that he could not fell a wild dog, then best he was dumped back in that fucking abaddon where he belonged.

Something kicked at Pitch's insides, the wildness moving about. The flame erupted in his palm. Now *that* was more like it. Daemon and beast leapt in unison. The red-eyed dog released a horrendous shriek, as though a hundred cockatrice screamed as one. The firelight emanating from Pitch's hand made it seem as though the beast's long lengths of fur quivered with its fear.

The impact came from out of nowhere.

A massive weight struck his side.

An unbecoming sound left him, a startled cry mixed with a violent exhale. Pitch was crushed into the damp grass with a weight pinning him down. Dirt stung his eyes, forcing them closed. The flame shot forth from his hand, ripping a glowing path along the ground.

'Pitch, stop. Please.'

Please? What kind of idiot said please at such a time?

The weight upon him shifted, and Pitch snatched at the freedom. He twisted like an eel, flipping onto his back, blinking madly to clear his vision. His flame had lost its blinding glow, but this close it would do damage enough to his foe.

'Pitch, stop!'

Silas's cry struck at Pitch's core, but it was too late to heed. He was swinging his arm already, the flame racing ahead in a deadly streak of destruction. The ankou vanished in the glare. His weight lifted, freeing Pitch, who choked on panic and memory and terrible mistakes.

'No. No!'

He slammed his hand into his own chest, sending the flame there. Fabric singed, melting beneath the touch of a dying daemonic light. He stamped it down inside himself, crushing it into the recesses it should have never left. *He* should never have left that godsforsaken room. The restlessness returned to its depths, leaving winter's bone behind. He curled in on himself, lifting his knees so he might ball himself up and disappear entirely.

'No, no, no.' He rocked against the heavy earth, eyes squeezed tight, the grass wet against his cheek and ear. But it was not a paltry graveyard where he lay. It was upon the scoured ground of the Hellfield.

Why was he in the way? Fucking idiot. Raph should not have been there.

'I didn't see him...I didn't see him in the way,' he whispered to the worms and dirt.

'Pitch?' A hand touched his shoulder and he flinched. 'Can you hear me? Look at me.'

The oaf was speaking. He was alive.

Pitch exhaled, and the Hellfield drifted away, taking the gore and grit and nightmares with it. He lay like a beaten dog upon the ground, but he was shaking too hard to unwrap himself.

'Pitch, please...say something...'

'Fuck off,' he told the worms and the dirt, and the ankou with his tender worry.

'Well, I'll take that to mean you are all right, shall I?'

Silas, damn him, would not let Pitch lie. A hand pressed to his shoulder, another to his waist, and he was pulled onto his knees. The moment he was upright, Pitch laid hands on the ankou's chest, pushing him away. Gods, he was rock solid.

'Are you entirely deaf? I said leave me be.' He darted a glance at the idiot's face. There was a redness on his cheek that might have been a burn. Pitch looked away.

'I'm not going to do that,' Silas said. 'I'm all right...if that is what is burdening you. Look, I am fine. No harm done. I shouldn't have lunged at you so –'

Pitch grabbed the ankou's jacket, large fistfuls of material, drawing him in close, making certain he would not mishear. 'Never, ever place yourself in my way again.' Pitch sounded no less of an animal than he was. 'Do you understand me, ankou?'

CHAPTER 31

S ilas understood very well. He'd do no such thing ever again, if he had
a say in the matter. Pitch was still ablaze with terrible beauty. His eyes
each a small inferno, bright as the flame that had pulsed from his hands.
Muscles at his jaw worked, and his warm breath fluttered against Silas's
lips. He'd thought his final moment had arrived, again, when Pitch had
rolled over, fist raised and blazing, teeth bared.

There, Silas had seen the soldier, the fighter upon a battlefield.

'I understand, Pitch.' Silas nodded, keeping the movement slow so as
not to accidentally cut loose one of the taut strings that seemed to hold
the daemon upright. 'I understand. And I'm sorry. It will not happen
again.'

Because he'd know the look next time. He'd recognise that fury well.

The daemon still held him, fists holding so much of Silas's jacket
the seams strained at his shoulders. Pitch blinked, as though something
stung at his eyes. The departure of his anger was as evident as its rise.
Slivers of gold settled into the depths of emerald. His breathing evened.
He relaxed the grip of one hand and, before Silas could ready for it,
touched his cheek.

'Does it hurt?' Pitch said roughly.

It did, a little. At the place where the flame had glanced against him.
The skin tingled, as though he'd leaned too close to a candle. 'No. Not
in the least.'

Pitch lifted his gaze, and their eyes met.

Christ. Silas was even less ready for this. His pulse stuttered. Damn it, they knelt too close. The drama of the past few moments still made the air hum. A bead of sweat traced the contour of Pitch's cheek, running down long lines that Silas wished to follow. He'd touched that skin once before, and now it taunted him. There was dirt upon Pitch's chin. Silas could brush it clear, run his thumb along that curve. A courtesy, nothing more. Something to soothe, perhaps, and chase away the shadows that plagued the daemon.

The quiet stretched as thin as Silas's held breath.

Pitch watched him closely. He kept his accursed finger touching Silas's cheek, moving it just slightly enough that gooseflesh rose, and the pulse in Silas's neck dashed out an unreadable Morse code. The corner of Pitch's lip twitched. He knew what he was doing, and better yet, was relishing it. The daemon was coming back into himself. Silas could see it, like the creep of dawn sweeping away the nightfall. Relief flooded him and very nearly pushed him to do something foolish, like cup his hands to that fearsome, astonishing face, and take possession of those lips, ensuring Pitch was well clear of the pall that had descended on him.

The terrible plan was laid to waste by the thrust of a wet, hairy muzzle between them.

'Fuck.' Pitch was on his feet in an instant.

The skriker growled low in its cavernous chest. The scent of damp fur clung to the air.

'It's all right, stay calm.' Silas rose, waving the beast back. He'd been so caught up with gazing at Pitch like an enamoured fool, he'd not given a thought to the animal's whereabouts. 'The creature intends no harm.'

'Really?' Pitch arched a brow and folded his arms across the scorched hole in his clothing that exposed alabaster skin. He was all delicate poise once more. 'What does it intend, then? I dare say it is not to fetch my slippers. Lucifer's sack, the stench is appalling.'

He pinched his nose, and the skriker seemed to take personal affront. The growl sharpened to a snarl, sopping lips pulling back to show off the onyx gums with their yellowed fangs. The beast hunched low down on its front quarters, as though it were actually considering the ludicrous option of attacking the daemon again.

'Go on then.' Pitch was not the least bit concerned. 'Come for me. It won't change the fact that you reek, and by gods you are awfully ugly.' He smiled his most disconcerting of smiles. The rage had gone, there was that at least, but really he was being most unhelpful.

'There, there, that's enough now,' Silas said, to both the creatures who glared balefully at one another. He dared touch only one of them. With a brief hesitation, Silas planted a hand on the skriker's thick neck and applied a gentle pressure he hoped would signal it to move away. Beneath his fingers the black coat was no less wiry than it appeared. 'Go on, away with you now. Some room would be appreciated.'

The skriker's reddened eyes were slow to shift from Pitch, and its black lips did not shift from a snarl. But at last, and with a disgruntled toss of its head, the creature backed away. Not so far, Silas noted, that it couldn't have set upon the daemon in a single leap.

'That is still far too close, you fleabag. You're making my eyes water.' Pitch flicked his hand as though the massive animal were but a fly.

'Leave it, Pitch,' Silas said. 'The skriker is my ally.'

'Your ally drools.'

That was not untrue. Long sinewy lengths of spittle hung from the hair beneath the skriker's jaw. Pitch wasn't entirely wrong in his assessment of the creature's lack of beauty.

'Well, so be it. I do not mind. Bess tells me the first ankou had a creature like this. A fae hound gifted –'

The twitch of Pitch's lip held no bemusement this time. 'Oh wonderful, another fae creature.' His words were tight as coiled string. 'I always have such a remarkable time with their kind. What with being fed upon by a horde of them, or tied to a bed and imprisoned in the home of another.' His laughter seemed to snag upon something in his throat, Silas could hear the hitch as though it were the crack of bone. 'Tell me all about your remarkable fae hound, my dear. I am so eager to hear of its merits'

Silas blasted his own thoughtlessness.

'I'm sorry, Pitch. I –'

'No, no, go on. Tell me of how you found your drooling ally hound while you wandered the wild road abandoned by your guardian.'

Silas eyed him warily. Pitch waited, tapping a toe against the ground. It was difficult to place his undertone. Sarcasm must be there, it so often was. But there rang another note too. And it could not possibly be the remorse it seemed.

'The skriker was a most welcome help when I was upon the road.' Silas paused. 'I don't know how much you've been told of the ash-men...the revenants that stalked us –'

'I understand you needed a piss-weak snip of a girl and a gnarled soothsaying bitch to haul you from trouble's reach. Honestly, how useless can a man be, if he cannot survive on his own one moment?'

Oh, Pitch was definitely well recovered. If Silas were like the daemon, he would have said something suitably cruel about *why* it was he'd found himself on his own. But one vicious tongue was enough.

'Lad.' Silas was categorical.

'What?'

'Charlie is to be referred to as a lad.' Silas glanced across the graveyard. Christ, he was hungry. And his pie must be stone cold by now.

'I suspect they don't care what you call them, so long as your prick finds its way between their legs.' Pitch's grin was wry, his tongue mean. The very place he so enjoyed. 'Really, you should charge for your services, Silas. We would all pay handsomely. I'm sure your *lad* would pawn his own mother so he could spread wide for you again.'

The skriker's growl rumbled along with the distant storm that hung over Harvington Hall. Perhaps the beast sensed Silas's own anger, hot and tight in his chest.

'Tobias, do not speak another word. I am done with your spite.' He turned on his heels, setting his back to the cursed bastard. 'Charlie is a good lad, and so very brave. At least he and Tyvain were at my side, when you were in no state to be so.' To hell with being considerate. Silas stalked away, raising his voice as he went. 'You may say what you like of me, mock me to your heart's content. You so often remind me of how pathetic I am, well then go ahead. I'm sure you are feverish with the desire to tell me how very disappointing it was to have me in your bed, of how inadequately I'm endowed, and cumbersome in my ways. I do not care, let your forked tongue run free.' He swallowed against the sting of it. 'But if I ever, ever hear you speak of Charlie in such a crass and vulgar way again, so help me, Pitch, I will chain you to that bed once more, and I will ride out alone. I don't care if your bloody Lord Enoch himself commands otherwise. I will survive. I proved I am capable of doing so without any assistance from you. Now be on your way. For it is clear you have no more wish to be here than I do to have you at my side.'

Christ almighty, if felt good to spew vitriol as he stomped away like a bruiser, releasing all the various tensions that plagued him. But his tirade had gotten away from him. The remark about the chain was a step too far. Too personal and vicious. He'd have burned down Harvington Hall rather than see Pitch so low again. And he had lied through his teeth about not wanting Pitch nearby.

But he could not apologise.

He *must* not, for what he'd said was not all wrong.

Silas weaved his way through the short expanse of graves, and still not a word came at him from behind. The skriker padded along beside him, silent upon paws as wide as side plates. They halted just short of the stone seat where the gingham-wrapped tin and small bundle of paper sat. But it was what lay on the ground that caught Silas's eye. He frowned at the bundle of royal-blue material with black trimmings. What in all the world was his coat doing here? The skriker's wide head lifted, and the beast peered over its shoulder, lips curled back in a silent snarl. Silas turned quickly.

Pitch had followed. He'd moved as silently as the beast had done, but Silas caught his last step and saw the limp there. The daemon saw him watching and straightened, clasping his hands behind his back, which only served to tug at the scorched hole in his vest, revealing bare skin. The lunatic had turned the flame upon himself, as though he sought to burn himself away.

'I'd rather you did not,' Pitch said, not much louder than the breeze.

'Did not what?' Silas's anger cooled at the sight of the daemon, whose skin was not so alabaster as he recalled. A greyness tinged its hue, darker in the rings beneath his eyes. He was not yet ready to be here, Silas saw it now.

'I'd rather you did not ride alone,' Pitch returned.

They were back at that quiet place, where breath and time stretched thin.

The beast shook itself, stepping forward. Silas stayed the skriker with the merest spread of his hand. The beast seemed to know his command and bowed its head, settling its great weight upon the ground at his feet. Neither Pitch nor Silas shifted their gaze from one another. The air brightened as the sun made a near successful attempt to pierce the thin cloud cover.

'And I would prefer that you were at my side,' Silas said with what air he could find to breathe.

'Though you have just said otherwise.'

Here, among the headstones, raw from the trauma of past trials, Pitch's slender form seemed less delicate, and more frail.

'I was angry with you.'

'And rightly so.'

Silas had no reply for that, least of all because the admission left him dumbstruck.

But Pitch was not done with shocking him. 'I apologise for the offence to your friend. Charlie was certainly far more useful to you than I have been.' He darted his tongue against his lips. His eyelids fluttering as though he fought not to look away. 'I am...I am sorry that I was not there when you were set upon. I should have been. What you must think of me, having seen that...deplorable wreck that hides beneath this skin, I cannot imagine. You've seen for yourself the folly it is to have made me your guardian. This game being played grows more ludicrous by the day, and whatever role we play, the two of us, ever more dangerous.' His irritation tightened his shoulders and pulled at the edge of his eyes. 'I mean, we have necromancers to deal with now? What absolute crud. You were supposed to be downing a few teratisms, and I was supposed to toddle along at your side to make a pretty picture. We have been duped, my dear. What's wrong? You look strange. Are you going to faint? I'm far too tired to lift you, and your dog will probably bite me.'

Silas flushed, aware he must have looked to be in something of a stupor. Because he damned well was. Pitch had just *apologised* to him. And revealed something of himself in the process. Bess had been right. The daemon thought himself pitiable and he assumed Silas did the same.

'Did you bring me my coat?' It was not in the least what Silas thought would spill from his mouth.

'What?' Pitch scowled.

'My coat. It is here.' Silas busied himself with collecting the swathe of blue material from the ground. It was damp in patches but otherwise none the worse for wear. 'And it was not me who brought it. Was it you?'

He readied himself for scorn and ridicule, for the self-deprecating mood couldn't last.

'I did.' Pitch was set to spend the day surprising him, it seemed. 'You need your trinket, do you not? And it was in the pocket.'

Silas touched the coat, tracing his fingers along the black trim at the collar, picturing the daemon trudging all the way here despite how his leg must have bothered him. Bloody hell. It was unbearably endearing.

'You are not pitiable, Pitch. I want you to know that.' Silas shrugged off his jacket. He shook out his coat and slid into it, relaxing beneath the familiar folds. 'I know you have faced terrible hardships in your past...that you have seen abominable things happen. Perhaps one day you'll see fit to share your troubles with me but know that I do not pity you for them. When I found you...in that room...I was worried for you and I saw you as weakened, not weak. There is a difference. Christ, if anyone is weak it is me. I mean, I'm trying my utmost, and I've learned much, but if I...if I were...more...if I did not rely on you so heavily...you'd need not have pushed yourself so far, as you did. I would truly not blame you if you refused to ride with me again. You've been given a thankless task, guarding a clueless man like me, and I'm sorry for it.'

He exhaled. He'd not looked up once while the words poured from him, well aware that Pitch had not made a sound all the while. Perhaps he'd wandered off, bored with his speech. Silas delayed the inevitable a little longer, brushing at his front, and when he lifted his head the daemon was there. Almost right upon him. Only a single step separated them, one that could not be surmounted, thanks to the presence of the skriker who was still settled at Silas's feet. But the beast's imposing presence did not deter Pitch. He leaned over the skriker, and his cool lips found Silas's mouth. The kiss was fleeting, barely there, bitter and sweet and gone before Silas could draw breath.

Pitch's smile lit up the sun-starved day, his eyes of purest emerald once more. 'It is not an entirely thankless task, Sickle. For though you might not yet be a warrior of note, you are talented in other ways I can appreciate.' His gaze darted downward, the aim plain. Christ almighty. This daemon was a whirlwind that had Silas in a spin. 'But you need not worry, you'll not be duty bound to lift me from a tiresome melancholy again. Your services were appreciated, don't misunderstand, but they shall not be called on again.' He snatched up the discarded grey jacket and wriggled into it. The size dwarfed him, which was quite charming. 'I know how much the whole thing bothered you. So fear not, I shall leave you to your adventures with your lad from this day on, and I will take my appetites elsewhere.'

Silas held still. Duty bound? Was that how the daemon saw their encounter? A service. That was not how Silas remembered it, but then he was not an incubus who must have bedded half the British Isles and a quarter of the New World combined by now. What had been an astonishing tryst for him was likely run-of-the-mill for Pitch. Silas was too slow to fill the pregnant pause, and the moment to speak sailed by.

Pitch lifted his shoulders in a grand sigh.

'Well now, what did you bring to picnic with?' He peered around Silas. 'Anything I can share in? I'm famished.'

To have the daemon think Silas wished to stay clear of his bed was not a terrible idea, the complications of such a dalliance were bound to be fraught with dangers. They needed their wits about them, not their hands upon one another's cocks, disappearing into each other's mouths as the world drew its blades, circling in. That would have been awful, indeed.

'Tarts...strawberry tarts,' Silas said, quickly. What harm though in showing thoughtfulness and consideration of his fellow rider's needs? 'I saw them in the bakery and thought you would enjoy them.'

The daemon was as delighted as Silas had imagined he would be, practically bouncing on his toes, setting his gold-streaked waves tossing. 'You bought them for me?' He also seemed a little startled by the fact. 'Oh gods, don't tease me. Do you truly have some?'

'I truly do.' Silas chuckled.

Pitch went to step around the skriker. The beast pushed to its feet, planting all four paws wide as though it sought to make its considerable frame larger still. Pitch glowered at the barrier now resting between him and the promised tarts. If Silas did not step in, he feared a return of the daemon's flame and the scent of dog meat on the air.

'Easy there, ah...well, I don't suppose you have a name do you?' Really, he needed to name the animal if it were going to hang about.

Pitch folded his arms, nearly eye to eye with the lofty beast. 'I had a valet once...in Arcadia...who was almost as unattractive as this thing, and as irritatingly loyal,' he said. 'Forneus, his name was. I think it suits your fleabag well enough.'

Silas considered it and grunted his approval. 'Right then, Forneus, out of the way. Let him by.'

But the newly-named beast was not heeding his command this time. Forneus held his ground. The animal lifted its shaggy snout, drops of slather raining from the rough fur. A convulsion took hold of its gut, its belly lifting and shuddering. A harsh cough sprayed spittle wide.

'Fuck.' Pitch stepped out of the way, unsteady on his troublesome leg. He wrinkled his fine nose. 'Is it dying?'

'I have no idea.' Silas hoped not. But it did not appear impossible.

The beast wretched, shoulder's lifting as its gut spasmed. The rough jarring reached its ribs, and Forneus hacked as though its lungs were filled with furballs. The creature's entire body was affected. Its thick neck contracted in time with a rasping, choking sound that pained the ears. Forneus opened its jaws wide, the widest Silas had seen it do so. The back of the beast's throat was bared, the inside as dark as the gums. But in the very depths of the throat something shone. Silas took a step closer to the ailing creature. Its haggard coat moved as though each hair were alive, such was the ferocity of its convulsions. The larger of the two red-eyes was radiant, ever more reminiscent of an ember at the heart of a well-set fire. The crimson sheen lit the interior of Forneus's mouth so well there could be no mistaking it. The creature was coughing up an obstruction. One so large Silas wondered if it would clear the canine's teeth.

'Careful.' Pitch's warning was a smidge too late.

The blockage shot forth. Silas wrenched his head clear barely soon enough. Whatever propelled from the beast's mouth skimmed his temple, catching a few strands of hair and tearing them free as it continued on over his shoulder.

Pitch cursed behind him, and Silas spun to find the daemon clutching at his thigh. 'Gods damn that foul piece of shit. As though this bloody leg isn't enough of a pain in my arse.'

'What happened?'

'That.' Pitch stabbed a finger down at the ground in front of his feet. A length of ebon wood lay there, at least as long as Silas's arm. 'Your dog just tried to impale me with it.'

Forneus sat on its hindquarters, long grey tongue slithering around the perimeter of its lips. The beast lifted a paw to swipe at its jaw. It looked as displeased as the daemon, panting in heavy gasps.

'What on Earth is it?' Silas crouched to one knee.

'I'm sure I'll be fine, by the way,' Pitch muttered.

'I'm sure you will be too.' Silas touched at the wood gingerly. One end lay buried in grass grown long enough to conceal it. He pinched his thumb and forefinger about the middle and lifted the slobber-drenched projectile. His eyes narrowed. 'Bloody hell.'

The skriker had thrown up a walking cane. And not a simple one at that. Silas suspected the wood to be blackthorn, a dark and sturdy grain. The shaft was smooth and gleaming beneath its lathering of bodily fluid, while the collar and handle were an exquisite work of silver and niello. There was much detail in the metalwork at the collar, embellishments he'd study later, but it was the handle that captured him. The end of the curve was shaped into the head of a fox. Ears erect with focused attention, its triangular snout ground to a sharp enough point it would make a handy weapon on its own. Green stones were inlaid in the eyes, their hue near Pitch's own.

Silas rubbed his thumb between the fox's ears, wrinkling his brow with thought. 'I've seen the likes of this before. I'm sure of it.'

'Well good for you, then.' Pitch still rubbed his thigh. 'Could we return to the tarts?'

Silas shook his head. 'At The Atlas.' He recalled his first visit there, and the long journey the house had led him on. 'Mr Ahari, he has one just like it...though it is ivory, not this silver.' He glanced over at the skriker. Forneus paid him no mind. The beast was fixed on Pitch. In turn, the daemon had eyes only for the gingham-covered parcel on the stone seat.

'I'm sure you will look most fetching with it, dear Sickle. Now, might we eat?'

He stepped around Silas. The skriker was on its feet at Silas's side in an instant. The beast snatched the cane from his grasp and lunged forward with the length of wood protruding out either side of its jaws.

'You bloody stupid hound.'

Pitch balled a fist, as though he meant to punch the animal into submission. Forneus angled its head, and the metal head of the cane touched the daemon's knuckles. Pitch drew in a sharp breath. His shoulders slackened, and his eyes fluttered as though he struggled to keep them open.

'Pitch? What is it?'

In answer the daemon uncurled his fingers and wrapped them about the head of the cane. He touched at the collar, seemingly lost in thought. Forneus released its mouthy grasp and backed away. The glow of the beast's eyes had dimmed. They settled on Silas a moment, and a growl followed, but it was higher pitched, a different sound entirely to those that came before. The creature turned and loped away through the headstones, with narrow ribbons of weak sunlight glancing against the dullness of its coat.

'What the hell was that all about?' Silas said, exasperated.

Pitch was watching the creature go. There was a lightness about him that had been absent before, fewer lines about his eyes and at the edges of that impossible mouth. 'Me, I believe.' He set the tip of the cane upon the ground and settled his hand about the fox's head, tilting his hips like the showman he was. 'I think I look far too quaint myself, but I suppose I can make it work. What do you think?'

Silas thought it looked incredibly fetching. 'It is not terrible.'

'High praise. I shall tell Mr Ahari when we next see him that you don't think much of his offering.'

'Good grief, it *is* from him?'

Pitch nodded. 'His delivery method leaves much to be desired.' Silas would not disagree there.

'How are you so sure of it? Is there some kind of enchantment upon it that has let you know?'

'Yes, it's called a note.' He slipped his finger underneath a scrap of leather that had been stuck flat with all the moisture to the intricate metalwork at the collar. 'Cut into leather so your dog's gut didn't ruin it. Dear Mr Astaroth, This is the best we can do for now. I do hope it is enough. We will keep searching, best regards, Tejin Ahari. Astonishingly magickal, wouldn't you say.'

'No need to be quite so dry about it.'

'You can read it for yourself if you like.' He held out the cane.

Silas waved him off with hurried, feigned disinterest. 'I will take your word for it.'

Pitch dug the cane into the damp grass, fingers so tight around the handle his knuckles turned a whiter shade of pale. 'But I fear they pin too great a hope upon too slight a cane. You have an unsteady guardian, my dear Sickle.'

Silas longed to wrap those pained fingers in his own, to ease the unspoken hardship. 'And you have me, an artless charge, so I suppose we are even really. We will just have to make do, seeing as neither of us are able to do anything else. Besides, as I told you, I've learned a bloody great deal since Black Annis. I think you'd be surprised at how adept I am with the scythe now. I cut a man in half, don't you know?'

The grip upon the cane relaxed, and Pitch's smile was lopsided and genuine. 'I did know, and I must say, Sickle, I had a moment of pride on hearing the news. A beheading too, I'm told. Well done, my fine fellow.'

The moment was ridiculous, and Silas relished it. 'Why thank you, Mr Astaroth. Most kind. Now shall we eat?' He swept his arm towards the stone seat with its two packages. Perhaps pigeon did not taste too awful when it was as cold as the day around it. He could hope. 'We can go back to the hall, if you'd prefer, or to the pub maybe? We could have an ale with our tarts and pie?'

Pitch started towards the seat, his weight upon the cane. To Silas's eye it did not seem he limped so badly as he walked. His hips swayed very nicely. He did not look quaint in the least.

'I interrupted your visit to your beloved graveyard, so I'm sure you'd rather spend a little more time with your corpses. This is where you find some peace, is it not?'

'It is.' And it did not seem an odd thing to admit.

'And I will not disturb that peace if I stay?'

'No. You will not.' Not, at least, in the way he might imagine.

Pitch let his cane drop into the damp grass. They settled beside each other, Silas delivering the gingham-wrapped parcel into Pitch's eager hands and saving the pie for himself. There was not much room to be had upon the seat. Their thighs touched as they made themselves comfortable as possible on the cold slab of stone, and Silas struggled to submergè a dangerous memory of Pitch's bare leg draped over his.

'So, are we to follow after Sybilla then?' Pitch's gaze fixed on the opened tin, fingers wriggling as he hesitated over his pick of the pastries. 'We're bound for Shrewsbury and your necromancer?'

'No. I believe we will have our own path to follow.' Silas had no idea where the certainty came from, but he was beginning to see that some things need not be questioned. Things that were an innate part of him. 'Lalassu hasn't shown me the way yet, but she will.' He frowned down at his pie. 'And Christ knows what that journey will entail.'

'Very likely not a lot that we will enjoy. I'd say we are going to have a bloody wretched time, really. But not today. This day is for strawberry tarts and whatever that stinking thing is you are about to eat.'

Silas laughed, the brightness of the sound surprising him. 'It's pigeon, and it smells bloody wonderful.'

'I fear for your sense of smell, I truly do.'

A tiny, brave sparrow landed on the grass near to Pitch's feet. Hopping far closer than Silas thought wise. He waited for his easily-irritated guardian to send it fleeing for its minuscule life, but Pitch had surprised him many times today, and was not done yet. The daemon pinched a piece of the golden crust between slender fingers and leaned down. To Silas's utter astonishment, the sparrow edged in closer and darted its beak at the morsel, swallowing it in an instant, and then flitting away.

'What?' Pitch raised the rest of the tart to his mouth. 'Did you want to put that bird in your pie too?'

'Certainly not. I just didn't figure you for a birder, that's all.'

'I dare say there are many things you do not figure me for.'

'I dare say.'

Pitch bit into the tart and hummed into his mouthful, as terrible a songster as ever, but clearly delighted with the pastry. Silas took a mouthful of the pie, finding it still warm at its centre, and thought the moment so very near to perfect.

A blissful lull before a brewing storm.

A quiet, troublefree moment certainly not made to last. But he would take it as it was, and relish it all the more.

CHAPTER 32

The soothsayer didn't think much of staying so long at Harvington Hall, near on two weeks now. The fresh air hurt her head and made her eyes water. She was certain those bloody chickens scratching about gave her a rash. And the nights in the countryside Sanctuary? Curse the Holy Mother's bubbies. It was like the hall went out of its way to be quiet as a bloody tomb in the witching hours. Which made waking in a cold sweat, ears ringing and tongue aching from being chewed on, even more nightmarish than the feckin' nightmares that had startled her awake. That kind of silence lay on a person like a funeral shroud and made it damned hard to breathe. She missed the hue and cry of London something fierce.

'Pissing 'ell. Make yourself bloody clear, won't ya?' She scratched at the tangled nest that was her hair. The same dream had woken her in a breathless mess three nights in a row, and it made her skin crawl each time. But she was buggered if she could remember any detail, save for one.

All the dreams had the same bloke in them. A fellow she'd not seen in months and had only met twice, at the most. Tyvain swiped at her face, her fingers coming away damp. Why him? He was a bloody purebred, not bad to eye up but quiet as a mouse, and had this pained look about him, like his insides ached. He wasn't interesting enough by half to be dreaming about for a fancy, which meant it was something else bringing him to mind.

Tyvain threw back her covers, shivering as the night air glanced across her damp skin. She hadn't had a dreaming sign in feckin' years. A pity, because they were a damned sight more pleasant than a belly swollen with hot air. She pulled on a robe, deciding that wandering about the house naked was likely a recipe for disaster, even at this late hour. Not that she gave a damn about having her cunny bared, that was the worry of other people and they could deal with it themselves, but it was a mite too cold for baring flesh, and her nipples were tight enough to burst. Tyvain shrugged on a green velvet robe, one that was too long for her, and swept from the room like a hobo empress.

She made her way down the hall towards the section of panelling that hid the opening to the backstairs used by the house staff. Her intention was to head down to the basement, where she knew the housekeeper, Mrs Tinkler, wouldn't mind her taking a tipple of the 'moonshine' she kept stashed in her office drawer.

As soon as Tyvain released the latch and the panel swung open, she heard it. Fluttering moans, delicate squeals that barely caressed the air. She rolled her eyes, cursing under her breath.

Someone was fornicating further below in the stairwell. They had the whole damned house, a massive spread of rooms, and they chose this spot? She peered over the railing. These stairs had some of the rare gaslights in the place. Old Bess was a stickler for his flames, but Mrs Tinkler knew how to handle her master and had scored an impressive victory in having gaslights installed in all the domestic areas. So it was a steady glow that caught at the man's hair, waves of light-brown glinting with unmissable gold threads. She'd know the coif anywhere.

Tobias Astaroth.

By all that was unholy, he was a piece of work. She'd not met a lot of daemons, but she knew they nearly all had incubus blood and grew as fat off a good fuck as she did a decent turkey leg. And this Tobias bastard had an appetite and a half. At least, he had until whatever malady it was that had struck him down. Back in London Mr Astaroth had a reputation for sticking his truncheon in any hole that would have him, screwing about like every day was his last. Tyvain leaned out a bit further, trying to catch sight of whom he was hammering against the wall. She wouldn't have been half surprised to see the ankou there. What a fecking sight that would be. It would sure give a woman something to keep herself warm at night.

Well, it was a sight alright.

No sign of Silas, but the daemon had his hands full nonetheless.

A housemaid was pressed up against the wall, hands splayed against the brickwork, white mob cap concealing her face, with the man driving into her from behind covering all else. But it was not the daemon doing the driving there. Tyvain knew the onyx hair well enough. Ronin was getting that fucking he'd been moping over for days, after getting sent running with his tail between his legs from Tobias's sickroom a couple of times. The daemon hadn't been interested in having his cock sucked in the early days, which had Sybilla all grim-faced and unhappy, and Ronin fuming over the rejection. But all was forgiven now it seemed.

While Ronin worked the housemaid, Tobias worked him. The daemon had one hand planted over Ronin's mouth as he pounded his hips against the tsukomagami's arse. Thank all the gods and their salty bollocks Tobias's flowing dressing gown of burgundy velvet covered up the eye-watering sight nicely. But the wet sounds and slapping flesh would take some getting over.

'Jesus wept,' she muttered, hesitating where she was still concealed. 'No other place for this shit?'

Her bet with the groundskeeper that said the ankou and daemon were more than just riding companions wasn't looking like it was going to pay out anytime soon either. She doubted the bashful Mr Mercer was the type to enjoy an orgy or two, so if Tobias were here, it meant his needs hadn't been met elsewhere. Gods, she would have sworn black and blue those two were tupping each other stupid, with the way the air went all prickly when they were in the same room, and the colour rose to Silas's cheeks every time the daemon crossed his path. She, along with most of the housestaff, had spent more than a fine minute or two over the past week watching them in the gardens, training at swordplay. She saw plain how the daemon found countless reasons to put his hands on Silas, all in the name of showing him how to hold his weapon. She was damned sure it wasn't that particular weapon he wanted the ankou to hold.

Well, whatever. No business of hers, and saint's tits, there was more important stuff to fill her head with, with all that was going on. And this orgy could move elsewhere, or at least let her pass. She was bloody thirsty.

Tyvain started down the stairs, the rutting trio oblivious to her approach. She was impressed with how well Tobias could swing his hips when he needed. He required a cane these days to move about, but put a sword in his hand or a tight hole around his cock, and he was lithe as a mist. No wonder Silas seemed so rattled around him. Nice fellow, that ankou. She'd not say it to his face, but he was all right. Strangely calming kind of lad, even though he himself looked startled out of his wits most of the time.

Tyvain charged down the stairs as the whimpers and moans rose higher. Tobias hung his head back, full pink lips parted. Beautiful thing, he was, no denying it, but he reminded her of hemlock. Delicate-looking but deadly.

'Come on you lot!' she snapped. 'Twenty bedrooms in this place, and ya can't use one?'

The maid squeaked, wriggling her way free of the man impaling her. She scratched at her hair, pulling it forward so it covered some of her face, like Tyvain gave a fuck who she was, or whom she was under. Ronin carried on as though the maid had not just jumped off his whore-pipe and raced away. He rocked back into the daemon his eyes rolling back in his head. But though he might act like he'd not heard Tyvain at all, the same couldn't be said for Tobias. He pulled away. And out. Ronin whimpered, staggering.

'Why are you stopping?' he moaned.

'Because we are done.' Tobias flared out his gown before wrapping it tight about his slender waist, and in that brief moment Tyvain was blinded by the glare of Ronin's damp arse cheeks.

'Feckin' 'ells,' she grumbled.

Ronin was equally displeased, snatching at his trousers where they bunched at his ankles.

'You needn't mind her.' He tucked himself away with smooth efficiency and turned to reach for Tobias. 'You weren't yet done.'

The daemon's glare flashed. 'I don't need you telling me my own mind. Go on with you.'

He dismissed the tsukomagami like the house servant he was. Tyvain winced. Feck, that would put Ronin in a right mood. She'd not get a decent game of billiards out of him anytime soon. Ronin muttered something dark beneath his breath and glared at Tyvain as he stormed past her, heading back up the stairs. She was left with the daemon.

He sighed, touching at the curls that played at his temple. 'Do you normally skulk about watching others fuck, Hag?'

She kept her eyes averted from his. Nothing but trouble in those emeralds. They could tempt the robe off the Archbishop of Canterbury, and likely had.

'Skulk? I could 'ave blown Raphael's trumpet, and I doubt any of you lot would 'ave 'eard a thing.'

'Now, that I would like to see, your fish lips wrapped about his trumpet.' He laughed, a sound like fine champagne glasses meeting.

Tyvain's head jerked, as though drawn to the sound. She ground her teeth. Bloody incubus. 'Take your charming claws out of me, will ya?' she snarled. 'You ain't my type.'

'Oh, sweetheart, I'm everybody's type, don't you know?'

His wiley enchantment tugged at her, sent shivers down into her bits where she didn't want them. Had her wondering what those swollen lips of his might taste like. Shit. Why hadn't she just used another stairway to the downstairs? Now she'd pissed him off, and he was going to have her moaning like a whore, just because he bloody could. Tyvain grabbed at a clear thought before it drowned in slick juices.

'If that were so, you wouldn't 'ave been mewling like a lost kit at 'is door the other night, beggin' 'im ta open up. Woke me, you did, with your drunken nonsense. Not a wonder 'e didn't let ya in.'

That had been the first time she'd doubted her bet with the groundskeeper would pay out. Two nights ago, when a staggering daemon had pounded on Silas's door at midnight, and been met with curt refusal.

'Go to bed, Pitch.'

'I'm trying to. My back hurts.'

'You are lying. You said today how well you felt. That we were ready to ride out.'

'Things have changed suddenly. Now it's too painful to sleep.'

'Then have some more wine.'

The heat of arousal left her with a shocking snap, and gooseflesh rose along her arms. Tyvain shook her head, her thoughts full of hemlock. She was a damned fool, likely having stepped from one fire to another by goading him. Tyvain kept her eyes down, considering the stairs ahead. To go further down, she'd have to practically brush by the daemon, which wasn't an appealing idea right then.

'This damned place is intolerable,' Tobias growled. 'We cannot leave it soon enough.'

She wouldn't argue with him there. Tyvain edged against the railing, making enough room for him as he swept past that they didn't need to touch.

'If you value those fish lips of yours,' he said, in that way that lay between snarl and hiss he did so well, 'it would serve you to keep them shut about...this evening. Mr Mercer has enough on his mind without the gossips of a household.'

She stared at his back as he made his way up the stairs, his limp well pronounced. What the bloody hell was that about? Since when did Tobias give a shit who knew what he did with his tackle?

She huffed her way further down the stairs, tempted to mention that he had twenty fucking bedrooms to hide away in if he wanted to keep himself secret, but deciding he wasn't worth the breath it would take. She was well on her way to putting some distance between them when her stomach clenched so hard she nearly tripped down the steps.

Twenty bedrooms.

She stopped. In this enormous house, at an ungodly hour, she'd run smack bang into the very person who had a direct link with the man in her dreams.

'Saint's fanny.' She smacked her forehead. 'You're a stupid 'ag sometimes, Ty.'

Really, she was. A soothsayer who couldn't see things set straight in front of her. Things that probably stood out like candles in a cellar to anyone else with half a wit of sense, but to her were just a hodgepodge of random signs that rarely made much sense. Still, she couldn't deny that since the Blight started playing up this time, the blurry edges were fading. That blasted residue of the angels' war stirred up her senses like the bloody chickens roused a rash.

'Hey,' she called out to Tobias. 'What was the name of that friend 'a yours? That lad in the military you flirted with for a season. Edward, weren't it?'

Oh and feckin' hell, there was another thing she'd missed. She'd drawn a medallion in her journal a few months back. A fancy thing with green enamel. Bess told her she was a terrible artist, and it was quite true. The design came out more like a button melted by a fire. But Tyvain saw it clear as cut crystal now for what it was. A war medal.

Tobias was quiet for so long she turned about. He watched her like a hawk. She shouldn't have put herself a few steps below him. It wasn't a comfortable place to be.

'Why do you ask?'

For a pretty thing he had a voice like a snake slithering. Tyvain's sleepy mind scrambled for a reply. She'd not expected him to get the shits about being asked. Her gut flipped like it did when she was headed in the right direction.

'I'm tryin' to set that Charlie friend of Silas's up with someone decent, ain't I?' Tyvain sniffed through her thin excuse. 'Get him away from this place, back with the purebreds. Old Bess is a silly tart wantin' 'im to stay 'ere. Why you so put out? You lookin' to marry the lieutenant yourself, then? Sorry to break it to ya luv, purebreds 'ave got a real twist in their cocks about that idea.' She cackled.

'Do I seem the marrying kind to you?' They both knew the answer. 'I dare say you are setting yourself up for failure there though. The lieutenant isn't fond of what's between Charlie's legs.'

'Hmph.' Tyvain scratched at her ear. 'Well, I don't think Charlie's that fond of what's there neither. But you're right, forget I asked.' She had what she needed anyway. Just the mention of the mousey fellow had caused Tobias to get all prickly. More so than normal, anyways. And her guts were churning. Her artistry may well be shite, but the medal was the lieutenant's, she was sure of it. And the green enamel a pale imitation of the daemon's eyes.

'Now do be a good hag and fuck off,' Tobias said.

'Eat 'orseshit and choke on it.'

With their nighttime farewells completed, they went their separate ways. Tyvain marched down the stairs, breathing easier with each step. Hell's bells, how did the ankou stand it? Tobias made it hard to breathe, and not in a good way. Tyvain found the basement at last and was marching through the dimly lit servants dining room when she halted once more. Heaven's crotch, it stank like a fish market.

Something stirred by the low narrow window that filtered light into the subterranean basement. Her gut gurgled.

''O's there then?' she barked.

'Oh god, you scared the life out of me, Tyvain,' a warm voice returned.

'Charlie?' Tyvain padded nearer, regretting her decision not to wear slippers. The stone floor was icy.

'Yes.' There was a scraping sound and a point of orange light bloomed as Charlie lit a candle in a tarnished silver chamberstick. He sat at the long table used by house staff for their meals. 'Sorry, I heard someone coming and wasn't sure if I should be here so...'

'You'll be needing to throw out that bloody concoction, then, if you want to stay 'idden.' Tyvain tugged her robe tighter around her. 'What in sweet 'ell are you eatin'?'

He had a broad smile, warm as the flame that flickered beside him. 'Cook made me a Cullen skink yesterday.'

'I'm sorry to 'ear that.'

Charlie laughed, a far more pleasing sound than when the daemon had done so. 'It's Scottish, and delicious, I assure you. I used to have them every day when I was young.' Like the lad was ancient now. 'I couldn't sleep, and I always found it helped in the past, so I thought I'd sneak down for a bowl.'

Another chance encounter, and Tyvain doubted it was not without its meaning. The night had that feel about it, as though the fates were bustling about and rearranging things like a housemaid did the furniture. The gossamer grey light that came before the dawn was evident through the dirty panes. Tyvain's gut swirled and messed about. She pressed a hand to her belly. 'Righto, righto, I get ya. Just keep it down,' she mumbled.

Charlie looked confused. 'I didn't think I was making any noise...'

'Nah, you're all good, laddie-lass. I'm just talkin' to me gut.'

'Oh, if you're hungry we could share?'

Of course they bloody could. Charlie was decent. Every bit as good and pleasant as the ankou. It wasn't right that he had to skulk about on his own along the rough roads of England. Tyvain had lied to Tobias about wanting to get Charlie out of here. Old Bess's idea that the lad should stay was a good one, though she'd drink cow piss rather than tell the old bastard so.

'I'll pass. But thankin' ya, all the same.' She leaned a hip against the table. 'Ya from Scotland, then?'

Whatever Charlie was chewing on seemed to take forever to grind away at. 'Yes, a long time ago.'

That accounted for the odd lilts, the way some words seemed all messed up and not sure how to sound. He was talking around a hidden accent. 'Don't sound much like a Scot.'

Charlie swirled the wooden spoon about in the bowl. 'Good. I've worked hard at it.'

'Why's that then?' Normally, Tyvain wouldn't have cared less. But there was nothing normal about times at the moment. 'Who you runnin' from? They 'urt ya?'

'No...well, not the way you might think.' Charlie's spoon tapped against the side of the bowl, as though he were metering out the value of saying more or not. 'The life I had looked so wonderful on the outside, I'm sure. I grew up in a castle by the lake, with all the dresses I could want, and all the jewels I'd need. Along with countless hours of embroidering and deportment lessons.' A roll of blue eyes. 'But there is no room in a family like that for someone like me. They couldn't tolerate me wishing to ride a horse with my legs spread, let alone not wishing to wear a dress and submit to a marriage and bear children.' He swirled the spoon through the reeking broth. 'They engaged me to a man double my age with a reputation for making those around him bleed. Lovely, don't you think?' Charlie stabbed at one of the floaty pieces in his bowl. 'What else could I do but run? I have the family history that proves how it will all end if I wish to live life as I want it.'

'And 'ow is that, then?' Badly, Tyvain was guessing.

Charlie gazed at the candle. 'My grandfather only inherited the estate through an awful tragedy. His older brother, a chap called Gilbert, caused a shocking scandal when he fell in love with entirely the wrong person, of very much the wrong sex and class. I've never heard his name said, but I believe he worked on the estate. Gilbert refused to take a wife to produce the sons required of the estate's heir. He simply would not betray his lover. Have you ever heard of anything quite so romantic?'

Romantic inclinations were not Tyvain's forte, so she just grunted, hoping that would suffice.

'Gilbert went to the military rather than marry. Perhaps he thought it would give him more time. His father had sired his children late in life, so maybe he hoped the man would die before he could force his son to wed.' Charlie was enthusiastic over that idea, perhaps imagining it for himself. 'The war with Napoleon was over, or so they thought, and it was peacetime. He joined the Royal Navy, only to have that dreadful Frenchman throw Queen and country back into wartime a few weeks later. His ship ran aground off the coast of Brittany, if I recall. Gilbert was taken prisoner by the French and would never be seen again. A month after the ship went down, his lover was found battered and drowned on the grounds of the estate. Took his own life so it was said, but the rumours whispered of murder.' He shivered.

'Feckin' 'ell, ya don't like tellin' a cheerful tale, do ya?' Tyvain said. 'Well, then, the lesson ya can learn from all that is not to go runnin' off to join the Royal Navy. And seeing as them roads out there ain't pleasant, I guess you'll just 'ave to take Old Bess up on the offer to stay, then?' She'd like to get that bleak look off the lad's face. 'Just make sure you don't 'ave Cook make that godsawful dish when I comes callin'. I don't know me gut can take it.'

Tyvain's nose wrinkled at the stench. Haddock, she was guessing. Hated the fish herself. But at least her comment caused Charlie to smile.

'Honestly, you should try it. You'll be surprised.'

'Don't like surprise much.'

A happy chuckle, and Charlie slurped another mouthful. 'It is so very kind of Bess to offer. Highwaymen and lecherous publicans seem a little tame after being with you lot.' He grinned, eyes bright again. 'I don't know what possessed me to head into the forest that day I met Silas, but I'm not sorry I did.'

'You seem to get along well enough.' Tyvain winked.

'Oh, no, no. That was just once, and we were convenient for each other.' Charlie waved off the insinuation, unabashed. 'He's lovely, but we're treading very different paths. And that's fine.' The lad rubbed at the bracelet around his wrist, tracing the intertwined rowan wood and slender twig of holly with leaves still as green as though they'd just been picked.

'Where'd ya get that, then?'

'Silas gave it to me. He said it was a good luck charm, I think. Lovely, isn't it?'

Not the loveliest Tyvain had ever seen, but the lad seemed fond of it. 'Guess so. Looks like somethin' that would get shoved on ya at a May Day fair.' Tyvain sucked at her teeth, thinking on what Charlie had said. 'You weren't intending to 'ead into that forest, then?'

'Not at all. In fact, I was well beyond it when I decided to double back.' He lifted the bowl and slurped the dregs. 'I make a habit of finding out where some good spots are for sleeping. Abandoned places just like the mill. But I was headed further north to where I knew a decent barn to be, and then...I don't know. I just had a change of heart. Strange really, must have been the forest faeries.' He giggled, wiggling his fingers, as though there were some spooky magick at play. Gods, if only the lad knew. 'Do faeries actually exist? I wouldn't doubt anything anymore.'

'Yeah, they do, ya should go ask Old Bess. The boring old fart will prattle on about how wonderful they are till the cows come 'ome.'

Tyvain perched herself on the table before her feet went any more numb from the cold. Gods, she'd known at the start there was something about this laddie-lass and Silas meeting. Her waters had been bothering her since she'd come across them. It wasn't bloody faeries that turned the lad's head towards the forest. Not serendipity either. Tyvain was bloated so full it hurt to hold it in, which she wouldn't do for much longer. Seemed she was going to have to trust her sight more these days, because it wasn't half the jumbled mess it used to be. Maybe having maleficium about had made her own peculiar talents more focused, alert to the threat. Whatever it was, she saw her way forward now, clear as cut crystal.

'I'm gonna ask ya to do somethin' for me,' Tyvain said. The unhappy gurgles in her belly fell silent. 'Somethin' for the Order.' Didn't hurt to fancy it up a little, though truth was Tyvain was handling this on her own for now. Mr Ahari was always saying it. Learn to trust your gift more, Tyvain. And it wouldn't do to bother the Lady Satine on such things. Her Ladyship was bothered plenty enough if she was raising her Horsemen.

'Oh my gosh, truly?' Charlie pushed the empty bowl away. 'How exciting. What do you need me to do?'

Tyvain gave the room a quick once-over, assured herself they were alone, and leaned in. 'I need ya to find someone for me. And bring 'im 'ere. Quiet as ya can, I don't want anyone knowin' where 'e's going to. Can you do that for me?'

It wouldn't do to handle it herself. Too many people knew the Hag of Beara, for better or worse. Meandering about with a lieutenant would draw too much attention. This felt like a secret worth keeping.

Charlie's blue eyes looked set to pop from his head. 'My father hired half the detectives in Scotland after I first bolted, and not one of them found me. I can do it. But I'm not sure I can drag whoever it is here...I mean, I'm no pushover, but I can't exactly force a grown man across the country.'

'Won't need to. He'll come all on his own.'

'Alright, so who is it?'

'A lieutenant, name of Edward.'

Charlie looked dubious. 'And what? I just say, come on dear officer, follow me. No bribe or anything?'

'Oh there's a bribe you can use that will get 'im followin' you.' Tyvain grinned with the relief of a belly settled at last. 'Say Tobias Astaroth is asking for 'im. 'E'll follow wherever you lead.'

'The author truly created a world that is unpredictable, intense and hauntingly human. It is an action packed short story that fosters a lot of curious thoughts of a futuristic and desperate society.'
Goodreds Review, 2021

ABOUT THE AUTHOR

Danielle K Girl is an Aussie who lives in stunning Tasmania with her three furkids, cats Luffy, Sweetie (@sweetiebyname) and Ren.
Her idea of heaven is a farm full of rescue animals, with a vegie garden that sprouts peanut M&M's and chocolate wheaten biscuits.
When she's not keyboard-deep in mysterious, beguiling worlds, she is binge watching K-Dramas, listening to K-Pop or hiking through the beautiful Tasmanian wilderness.
Join the newsletter - Get a FREE D K Girl novella!
If you'd like to receive DK's monthly newsletter, and be first to know when a new book is ready, then you are in the right place.
Head to, https://daniellekgirl.com/subscribe/ and score yourself a
FREE Dystopian novella
in the deal.
Find D K Girl online:
https://daniellekgirl.com/
https://www.instagram.com/daniellekgirl/

Lightning Source UK Ltd.
Milton Keynes UK
UKHW011646031022
409847UK00004B/1106